# Dedication

***For Jesse***

*The Charles Taylor to my chaos—*
*loyal and unshakeable, even when the weight is unbearable.*
*Thank you for being my rock—and for being exactly the same kind of weird.*
*Even when I start a sentence and don't know where it's going,*
*you always manage to help me find it along the way.*

# A Dramatic Debut

## Love and Legacy in the Deep South

Lucine Elizabeth Watson

ROUGH &
TUMBLE
HOUSE PRESS

Rough & Tumble House Press

**A Dramatic Debut**© 2025

Lucine Elizabeth Watson

First published in Great Britain in 2025 by Rough & Tumble House Press, an independent imprint.
For inquiries, please contact: contact@roughandtumblehousepress.com



Ebook ISBN: 978-1-0684776-0-7

Paperback ISBN: 978-1-0684776-1-4

Cover design by Samantha Sanderson Marshall

Printed and bound in the United Kingdom.

*"How long not to speak the truth*
*when it is burning in you?"*

—Seneca

*"Act well your part; there all the honor lies."*

—Alexander Pope

# A Historical Note

As with most things, timing and context are important—so let's start there, shall we? This story takes place in what is commonly referred to as the antebellum South—specifically, the period between the War of 1812 and the Civil War. A time of transformation, ambition, and yes, a fair share of grand contradictions.

While this novel primarily revolves around the personal dramas, romantic intrigues, and societal machinations of its characters, it's essential to acknowledge that much of the wealth and privilege these families enjoyed came from a rather grim source: slavery.

Slavery is not the central focus of this story, but it is undeniably present in the world the characters inhabit. Some of the families in these pages were slaveholding families, which, unfortunately, was not an uncommon reality among the Southern elite. This is not to excuse or glorify their actions—far from it—but to present an honest picture of the historical context that shaped their world.

Historical fiction, as many know, tends to walk a fine line. We strive to capture the world as it once was, while telling a story meant for the world we live in today. I won't pretend to have gotten this balance perfect—but I have approached it with as much care and thoughtfulness as possible. There's no intention to pass modern judgment on these characters; rather, I invite you to read with the understanding that these stories unfold within their time, and that time had its own set of rules, however flawed they may have been.

Worth noting is that many women of this era—particularly younger ones—held anti-slavery sentiments. Quietly, and often hypocritically, but with a sincere sense of moral conflict. Women, though rarely granted legal or social power, often carried the emotional and moral weight of their communities. This tension is something I explore throughout these pages.

At its heart, however, this is a love story. A chance to escape, to find joy, and to celebrate the complexity and strength of women—especially those navigating a world not made for their independence.

If the world I've depicted doesn't sit well with you, I understand completely. There are countless stories out there, and I hope you find the ones that resonate most with you. But, if you choose to stay and keep reading, I invite you to join me on this particular journey—one full of twists, scandals that will make you gasp, and more than a surprise or two.

Yours, as always,

Lucine Elizabeth Watson

# The Record of Events

*Being a Faithful and, Where Necessary, Embellished Account*

**As Compiled by Miss L. E. Watson**

# Act I

## *The Presentation of Miss Taylor*

# The Richmond Review (excerpt)

*A formal announcement of Miss Mary Taylor's debut—accompanied by economic prospects, polite observations, and a gentle reminder of the family's influence*

## An excerpt from *The Richmond Review*

## High Society (social update)

William and Anne Taylor of Richmond announce with pleasure the debut of their youngest daughter, Miss Mary Taylor, into society on the evening of the 24$^{th}$ of March. The celebration will be held at the Taylor family plantation of Cana, and the Taylors are humbled to include amongst their guests a number of esteemed families who have travelled far and wide to welcome Miss Mary Taylor into society, including but not limited to the Defours of New Orleans, cousins to the Taylors, the Riveras of New Orleans, the Walkers of Charleston, the Sinclairs of Savannah, and the Brynes of Atlanta.

Miss Taylor will be chaperoned by her eldest brother Charles—a graduate of the College of William and Mary and now the proprietor of the newly established Taylor Mutual Fund of New Orleans. She will also be joined by her twin siblings: Edward, recently of the University of Virginia, and Elizabeth, who has journeyed from North Carolina, where she is engaged in charitable works.

All of the Taylor children remain unwed.

The debutante has recently returned from boarding school where she excelled in literature, history, arithmetic, and religious instruction, with a proficiency in dance and music appreciation. Yesterday morning when I spoke with the lovely Miss Mary Taylor, she expressed her excitement to be back once again amongst her fellow Virginians and eagerly awaits her entrance into society.

Miss Mary personally wishes to sincerely thank all those who have extended their congratulations and blessings to her in the lead up to her special night, and the hosts remind readers that the celebration is strictly by invitation.

## Fiscal focus (economic update)

Following Mr. Whitney's highly speculated invention, the price of cotton has tripled in the past quarter and is expected to continue to rise. Recent reports suggest that cotton is the fastest-growing export to Europe from the South, though it is unlikely to overtake tobacco.

Taylor Mutual Fund of New Orleans is offering preferential borrowing rates for those interested in investing in technological transformation for their plantations. For those struggling with collateral, a profit-share investment might also be considered on a situation-by-situation basis.

The James River Atlantic Shipping Company has recently expanded its extensive routes to include the Spanish-controlled Caribbean islands, which will be navigated in partnership with the Walker Shipping Company of Charleston. The James River ASC also works closely with the Defour-owned Aigle des Mers of New Orleans.

Inquiries in relation to trade routes or banking arrangements may be made in Richmond at any of the Taylor-owned premises, including the offices of *The Richmond Review*.

# Chapter I

A sense of impending doom overcame Mary Taylor as she sat at the dressing table, staring at the reflection it produced. She carefully inspected the figure's hair, the tight curls that had been primly pinned either side of the head and gathered with a light purple silk ribbon tied into bows. Her eyes travelled down as she considered the skin—the Taylor family was known for their fair English skin, and Mary was no exception. She guarded herself from the sun as her mother had taught her, as any Southern lady should. She had seen it at school more than once, young ladies venturing outside without a shawl for their shoulders, a hat, or even a parasol, as though they didn't care in the slightest if their skin browned and freckled like a field hand's. The exception to this rule was, of course, Elizabeth, who seemed to challenge the sun with the haughty entitlement of a baroness, and maddeningly, always seemed to defy nature, her skin remaining pristinely white, like porcelain.

Not all are so fortunate.

Mary sighed at the thought of Elizabeth, continuing her critique as she inspected her bosom. Despite her seventeen years, her frame was slight—her shoulders knobbly, her breasts barely creating a mound in her dress. Cupping them, Mary roughly tried to push them upwards, watching with anticipated dismay as they stubbornly stayed in the same place, not even providing her the dignity of a small bounce.

*I might stuff the bottom with tissue*, she thought wildly, biting her lip in guilt as she looked around to check if anyone had witnessed such a thought.

A sin of desperation.

It was well-known that good Southern girls would never do such a thing—even rumors of it were considered a scandal.

It was also well-known that plenty of good Southern girls did exactly that.

A detail of which Mary was unfortunately ignorant.

She shifted back in her chair to better glimpse the entire top of herself, from the waist down. The lilac purple of the dress complimented her brown hair, mousy though it was. While her arms were bare, the sleeves bunched three inches off her shoulder in an attempt to give her some shape before plunging into a deep neckline that cut across her chest.

*If only Elizabeth hadn't been gifted all the chest in the family. Couldn't she have spared a little?*

Mary winced immediately. To covet was a sin, she knew—though technically it was coveting another man's wife. And Elizabeth wasn't anyone's wife.

Yet.

Off on a technicality, she consoled herself grimly. Though she knew deep down that the coveting of another woman's breasts was no way to ensure one's place in heaven.

Especially when the breasts belonged to her own flesh and blood.

At the thought of Elizabeth, Mary could feel herself shrinking, her shoulders hunching forward, threatening to collapse in on themselves, as though there was not enough room in the world for two Taylor ladies.

And she was far from alone, for when Elizabeth entered a room, she was the object of resentment for all of the women, and in turn the object of affection for the men.

She was an undeniable beauty: tall and shapely with a waist that went in at exactly the right place, and an upper and lower body that confirmed she was very much a woman. Her hair, so dark it was nearly black, juxtaposed her creamy skin, and her green eyes danced with a merriment and carefree attitude that drew men to her like fish after a worm.

Or rather, like flies to a honey trap.

They ran to her beck and call, competed for her affections, and physically grew taller at her thanks and compliments.

Mary would watch these exchanges closely, mesmerised, as though her sister employed some witchcraft that extended past the men and affected anyone who happened to find themselves in her proximity.

And to make matters even worse, it was all clearly so effortless for her.

Another sigh escaped Mary's lips as she raised a hand to untangle her curls, repositioning each so that it bobbed as its own separate cylinder.

Did it look sophisticated, or did it look childish? She fretfully patted the sides with her gloved hands as her heart sank into the pit of her stomach. In despair, she held her hand out in front of her, scrutinizing it for a fault.

But the little white gloves folded about her hand perfectly, like a delicate web of lace.

She did have very small pretty hands, she conceded to herself, holding them up and inspecting them.

She reached for the folded paper fan sitting on the table in front of her, and with a slight flick of her wrist, unfolded it to reveal individual panels, each numbered and designating the order of the dances for the evening. She stared at the columns, still blank, where aspiring beaux would write their names, and her heart pounded.

Imagine the humiliation—waiting idly while other girls were swept away by eager partners.

Worse still would be the pity of uncles or brothers, sacrificing their own promised dances to save her from disgrace.

*"Dear, don't be ridiculous,"* Mary recalled her mother's soothing but firm tone the last time she confided these fears to her. "*The dances have been specifically chosen with you in mind to highlight your charms and abilities. You will start the evening with a dance with your father—you know he is so proud of you, Mary.*"

The thought of her father caused Mary to sit up a bit straighter. It was true that Mary and her father had a special bond. While some fathers discouraged talk of business around their daughters, sending them from the room with condescending promises that it would be of no interest to them, William welcomed it, encouraged it, even—gifting her books with a generosity only known by a father towards his daughter (though not so generous as to spoil her and risk that ever so important value of Protestant frugality), and teaching Mary from an early age the economics of running a plantation, especially one the size of theirs.

Having grown up in a home that praised her erudition, Mary had been shocked when she was finally sent away to school, the juxtaposition of her interests and those of the other ladies forcing Mary to learn (and quite quickly, mind) that there was something about her that was, well...perhaps a bit queer. For it was clear—blinding, some might say—that her pastimes were different from that of the other ladies.

Her early attempts to engage her peers with talk of foreign policy—was no one else curious about Canada, or the trouble with Spain in Mexico?—had fallen flat. Her invitations to the library were met with high-pitched tinkles of laughter and... were those pitied stares?

Yes, by the God who created the Earth, they looked at her with pity—as though she were the most pitiful creature they had ever seen.

And what was worse, they believed she did not even know it.

But Mary did know it, and the knowledge of it created a panic deep in her chest, for Mary did find herself bound to that all-too-human desire, especially for young ladies, to be socially accepted.

The fact that it was expected that she should desire such a thing was obvious.

The fact that such a thing did not come naturally to her in the slightest was also obvious.

Had it not been for Elizabeth, who had early on established herself as an adversary no young lady desired, Mary was certain she would be somewhere near the bottom of the social hierarchy carefully woven and guarded by the ladies of Southern standing.

And so she had learned, also from an early age, that quality well-known to Southern ladies—passivity. She had learnt to smile, to nod, and to allow the conversations to occur around her, though she rarely engaged herself.

In Mary's experience, if in chaperoned or polite company, ladies generally defaulted to complimenting one another, mentions of beau—though only in the most chaste terms—discussing their church's charity work, and perhaps comparing the latest fashions, if they were feeling ever so indulgent.

Whereas in unchaperoned company, the conversation could quickly descend to mooning over gentleman (in terms that were not strictly... shall we say, appropriate), bickering, plotting, stories of scandal, and not to mention, that most loved Southern tradition of exchange: rumors and gossip, a currency second only to a state's bank notes.

It was Elizabeth who credited herself with the hierarchy of social exchange—a rumor was hearsay, often of interest, though lacking the appropriate evidence to adequately elevate it to the level of gossip. Whereas gossip had met the bar of corroboration, at least to some extent, and generally brought with it promises of further fallout.

Rumors brought with it speculation of truth.

Gossip brought with it speculation of consequences.

Neither appealed much to Mary, for they both left a sour taste on her tongue, and she could not help but feel that when the Taylor sisters were not in the room, she became a topic herself.

*"Of course we are being spoken of,"* Elizabeth had said, throwing her hair over her shoulder in the most dismissive of manners when Mary had confided her fears. *"I should be offended were we not!"*

It was for this reason that Mary tried her best to blend in—she could not exempt herself fully from the social interactions expected of a lady of her upbringing, but she could do her best to remain discreet, to be present without a presence.

And besides, it was not so much that she did not care at all for those things which occupied the minds of most of her peers, for she appreciated a beautiful gown and a lovely trinket as much as the next well-bred Southern lady should, but it was not the sole content of her attention.

In fact, far from it.

Her father had managed to raise a daughter completely contrary to the expectation of Southern ladies.

And despite being a man who held great reverence for social norms, it was in this one respect that he did not seem to care in the slightest.

Yes, the notion that such an esteemed man as William Taylor held such a high opinion of his youngest daughter always managed to grow Mary a few inches in confidence, even if only momentarily. And it was not simply by virtue of being his daughter that tendered her father's heart towards her, for Mary had watched her eldest brother Charles tread in the long shadow cast by their father and his successes. And she had listened, with ears pressed to closed doors, to the reprimands levied towards her elder brother Edward, and the cool admonishments that often turned to raised voices when Father tried to chastise Elizabeth into more appropriate behavior.

That William Taylor expected Charles to lead by example for his younger siblings was obvious—that the brilliance of his example had obviously not rubbed off on his two closest siblings in age was also obvious. As a result, Charles had turned keenly to Mary, intent on ensuring that she was not led astray, that she took seriously her education and became an upstanding young lady that any Southern elite would be proud to call his wife.

The thought of her father and eldest brother forced Mary's eyes closed. She could imagine the scene clearly: her dance card bare, Charles would declare how fortunate he was to dance again and again with the prettiest girl in the room.

And in doing so, inadvertently reduce her with his niceness into an even smaller creature than she was.

Elizabeth's debutante ball had been another matter entirely.

Of course, Mary was not there in person as she was too young, but there was hardly talk of anything else for months following the *extravaganza*, as the papers the next day had described it. Not *The Richmond Review*, of course, and Father had made no bones about expressing his disappointment at the scandalizing nature of newspapers in this day and age.

Mary did not often find herself disagreeing with her father, and if she did, she had the good sense to know better than to express it, which was why she had the decency to wait until Father had discarded the morning's newspapers to retrieve them, scurrying off to her room to hide her curiosity.

There, seated cross-legged on her bed, Mary read how men had gasped when Elizabeth Taylor had walked down the grand staircase on Father's arm.

Her deep green velvet dress was tiered and one of a kind, having been made in Paris, with a skirt so large it ballooned around her dramatically, in turn juxtaposing the size of her waist and giving her the illusion of the most defined hourglass shape anyone had ever seen. At her neck she wore a pearl and diamond choker of her mother's, a gift from their father on their betrothal.

The articles elaborated at length on the manner in which the gentlemen of the room could not, for love of God or country, take their eyes off of the debutante, the way her *supple* (Yes—supple!) skin glowed under the candlelit chandeliers—*Miss Elizabeth Taylor need only ask, and the gentlemen were only all too happy to oblige.*

Mary recalled sitting at the foot of her sister's bed as she had prepared that evening, gripping the bedpost tightly as she watched Elizabeth transform from a swan into a...

Well, somehow even more beautiful creature.

What was more beautiful than a swan?

And when her sister turned around, Mary's eyes widened as she gaped at the plushness of her sister's porcelain breasts on display in the most regal manner.

"*Father will be furious.*" The words came out before Mary could catch them.

"*I know.*" Elizabeth's eyes had danced with delight at the thought.

And indeed, he was.

As she read the words, Mary understood her father's anger, for there is a certain frustration that can only be borne of a story that is regrettable both for its contents, and because it is utterly true.

But it had not ended there.

According to tale, Elizabeth had whirled around the room so gracefully in the arms of William, Charles, and Edward Taylor respectively, that by the time it came to dinner, there was a queue of every available bachelor young and old to fill up her dance card. Those in the back of the queue jostled those further up, nervous they would not get their opportunity to dance with the young and beautiful Elizabeth Taylor. And Father was especially appalled when some of the fathers, his friends, approached him on behalf of their sons, asking if he could help their sons move up the queue!

It was actually a borderline scandal. Elizabeth had laughed with delight, as though in disbelief and awe of her own charms.

Now of course, Mary didn't want *that* kind of attention, for no good Southern lady should desire that kind of attention.

All she wanted was a tiny, minuscule portion of that.

Imagine the talk tomorrow: When Elizabeth Taylor was presented to society, she received so much attention it created a scandal.

When Mary Taylor was presented to society, she received so little attention it also created a scandal.

Mary sighed again, smoothing the silk of her dress from her neckline down to her waist before gazing once more into the mirror.

A small, scared-looking girl stared back at her, her eyes wide yet forlorn, as though while petrified, she had accepted her fate.

*I look like a child playing dress up*, she concluded, smashing her eyelids together as she fought the hot prick of tears that bubbled to the surface.

It was so unfair.

In what world could she and Elizabeth have come from the same parents?

And if Elizabeth did have to have all the beauty, why was she also so effortlessly intelligent (even if she didn't care for people to know it, for no gentleman, according to her sister, was looking for a study partner), carefree, and confident.

Her beauty was her freedom, Mary had concluded long ago.

Her entitlement.

And by the same logic, Mary's lack of beauty was her cage—the thing that tethered her to a future of compromises and *good-enoughs*, a future that had been decided for her long ago, a future in which she was entitled to no say but was forced to accept.

She would never be courted like the other girls. Late at night at boarding school and during naptime at barbecues, she would sit up and eagerly listen to stories of gentlemen coming to call, of extravagant gifts from overseas, declarations of love, and threatened duels with family members if a man could not see his beloved or ask for her hand in marriage.

The rational part of Mary's brain knew these stories were exaggerated, or at least, that some of them had to be—any story worth its salt required at least a little bit of embellishment—but then again, Mary was the sister of Elizabeth Taylor and she knew firsthand the lengths men would go to for the object of their affection.

And it was not even solely the grand gestures—that was of course appealing, though part of Mary felt she might disappear into a puddle of her own embarrassment if a gentleman appeared at her door with a wrapped box from Paris for her—but it was the notion, the knowledge, of being sought, being desired, and ultimately, being appreciated, that Mary dreaded, deep down, would exist for her only in the stories of others.

Of course, her situation in life didn't necessarily mean that she would end up alone, for she was not totally helpless and came from a family of good-standing. She might be married off to a distant cousin, or perhaps—

Her train of thought halted as she clutched the dance card in her hand tightly, fighting the tears that began to stream down her face, leaving streaks of wet lines and ruining her pearly complexion.

*It is all going to be terrible—I have been away at boarding school for nearly three years, and I have no idea who's even going to be here tonight, let alone who Mother and Father might approve of, or who would even be interested in me—*

"And what is this all about?" Mary's eyes shot open as the light voice pierced through her self-loathing. In the reflection of the mirror, Elizabeth stood behind her, staring at her with a look of concern and....Was that pity?

Yes, it was definitely pity.

Perfect.

"Why are you crying?" Elizabeth was at her side, holding a handkerchief out for her sister with one hand, her other squeezing Mary's shoulder.

"I'm afraid," Mary admitted in a faltering whisper.

"It is perfectly normal to be nervous." Elizabeth delicately untangled one of Mary's curls with her slender fingers.

"You wouldn't understand." The comment escaped before she could stop it.

The suggestion that Elizabeth Taylor had any idea how she was feeling was, quite frankly, absurd.

"Why wouldn't I understand?" Elizabeth demanded forcefully, placing a hand on both hips and cocking her head in challenge. "I did have a debutante ball myself, you know."

"Yes, I do know," Mary snapped, "and as I remember it, the men were literally fighting over you!"

At the harshness in her sister's voice, Elizabeth's eyes softened. Kneeling down, she turned Mary around so she was facing her, and with a thumb caught another tear that threatened to cascade down her cheek.

The sisters stared at one another for a moment before Mary finally spoke again.

"You are late," a soft accusation.

"I know. I am sorry, the trains were late." Elizabeth sounded genuinely apologetic, prying the dance card out of Mary's hands, placing it on the dressing table, and taking both her sister's hands. "I wanted to be here to get ready with you.

"Please Mary, tell me what's wrong," Elizabeth encouraged, squeezing her hands lightly. "What are you afraid of?"

"I'm afraid that no one will wish to dance with me," Mary whispered. "That my dance card will be bare all night, and that Father, Charles, and Edward will be my only partners, and I'll be a laughing stock and no one will wish to marry me. And I will end up with an arranged marriage to some distant cousin, or worse, a spinster." The words came out quickly, like a sinner finally making her confession.

"Oh, for goodness' sake," Elizabeth rolled her eyes. "Is that really what you're afraid of?" She shook her head in that condescending manner that Elizabeth always utilized.

Though Mary had learnt to try not to take it personally, for Elizabeth spoke to most people in such a manner.

"Mary, for as smart as you are, I have no idea how you've made it this far in life without understanding the power you have. Actually," Elizabeth paused, "I do, because the world does not really wish women to know what power they hold, and you are no exception. But Sister, please," Elizabeth smiled, brushing Mary's curls off her shoulder.

"You are the daughter of William Taylor—do you have any idea what that means?"

Mary stared at her sister blankly.

"I thought you were smart," Elizabeth chided playfully, rolling her eyes again. "Little sister, listen to me when I say to you that at this moment, you are the most eligible bachelorette in the South."

Mary continued to stare, her expression morphing to one of skepticism.

"I am being sincere!" Elizabeth insisted. "Not only does our family run the largest tobacco plantation in Virginia," Mary shifted in her seat uncomfortably, for while it was true, the Taylor family was not gauche enough to declare such a thing aloud.

Or at least, they should not be.

"And not only is our father an esteemed member of Congress, just like the men of our family before him for generations, but our family have retained our connections in England. We have one of the oldest and most established shipping companies in the country. Not only that, but your brother has gone and opened up the first bank in the South with the help of local and foreign investors linked to, you guessed it, a bank in England. Mary, our family controls the tobacco market, the shipping, the financing, and the government. And you are one of two daughters of this family who are becoming of marrying age.

"So you tell me, in what world, are you going to be standing against a wall tonight or be stuck dancing with some old uncle or cousin?"

"But I do not wish someone to want me because of our family's money and power—"

"Of course not," Elizabeth dismissed. "But they will. It will be a partial motive, regardless of whatever pure honorable ideals you harbor. But what I'm saying is, you will have options—more than almost any lady in the South."

"Except for—" Mary halted, swallowing the last word as she chastised herself for her own pettiness.

"Ha," Elizabeth laughed. "I have seen over twenty summers now—I am basically an old maid."

"You don't even believe that."

"No, I don't," Elizabeth admitted, smiling mischievously and casting a glance at herself in the vanity. "But it felt like the appropriate thing to say.

"But honestly Mary, this night is about you. All these men have journeyed across multiple states for the chance to dance and flirt with you! It is something to be enjoyed, not dreaded."

"I've been away for three years." Mary wrung her hands. "I barely remember who's who."

"I'll help you," Elizabeth assured her, putting her hands on top of her sister's. "I'm up to date with all the gossip. I'll be by your side the entire evening if you wish me to.

"Or I'll trip and break my nose if that's what you prefer." The laugh escaped Mary's lips before she could catch it, too hard, perhaps because there was the smallest touch of truth in her sister's words, and Elizabeth knew it too.

"And don't forget," Elizabeth smiled. "You bear the name of a Queen."

"Queen Mary lost her head," Mary said flatly.

Elizabeth sighed.

"Well, with an attitude like that, you'll never find yourself a husband."

Clutching the crook of her father's elbow, Mary tried to stifle the trembling of her body. The long dress shuffled noisily under the vibration of her limbs, her knees buckling together. She could feel the beads of sweat as they pricked her back, running down her thin spine as she worried for the fate of her dress. The material was fine but thin—it was a spring ball, after all.

A steady warm hand rest atop hers reassuringly, and William Taylor smiled down at his youngest daughter.

"Mary," he said, soothingly but firmly, squeezing her small hand in his. "You needn't be so nervous."

"Yes, Father," she nodded obediently, hoping her words were convincing, but he laughed softly.

"It is of course normal to be nervous, but I mean it when I say, you needn't be." William guided his daughter away from the double doors that led to the grand staircase where Mary would make her debut, and where Elizabeth had made hers before.

"But Father, won't we be late?" Father was a strong believer in the importance of being prompt—not too early, as that was equally inconvenient for the other party, but exactly prompt. He was known to wait outside of rooms before meetings or houses prior to calling, perched against his carriage as he held his pocket watch and considered as the seconds and minutes ticked by so as to determine the exact moment it was appropriate to knock.

*If a gentleman gives a time, he is obliged to keep it*, Father missed no opportunity to remind his sons.

William chuckled at his daughter's propriety.

"Usually yes," he conceded, "but today is a rare occasion when they are happy to wait, for the party cannot start without you." They stopped in front of a large, ornate full-length mirror. "Look at you," William smiled warmly, patting her hand that still clutched his forearm. "No father could be prouder of a daughter," he promised, beaming into the mirror. "The way you love books and politics and resent the sewing and knitting that most Southern women love." The base of Mary's neck flushed scarlet, the colors rushing through her cheeks.

"Did you think I did not know?" Her father chuckled softly. "You are a true martyr, Mary, doing the things you know you should despite the fact you find no fulfilment in them. And even more so, never a complaint from you. Sometimes, this is what life demands of us, and you navigate this with grace. But you should ensure you find a balance. Some men will love a studious wife. They will appreciate and treasure you all the more for it, for in you they will find not just a wife but a companion. I cannot imagine life without Mrs. Taylor and the head she has on her shoulders.

"And some men do not care for what is in your head, and that is okay too. Consider the different wives both your brothers will bring home one day."

Mary nodded, silently internalizing her father's words as she stared at the ground, her little silk slippers sticking out from the layer of petticoats of her gown.

She understood that she should appreciate his kindness, even if it made clear her father did not understand her situation at all.

He was blinded, as many men in his position would be, with their love and adoration of their daughter.

"Do you understand what I'm trying to say?"

"Yes Father." Mary met his eyes in the mirror.

"I'm telling you all of this because there's a room full of eligible young men who have come here to meet you, to dance with you, and to try and win your affection. Only you can make the choice best for you, and your choice may be different from others." Mary did not need to read between the lines. She could understand exactly what her father was saying.

Her debutante ball would be a very different experience from Elizabeth's—so she should try not to be too disappointed.

"Just look at you, my dear," William sighed, gesturing with his head for Mary to look in the mirror. Reluctantly, she considered the pair who stared back at them.

William Taylor stood tall and broad, beaming at Mary.

She tried her best to see herself through her father's eyes, through that obviously proud and pleased smile that brought his face to life. She considered herself, the fine dress that cinched at her waist and then plumed in a large balloon, tiers of material creating a cascade effect that was cinched with black ribbon and adorned with pearls, matching the teardrop pearl necklace at her throat and the ribbon which tied her curls. She wanted with all of her heart to see a grown woman, a lady of confidence.

But she could not.

"Make good choices," her father counselled. "You always have, and I trust you always will."

Mary cast her eyes back to the ground.

That was assuming she would find herself in a position of choosing at all.

# Chapter II

At the sound of the hinges, a hush descended over the crowd as the large walnut door swung open. A small gloved hand appeared on the banister of the stairs, sliding slowly along in line with the substantial tread of William Taylor and the light pad of slippered feet. Father squeezed her hand as they rounded the hall and reached the head of the grand staircase, which led into the parlor where all the guests stood waiting, silently, expectantly.

Judgingly, Mary thought. From their height she stared down at the nameless faces, searching for someone, anyone, she might recognise.

Her eldest brother Charles stood at the bottom of the steps and slightly off to the right, flanked by Edward and Elizabeth. And standing in front of him was Anne, so short compared to her sons that Mary had missed her own mother on her first scan of the room. They all smiled back up at her, warmly, happily, supportively, as though this were a moment to be celebrated, as opposed to the worst of her life.

"Smile, darling," her father reminded her, leading the descent down the red carpeted steps with Mary hanging off his elbow for support. She fought the urge to stare at her feet, despite the horrible fear her presentation to society would begin with a face plant. But after the first step, the second, and then the third, she began to remember that she had been walking for nearly the past seventeen years, and it had never caused her an enormous amount of anxiety before.

Moving more confidently, she dared to pry her eyes from her family, even nodding to them in acknowledgement, before returning her gaze to the rest of the room.

There were twenty-four steps to the grand staircase, with a landing in between at twelve and thirteen. William and Mary paused, directly underneath the large ornate golden chandelier. It hung above their heads, the light from the dancing flames catching the cut glass and making it sparkle. From here, Mary could better see their audience.

She inhaled sharply, the full extent of her father's and sister's words finally registering.

Of the hundreds of people in the hall, their attention was directed solely and exclusively on her—Mary Taylor. A shiver ricocheted through her shoulders, but caught in her chest as something else in her began to swell.

For the first time, Mary understood her own significance, a significance that she had applied to everyone else around her, but not to herself.

As they descended the second flight of stairs, Mary started recognizing other faces: some of mother's old friends from church who had taught her in Sunday school, their old family doctor and his wife—And the men! Dozens of them—some near her age, others a decade older—all watching her with quiet interest, as though they had been waiting for her all evening.

And indeed, they had.

Having successfully scaled the steps, Mr. Taylor and Mary continued through to the ballroom, the guests hot on their heels. As the lead in Mary's feet dissipated, she allowed herself to be swept by her father into the centre of the room, waiting patiently for the room to fill as the guests crowded in, surrounding the pair and encircling them in anticipation.

"Ladies and gentlemen," Mr. Taylor finally began. "As some of you may know, I am not one for making speeches." He smiled a bit ruefully, the room bubbling with laughter; in Congress, he was known as a man of few words but great influence. "And I will, for the most part, maintain my reputation and allow the grace, beauty, and brilliance of my youngest daughter, Mary, speak for herself.

"Mary," he held out his hand, "will you allow me the privilege of this first dance?"

On her acceptance of her father's outstretched palm, the orchestra struck up a waltz.

And it was then, less than a minute into her debut to society, that Mary tripped over her own feet.

Despite her belief that she would melt into a puddle of her own shame if she did anything as utterly embarrassing as tripping—let alone on the first dance, let alone a dance chosen to showcase her abilities—the music did not stop.

The chandelier did not crash from the ceiling and smash her into a million pieces.

The earth did not open and swallow her up.

Instead, Mr. Taylor caught the fall and helped mask it to the best of his abilities, with a calmness that almost made Mary suspect he knew it was going to happen.

Or perhaps, that it had at least been a possibility.

"Keep going," Mr. Taylor urged placidly through an adoring smile. "You dance like a swan floating over water when you are not so nervous."

"That is a little bit of an exaggeration, don't you think, Father?" Her grin emerged slowly from her mortified expression.

"If I did not think so, I would not have said it," he replied, playfully but with mock sternness. "Have you ever known a Virginian to exaggerate his speech?"

"In matters of great importance, no," Mary conceded, her steps becoming more effortless now as she allowed her focus to slip from the movements of the dance, her limbs becoming less stiff as they adjusted into auto-pilot.

Of course, she knew how to waltz. She had waltzed a thousand times before.

"But in matters relating to the Taylor women and their graces, almost certainly."

"When it comes to their belles, Virginian men never need to exaggerate," he said, with that particular pride known only to Southern fathers.

And perhaps because she had already embarrassed herself beyond repair, Mary Taylor twirled around the dance floor, moving with the effortless grace of a woman who, for the first time in her life, had nothing to prove.

"You look beautiful, little sister," Charles beamed, accepting her hand from his father as he stepped in to lead her in the reel. "And I am flattered to have been selected as your chaperone."

"Who else would it have been?" Mary evaded his compliments, staring up at her eldest brother and recalling the day she had believed him the tallest man she had ever seen.

That was, until Edward had not only caught up to him, but passed him by a further two inches.

"Last time I checked, you have another brother," Charles chuckled, fixing his glasses before bowing to his sister.

"Yes, but he chaperoned Elizabeth." Mary curtsyed back.

"Ha, well, yes, in a sense." Charles rolled his eyes, trying to mask embarrassment with playfulness.

"What do you mean?" They joined hands as the conductor raised his hands.

"I will tell you another time." Charles dismissed her inquiry with a smile. "Tonight is about you. Not Father, not Elizabeth. You."

"I see that Charles is the favorite brother." Edward feigned offense when it was his turn, meeting Mary on the dance floor with crossed arms and the most outrageous lopsided smile.

"Edward, do not say such a thing! I had to pick an order, and by age seemed the most fair. I cannot help it if you were born last of the Taylor men."

"That's a mighty fine excuse," he relented, dropping his arms and bending down to greet his sister with a kiss on the cheek. As he straightened up, a wisp of hair fell over his eyes, which he brushed aside carelessly, his full set of teeth gleaming in the glow cast by the candles. Mary could hear the sharp intake of women's breaths at the devilish grin of Edward Taylor.

Much like his twin, Edward had that lazy confidence born of knowing he was the most handsome man in the room. Unlike his twin, however, he cared less that everyone knew he knew it. Which was perhaps what made him so maddeningly attractive to the women, their compliments washing over him with barely an acknowledgement, and heinously irritating to the men.

For how could any real gentleman show up to the races unshaven, smelling of alcohol and tobacco and with a shirt so crumpled, it was obviously the same one from the day before... and yet, *still* manage to be the desire of every woman.

"Plus, you did escort our sister to her debutante ball," Mary fished, desiring the punchline which Charles had been too proper to provide.

"HA!" Edward threw back his head in laughter. "Well, yes, in a sense."

"What does that mean?" Mary asked, feigning innocence, though it did make her feel the tiniest bit guilty.

For the art of manipulation did not come as easily to her as it did her sister.

"I fear I am not supposed to say, for it brought great shame on our family name," Edward spoke with mocking gravity, bowing his head in contrition. "But seeing as you are a lady of society now, and the subject is your sister, I see no reason why it should be kept from you." The faux severity was gone from his brow as he reached for her hands.

"I did indeed chaperone our dear sister to her debutante ball, though I was not alone, for in the end she had five chaperones..."

"Five?!" Mary balked, pausing in her steps.

"Or perhaps it was six..." Edward thought aloud, dragging Mary along with the music. "I cannot exactly recall. Besides, it was Father's fear of a scandal that meant I was named her chaperone, it was bestowed by decree, not by choice, so it is hardly something deserving of brag.

"But she was clearly displeased with this outcome, and so being the resourceful lady she is, collected herself some other options.

"Yes, that was more or less the look on Father's face also." Edward chuckled at Mary's disbelief, "Multiple young men turned up early to the house and insisted they were her chaperone."

"Wh-what did Father do?" Mary leaned forward in a conspiratorial manner, knowing he had already divulged information which was not for her consumption.

"What could he do?" Edward shook his head. "He swore them to secrecy, dismissed them to wait in the parlor, and promised them dances..." Edward's voice had transitioned from playful to conciliatory as he smiled down at Mary reassuringly.

"I know it makes an entertaining story, but that does not mean it is something to which one should aspire."

Edward, perhaps better than anyone else, seemed to understand Mary's love and loathing of her sister.

Elizabeth had been shipped off to North Carolina following an incident in the barn with one of Charles's university friends, or shall we say, *former friends*, for the young man (one could hardly call him a gentleman, for it was little known and wildly speculated what exactly had transpired between the two, but it was understood no gentlemanly behavior would have led to a fallout of such a degree) in question had been sworn to silence, forced to accept payment, which was an absolute affront to his honor, and banished from Cana never to return. It was a day Mary remembered vividly. The roaring of her father's fury, especially terrifying to Mary, who rarely heard her father raise his voice; the high-pitched retorts from Elizabeth as she vehemently refused to marry the young man; and the pleading of her mother as she insisted Mr. Taylor remained calm and begged Elizabeth to see reason.

Mary could feel her body physically tensing at the exchange, scrunching smaller and smaller as she stared at the pages of the book that shook too violently in her hand for her to make words from the letters which jumped all over the page. Finally she gave up, discarding the book on the couch next to her and bringing her knees to her chest, wrapping her arms around them.

Across the room, Edward had sat in a chair quietly, listening intently through the walls.

*"I wish they would stop," Mary finally breathed, resting her head atop her knees.*

*"Worry not, it will be over soon."*

*"Are you not worried?"*

*"No," Edward answered simply, definitively.*

*"But how?" Mary raised her head in bewilderment.*

*"I do not worry for Elizabeth," he replied after a moment, "because even though she may get herself into trouble, she can handle herself. Honestly, I worry more for you."*

*"For me?" Mary looked up. "Why?"*

*"Because," Edward turned towards her with one of the most serious expressions she had ever seen cross her brother's face. "You choose to live in her shadow."*

*Mary gaped at his words.*

*"Wh-what do you mean?"*

*"I mean you emulate her while obviously feeling like you will never be her."*

*"I-I'm not trying to be her," Mary insisted. "I couldn't be even if I wished to."*

*"And that is what I'm talking about," Edward pointed. "I know better than anyone the shadow Elizabeth Taylor casts. I grew up standing right next to her. For Christ's sake, she was reading at the age of three." Edward shook his head. "And I struggled with my letters until I was almost ten."*

Not a year earlier, Edward had dropped out of university—despite the immense strings their father had pulled to get him in, Edward's grades from school having been deemed by teachers and tutors "unremarkable".

Completely oblivious to the great lengths his father had gone to on his behalf (or perhaps if not oblivious, simply dismissive of, though no one in the family dared suggest that for the affront it would be to both Mr. Taylor and his son), on dropping out of school Edward had told no one save Elizabeth and had journeyed to Georgia, where he passed (*wasted,* according to Mr. Taylor, *squandered*) his days in bed, and his evenings gambling, betting, and generally seeking out the most reprehensible company he could manage. Once the stipend father had given him had dried up (not, to be clear, because Edward Taylor was a poor gambler or inept when it came to choosing a horse, but because his proclivity for drink and frequenting of houses of ill repute had regrettably outpaced his earnings), Edward had turned to making his bread at underground street boxing, a sport not technically legal but too entertaining to be fully regulated.

Edward's plan to return home at the end of the semester, his parents none the wiser, had been foiled by an untimely letter from one of Father's fellow Congressman, who had seen the reputable speaker's son stumbling out of the door of a certain establishment in the early morning hours of a Tuesday.

No one had thought to ask what this Congressman had been doing up at such an hour himself, let alone in proximity to such an establishment. No one apart from Edward Taylor, that was, who maintained to this day that the man had played Judas to extract his son from a considerable debt he had owed to Edward.

Though these reasonings (*attempted diversions*, according to his father) did little to quell Mr. Taylor's rage, for he, once again, found himself in one of those peculiar hells known only by those blessed (*cursed*) enough to be parents, of not knowing which discretion to punish first.

*"I know I need not explain that stipend was for your living expenses, Edward,"* Mr. Taylor had remarked from

where he stood at his drinks cabinet, his hand shaking with frustration as he poured himself a brandy. It was a rare and terrible thing to drive Mr. William Taylor—a man who had weathered the trenches of warfare and the corruption of Congress—into a drink.

But Edward Taylor had accomplished it with almost no effort at all.

*"Of course, Father, and I am internally grateful, for your generosity lasted me the better part of a month in Savannah,"* Edward had sincerely acknowledged, nodding his head with a deference that Mr. Taylor could hardly believe for its graveness.

Either his son was an idiot, or he mocked him in the most unforgivable manner.

It was one of the most vexing qualities that this particular son of his always met his disapproval with a calm respectfulness that made it impossible for Mr. Taylor to raise his voice, for he would then be cast as the unreasonable one in the exchange.

Second only to the fact that his disappointment and stern talks did nothing to change his youngest son's behaviors, for Edward Taylor seemed serenely resigned to constantly disappointing his father.

He did not argue.

Nor did he make any efforts to alter himself.

"What I am saying, Mary, is that you're much better off just being yourself and doing what you wish to do—if you try to constantly measure yourself against others, you will always come up short."

"Mary?"

"Yes?" She still clasped her brother's hands, though the music had stopped, her attention firmly planted on his chest.

"Did you hear me?" He leaned forward, speaking into her ear as Elizabeth and Charles joined the pair on the dance floor, along with two other couples for the quadrille.

"Yes," Mary raised her head to meet his eyes, filled with something like concern and...was that regret? Did he really believe her so fragile that she could not tolerate the truth?

"And I know." She forced a smile to his original question, turning her attention to the other guests who had joined them on the dancefloor. One of the men was a son of the Walker family of Charleston, South Carolina, though which she was not certain, and another her distant cousin, Michel Defour of New Orleans. At her glance, the Walker son made eye contact with Mary, lingering perhaps a bit longer than was appropriate, and bowed low, a show of respect and interest, before bowing to his dance partner.

At the demonstration of attention, Mary blushed.

# Chapter III

Mary found herself in a stupor of excitement as the formal dance came to an end. Her face was flush, and her cheeks glowed with the exertion of the movement of the last hour. Despite this, she stepped lightly from the dance floor, invigorated by the evening so far. After catching the lingering gaze of the Walker son, Mary noticed more men trying to meet her eyes. At first, she assumed something was amiss—perhaps a wardrobe mishap. But as she spun around the room, she grew bolder, even offering a smile or two in return.

"Well done, Sister." Elizabeth intercepted Mary, slipping her arm into the crook of her elbow and leading her from the floor. "You are positively glowing!"

"Miss Taylor." A man appeared in front of them. "It has been many years, but do you remember me?" At first, Mary did not answer, assuming he was speaking to Elizabeth. Instead, Mary studied him semi-curiously: tall with thick black hair, tanned skin, and cheekbones so devastatingly high, they flirted with his eyes. Undoubtedly handsome, and from his posture a man of standing who knew it, exactly the type of gentleman Elizabeth might wish to hook and subsequently humble.

And yet...

Something about him did seem familiar.

"Well, Mary," Elizabeth squeezed her arm. "Do you remember your old childhood playmate?"

Mary's eyes grew wide with recognition, clapping her hands together in glee.

"Manuel Rivera!"

"Yes, ma'am," Manuel's face beamed at her remembrance. More emboldened now, he extended his arm and reached for her gloved hand, which he kissed lightly. "I am flattered you have left space in your memories for a simple New Orleans boy like myself."

"Don't be silly. You were my best friend for many summers! How are your siblings? And how is your father?" Mary remembered Mr. Rivera as a kind, soft-spoken man, who always treated the children to oranges and citrus fruits from their plantations. The Riveras had some of the largest rice plantations in the South, but Mrs. Rivera had loved her orchards, and Mr. Rivera tended to them still out of love for his late wife.

"We are all well, Miss Taylor. Everyone's come along, and I'm sure they're all hoping for a word with you before long. All of us, apart from Catalina, that is. Did the news reach you at school, Miss Taylor, about my brother-in-law?"

"Why, no. What happened?"

"Oh Miss Taylor, I'm not keen to bring down your mood on your day—"

"Please Mr. Rivera, the mortification of not knowing is worse than the alternative."

"If you insist, Miss Taylor, but only because you have. My sister lost her husband in his final service to the Spanish crown, and she is still in mourning."

"Mr. Rivera, I am so sorry for your loss." Without thinking, Mary reached for his hand before blushing at her own forwardness. At the gesture, Manuel smiled, accepting her hand and squeezing it lightly.

"Thank you, Miss Taylor. That is so kind. She loved that man more than I've ever seen a woman love a husband," he sighed. "All I can hope is that I find a love as strong as hers, or a woman who would miss me the way my sister misses Mr. Sandoval.

"Miss Taylor, now I know I've been an awful gentleman and ruined your evening with my somber news, but I always remembered you as a lady with a forgiving heart, and I hope you will do me the honor of saving at least one dance for me." Manuel clutched her hand hopefully.

"Of course!" Mary's heart thudded at the feeling of her hand in his, her mind still lingering on the sincerity of his words. "Regretfully, I do not have my dance card on me at this moment—"

"I have it here," Elizabeth interjected, opening the fan so the panels faced her. "The third dance after dinner is free, Mr. Rivera, assuming you have not promised that to someone else?"

"No, ma'am," Manuel nodded eagerly. "It would be my honor."

"I'll put you down for that one then," Elizabeth nodded, reveling in her role as gatekeeper.

"Why did you say the third dance after dinner?" Mary asked as they navigated through the crowd.

"Because knowing you, my dear sweet and too-honest-for-her-own-good little sister, you'd have told him that all your dances were free!"

As was often the case, Elizabeth did have a point, even if Mary was not about to admit it aloud.

"Besides, the Riveras are undoubtedly a good family, but you cannot spend the entire evening dancing with Manuel Rivera."

"And why not?" Mary protested, looking back over her shoulder she caught Manuel watching the pair of them walk away. At having been caught, Manuel quickly diverted his gaze down into his glass before looking back up and smiling nervously. At the curvature of his mouth, Mary could feel her heart pound.

Manuel Rivera was smiling at her.

"Well, for two reasons. One, because, you cannot marry the first man you dance with. What if there's something else better out there?"

"And what if there's not?" Mary protested.

"All I'm saying," Elizabeth soothed, "is that you have no obligation to pick the first man who gives you a bit of attention. Consider this evening window shopping, a chance to see plenty of options. You don't buy the first dress you see, do you?"

"Elizabeth!" Mary raised a hand to her mouth in horror. "Are you really likening finding a husband to dress shopping?"

"Yes," Elizabeth answered simply, without hesitation. "It's not enough to just like the look, the cut, the color.

You have to like the material, the way it feels in between your fingers, and the way it fits on your body."

"Elizabeth," Mary flushed with embarrassment. "I'm not sure I know what you're talking about exactly, but I know it's not good."

"You'll know soon enough," Elizabeth laughed lightly. "Oh, stop looking so scandalized!"

"And what's the second?" Mary tried to pivot the conversation. "You said there were two reasons I could not spend the entire evening dancing with Manuel Rivera."

"Oh, because of the Defour and Rivera feud, of course," Elizabeth said it matter-of-factly, as though it were the most obvious thing in the world. "The Defours are our family, after all. That's not to say you cannot dance with the Rivera men, but you should be mindful of how it looks."

"It's quite amusing, sister, for you to be lecturing me on the appearance of our actions," Mary teased.

"Oh, look who's an adult with adult humour!" Elizabeth raised her eyebrows, clearly entertained. "And for the avoidance of doubt, little one, I am always aware of the appearance of my actions and their consequences. I do try not to act in utter ignorance."

"Enlighten me, then. What is the Defour-Rivera feud about?"

"Oh, what are any feuds about? Love, money, honor, or a combination of all of the above." It was so like Elizabeth to share enough information to pique one's interest but hold back the revealing details. Mary always thought it was a bit malevolent how much her sister appeared to take such joy in watching her audience beg.

"Elizabeth, please! Tell me."

"Tell you what, dear Mary?" Both Taylor sisters turned, their heads tilting in tandem as they met the ever-composed stare of Elizabeth Walker.

"Ah, Beth," Elizabeth pronounced her name with a practiced condescension. "You did just interrupt a private conversation between sisters—though how could you possibly know." They wore the same name like a stain—unspoken, unwelcome, and impossible to ignore as they traded glances soaked in contempt.

Neither made any effort to stifle it.

"So sorry, Eliza," Elizabeth Walker cooed, her smile sweet as tea left out in the sun—and just as bitter.

"You will be so kind as to address me by my Christian name in my own home." Elizabeth let the silence settle before adding, with a pointed little cock of her head,"I understand things are done differently in Charleston—but here, we do try to mind our manners."

Elizabeth Taylor and Elizabeth Walker had despised each other for as long as polite society could remember. As far as Mary could tell, it all traced back to a long-forgotten quarrel over which of them had rightful claim to the name "Elizabeth"—a dispute that had never been settled, only sharpened with time. "Miss Walker," Mary interceded. "So lovely of you to come. And that gown—such a divine shade," she added, feigning a study of the soft pink silk.

"Oh yes," Elizabeth Taylor chimed in, her smile sweet and sticky. "Absolutely charming. Possibly even lovelier than when you wore it to the Byrnes' barbecue last summer." She leaned in slightly, voice lowering to a stage whisper. "A small tip, dear—skirts in Paris are getting wider this year, not narrower. But of course, you couldn't have known. Charleston must be simply ages behind."

Elizabeth Walker's face hardened into a grimace, her distaste at the sight of her nemesis so apparent, Mary wondered if she might actually spit on her sister.

"You have always been so resourceful, Miss Taylor, being able to keep up to date with the latest fashion trends even when being hidden away in North Carolina. Though I suppose there is probably not much else to do there other than read fashion magazines.

"At your sister's current rate, Mary," she turned towards the debutante, "I expect you'll be married before her!"

Mary shot a glance at her sister, knowing the reference to North Carolina would have irked her. The story promulgated, which was that Elizabeth Taylor had gone to stay with distant family to carry out charity work at a children's orphanage, had been accepted at face value when their parents shared it, the selflessness of their eldest daughter being praised to no end—at least, in the Taylors' company.

But behind closed doors, the whispers had spread through Virginia like a biblical plague—crawling through drawing rooms and parlors, carried on lace fans and pursed lips, all the way to Florida and as far west as Louisiana. Elizabeth, for her part, did not seem in the least bit distressed by such talk, declaring to those who asked that "gossip is for those with nothing better to do," but saying it with a twinkle in her eye that left the inquirer knowing there was more to be told. It was this feigned sanctity, combined with the intrigue of her reputation, that had quickly allowed Elizabeth to once again rise to the top of the social hierarchy of her new town—though this was hardly a prize, for Wilmington, North Carolina, was "the dullest place you can imagine" according to Elizabeth's infrequent correspondence, a description which pleased her parents greatly.

"Oh, it's not as bad as all that," Elizabeth dismissed. "In fact, Beth, I think you'd adore it. It's full of strangers—not a soul would recognize just how often you recycle your ball gowns."

"You were unforgivably rude," Mary condemned her sister as they strode towards a table laid with crystal tumblers and champagne flutes. "Mother would have died if she heard you speak like that to a Walker."

Or near enough anyone, for that matter.

"Beth Walker is a stupid cow," Elizabeth said definitively, as though that was enough to end the conversation. "She's just mad—"

"Who's mad?" Edward appeared at his twin's side, holding a tumbler of brandy.

"Beth Walker."

"What'd you do this time?"

"Why must it always be me?" Elizabeth snapped.

Edward shrugged, amused. "Because it usually is."

He took a sip and glanced over the crowd. "Good turnout for you, sister."

"They're not here for me," Mary said quickly—by reflex, more than conviction. "They're here because Father invited them."

"Aye, that's true," Edward nodded.

"Aye? Have you spent so long with the Brynes family that you're starting to speak like an Irishman?"

"The Brynes are good folk. They've done very well for themselves in Georgia. And they're kin to the Walkers, so maybe do us all a favor and stop setting fire to every bridge in the county."

"Oh, Charles has done that well enough already."

"What?" Mary blinked. She could hardly imagine Charles being anything but gracious. He was far too dutiful for scandal.

No, Elizabeth did plenty of that for the family.

"Don't you know about the ruined fortunes of the Walker family?" Elizabeth asked in disbelief, failing to mask her delight.

"It's really not the place—" Edward began to protest, but Elizabeth waved him away.

"Edward, it is our job, nay our duty, to ensure our little sister has all the information necessary to navigate the terrain of entering society and finding a husband."

"And are you—sister of twenty-one, which is essentially a spinster—the right person to be providing her with this guidance?" Edward asked, grinning in the cheekiest of manners.

"I am unmarried by choice, as you well know," Elizabeth responded with a swat to his arm.

"I reckon that wasn't made readily clear from the announcement in Father's paper," Edward dared. ""Remains unwed" were the words used, which if not an Englishman's way of criticizing, then I know not what is."

"I believe, dear brother, that comment was in reference to all of us," Elizabeth clapped back. "Besides, I can hardly bring myself to trust a source that drips of such obvious propaganda, especially with the advertisement for Charles's bank and the new shipping routes wedged into literally every section. Completely shameless!"

"It is Father," Edward chuckled, shaking his head knowingly and bringing his drink to his lips.

Mary studied her siblings, irritated with herself that she had been so distracted anticipating the impending doom of her debut that she had broken with her usual routine and had failed to read the paper this morning.

"As I am sure even you will be aware, little sister, the Walkers are some of the largest indigo producers in the South." Elizabeth finally returned to her original subject.

Mary nodded in acknowledgement.

"But are you also aware that the introduction of the cotton gin has completely changed the hierarchy of cash crops in the South?"

"You always tell a story as though it should be obvious," Edward chided. "If it were obvious, there would be no need to tell it."

"Well then, you tell it if you don't like the way I do it." Elizabeth rolled her eyes as though it were of no consequences to her, as though she had not been the instigator of the entire conversation.

"What's this?" Charles appeared on the other side of Mary.

"Gossip, Charles," Edward confirmed. "You wouldn't be interested."

"Call it what you like, but I do seem to be the only one here who has any interest in our sister's future marriage prospects," Elizabeth declared with a faux self-righteous air which was all too familiar to her siblings.

"I think it's safe to assume that if Father invited them, he considers them a reasonable match." Mary smiled at her eldest brother's level-headedness. There was something comforting in the way Charles saw the world as less complicated, as though others made it that way.

"Before you dismiss it all, you might be interested to know the part you played in this story."

"Elizabeth was just telling us that you burned our bridges with the Walker family."

"Excuse me?" Charles scoffed, staring at the twins in disbelief. "And how might I have done that?"

"I don't know," Edward feigned nonchalance while clearly amused at his elder brother's reaction. "Elizabeth was just about to tell us."

"It is no secret that the Walkers and Sinclairs have been in competition for years, by virtue of both growing indigo."

"Yes..." Charles answered slowly and skeptically. "A little bit of friendly competition never hurt anyone."

"Until," Elizabeth pointed at him accusatorily, "a third-party comes in and tells his old school friend, who happens to be a Sinclair, about this brilliant new invention he's heard about while travelling up North that can separate the seeds and fiber from cotton much more easily."

"Go on."

"Now the Sinclairs see the writing on the wall and know that textiles will move towards cotton, but they need a way to finance these cotton gins. Good news for them, that this same unnamed third party also recently opened a bank in New Orleans, and he can help them finance their new machinery at a very competitive rate of interest.

"And soon we see that as the Sinclairs' fortunes go up, up, up, the Walkers' seems to be going down, down, down at a comparable rate."

Charles, clearly furious, studied his sister with what he believed was a measured caution. Finally, after a moment, he inhaled deeply, choosing his words with care.

"The Walkers are a very respectable Southern family. I do not consider myself an influential enough man to have in any way impacted their fortunes."

His words, quiet but stern, could have been those of their father.

"But is it not true that the Sinclairs adopted the cotton gin, which was a recommendation of yours and financed by your bank? And is it not also true that their fortunes have only risen since then? I mean, cotton is exported everywhere. I believe our shipping company even takes theirs to England. And is it not further true that the rise of cotton has meant the severe decline in the indigo market?"

"You know, Elizabeth, not all things that are true need to be said aloud." Charles looked unsettled, perhaps the discomfort of the consequences of his actions being spoken into existence.

"I'm sure even if that was an outcome, it was unplanned and unintentional." Mary tried to ease the tension. "I mean, who would have known that the market for one of the oldest crops would nearly disappear overnight?"

"Well, Charles did, apparently."

"I would greatly appreciate if you did not go around spreading such untruths," Charles spoke with no room for negotiation—an order, not a request. "The Taylors pride themselves by remaining above family feuds and town squabbles. Whatever story you've woven together, I suggest you keep it firmly in your head where it was created.

"Edward." Charles turned stiffly towards his brother. "I would like to introduce you to someone."

And with that, the conversation ended.

"Must you provoke him so?" Mary turned back to Elizabeth, who looked entirely too pleased with herself. Charles's retreat wasn't just a sign of irritation—it was a surrender, and all three siblings knew it.

"I don't provoke. I reveal," Elizabeth said, entirely too pleased with herself. "The reaction is never my responsibility."

Mary sighed. She hated when her siblings fought—second only to being made the unwilling referee.

"To be clear, you *do* still want my guidance on eligible bachelors this evening?"

"Of course I do," Mary huffed. "I just don't want it to come with a side of family ruin."

Elizabeth smiled, unbothered. "Oh, darling. That depends entirely on the bachelor."

She linked arms with her sister and steered her toward the crowd, the tension behind them unraveling into the hum of string music and society's chatter—for now.

# Chapter IV

Over the next hour, as the ballroom buzzed and the Taylors awaited dinner, Mary found herself approached by nearly every eligible young gentleman in attendance. To her great relief—and mild disbelief—her dance card filled faster than she could glance toward Elizabeth for guidance.

Fortunately, her sister was never far. Acting as both social sentinel and oracle, Elizabeth dispensed intel on each suitor with practiced precision: the official (lineage, fortune, career) and the unofficial (rumors of rakishness, past attachments, and any whispers currently making the rounds). With each passing introduction, the anxiety that had knotted Mary's stomach earlier in the evening began to ease. Even her earlier stumble on the dance floor had faded to nothing more than a faint blush of memory.

"Miss Taylor and Miss Taylor." The forms of Thomas and John Walker bowed low to both Mary and Elizabeth.

Despite her sister's earlier slander of the Walker name, Mary had to admit the brothers presented themselves well—perhaps even *too* well. Tall, strikingly handsome, and possessing that rare combination of formality and Southern ease, they were the finest farm boys the

South had to offer. Their voices carried a faint country drawl—just enough to knock a lady slightly off balance.

They were twins, of course—which only added to their appeal—and it was precisely *because* they were twins, and *because* their sister was also named Elizabeth, and *because* they hailed from English stock nearly as old as the Taylors, that Elizabeth Taylor had taken to calling them 'the poor Taylors'.

"Charles will *die* if he hears you say that. As will Father. As will Mother," Mary had whispered as they approached, hoping to appeal to whatever shred of propriety might still exist within her sister.

"Mr. Walker and Mr. Walker," Elizabeth declared now, one hand landing on her hip in a sharp show of disapproval. "We've been waiting all evening for you to come say hello."

She did not offer her hand to be kissed—a clear sign of her annoyance.

"Do you find it amusing," she went on, voice lilting ever so slightly upward, "to keep a pair of simple Virginian girls waiting?"

Both young men flushed at the mild scolding—but practically glowed beneath it, delighted by the idea that their absence had caused such disappointment.

Mary, on the other hand, gawked at her sister's effortless duplicity.

"Well, ma'am," John Walker began, the slightly larger of the twins who had been sweet on Elizabeth for as long as Mary could remember, "we know you and Miss Taylor are always the belles of any ball. And seeing as this one belongs to Miss Taylor, we didn't want to be causing you any annoyance by clinging to your side like a saddle to a horse."

"But that's not to say we weren't itching to come over here the moment we saw Miss Taylor leave the dance floor," Thomas insisted. "We were just trying to be respectful, ma'am."

Elizabeth softened, if only slightly. "Well, while I wish you hadn't, I do understand your reasoning." She leaned forward, fingers brushing John's arm in mock-conspiracy. "Now, tell me—is it true?"

John blinked, clearly thrown by both the question and the nearness of her neckline. "Ma'am?"

"That you're the best horseman in the South," Elizabeth finished with a sly smile. "Or perhaps it's your brother?"

Both men laughed, pleased and flustered.

"Well ma'am, I reckon we both have a different view of that, and it'll depend on which one of us you ask," John replied good-naturedly.

The Walkers of South Carolina might be known for their dwindling indigo crops, but they were also known for their horse breeding. There were no finer colts in the South than those that came out of Charleston, nor was there anywhere better for horse racing. All the Walkers were accomplished horsemen and horsewomen, a point they defended with fierce and brazen pride, despite the fact few would have been bold enough to argue otherwise.

"You will both have to grace us with your presence at the races this year," Thomas Walker insisted, turning his full attention to Mary. "We would be honored to host you. And Frances, my dear sister, would be so delighted to see you, Miss Taylor."

"Oh, it will have been ages since I last saw Frances! How is she?"

"She's well, Miss Taylor, thank you for asking. Heartbroken to be missing your debut, of course. But hers isn't until winter."

Mary nodded sympathetically. "Please send her my regards. I've been a terrible friend—I meant to write."

"Well Miss Taylor, she hasn't written to you either," Thomas offered, a silly sideways smile taking over his face. "And I reckon correspondence goes both ways. But I will of course pass on your regards.

"Well, the men will be looking to skin us if we monopolize your time for too long, but would each of you do us the honor of a dance?" Thomas asked hopefully.

"Why, of course—" Mary started, but her voice caught. Thomas Walker hadn't looked away from her once.

The way he stared—like she was the most fascinating thing he'd ever seen—sent a strange twist through her stomach. Not nerves exactly.

Something else.

Something like... anticipation.

He wasn't the only man who had looked at her that way tonight, but he was the tallest—and his eyes had a weight to them, as if they meant to pull her under. She fought the urge to glance at the breadth of his shoulders.

"I'm afraid we're all booked up," Elizabeth cut in crisply, arms crossed and chin lifted.

Panic bloomed in Mary's chest. She opened her mouth to protest—but Elizabeth shot her a look so sharp, it snapped her lips shut again.

"Oh Miss Taylor, don't say that," John Walker protested, reaching for one of her hands. "You'll break our hearts if you carry on like that."

Elizabeth allowed the contact but gave no ground. "If your hearts are so fragile, why wait so very long to come and ask us?"

"You know why," John pleaded. "You must."

Elizabeth placed a hand on her hip. "If I did know, I've quite forgotten. Please, remind me."

Thomas stepped in, gaze still locked on Mary. "It's no secret that Virginian women are the most beautiful in the South. We've been trying to summon the courage ever since Miss Taylor left the dance floor."

Mary inhaled sharply.

Had she just... intimidated someone?

Was *this* how Elizabeth felt all the time?

"I suppose," she heard herself say, her voice steadier than expected, "we can make an exception."

She turned to Thomas. "Are you free, Mr. Walker, for the opening reel?"

Thomas's smile softened. "Miss Taylor," he said, almost reverently. "I would be honored."

"That was splendidly done!" Elizabeth congratulated Mary as they took their leave from the Walker brothers. "Now, a tip," Elizabeth linked her arm into Mary's, leaning her head towards hers. "The Riveras and the Walkers are close business acquaintances. So, when you're dancing with Thomas Walker and Manuel Rivera, make sure to mention the other, just to ensure they both know of the options available to you." At the suggestion, Mary gasped, but Elizabeth continued, a finger plunging into the air in glee.

"And Beth Walker will be furious that we open the second half of the night with her brothers!"

"What exactly is between you and Beth Walker?" Mary ventured, deliberately using the name Beth in an attempt to win her sister's favor, and in doing so, more information.

"Don't worry about that cow," Elizabeth dismissed. "Actually, speaking of her, I do need to go find that Brynes boy she's sweet on and steal him for the dance he's promised to her." Were it anyone else, Mary would have assumed it was a rude joke, but Elizabeth, true to her word, scanned the room on tiptoes, and having identified her target, made a beeline for Eamon Brynes, leaving Mary alone for the first time in the evening.

Elizabeth was so fearless, Mary marvelled, torn between admiration for her sister and disapproval for some of the ways she wielded her powers.

And yet, she should hardly criticize, for she had learned so much with Elizabeth by her side.

She had been right. It was silly to be so anxious, Mary acknowledged, and gently flicking her wrist, she stared down at the fan, the names of her future dance partners neatly written on each pane.

Her card had filled quickly, as Elizabeth had promised it would, all with eligible young men who had sought her for a dance. Mary had always found herself desiring male attention (even if she knew that no well-brought-up

Protestant young lady should admit to such a thing), and now that she had experienced it, she had to confess that she really did see what all the fuss was about!

Scanning the names, her eyes lingered at the top pane.

Thomas Walker.

Mary thought back to his eyes, the way they seemed to consume her... A hot flush raced through Mary's body, causing her to shiver.

"Mary," a hand gently rested on her shoulder, pulling her mind back from...well, from where Mary was not entirely sure, but she was entirely sure that it was not the kind of place a young lady should be contemplating.

Particularly in a room full of people.

"If you have a moment, there is someone I should like you to meet."

"And is there anyone here you might be interested in, dear brother?" Mary asked, tucking her hand into her brother's elbow as he led her across the room. She tried to sway her hips as she walked, subtly and delicately, the way she had seen Elizabeth do and had never been daring enough to try.

Until this evening.

"Ah, you know me, I am so busy with the bank," Charles dismissed.

"You are nearly thirty, brother, which is well within marrying age for a gentleman."

"Your first evening on the market and you are already lecturing me as though you're an expert!"

"I only wish for your happiness."

"And I yours, dear sister, above all else," Charles smiled down at her, patting the hand that rested on his forearm in a paternal fashion. "We are so proud of you, you know—Father, Mother, and I. I know, it is not always easy to be...different, but if you ever have a doubt, remember that we are made in God's image: equally loved for our uniqueness. And I truly believe that he will help us to find those on this Earth who sees us as he does."

"That is exactly what I wish," Mary breathed, seeing herself reflected in Charles's understanding eyes.

"As do I, sister. I believe it will take more time, but I implore you not to let that trouble you—the best things this life has to offer often require a wait. It is the reason patience is a fruit of the spirit.

"And speaking of someone who might benefit from some patience, Mary, this is Leander Doucet," Charles announced, interrupting her thoughts. At his words, a man turned, extracting himself from a nearby conversation, and the full beam of his attention hit Mary like a sandbag to her stomach.

Gone were her wholesome musings on the gifts of the Lord, a heat flushing through her body as she gazed at Leander Doucet.

"Miss Taylor," he smiled brightly, reaching for her small gloved hand and kissing it. Mary's insides fluttered, and she stared, captivated, at the tall and built man who stood before her. "I do hope you know that whatever tales your brother is telling of me are categorically false, for any man who speaks of another without the subject there to defend himself certainly speaks untruths."

"Leander, don't fill my baby sister's head with nonsense." Mary winced at the use of the word "baby." The last thing she wished was for this man to think of her as anything other than a woman.

And an available woman at that.

"And besides, it is patience of which we speak, a virtue which we know the Lord had run short of by the time he made it to you."

"Your brother, Miss Taylor, speaks hogwash, for what he crudely dubs impatience, I prefer to think of as ardour."

"You will forgive Mr. Doucet, dear sister, for by virtue of his French ancestry, he suffers from the misfortune of a devastatingly high opinion of himself, when in fact it is my sister Mary we are celebrating this evening."

"I am not only so glad to make your acquaintance, Miss Taylor, but also relieved you are here to bear witness to your brother's assault on my character."

Handsome and quick-witted.

Mary racked her brain, desperately searching for her own equally impressive remark, something to elicit a chuckle and perhaps an eyebrow raise, but words, which were usually such good and dependable friends to her, seemed to elude her under the penetrating gaze of Leander Doucet.

*Lord help me.*

"It was so kind of you and your family to make arrangements for me, and at such short notice, to attend," he nodded, returning Mary's hand lightly to her side.

"Oh, of course." Mary could hear her own words, but was sure it was someone else forming them and shoving them through her lips. "Have you come from far, Mr. Doucet?"

"Mobile."

"All the way from Alabama!" Mary exclaimed, running the math quickly in her head. "But that must be nearly nine hundred miles!"

"Yes, ma'am." He smiled modestly. "But it wasn't a bad journey at all, well worth it, of course. This is a splendid evening, indeed! You wouldn't find anything like this in Alabama, I can tell you that for sure!"

"And are you a friend of my brother's from university? Or perhaps you met during his time up North?"

"Leander is actually one of my business partners. Though, you are right, we did meet up North. It was word of the cotton gin that made us both think this could revolutionize the South, if folk had the money to procure one."

At her brother's words, Mary started, for she had, momentarily, forgotten he was there.

"It is amazing, Miss Taylor, how many people in the South do not trust banks, which is why we were able to be one of the first."

"Well indeed," Mary nodded. "But surely that cannot be any surprise?"

"And how do you reckon that, Miss Taylor?"

"Well, after the disaster of the First National Bank, the public lost trust in the institution. Plus, the second one is largely concentrated in the North and run mostly by Northern politicians. Southern society has always been more isolated and independent, not to mention concentrated in assets as opposed to capital. We are a less liquid society. Which is why I say I am not sure it surprises me that there is a natural distrust among Southerners of a formalized banking system. Which is fascinating, considering the levels of debt that exists in many Southern states." Mary finished her thesis abruptly, remembering all at once where she was and who she was speaking to as she cursed herself for forgetting.

"I told you she was brilliant, did I not, Leander?" Charles chuckled. "Can you tell she is the daughter of a politician?"

"I happen to agree with you, Miss Taylor," Leander nodded through a lipped smile, clearly amused. "It is rare to meet a woman who enjoys such topics of conversations, let alone one who can engage so thoughtfully."

"Yes, well," Mary tried to mirror his amused smile with her own, desperately searching for something charming and quippish to say in return. "It is always nice to hear that a woman's mind may be valued as much as her virtues and ability to sew."

"Of course, Miss Taylor," Leander nodded thoughtfully. "Looks fade, but a sharp mind keeps a man company all his life."

*Do not gape, for it is not ladylike*, the admonishment of her mother rung in her ears.

Though, I am sure were Miss Taylor able to speak for herself, she would desire it made clear that this was most often than not a critique levied towards Elizabeth, for unlike her sister, Mary had inherited the appropriate dose of shame expected of a well-brought up Christian lady.

Perhaps even more than was necessary.

Her heart thrummed in her chest as she studied Mr. Doucet's face, searching for something—anything—to decode his intent.

Because even now, even *after* all this, her thoughts kept returning to Thomas Walker. To the way he had looked at her—urgent, hungry, as though he'd stumbled upon something he didn't know he needed until that very moment.

It was a look she'd never received before. A feeling she hadn't dared hope could be hers. And yet, Leander's words, his gentle regard for her mind, had stirred something just as unexpected—a recognition.

A reverence.

Was it truly too much to ask for both?

A man who saw her mind.

And a man who saw her body.

Mary dared not name the latter. But she knew it when she felt it.

Leander held her gaze with that calm curiosity—the kind a gentleman offers his friend's younger sister on her debut—warm, polite, and perfectly appropriate.

He looked at her exactly as a gentleman should.

Which was, of course, the problem.

Because though her heart had steadied, something deeper stirred—not in fear, nor even in excitement, but in the quiet realization that the world was suddenly more complicated than she had prepared for.

And as she stood beneath the glow of a dozen chandeliers and a thousand expectations, Mary found herself wondering what it might feel like to be looked at... differently.

She understood Elizabeth now better than she ever had, Mary reasoned, as she made her way toward the ladies' retiring room, her gloved fingers brushing along the silk of her skirt.

There was something about being wanted—*craved*—for one's beauty and charm that felt... was the word *delicious*?

The thought startled her, and a flush of embarrassment crept up her neck. To think it—let alone feel it—made her suddenly and deeply guilty. It was not the sort of thing a well-raised lady was meant to desire, let alone pursue. And yet, the sensation lingered, warm and unfamiliar, curling somewhere just beneath her ribs.

Mary turned the knob of the lavatory and quickly shut the door behind her. Confident the latch was secure, she exhaled and reached behind her back, fumbling with the ties of her petticoats.

It would be a nightmare to get everything back on again—but she had to know what was happening.

She had stood beside Leander Doucet for as long as she could bear it, trying to make polite conversation while her thoughts tangled and twisted like the ties of her corset. His smooth, handsome features danced in her mind, but it was the ghost of Thomas Walker's stare that clung to her—lingering in a way that made her knees unsteady.

The heat building between her legs had become unbearable. She was sure something was wrong. And worse, she had no idea what to do. She couldn't imagine asking Mother. Or Elizabeth.

For how would she even explain it?

Panicked now, she let the heavy skirts fall to the floor. She couldn't remove the dress entirely without help, but without the outer layers, she could at least examine herself — confirm that nothing was... *broken*.

*Why... wet?* she wondered in horror, running her fingers across the fabric of her cotton pantalettes. Her courses had come only two weeks earlier — it couldn't be that. Perhaps sweat?

But no. Not like this. Not there.

With trembling hands, she tugged the pantalettes down and examined herself. Everything looked normal. Carefully, she parted a bit of hair, checking for a rash, a mark, *anything* to explain the burning ache that pulsed steadily in her core.

Driven mostly by panic, Mary let her fingers brush gently over her most sensitive skin—and gasped. A tremor ran through her entire body, and she had to clutch the wall to steady herself.

The feeling wasn't pain. Not exactly. But it bloomed hot and sharp and sweet all at once.

She flushed, mortified. As if she'd uncovered something she was never meant to find.

And yet... when her fingers found that little knot of skin again, the ache intensified, a growing pressure she didn't understand but couldn't ignore. It felt like... like something waiting to be undone.

*Released.*

She looked around the room, frantic. Her skirts tangled around her ankles. Using the hem of her dress, she fanned herself desperately. The heat was dizzying. How could she be so warm when it was barely spring?

She begged silently for an answer—from God, from reason—*from anyone.*

But instead, she saw Leander's face.

It shimmered behind her eyes, overwhelming every effort to still her breath. If he wasn't the Devil himself, then surely he belonged to him. Who else could make a woman feel so entirely undone?

*What is this?* Mary thought, pressing a hand to her chest. She had always imagined courtship as walks through manicured gardens, lively debates over literature, a surprise bouquet or note of affection.

She still wanted all of that. But now... now it was overshadowed by something else. Something urgent and consuming.

She closed her eyes.

And imagined Leander Doucet standing there with her.

His eyes bore into her, as Thomas Walker's had—only here, she didn't look away. She reached for him, her fingers threading through his. He stepped closer, towering over her, his body warm, his smile a promise.

He touched her chin, lifting her face toward his, and pressed a kiss to her lips—light as air, yet it stole her breath.

Her exhale was almost a sob.

She needed more.

She absolutely required it.

He kissed her again, not gently this time, but with purpose. His hand slid to the back of her neck. His mouth grazed her collarbone. Her body shivered, lit with sensation. She leaned into him, feeling the firmness of his chest, the power in his arms. Even through their clothes, she could feel the shape of him—the strength, the tension.

She didn’t understand it.
Only that she didn’t want it to stop.
Not yet.

# Chapter V

Mary emerged from the bathroom flushed, grateful that no one at the party—so far as she was aware—had the ability to read minds. She would have died of embarrassment, both from her discovery and from what was surely a sloppy attempt to put herself back together.

She had splashed her face with cold water until the crimson in her cheeks dulled to a respectable rose.

*Was that what Elizabeth and Charles's friend had been caught doing in the stable...?*

She flushed again at the thought, but oddly, a calm had overtaken her. A soft cloud of peace dulled her nerves as she let her hand trail along the banister. She had performed the same motion only hours before, clinging to her father's arm like a lifeline.

If only she could go back and tell that girl it wouldn't be as bad as all that.

Yes, she'd tripped during the opening dance—but everything had worked itself out.

"I've already told you, I have the first dance."

Mary froze.

The voice—sharp, clipped—belonged to Thomas Walker. It drifted from a room just up ahead.

"Only one dance?" an older man responded, irritation bleeding through every syllable.

"We have one each, isn't that right, John?"

"Yes, one each with the Taylor sisters," John confirmed.

Mary crept forward, instinctively avoiding the parts of the floor that creaked. Through the sliver of a barely ajar door, she peered into the room—what had once been the children's playroom, now an overflow library, stuffed with volumes from her father's downstairs collection.

Thomas leaned lazily against the fireplace. Across from him, two men sat in twin chairs: John Walker and their father.

"Why only one each?" Mr. Walker growled. "Do you not understand the stakes here, boys? Have I not explained it enough?"

"Yes, Father, we understand," Thomas muttered, rubbing his temples. "She offered me the first dance. I didn't even have to ask. I assure you, I have it under control."

"And what about you?" Mr. Walker snapped at John. "You leaving your brother to do all the work?"

"I am pursuing Elizabeth Taylor, as you well know," John replied, his voice quiet and wounded.

"Well, clearly you're not doing it very well," Mr. Walker barked. "She's been of marrying age for nearly four years, and you've still got nothing to show for it. Have you even asked the question?"

"Miss Taylor is one of the most sought-after Belles in—"

"The way I hear it, she's ruined goods."

At that, both John and Mary inhaled sharply—in unison.

"She is not a hussy!" John exploded, rising to his feet.

Mary's entire body tensed.

"Calm down," Thomas said, catching his brother's sleeve. "John, look at me."

John turned, jaw tight.

"You need to come to terms with the fact that Elizabeth Taylor may never agree to marry you. And if she doesn't, she'll marry someone else."

"I *know* she has feelings for me," John said desperately. "I just need more time to win her heart."

Mary blinked back sudden tears. The sincerity in John's voice—his devotion to Elizabeth—was touching, even beautiful. If only her sister could hear him, maybe she'd...

"We don't *have* time," Mr. Walker snapped, shattering her thoughts. "While you're off dancing around with some tart, your brother's out here doing all the work. Do I not have *two* able-bodied sons?"

Mary's chest burned. *How dare* this man speak of her sister like that—*twice!* And in *her* home?

"Father, this isn't helping," Thomas said, stepping in.

Not exactly a defense. But better than silence.

"John, you know the family's finances," Thomas continued, voice lower now. "We need to clear some of the debt. You and I are the only ones positioned to do that.

"And before you say 'what about the horses'..." he raised a hand, stopping John's objection before it began. "You know that covers a fraction of the hole. We need capital. Real capital. And the fastest way to get it is through a dowry."

Her breath caught in her throat. A quiet, unladylike sound escaped her lips—not quite a sob, but something sharp and involuntary.

She didn't want to believe it.

But there it was.

They didn't see her.

They saw a dowry.

A way out.

She wasn't there to be loved.

She was there to be leveraged.

"If you can't marry Elizabeth Taylor—and soon—then you need to find someone else."

Mary's legs wobbled. And to think, Charles had flat out dismissed Elizabeth's suspicions.

"That's easy for you to say," John muttered. "You've never been in love. If you had, you wouldn't ask me—"

"I'm not asking," Thomas cut in. "I'm *telling*."

He paused, then added, "And John, before you paint yourself a martyr—don't forget that I too have danced with Elizabeth Taylor. I *like* her. I stepped aside because you asked me to. And now, I'm expected to pursue her mouse of a sister."

Mary froze.

"She's hardly a wisp of her sister. You'd barely notice her if you passed her in the street. And in that gown today, with those ridiculous skirts from Europe, she looks like a child playing dress-up."

Thomas's voice didn't falter. The words came smooth, practiced.

Mary's tears fell silently.

Everything she'd feared was true.

They didn't *want* her.

They tolerated her.

For the name.

For the money.

But truly *desire* her?

Don't be absurd.

"What I'm saying," Thomas said more gently, placing a hand on John's shoulder, "is that you're not the only one being asked to make sacrifices."

*Marrying me would be a sacrifice,* Mary thought. She pressed a hand to the door frame, barely able to hold herself upright.

"For what it's worth," John offered, "she seems quiet. Docile. I imagine she'll make a good wife."

"Then *you* marry her!" Thomas exploded.

Mary doubled over, her stomach wrenching violently.

*Not like this. Please, God, not like this.*

She stumbled back from the door, hand to her abdomen, fighting off the urge to vomit.

She had to leave. *Now.*

Bracing herself against the wall, she staggered down the hallway toward the only sanctuary she could think of: her bedroom, at the far end of the house—tucked away, because she was the youngest.

Tears and sweat blurred her vision. Her legs were numb. Still, she moved.

At last, she reached the door. The knob slipped in her clammy grasp. She gritted her teeth, grabbed a fold of her dress, and used the fabric to twist the handle.

It turned.

She flung the door open and slammed it shut behind her with everything she had.

Mary lay face down, tears soaking into the cushions of her bed. She'd heard voices in the hallway—the slam of her bedroom door had clearly alerted the Walker men to someone's presence.

*Good,* she thought bitterly. Let them stew in the shame of knowing they'd been overheard. Let them feel even a sliver of what they deserved—for their plotting, their presumption, for wandering the upper floor of their host's home uninvited.

They could leave her alone. Alone, to die of embarrassment and despair.

She sniffled and twisted, rolling onto her back and staring up at the canopy of her four-poster bed.

*A mouse.*

They had likened her to a mouse.

But a mouse who might make a good wife, apparently—for her docility. Mary laughed bitterly.

*How could I have been so utterly foolish?*

Tears welled again, grief returning in waves. Her imagination leapt ahead: the endless parade of attempted matches her family would force upon her, once it became clear she was incapable of finding a husband herself. The moment would come—she could feel it already—when she would be made to choose between marrying someone she could not love or choosing solitude.

It felt horribly unfair. She wasn't cruel, or dim, or poorly bred. True, she didn't shine like Elizabeth—but she couldn't be *that* hideous, could she?

*A rodent,* she reminded herself. *Thomas Walker called me a rodent.*

Even he—the poor version of a Taylor—wouldn't have her.

Only what came *with* her.

Her chest tightened as her mind returned to the way Thomas had looked at her—how she had felt, for a moment, as though she were truly seen.

And to think it had all been an act.

Mary shook her head and laughed bitterly at her own idiocy, even as the tears spilled again.

"What's going on?"

Mary turned her head slowly, not even startled. She'd been so consumed with her own despair, she hadn't heard the door open.

"Are you laughing or crying?"

"Both," she squeaked, squeezing her eyes shut as a fresh wave of tears slipped down her cheeks, pooling in the dip of her bodice. The front of her gown would have been soaked if it hadn't been so low-cut.

Elizabeth perched on the edge of the bed and gently brushed the tightly curled tendrils from Mary's forehead, framing her face as delicately as a portrait.

"What's happened?"

"Can I ask you something?" Mary blinked back the tears.

"One question, and then we must return downstairs. They're waiting for you."

"What happened with that boy in the stable?"

Elizabeth blinked. "What?"

"Charles's friend," Mary clarified. "The one they found you with, before Father sent you to North Carolina."

Elizabeth raised a brow. "Why are you asking about that?"

"Please tell me." Mary's voice cracked. "Please."

Elizabeth studied her for a moment, then nodded. "I'll tell you—if you swear never to repeat it. Not to anyone. It could ruin my reputation, and you know how a woman values a thing like that."

Mary managed a shaky smile and nodded.

"We were kissing," Elizabeth said calmly, watching with amusement as Mary's eyes grew wide. "With tongue. Among other things."

Mary inhaled sharply. "Tongue?"

Elizabeth laughed. "It's not as dreadful as it sounds."

*Surely*, Mary thought, *a well-bred girl isn't supposed to let a man kiss her like that. And certainly not be caught doing it.*

And as for the "other things"... *what other things could there be past kissing?*

"You'll understand soon enough," Elizabeth said gently.

The tears resumed.

"For heaven's sake," Elizabeth muttered, brushing them away. "What now?"

"I'll never understand," Mary sobbed.

"Don't be ridiculous, of course you will."

"Thomas Walker thinks I'm a mouse," Mary choked.

"He *said* that to you?"

"I overheard him speaking with his father and brother. He was only pretending to be interested in me—for our family's money."

Elizabeth's expression hardened instantly. "Those plebs," she spat. "As if a Taylor would ever stoop to marry a Walker."

But Mary barely heard her.

"I can't marry," she whispered. "I'll never know if someone loves *me*, or just what I come with."

"That's stupid," Elizabeth said flatly, though without cruelty. "A man will *always* be at least partially interested in the Taylor fortune. You might as well accept that now."

"For *you* it might be partial," Mary said, sitting up. "But for me..." Her voice cracked. "For me, it's the *only* relevant factor."

Elizabeth rolled her eyes, though there was no malice in it. "Mary, really, who cares what a stupid country boy thinks? Just because Thomas Walker said something cruel—"

"I *care*, Elizabeth!" Mary cried. "I thought he liked me."

"What's going on?" Both sisters turned at the sound of Edward's voice as he stormed into the room, his face full of alarm. "Who did this?"

Mary shook her head, unable to say it aloud.

"Thomas Walker is a bastard," Elizabeth said coolly.

"*Did he touch her?*" Edward's voice thundered.

"They're *emotional* bruises," Mary said quickly.

"That's still too many." He crossed the room. "What did he do?"

Elizabeth stood. "He implied he was courting Mary—only to secure her dowry."

Edward's face flushed red. "He said this to you?"

"He didn't know I could hear," Mary whispered. "But yes."

"This South Carolinian insults my sister, in *our* home, on the night of her debut?" Edward thundered. "I'll kill him."

"Stop!" Elizabeth grabbed his arm. "Where are you going?"

"To find him. If he's any kind of man, he'll agree to a duel—"

"Absolutely not!"

"You think I'll let him insult our family without consequence?"

"You'll ruin her night," Elizabeth snapped. "And worse—you'll immortalize his words. The embarrassment would be unbearable."

Edward exhaled sharply.

"I would happily put a bullet in his chest," he said, as if offering his youngest sister a cup of tea.

"Thank you," Mary whispered. "But if anyone finds out, I'll die."

He nodded solemnly. "I won't forget this."

"I have an idea," Elizabeth said, turning back to Mary. "You need to return downstairs. They're waiting for you to open the second half of the evening."

Mary shook her head. "I can't face him. He's my first dance. I'll feel like such a fool."

"You don't have to dance with him."

"But he's the first name on my card." She gestured to the fan lying near the wall, where it had been hurled in anger.

"Then dance with someone else."

"It's not that simple." Mary protested. It was so like Elizabeth to be so reductive, as though it were the most obvious thing in the world and not the height of rudeness and impropriety to ditch one's dance partner without even the decency of informing him first.

Then again, Thomas Walker was not exactly entitled to any decency from her.

"It *is*," Elizabeth said breezily. "You were enjoying your conversation with Manuel Rivera earlier. Why not him?

"Oh, wait!" Elizabeth lit up. "No—You should dance with one of the Sinclairs!" Elizabeth looked delighted with her genius, clapping her hands excitedly. "Oh, that'll just kill Thomas Walker! Which of the Sinclair men are here?" she asked, turning towards her brother.

"Shouldn't you know?" Edward asked, raising a mirthful eyebrow. "I have it on good authority that all of the brothers are beaux of yours.

"And that you have promised dances with all of them."

"Go for the one nearest Thomas's age. Which one is that?" Elizabeth asked, placing her palms out to either side and scrunching her face in concentration. "I can never keep them straight."

"Archibald." Edward rolled his eyes. "Really, Elizabeth, you are unbelievable."

"It's not my fault." She waved a hand dismissively. "Really, I don't know what those parents were thinking, giving all their children names that start with the letter 'A'. They all now need to work twice as hard to be memorable."

"It makes sense you would understand their plight, considering you have a familiar situation with Elizabeth Walker."

"You—" Elizabeth pointed at him sharply. "Watch your tongue.

"So," she turned back to Mary, beaming. "Go down there and ask Archibald Sinclair for the first dance."

"But what if he already has a partner?"

"Then ask in such a way that he can't say no."

Which is exactly what she did.

Mary strode into the ballroom with such conviction that the attendees barely had time to open the doors for her. But she didn't pause—she walked with the hard-headed certainty that they *would* open, and that they would do so just in time to frame her grand entrance. As the doors flung open in a flurry, the room turned to see Mary Taylor standing in the doorway, pausing for a moment to allow the guests to take her in, exactly as Elizabeth had instructed.

*"Take a breath,'* Elizabeth advised. *"Survey the room, carelessly. Smile with your eyes, not with your lips."*

Mary obeyed. She let her gaze drift slowly, feigning disinterest, though her heart thundered in her chest.

*"Until, that is, you find the object of your attention."*

She had already found him. Archibald Sinclair stood tall beside his brother Alexander—easily one of the most handsome men in the room, with dark brown curls that flirted with his collar and a chest built to wear a jacket like armor. He was far out of Mary's league, so far as she could tell—but Elizabeth had insisted she set aside her doubts.

Her sister's tactics, after all, seemed to work rather well.

Allowing her eyes to land on Archibald Sinclair, Mary took him in, starting at the top of his head and slowly dragging her gaze down to his chest before trailing back up to meet his eyeline.

To her surprise—though it should not have been a surprise—the scene played out exactly as Elizabeth said it would, and when Mary raised her eyes to Archibald's face, his were already there waiting for her.

*"Hold his gaze, but only for a moment—long enough for him to know you didn't happen upon his face by accident, but not too long that it becomes a scandal."*

Mary held for a moment, allowing their eyes to linger on one another.

*"And then, once you've held his attention hostage, once you've allowed his mind to wander to what it might feel like to swim in your eyes, once you've made him like your attention and allowed him to feel fear at the prospect of it being taken away, that's when you finally abate his fears with the reassurance of a smile."*

Before she tilted her head to one side and allowed her lips to spread across her face, the rest of her features illuminating at the gesture.

*"And he will, without fail, smile back,"* Elizabeth guaranteed.

And did he?

Well, of course he did.

*"And that, my dear Mary, is how you will find yourself opening the second half of the evening in the arms of the South's most eligible bachelor."*

Before Mary could think—"*don't think*," Elizabeth had instructed—she was crossing the room at a slow and steady pace. The eyes of the room watched her in awestruck silence, holding their breaths so that the soft touch of her slippers could be heard on the wooden floor.

*Do not think*, Mary repeated to herself, knowing thought would dissolve whatever magic she'd summoned into being.

There was something discomfiting about femininity performed so deliberately—especially when designed to court male attention. It unsettled Mary, both on principle and because she had never believed herself to possess the kind of beauty that earned such attention.

Still, she swayed her hips just slightly, with the quiet confidence Elizabeth had promised her would come.

*"Mary, the men pay attention to me not just because I'm beautiful, but because I decided that it was time that they should.*

*"Your only limitation is your own opinion of yourself."*

Finally, Mary approached her target. Archibald Sinclair stood waiting for her, grinning radiantly in a dinner jacket of deep navy-blue velvet, cut short and buttoned at the waist, with long tails at the back swooshing dramatically towards the floor. Without hesitation he reached for her hand and swept into a low deliberate bow. His lips brushed the back of her hand—lightly, but with just enough pressure to send heat spiraling through her chest. He looked up from his bent position, his eyes fixed on hers, his smile unhurried.

He lingered, just a moment longer than was entirely appropriate.

Mary's skin flushed at his touch and the provocation that comes with pushing the boundaries of accepted social norms.

Though, if she were being perfectly honest, she did not mind in the slightest.

# Chapter VI

The next morning, Mary lay in bed on her back, staring up at the canopy overhead.

She thought of the last time she had been in this position—hours ago, drowning in humiliation, utterly convinced her life was over and that spinsterhood was her unavoidable fate.

It was astonishing how much could change in a single evening.

"Are you still in bed, Sleeping Beauty?" Elizabeth burst through the door and leapt onto the mattress, landing on her knees with a dramatic bounce.

"Are we not both still in our nightgowns?" Mary asked, gesturing towards Elizabeth's white cotton shift, the hem skimming the tops of her bare feet.

"How do you feel?" Elizabeth ignored the jab, flopping across Mary's legs and letting her hair spill in all directions.

"My feet have never felt worse," Mary admitted. "I can barely feel my toes."

"That's how it should be when you've spent all evening being whirled around the dance floor in the arms of handsome men. You'll get used to it," Elizabeth promised with a grin.

"Oh Mary, you were perfect. You burst through that door with so much entitlement, and the way you approached—what's his name again?" She tapped her chin theatrically. "That oldest Sinclair boy? Or is he the middle one..." She abandoned the effort. "Well, *he* was ready to melt."

*"Miss Taylor," Archibald Sinclair breathed, returning to his full standing position but still in possession of Mary's hand. "I regret that I had missed the opportunity to make your acquaintance this evening until now."*

*"Indeed Mr. Sinclair, I was rather disappointed we had not yet had a chance to speak," Mary agreed, her voice soft and coquettish. While she could imitate the voice she'd heard Elizabeth use on men, she could not quite bring herself to accuse Archibald of ruining her night with his absence, as Elizabeth had done with the Walker twins.*

*That was simply a bridge too far.*

*"But never mind," Mary smiled up at him through her lashes, blinking more than was strictly necessary. "We are now."*

*Archibald returned her smile—and more. He bowed again and kissed her hand a second time.*

*The crowd gasped.*

*Mary's heart pounded.*

*"Mr. Sinclair." Mary stepped forward, emboldened by his second kiss. "I suddenly find myself no longer engaged for the first dance of the evening."*

*"That'll make me sound pathetic," Mary had protested earlier, when Elizabeth rehearsed the line with her.*

*Only if you deliver it that way," Elizabeth replied confidently. "If you sound like you simply couldn't fill your dance card, then yes—tragic. But if you deliver it properly, he'll see it as both his good fortune and an opportunity to rescue a beautiful lady in distress. And men..."*

*"Men love helping helpless women," Edward chimed in. "It makes us feel useful."*

*"Exactly," Elizabeth said, unbothered.*

*"And you will, I hope, forgive my boldness," eyes lowered to Archibald's chest, "but I could not face the embarrassment of sitting out the first dance of my own debut ball." She studied the gold brocade embroidered into his shirtfront for another beat, then looked up again, her voice even softer.*

*"Which is why I was hoping—perhaps against hope—that you might escort me." Mary delivered her punchline demurely, smiling at him through her eyes, as though the fate of her very existence could be found only in his reply.*

*Just as Elizabeth had shown her.*

*"Miss Taylor." Archibald Sinclair took her hand, raising it to meet his mouth—his lips—for the third time.*

*The third time!*

*Mary need not look, for she knew eyebrows across the ballroom reached for the ceiling in delighted disbelief for having been gifted something to discuss over the coming weeks.*

*And as for his intended dance partner... well, Mary had not heard that Archibald Sinclair was a rogue, but perhaps she had not been paying close enough attention!*

*"It would be," he began slowly, finally touching her skin to his lips. "My absolute honor."*

"Part of me cannot believe I did that." Mary murmured, smiling at the memory—a memory that shot a hot pang of desire straight through her nightdress.

"Believe it, because it happened," Elizabeth rolled over beside her. "By the way, while you were causing scandal with Mr. Sinclair—"

"Can you still not remember his name?!"

"I'll remember his name if he becomes my brother-in-law," Elizabeth dismissed. "As I was saying, while you were playing Cinderella, I was standing next to a very furious Thomas Walker." Elizabeth giggled with delight at the thought. "Oh Mary, I wish you could have seen his face when you walked towards the dance floor without him. He was the color of a tomato!"

"Wh-what happened?" Mary sat up slightly, the lightness in her chest slipping away. She had known there might be consequences—even whispers—if it became known that she'd promised her first dance to Thomas Walker. But she'd hoped, perhaps naively, that embarrassment might keep him from saying anything at all.

As it happened, that was indeed *very* naïve.

*"What in the devil is this?" Thomas Walker demanded as he watched Mary and Archibald together, hands clasped, float towards the centre of the room to lead the Grand March.*

*"What in the devil is what, Thomas?" Charles asked.*

*"Your sister had promised the first dance to me." Thomas sputtered, utterly dumbstruck.*

*"Perhaps there's been a misunderstanding," Charles suggested hurriedly. "Mary would never meaningfully—"*

*"Actually Charles, Mary did meaningfully give her original partner the boot." Elizabeth explained calmly, lightly, as though it were of little consequence.*

*"And why might that be?!" Thomas demanded.*

*"I suspect, Mr. Walker, it is because she happened to overhear a conversation in which you likened her to a mouse," she said coolly, staring up at him with hard, unflinching eyes. "And made same rather repugnant claims about desiring to marry her for her expected dowry." At these words, Thomas flushed red, his mouth opening and closing like that of a fish as he tried to find the right words.*

*"Can you really blame a lady for deciding to seek a different dance partner after hearing such a thing?" Elizabeth placed one hand on her protruding hip in challenge as she stared up at her victim, demanding an answer.*

*"It is not polite to listen in on the conversations of others," Thomas finally managed, his tone low and condescending.*

*"Nor is it polite to invite yourself to the upstairs floor of your host's home without their invitation," Elizabeth snapped back.*

*"Miss Taylor!" John Walker appeared at her side, practically breathless. "I believe it is time for our dance." The eagerness dripped from his smile as he reached for her arm.*

*"Thank you, but no." Elizabeth shook her head, wrenching her arm free with a flick of her wrist.*

*"But, Miss Taylor." John's eyes grew wide with distraught. "Please—"*

*"I'm afraid I've made other arrangements," she said, her lips creeping into a shamelessly supercilious smile. "Gentlemen." She curtsied sarcastically, tossing her hair over her*

*shoulder as she spun around and made her way to the dance floor.*

"Elizabeth!" Mary clapped her hand to her mouth in horror. "Did you actually tell him why?"

"It is better this way," Elizabeth insisted. "Now that the Walkers know you overheard their shameless and very ungentlemanly conversation, they will think twice about telling the South that they were mistreated in the Taylor household."

Mary couldn't deny it—she had a point. Elizabeth often did. Even if Mary didn't always like admitting it.

"Are you sure that you didn't just do it to slight the Walkers?"

"That was also an added benefit," Elizabeth conceded with a smile.

"Was there anyone else present for that exchange?" Mary tried to ask casually.

"Apart from Charles, no," Elizabeth confirmed. "Why?" she asked, cocking her head to one side and looking at her sister with interest.

"No reason," Mary answered quickly.

Perhaps a bit too quickly.

One eyebrow extended towards Elizabeth's temple, her face scrunching up in curiosity.

"Who is it you did not wish to hear?"

"No one," Mary insisted. "I was just curious. It is a very embarrassing situation, to have a man speak so poorly of your physical appearance and bemoan the idea of marrying you for your wealth. I would just like to keep it between as few people as possible."

"Mary, if you tell me, I'm certain I can help."

"It is nothing." Mary waved her hand, averting her gaze from her sister's and biting her lip.

She was afraid to speak it aloud, though exactly why she was not sure.

Perhaps because the idea of it felt *absurd*. Because the man in question was, by all accounts, out of her league.

Then again, Elizabeth never did laugh at her.

Condescend to her, yes.

Tell her she was worrying for nothing, yes.

Dismiss her deepest darkest fears as creations of her own imagination, yes.

But laugh, truly laugh? No.

For all her faults, she was a good sister.

And her advice had worked last night, had it not?

"Mary, tell me!" Elizabeth pleaded, her eyes wide with excitement.

Her sister loved a secret almost as much as she loved a scandal.

And fortunate for her, one usually preceded the other.

A moment later, Elizabeth's face flashed with recognition. "If you will not tell me a name, then at the very least answer me this—does the man in question reside in New Orleans?"

Mary's heart skipped. Her mouth opened, then closed again. She stared at the canopy above her, measuring just how much to confess.

For Mary knew her sister believed her to be thinking of Manuel Rivera. And indeed, Mary had enjoyed her dances with him immensely, but it would be a sin to fail to mention the other gentleman whose memory had refused to leave her thoughts since she had made his acquaintance.

It was irritating, really, for he had burrowed into her mind and refused to see himself politely to the door, despite the fact Mary knew he was absolutely out of the question.

Thoughts of him were an indulgence, at best, and torture at worst, neither of which any good Protestant lady should take part in. For indulgence should be severely regulated, and torture was purely reserved for the Lord to levy out as he saw fit.

Thankfully for Mary, her sister's self-proclaimed omniscience of all matters of love and legacy in Southern society led her to make her own assumptions.

Assumptions Mary declined to correct.

"I knew it." Elizabeth clapped her hands in delight. "And, if that is the case, then we better get ourselves an invitation to New Orleans!"

Which, as it turned out, was not actually a very difficult thing to do.

# Act II

## *Of Promises and Pretenses*

# La Libération (excerpt)

*A collection of society updates, advertisements, and carefully curated family connections*

**An excerpt from *La Libération***

## Crème de la crème (societal update)

The Defours of New Orleans once again extend their congratulations to their niece and cousin Miss Mary Taylor for her successful debut into society on 24th March. The Defour family were honored to be in attendance, and it is with delight that Henri and Genevieve Defour, owners and editors of *La Libération,* owners and operators of Aigle Des Mars Shipping Company, and owners and proprietors of Chêne Blanc, welcome Miss Mary Taylor and her eldest sister Miss Elizabeth Taylor to New Orleans, where they will be staying with their family for the summer.

## Engaging Engagements (upcoming events)

Ladies and gentleman, dust off your best frocks and party jackets, for the social season is once again upon us and will formally commence with the annual charity ball to benefit the New Orleans children's hospital, proudly sponsored by the members of Cathedral Basilica of St. Louis, King of France.

## Procurements and provisions (advertisements)

For all of your borrowing and lending needs, visit Taylor Mutual Fund, located at the top of the high street. English and French both spoken.

# The Verity (excerpt)

*In which the season's most anticipated races are duly forecasted*

**An excerpt from *The Verity***

## The Social Sundial (upcoming events)

The third weekend in May will once again see New Orleans host the annual races. With the return of old champions and the debut of unknown hopefuls, this will prove the social event of the season not to be missed.

# Chapter VII

Thank goodness for Elizabeth, Mary cast a glance at her sister out of the corner of her eye. The pair looked like mirrors of one another, sitting prettily in their seats, their large petticoats splayed either side of them and taking up nearly the entire cabin. Both their gloved hands were clasped in their laps, but their heads turned to watch out the window as the South simultaneously sprawled before them and disappeared as the train chugged towards New Orleans.

The whole scheme—Mary wanted it stated plainly—had been Elizabeth's idea. It was she who had invited themselves to the Defours. They were, after all, kin (by marriage—though the Defours made a point of reminding everyone of the connection, as if blood could be willed into existence through proximity to prestige), which made it a perfectly legitimate family tie to exploit.

Again, Elizabeth's description of the situation, not Mary's.

But Elizabeth had been coy, Mary conceded. She had watched her sister from across the dining table that very afternoon following her debut over dinner. The Defours, being family and having come all that way, were of course staying with the Taylors. Elizabeth had employed a well-practiced tactic, one she had undertaken many times when she was interested in winning the affection of a man's heart so that she could promptly break it: charm.

Genevieve Defour was a small yet regal woman. She had a thin face, a slightly pointed chin and even spikier cheek bones, with deep eyes and one eyebrow that appeared to be perpetually arched, somewhere between bemusement and disapproval. Her black hair was always immaculately pulled back into a tight and tidy bun. She was the sort of old money Southern woman who upheld tradition, Catholic values, and propriety as some of God's greatest gifts and gravest burdens.

Nothing good in life should come without some suffering, she would remind anyone who was silly enough to complain to her. If you were suffering, it probably meant you were doing something right.

Actually, scratch that, it absolutely meant you were doing something right.

"*Christ suffered on the cross for your sins. The least you can do is dress appropriately for the hour a week you find in your busy lives to sacrifice for him,*" she had said to her girls the last time they had questioned the necessity of wearing full sleeve dresses to church in June.

It was for this reason that she was both feared and admired—she oversaw the largest sugarcane plantation in the South with the quiet suffering of a woman who felt it her personal ordained gift to suffer.

And all of this was why when Elizabeth Taylor entered the dining room that afternoon, her plot was carefully arranged.

"Mrs. Defour." Elizabeth dropped into a deep curtsy, so deep Mary thought for a moment that her knees might have given way beneath her. "I cannot tell you how honored we are that you came all the way to Virginia for my sister's debutante ball." Her eyes still studied the floor boards, waiting for some indication from Aunt Genevieve that she should return to her standing position.

Mary, seated on the other side of the table, suddenly felt that her own "Good afternoon, Aunt Genevieve" had been grossly inadequate.

Anne Taylor, who had entered the room with their aunt, also stared, somewhere between confusion and disbelief.

"I do hope you will be staying with us for a little while," Elizabeth offered, chancing a look directly into her aunt's eyes.

"Not as long as I would like, sweet girl." Aunt Genevieve smiled at the deference, reaching out one of her ringed fingers towards Elizabeth's hands, a gesture to indicate she should return to her feet. "But it is always a pleasure to see this part of the family."

"And we feel so fortunate to name you among ours," Elizabeth insisted, elegantly seating herself next to Genevieve. "Why, when I was at school, you would not believe what the others girls would say when I told them I was related to the Defours of New Orleans..."

Later that day, Aunt Genevieve and Elizabeth strolled arm in arm through the estate. Elizabeth stood more than a head taller than the matron, but somehow made herself seem meek, dwarfed almost by the esteemed lady's presence. As they walked Elizabeth held the umbrella for both of them to keep the sun off of their luminescent skin. At one point, Aunt Genevieve threw her head back and a cackle escaped her small throat, so piercingly loud that everyone in the house reported having heard the laugh of Genevieve Defour for the first time ever.

By the time they returned from their walk, Aunt Genevieve was speaking to Anne about the girls coming to stay.

Of course to Anne, the prospect of her free-spirited daughter being taken under the wing of her somewhat severe, pious, and esteemed sister-in-law could only be perceived as a positive thing. Mary knew her mother must have hoped that some of Genevieve would rub off on Elizabeth.

Their mother did, however, ensure both girls left with their King James Bibles and reminded them both to be respectful of the beliefs of others, but that they had been born into, baptized, and raised in a Protestant family.

*"If you go to Catholic Church,"* she had explained gravely, *"do not eat the bread."*

Yes, watching Elizabeth work was a reminder that influence, in the right hands, looked an awful lot like grace.

"We'll be there soon," Elizabeth smiled, raising her eyebrows in conspiratorial anticipation. "Are you excited?"

"Elizabeth, please," Mary gestured towards Edward, who sat slumped in the corner on the far side of the seat from his twin. His face rested against the door into the hallway as he snored softly.

"He sleeps." Elizabeth waved her hand dismissively. "So tell me, what is your plan for capturing the heart of your intended beau?"

"I know not," Mary looked at Edward worriedly. "Can we please discuss something else?"

Anything else!

"Oh, we are going to talk about it!" Elizabeth raised her voice slightly. "I have been on this train for nearly two days, all so that we can get you close to— "

"Elizabeth!" Her own eyes were pleading—while Elizabeth's sparkled with unmistakable delight.

This, Mary realized, was not just a scheme.

It was sport.

Entertainment.

This entire thing was for her own entertainment.

"Fine, I won't say his name." She smiled proudly at her own benevolence. "Are you happy now?"

"Yes, thank you," Mary whispered, though why she was thanking her sister for not embarrassing her was not something she herself fully understood.

"But really Mary, if this is the man you wish to marry, you do need some sort of plan."

"Who says I wish to marry him?" Mary attempted to sound sincere.

"Oh, please." Elizabeth swatted the suggestion from the air effortlessly. "All women must marry, but some women are the marrying type, and some do it because they know they must. And you, my dear sister, are in the former category." She pointed a finger at her sister.

"Mary will make a man an excellent wife," Edward spoke from the corner, his eyes still closed and his arms crossed. "Do not torment her."

"I am not tormenting her. I am trying to coach her."

"You, a twenty-one-year-old spinster who firmly belongs in this aforementioned category of women who know they must eventually marry." Edward opened his eyes, rolling his head to face his siblings. "You are going to explain to Mary how best to find a husband?"

"Go back to sleep," Elizabeth snapped. "And for the avoidance of doubt, you should understand my lack of husband as a choice, as opposed to a lack of ability."

"Yes, you are very popular with the young men," Edward agreed. "But the mothers of your beaux, not so much." He closed his eyes and turned his face back towards the door, settling once again into his former sleeping position.

Elizabeth opened her mouth to protest, when a knock sounded on the door of their cabin. Edward jostled out of the way slightly, and a man in a uniform stuck his head in.

"Ladies and gentleman, we are approaching New Orleans."

Mary inhaled deeply, the warm spring air prickling her skin after days of confinement. She blinked at the sunlight, feeling as though she hadn't seen it in years.

She reached for the stair rail to descend from the train, bracing herself—

"Miss Taylor, allow me."

Her heart skipped.

No. It couldn't be—

Leander Doucet stood before her, offering his hand in gentlemanly assistance.

Mary tried to hide her surprise, tried to ignore the way her breath caught in her throat.

She could not, however, supress the buckling in her knees, and when she reached for his hand in startled excitement, she toppled over, face first down the stairs.

And into the arms of Leander Doucet.

He caught her with effortless grace, his hands braced at her waist. In her flailing, she'd grabbed his shoulders. Now they stood, pressed together, face to face.

"Why, hello there," he grinned. His voice was low, amused.

Far too close for propriety.

Though not near enough for Mary's liking.

She opened her mouth, but nothing came out. His shoulders were solid beneath her fingers. She could feel the warmth of him through his coat.

"Are you hurt?" he asked gently.

*Hurt? Was that what this was?* Mary's brain had vacated entirely. All she could register was the press of his hands, the flush in her cheeks, and the way his voice sent goose-flesh skittering down her spine. She might have stayed like that forever—If not for Elizabeth.

"Why Leander Doucet, I do believe you've swept my sister off her feet," Elizabeth's voice rang out from behind her.

Mary turned, mortified

"Miss Taylor." Leander looked up, raising an eyebrow coyly. "A humble Alabama man could only wish to be so lucky."

Mary inhaled sharply.

Could he actually mean what he just said?

"Well indeed," Elizabeth agreed, gathering two fists full of skirt in her hands as she made her descent.

Clearly having learned from her sister's blunder.

"I also don't know how you do things in Alabama," Elizabeth continued, "but you might wish to return my sister to the ground before people start to talk.

"Unless of course, you plan to carry her all the way to Aunt Genevieve's."

"Ha, a wise observation, Miss Taylor," Leander chuckled, returning his gaze to Mary and carefully lowering her to the ground.

"And are you sure you're alright to stand on your own, Miss Taylor?"

Was he teasing her?

Or did he think her so silly and incompetent that she could not even stand upright without assistance?

She wasn't sure whether to swoon or be offended.

"And why wouldn't I be?" she asked, lifting her chin slightly.

"Why, because of the nearly two-day journey you've just endured," Leander clarified, something flashing in his eyes. "It is enough to flatten anyone."

"Oh, of course," Mary insisted her understanding.

Was she mostly relieved that he clearly did not think her inept?

Or mortified that she had suggested he might?

"I believe I just stood up too swiftly," she clarified. "I am very grateful you were here, for your quick reflexes almost certainly saved me a broken leg, or a twisted ankle at the least."

"It sounds as though you are in my debt." His eyes twinkled.

"In debt to a banker?" Mary arched an eyebrow. "That must be the worst kind!"

Leander laughed softly and finally, regretfully, let go of her waist.

"I will have you know I am a *nice* banker, Miss Taylor." Leander explained, straightening his coat.

Mary's sides felt suddenly cold where his hands had just been.

"I hope not too nice." Elizabeth stuck a white gloved hand on a protruding hip.

"Do you disapprove of niceness, Miss Taylor?" Leander tore his gaze away from Mary towards her sister.

"In a banker? Absolutely," Elizabeth replied. "Imagine the disappointment a poor lady might feel, thinking she's married a banker and finding herself living in a house with no second ballroom."

"Well, I never claimed to be *that* nice," Leander responded coyly.

"But nice enough to collect two ladies from the station?" Mary teased, emboldened now.

"Well, not just any ladies, of course."

"Is Charles too busy to greet his own sisters?" Elizabeth asked, though it sounded more like an accusation.

"He sends his regrets, though it is my pleasure to see you both to the Defour household."

"You mean the three of us!" Edward called from the door of the train, where he stood laden with suitcases. "Heaven forbid anyone help the poor brother hauling half of Virginia in these bags."

Mary winced. "Oh Edward—"

"No, no, by all means," he continued. "You two enjoy your flirtation. I'll be here, breaking my spine on Mary's twelve petticoats."

"It's only ten," she murmured.

"Truly, I'm honored to serve as your pack mule," he called over his shoulder, stumbling down the steps with bags under both arms and trailing from each finger.

Leander, chuckling, stepped forward to help.

"There's more," Edward said ominously, vanishing back into the train.

He re-emerged moments later, more bags piled precariously in his arms.

"I am afraid I now must echo the sentiments of your brother." Leander turned towards the Taylor sisters. "Do you fear New Orleans offers no creature comforts, so you brought them all with you?"

"I was unsure of the weather," Mary offered sheepishly.

"I jest, of course, Miss Taylor." He paused, glancing towards the horse and buggy carriage. "Though I fear that we may require two trips."

# Chapter VIII

The ride to the Defour household was pleasant enough—the weather mild, the breeze soft—though Mary could imagine how, in summer, the thick air might become the swampish humidity she'd been warned about.

Still, the journey enchanted the sisters. Both leaned forward eagerly, eyes wide as the city unfolded before them.

New Orleans looked like something out of a painting: tall, narrow townhouses with wrought-iron balconies where stylish people stood, watching the streets like actors in a play. Flowers spilled from planters and vines curled around windowpanes. And the colors! Blue, pink, yellow—houses painted like candy boxes.

The streets buzzed with movement: people of every shade, size, and style swept past—some strolling, some gliding in carriages, some arguing cheerfully in French.

Mary's gaze snagged on a striking sight—a beautiful mulatto woman in a French-cut gown, arm-in-arm with a tall white man in a waistcoat of impeccable tailoring.

Mary had seen free negroes before, mostly in cities like Richmond. But never like this. Never so elegant. So public. So... *unapologetic.*

"New Orleans has many free negros," Leander explained over his shoulder. "Some with great wealth. Business owners. Good Catholics, like the rest of us."

"How interesting," Mary said, eyes still fixed on the passing couple. She'd heard tales of the city's uniqueness—but seeing it was another matter entirely. "Do you have any as customers?"

"Oh, yes," Leander nodded. "And our clerk Harrison was born to parents who bought their freedom. He can tally numbers faster than I can count fingers—and he always seems to know how the cotton price will shift. Don't ask me how. I've learned not to question it. I sign the checks and stay out of the way."

"Why, is that one of the Sinclairs?" Elizabeth gestured down the street.

"Likely it is, Miss Taylor. We do a lot of business with the Sinclairs, as I am told you are aware." Leander offered the last part nonchalantly, as though dangling it in front of Elizabeth to see if she would bite.

"Oh, so you have heard of my theory?" Elizabeth lit up. "And what do you make of it?"

"I hate to disappoint you, Miss Taylor, but I reckon the finances of another family are not much my business unless they require funds for a loan," Leander answered courteously.

"Oh, don't be such a bore!" Elizabeth threw herself back in her seat, her interest having disappeared as quickly as it had come.

"I do sincerely hope that you will be on better behavior under the roof of our aunt and uncle," Edward muttered.

His voice was low, just enough to be masked by the clatter of the carriage.

"I was not raised in a barn." Elizabeth met his comment with annoyance.

"No, but you do have a history with them," Edward offered darkly.

"You are lucky we are in public." Elizabeth hissed, pointing a white-gloved finger at him.

Mary turned her attention from the bickering of her siblings, daring to engage Leander in further dialogue.

"Mr. Doucet, I have been meaning to ask you something."

"Please do, Miss Taylor." He turned around in his seat, smiling encouragingly.

"Do you enjoy any sports?"

"Well, like most Alabama men, I enjoy horse-riding." He nodded. "In my youth, I might spend time wrestling and boxing."

"And do you swim?" Mary asked, resisting the small grin that pressed against her cheeks.

It was a purposeful question, a test of sorts, to see just how intelligent this Mr. Doucet actually was.

"On occasion," Leander answered, smiling. "Though I always take precautions, considering my namesake."

"What, is Leander Latin for "bad at swimming"?" Elizabeth asked, her expression all wide eyes and clueless charm. "Or does your family have some ancient feud with lakes?"

"Ah, your sister was referring to the Greek myth of *Hero and Leander*," Leander answered, politely, in that way men always do when they're explaining something to women. "He drowns trying to swim across the sea to his beloved's tower," Leander explained. "A classic tale of love, water, and poor decision-making."

"How horrible." Elizabeth put a hand to her chest. Edward rolled his eyes at his sister's feigned ignorance, a propensity of hers, particularly when amongst young men, that he despised greatly.

"Perhaps Leander should have built a bridge," Elizabeth offered.

"A bridge?" Edward demanded, clearly unamused by his twin's airs of stupidity. "How easy do you think it is to build a bridge?"

"Well, clearly swimming wasn't an especially brilliant idea.

"Mr. Doucet, why would your parents give you a name so full of tragedy?"

"I suspect, Miss Taylor, that they just liked the way it sounded," Leander confessed. "And they liked the idea of giving their firstborn a less common name—and by common you will I hope not think that I mean poor, but rather not in circulation. I think they thought it would make me memorable, though I am not sure how much good it has done."

"I think it does," Mary said before she could stop herself.

Leander turned back, tipping his top hat toward her with a warm smile.

"I'm very flattered you think so, Miss Taylor."

Henri and Genevieve Defour lived in an area that Leander explained was known as The French Quarter. As their carriage pulled up, Mary tilted her head to take in the full view. The house stood two stories tall, painted a soft clay pink, stretching nearly the length of the block. Wooden steps led from the street to a veranda that ran the entire front of the house, mirrored by a second-story balcony above. Double windows framed each floor, their shutters painted a vibrant Kelly green that matched the narrow iron gates lining both verandas.

"What a beautiful home," Mary breathed.

As though if on cue, the doors to the grand townhouse opened and there stood Aunt Genevieve and three of her daughters: Gabrielle, Amelié and Antoiné—lined up behind her like matching porcelain figurines. Though each girl stood nearly a head taller than their mother, they were unmistakably Defours: sharp-featured, coolly elegant, and impossibly poised.

Mary's eyes lingered on Gabrielle, whose famously pale hair was so light it looked almost translucent in the sun.

"Merci, Monsieur," Aunt Genevieve spoke to Leander first once they were all safely inside.

Leander took her hand with practiced charm and kissed it lightly, replying in smooth, fluent French.

Genevieve raised a brow and offered a conspiratorial smile—a glint of mischief in her dark eyes. Then she leaned toward him, murmured something, and the French speakers—herself, her daughters, and Leander—all laughed.

"Ah, Madame Defour," Leander replied, his tone teasing as he clicked his tongue before continuing in French.

"Perhaps you are right," Aunt Genevieve resigned, returning to English. "You are our guests after all, but please be aware—in this house, we speak French."

If her goal was to make her guests feel inadequate, she had succeeded.

"Please forgive us, Auntie," Elizabeth jumped in. "We are from Virginia, after all. The most culture we've ever really been exposed to is Richmond."

Genevieve snorted softly, half amusement, half judgment. She gave a slow, regal nod of acknowledgment. "It is not your fault," she said, with the graciousness of someone offering mercy they felt was wholly undeserved. "Now— " she turned, motioning them all into the parlor, "the three pillars of our home are Faith, Family, and Tradition. In that order." The group began to move again, following her lead.

"Amelié," Mary whispered as she lagged slightly behind the others, "what did Auntie say that was so funny?"

"She said," Amelié replied without pause, "that only the English wait for everyone else to learn *their* language."

Mary blinked, then smiled—unsure whether to be offended or impressed.

It wasn't polite.

Then again...Perhaps it wasn't meant to be.

"Leander Doucet is very handsome," Amelié whispered with girlish glee as she, Mary, and Elizabeth filed out of the front door. "But so is your brother."

After the sit down in the parlor, Leander excused himself for work, and Edward had used the opportunity to make his own exit.

*"Oh, ma chérie, do you mean to tell me you are not staying even one night?" Aunt Genevieve had cried. Despite her strict nature, she had always had a soft spot for Edward—it was, Mary suspected, his old-fashioned charm laden with a hint of country that Aunt Genevieve found so mystifying.*

*Nor was she the only woman who thought so.*

*"I am afraid not, Auntie." Edward put a hand to his chest in regret. "We have fields ready for planting, and because my brother is out here gallivanting in your lovely city, I must return to my father to help oversee the process."*

*"Uneasy is the head that wears the crown," Aunt Genevieve nodded, forever approving of the concept of personal familial sacrifice. "My Henri and Michel are finishing the fields as we speak, and will join us soon, God willing."*

"Come now. I know he is your brother, but surely you know how handsome he is?" Amelié insisted with a coy smile as the ladies stepped out into the New Orleans sunshine. After their journey, the Taylor ladies had retired to their shared room for a nap, and now refreshed, they eagerly sought to explore the town.

"If I didn't know better," she continued, "I'd say Mother looked positively *bereft* at his departure—likely hoping he might take a liking to Gabrielle.

"Which would be all well and good of course, if Gabrielle were not in love with your other brother," Amelié said it as though it were the most obvious thing in the world.

"Is she now?" Elizabeth delighted at the gossip. "And is Charles in love with her?"

"Well, I do not know for certain. All I have heard are rumors."

"Rumors would not exist if they did not desire to be shared." Elizabeth looped her arm into Amelié's and brought her under the shade of her parasol. "So tell me, *ma chérie*," Elizabeth feigned an exaggerated French accent. "What have you heard?"

"Well," Amelié began, dramatically saying the word with considerable emphasis, "I have heard that he is sweet on Catalina Rivera."

"No!" Elizabeth gasped, "The widow?"

"Yes!" Amelié concurred, the clear excitement in her voice overlaid with a tinge of scandal. "From what I hear, she mourns for her dead husband everyday. She rarely leaves the house, only for church. And when she does leave, she still wears the full mourning—plain black gown, and when I say plain I mean *plain*. No cuffs, no ribbons or lace, just the black dress like a nun might wear, and a long black veil that covers her head."

"I think that sounds rather tragic," Mary said gently. "I spoke with her brother Manuel at my debut, and he said she loved her husband more than he has ever seen a wife love a man."

"Even more tragic for your brother," Amelié responded brusquely, clearly far from delighted at Mary's reproval. "If he does find himself in love with a woman who is devoted to her dead husband."

Mary opened her mouth to respond but caught the look Elizabeth was shooting her—a silent *don't start* across Amelié's shoulder.

"Well then," Elizabeth pivoted cheerfully, "perhaps we ought to help Gabrielle and Charles spend more time together. And maybe he'll think less about a woman who isn't even on the market."

"Not to mention, she is a Rivera." Amelié' rolled her eyes. "Between us, I know Father is disappointed he has not asked for one of our hands in marriage."

"Oh, did he make suggestions that he might?"

"Well, no," Amelié admitted. "But when Mr. Doucet and Charles arrived in New Orleans, they called on Father first. He helped introduce them around town, brought them clients. You might think that kind of generosity would earn more than polite thanks, but I suppose—"

"As far as I understand it," Elizabeth interrupted, halting mid-step and releasing Amelié's arm, "your father is an *investor* in their bank."

Her hand flew to her hip.

"And from what I hear, his investment is far from charity. I would kindly request, *dear cousin*, that you refrain from suggesting my brother is anything less than a gentleman. He would never leave a debt unpaid—*that*, I know for a fact."

Amelié blinked, caught off guard.

"Yes, of course," she stammered. "I apologize, cousin. I didn't mean it that way. I only meant it would be lovely... you know... if we became sisters."

Elizabeth held the pause just long enough to be intimidating, then gave a gracious nod.

"You are, of course, forgiven," she said with a smile. "And I agree. It would be lovely if we became sisters."

Mary had been surprised by the outburst at first—especially considering how little Elizabeth and Charles usually had in common beyond a surname.

But on a moment's contemplation further, perhaps that was enough.

Despite their differences, Mary knew Elizabeth would do absolutely anything for her siblings.

*And I would too,* Mary told herself.

At least... she *wanted* to.

But unlike Elizabeth, she lacked that one crucial quality that made such things possible.

Fearlessness.

# Chapter IX

The ladies strolled in leisurely fashion, parasols propped on their shoulders, white-lace gloves clutching the handles, their skirts swishing in rhythmic unison. As they made their way, men tipped their hats and paused to make introductions, while women extended invitations for tea. Everyone seemed to know Amelié Defour, and, more importantly, everyone seemed eager to extend nothing short of the utmost politeness to her Virginian cousins.

Hardly a surprise. The Defours were something of an institution in New Orleans—steeped in wealth, tradition, and that specific brand of grandeur that came from an old Catholic name.

"Why, Amelié Defour!" A young lady in a dusky pink dress intercepted them, her curls bouncing with each breath. "Are these the Virginian cousins I have heard so much about?"

"They are indeed! Elizabeth and Mary Taylor, please meet my friend Miss Madelyn Woodrow."

"A French mother and an English father," Madelyn explained the curious compilation of her name without invitation. "I am so pleased to meet you both.

"You must come to our sewing circle. We meet on Mondays! The other ladies will just love to meet you, and we need all the help we can get. We are knitting socks for the less fortunate."

"We will be there," Amelié confirmed. "We pick a different charity or organization in need of service every quarter," she explained. "This month it is for the children's hospital."

"How do you decide which organizations or charities to choose?" Mary asked.

"Oh, well when I say "we", I mean the elder ladies in the church," Madelyn clarified, brushing a speck from her sleeve.

"In the church?"

"Oh yes, the group is a part of St. Louis's, or, Cathedral Basilica of St. Louis, King of France, if you asked Mother."

"Your king was canonized?" Elizabeth arched an eyebrow.

"I mean, we have no king," Amelié sniffed in her usual clipped tone. "But King Louis IX was canonised for fighting in the Crusades.

"You have heard of the crusades, I hope?" Amelié asked with a haughty sincerity.

"Is this what we will be spending our time talking about in the sewing circle?" Elizabeth asked blandly.

"What my sister means," Mary jumped in, "is that yes, we did learn about the crusades at boarding school, and that is so interesting about King Louis." The girls laughed at her pronunciation of Louis with a hard "s".

"It's pronounced like "Louie"," Madelyn explained. "But do not worry, there will be no exam." She giggled in a playful manner with just the tiniest note of condescension. "Can we count on your attendance?"

As the trio turned away, Elizabeth pushed her head close to Mary's and whispered in her ear,

"Are we allowed to go to Catholic sewing circle?"

"I honestly don't know." Mary shook her head. "Maybe we can stop in the bank and ask Charles.

"Amelié, do we have time to stop in to see Charles?"

"I think we should—"

"Miss Taylor!" A familiar voice called from across the street.

All three women turned.

"It's—"

"Manuel Rivera," Amelié stated with contempt.

"Mr. Rivera!" Mary called back, waving—just as he began crossing, dodging horses and carts like a man on a mission. "Pardon me, excuse me," Manuel jostled through the labyrinth of horses and buggies.

Mary blinked in wonder.

*Is he really rushing to see me?*

Finally having successfully navigated the street, he sighed deeply, gaining his composure before sweeping his hat from his head and beaming down at her.

"Miss Taylor," he declared again, reaching for her hand and kissing it. "What a delightful surprise. I thought my eyes must be deceiving me."

"On the contrary, it would appear your eyes are in excellent working order." Mary returned his smile. "Though, I assure you it was not necessary to risk being trampled in order to greet us."

"Pardon me, ma'am, but I do respectfully disagree. A man who does not risk the road to greet you properly is not a man worth having around."

Mary blushed furiously.

"Oh, very well said," she finally managed.

"Please Mr. Rivera, the last thing my sister needs is more flattery," Elizabeth jumped in. "She has had enough of that for one day."

"She is making a jest—," Mary tried to insist before being interrupted.

"I do not doubt she is the subject of flattery, though I respectfully disagree that she has received too much.

"Miss Taylor, please forgive me my manners," Manuel reached for Elizabeth's hand also, kissing it lightly and returning it to her side. "And Miss Defour, I do believe," Manuel turned to their cousin, his tone cordial, if slightly forced. "How do you do, ma'am?" He asked, tipping his hat briefly.

"Fine, Mr. Rivera, thank you for asking," Amelié answered stoically, her lips tightened into a grimace. "You'll have to excuse me, but I see someone I know and must extend my greetings."

"I'll join you. Lovely to see you, Mr. Rivera," Elizabeth curtsyed. "Mary, we won't be far." She gestured towards a group of nearby ladies.

"I apologize for my cousin's demeanour—" Mary began to explain, but was once again cut off.

"Oh please, Miss Taylor, you needn't. Our family matters need not extend to yours. Though, I hope it does attest to my desire to speak with you that I approached you while you are in the company of your cousin."

"Ha, indeed Mr. Rivera," Mary smiled at the flattery. "Your valour and determination is duly noted."

"I am glad to hear it. And what brings you to New Orleans, Miss Taylor?"

"Oh, we are staying with our cousins. My Aunt Genevieve invited us after my debutante ball."

"How wonderful. And how long will you remain?"

"Through the summer, at least."

"I cannot tell you how pleased I am to hear that," Manuel confessed, rubbing the brim of his hat between his fingers.

*Is he nervous?* Mary wondered.

"I...regret," he chose his words carefully, "that I cannot call at your aunt's home, for fear of being unreceived."

Perhaps it was as dramatic as Elizabeth had made it out to be!

"I cannot imagine that would be the case."

Manuel looked slightly uncomfortable, scratching the back of his neck nervously.

"Well, Miss Taylor, I suppose as with most things in life one does not know until one tries, but it would upset my family greatly if I did. I hope you won't take that as a sign of disrespect towards you personally, if I do not call at the Defour residence."

"No, of course not. I would never wish you to do anything to upset your family. Family is so important, after all.

"Which reminds me, on our way from the station this morning I noted sales of *The Verity*. Am I mistaken, or is this your family's paper?"

"That it is, Miss Taylor." At her recollection Manuel beamed, nodding his head in pleasure at her acknowledgement. "Are current affairs of interest to you?"

"Greatly. One of the most unfortunate aspects of attending boarding school was my inability to read my family's paper daily, though, as I have grown older, I understand that I need only speak with my father, and it is more or less equivalent to reading *The Richmond Review*."

"Well, in that case, Miss Taylor, you may be in luck, for I am the chief editor and operator of *The Verity*," Manuel announced, almost sheepishly as he smiled slightly before casting his gaze towards his shoes.

"Mr. Rivera, I had no idea!" Mary's voice rose in excitement, causing Manuel in turn to grow under the light of her praise. "Editor-in-chief, and at such a young age!"

"Perhaps, if it were pleasing to you, Miss Taylor, I might fill you in on the affairs of the day, though I confess to not be terribly close to the social section, but I will become more familiar if it were your desire to hear about it," Manuel declared, casting his eyes upwards as he waited, expectantly for her response.

"I am certain your current expertise will suffice, for I rarely read the social section," Mary confessed quietly, though through a smile that stretched the length of her face. "I should love that, Mr. Rivera," she finished, her insides stirring with the way Manuel stared at her.

"Very well, then it is a date," Manuel promised, reaching for her hand. He kissed it softly, lingering just long enough to steal her breath. "As much as I do not wish to, I expect it would be most appropriate to allow you to get on with your day. The last thing I would wish would to be in the bad books of your sister, or your cousin for that matter."

"With respect to Elizabeth, I do agree, but when it comes to Amelié, I regret to say that it appears as though you are in her bad books already."

"I believe you are quite right," Manuel laughed softly, a tuft of his black hair falling over his eyes.

"And will I see you at church?" Manuel asked hopefully.

"Church? Do you attend Saint Louis?"

"No, ma'am, my family goes to Santiago San Ignacio—do you know it?"

"I am afraid I do not."

"Oh, it's a beautiful building. Perhaps I can show you sometime."

"That would be lovely."

*Are we allowed to tour Catholic churches?* Mary made a mental note to add that to her list of questions for Charles.

"I look forward to it," she said, taking his offered arm. His bicep was solid beneath her touch. As they walked, she glanced up—just in time to catch him looking at her.

Undoubtedly, Manuel Rivera was incredibly handsome.

And the way he looked at her...

Something in her chest fluttered. As though all the things she'd once quietly hoped for... might actually be possible.

They returned to the others.

"Ladies, forgive me for keeping Miss Taylor so long," Manuel said, reluctantly releasing her hand. "Miss Taylor," he added softly. "It's been a pleasure. I eagerly await our next meeting."

"As do I," Mary replied, her voice catching just slightly.

He bowed low, then straightened and replaced his hat with a flourish before turning and walking away.

"Well, someone has a beau already!" Elizabeth squeezed Mary's arm. "And with what, having been in New Orleans only a matter of hours? Bravo, sister."

"I'm not collecting them," Mary insisted, blushing. "I like Mr. Rivera."

"Really, Mary, do you like him or do you like the attention he gives to you?" Amelié asked in annoyed disbelief.

"I—both!" Mary insisted. "And if he called at the Defour house, would he be received?"

"No, of course not." Amelié rolled her eyes, as though it were the stupidest question in the world. "If you want him to be received, you better be answering the door yourself!"

The ladies continued through town towards the bank.

"Elizabeth." Mary pulled her back as Amelié paused to speak with another passer-by. "Do you know why the Riveras and the Defours hate one another so deeply?"

"Did I not say before? All feuds are born of the same three things—money, power, love—"

"No, but do you know the actual origins?" Mary insisted, slightly impatiently.

Elizabeth perked up. "Well, well. Someone's finally interested in a bit of gossip."

Mary frowned. "It isn't gossip—it's just… to refuse a call from Manuel Rivera suggests something *grave.*"

Mary had only ever heard of someone being "unreceived" once before. It had been the talk of her boarding school for weeks—passed from girl to girl with delighted horror.

The story, as best as Mary could recall, involved the unmarried cousin of a friend's friend. The girl had fallen pregnant—scandalous enough, as even married women disguised their pregnancies beneath high-waisted skirts and self-imposed isolation. To be seen *with child* was bad enough. But to be *with child* outside of marriage?

Her condition had gone unnoticed at first, dismissed as a loss of appetite or an unsettled stomach. But when her waistline began to grow and her dresses no longer fit, her mother finally pieced it together. The scandal broke just as the social season was beginning—when a husband *needed* to be found.

Her father, desperate to contain the fallout, demanded the young man responsible take her hand in marriage.

Which he unequivocally refused to do.

And with that refusal, he didn't just ruin the girl—he ruined *himself*.

It was said that he called on his own father's house not less than a week later and was unreceived.

*"Unreceived!"* the girls had gasped in chorus. *"By his own family!"*

*"Well of course they had to,"* someone had reasoned. *"To receive him would be to invite shame upon them all."*

All the girls became experts in proprietary behavior, knowing without thinking what they would have done if they had found themselves face to face with such a man.

Mary remembered the other girls dissecting the event like scholars, each one eager to offer her analysis as though gossip were an academic subject. And yet, such behavior would never have been officially tolerated at school. The headmistresses—severe, upright women in stiff collars and sharper expressions—referred to gossip as *the devil's work,* and insisted that any young lady who indulged in it risked her soul, her reputation, and her future.

Still, they suspiciously allowed certain stories to linger.

Cautionary tales, dressed up as scandal—delivered not for amusement, but as moral instruction.

And it worked.

Even more shocking was the rumor that the girl's brother had challenged the rogue to a duel. But the rogue had never shown.

Which was the worst sin of all.

To compromise a woman was one thing. To refuse her hand was another. But to not show up for a duel when challenged by her brother? That wasn't just dishonor. That was *cowardice.* And cowardice, in Southern society, was death by a thousand whispers.

*"The only excuse for not showing up would be that he is already dead,"* one of Mary's classmates had declared at the time. *"And for his family's sake, I hope he is."*

At the time, Mary had sat in silent disbelief. Even now, the story made her stomach churn. Not for the scandal, but for the sadness of it. She didn't know exactly where babies came from, though she suspected it had something to do with why a young woman mustn't ever be alone with a courting man.

But she didn't believe for one second that the girl in question had been reckless for sport. Surely, she had thought herself in love. Perhaps her heart had won a battle her head had tried in vain to fight.

And Mary couldn't help but think of her sister—of what might have happened in the stables that night. She thought of Thomas Walker, how easily he had swept her up, how nearly she had believed he saw her.

If she hadn't overheard the truth, hadn't been warned by chance, would she be here now?

*No.* She would still be in Virginia, still mistaking flattery for affection.

It terrified her. How easily a woman's future could be decided by the illusion of a man's intentions. How quickly she could fall, and how slowly society would forgive her.

She thought of that nameless girl again. *Did she keep the child? Was she sent away? Did she ever find love?*

Mary would never know. She could ask Elizabeth—but somehow, she wasn't sure she wanted the answer.

"I do so admire your attachment to social propriety," Elizabeth mulled, tugging at Mary's hair as though she were a small child and returning her to the present.

Ah, sisterly affection—never complete without the faintest whiff of mockery.

"You do not know the origins, do you?" Mary accused, her delight at the realization competing with her disbelief.

Elizabeth huffed, her eyes narrowing at the accusation.

An accusation which just so happened to be true.

"Oh alright," she conceded. "Honestly, Mary, I am dying to know!"

"Really, Elizabeth, you're dying?"

"Literally dying." Elizabeth nodded furiously. "I first heard about it at school, but none of the girls knew the real story—only that if a Defour and a Rivera pass on the street, it's a race to cross first and snub the other.

"Amelié's maddeningly discreet, like she's been sworn to secrecy—but not the *fun* kind. The *boring family duty* kind. You know. The kind I avoid at all costs."

Mary laughed despite herself.

"And Gabrielle would *never* spill anything. But Antoiné—she might be young enough to bribe."

Elizabeth's grin turned devilish. "Which is why I'm so invested in your budding romance with Mr. Rivera. Perhaps *he'll* tell you—if you offer something in return."

Mary's eyes widened. "L-Like what?"

"Dear sister, you are as sweet and innocent as the Virgin Mary herself," Elizabeth said, her voice honeyed, her eyes glinting with the kind of amusement that always made Mary feel vaguely like the punchline of a joke.

# Chapter X

Taylor Mutual Fund was situated in the middle of town, right between the hustle and bustle of the city. A small bell tinkled as the sisters entered the bank. It should, of course, have been the three of them, but Amelié had found herself fluttering her eyelids at a would-be beau in a manner that was, according to Elizabeth, "an ill-masked act of desperation".

Heavens Miss Taylor, tell us what you really think.

On their entrance, a stout African-American man stood up from his desk and walked over to greet the ladies. He was dressed in a fine grey suit, a purple shirt, and silver kerchief tucked into his collar. "You must be the Taylor sisters," he declared. "I am Harrison Treewell, the clerk here at Taylor Mutual Fund."

"It's a pleasure to meet you, sir," Mary dipped into a curtsy. "I have heard tales of your prowess when it comes to numbers. It sounds as though my brother and Mr. Doucet would not manage without you."

"It is true, and it is not a notion I am even willing to entertain." Leander emerged from an office towards the back of the main reception area. At his sudden appearance, Mary inhaled sharply, her heart beginning to pound against her chest in a most inconvenient fashion. "I have made it very clear that if anyone in this town tries to poach our Mr. Treewell here, they will have to go through me."

"And as it happens, Mr. Doucet is not at all intimidating because I receive offers near enough every other day!" Harrison nudged his elbow into Leander's side as the ladies laughed.

"Really, Harrison, must you embarrass me in front of our guests?" Leander bemoaned playfully.

"It is, in my opinion, the best and most appropriate time to embarrass you."

"As you can see, our dear Mr. Treewell is not only a wizard when it comes to numbers, but he also keeps us humble."

"A very important role you play indeed, Mr. Treewell." Elizabeth nodded sagely. "It is my experience that most men would benefit greatly from someone who can keep their opinion of themselves firmly planted on the ground where it belongs."

"Well, at least in the case of Mr. Doucet, it appears to have worked." Mary's eyes twinkled. "For he never told us he was fluent in French!"

Leander cocked his head slightly, extending his hands either side of his body.

"I assure you, Miss Taylor, had an opportunity risen organically, I would have taken it without delay.

"And perhaps, had I known it would have been so effective, I would have orchestrated an opportunity sooner."

Leander winked.

Mary gulped.

"Oh Mr. Doucet, you are such a rogue," Elizabeth chided.

"That he is," a familiar voice sounded as Charles also emerged from the back offices. "My dear sisters." He embraced them both warmly. "I have just seen Edward back to the station. How are you both?"

"Well, Charles, I must confess, I am furious with you." Elizabeth, never one to mince words, got right to it. "I have it on good authority that Father sent Mary with an allowance, and I received no such thing. Now, I know this must have been an oversight, for I cannot believe Father would wish me out there, begging on the street to put clothes on my back. Or worse, imposing on the hospitality of our family."

"The matter of our family's finances is private and should not be discussed in the open." Charles went rigid, taking on a softly scolding tone. "Let us discuss it in my office." He gestured for Elizabeth to go first. "Leander, Harrison, are one of you able to keep my little sister company for a few minutes?"

"I had asked Harrison to take some paperwork over to the Richelin house before he heads home," Leander explained. "But I will happily keep Miss Taylor company."

"Charles, really, how can you suggest such a thing, especially after we have just established what a rogue he is?" Elizabeth playfully protested.

All the men laughed.

"I know Mr. Doucet would never do anything to bring shame on himself."

"Debatable." Harrison jibbed.

"And I know for certain that he would never do anything to bring shame on my family."

"Of course, Charles." Leander nodded, more seriously this time. "Any sister of yours is a sister of mine."

At his words the breath left Mary's body, summoned from her lungs by the sting of disappointment. She stood there stupidly as everyone else moved around her—Harrison left with his papers, Elizabeth and Charles filed into his office, the door remaining slightly ajar as Charles spoke in hushed tones and Elizabeth responded at full anger.

*Any sister of yours is a sister of mine.*

How stupid she was.

How absolutely utterly absurd of her, to think that Leander Doucet was doing anything other than playfully flirting with her.

As any unmarried man might with an unmarried woman, within the appropriate boundaries of social norms.

But the issue for Mary was it did not feel "playful". She found no currency in words that appeared to make suppositions and insinuations when there were actually none to be found.

She wanted the words from a man to mean something.

"Miss Taylor?" She looked up, the sound of her name breaking her from her rumination. "Are you alright?" Leander asked.

"Yes, thank you," Mary answered, a bit coldly. "I think I might just wish to sit down for a bit," she explained, finding the nearest seat by the door and settling herself into it delicately. As she sat, the petticoats of her skirt ballooned either side of her, causing her to take up an absurd amount of space on the small bench.

"Are you feeling alright?" Leander insisted again, concern in his voice as he approached and took the seat next to her, carefully gathering the side of her dress so as not to sit on it. Mary watched his hands, still holding the fabric between his fingers even after he had seated himself.

Perhaps he was unsure of what to do with it.

Or perhaps he knew exactly what he should do with it.

"Yes, thank you. Please do not let me be a hindrance to continuing with your work."

"Miss Taylor, if you do not mind me saying so, you do look a bit flush." Leander absentmindedly ran the material of her skirt in between his fingers, a physical manifestation of his concern.

"I am fine, thank you for your concern, Mr. Doucet." Mary could feel her words coming out short and crisp, all the while staring at his fingers.

"I have just sworn to your brother to look after you."

Yes, as a sister.

"So I will have failed miserably if on return of his match with your sister, which between us," Leander leaned towards Mary and cupped a hand to her ear, "I am certain he will lose..."

Mary fought a smile as it flickered on the edges of her mouth.

"He finds you sitting here by yourself, abandoned and unwell."

"I thank you for your concern, Mr. Doucet," Mary chose her words carefully. "I believe I am just tired from the day of travel."

Leander nodded in understanding.

"Perhaps you would feel better if you took off your gloves and bonnet," Leander suggested, finally releasing the fabric of her dress, draping it carefully over his knee.

Mary raised her eyes cautiously, considering his words. It was not a suggestion altogether unreasonable, though it might offend some of the more conservative ladies.

But combined with the intimate act of touching her clothing, the suggestion gave Mary pause as her heart quickened.

"Oh, not like that, Miss Taylor," Leander responded to her measured consideration with a start as he nudged a bit closer towards her. "If you were calling on someone in their home for tea, perhaps, you would not sit as near to the door as possible, still bundled up in your gloves, bonnet, and outdoor overcoat, let alone holding the neck of your parasol so firmly, it almost seems as though you are intent on strangling it." At his words, Mary looked down. She had forgotten she was holding it, her hand clutching so tightly that her fingers had turned red.

"That is true," Mary reasoned, propping the parasol on the seat beside her. "But the fact remains that this is not your house, and I have not been offered a cup of tea."

"You are right, of course," Leander conceded. "Where are my manners?" He made a show of straightening up, clearing his throat dramatically, and turning towards Mary again, as though he were starting their interaction over.

"Miss Taylor, what a pleasure to see you. Might I offer you a cup of tea?"

"Why, thank you Mr. Doucet. I just have one question. Do you know how to make a cup of tea?" Mary asked, one eyebrow raised.

Damn his charm to hell, she was going to embarrass him the way he had her.

"Well Miss Taylor, you will just have to find out," he responded softly.

Coyly.

"But first, won't you please make yourself more comfortable?"

"I am quite fine the way I am, thank you," Mary insisted, her heart beating wildly in her chest.

"May I?" he asked, gesturing towards her hand. Mary eyed him suspiciously for a moment before placing her small hand into his outstretched palm.

Leander studied her hand, turning it over in his. Softly, with the thumb of his other hand, he began caressing the inside of her palm, moving his thumb in a circular motion.

Mary inhaled sharply at his touch, the sensation of his roving finger electrifying.

Suddenly she felt extremely flushed, as though she were indeed overheating.

And she was certain that the touch of Leander Doucet was the cause.

That aching she had felt the night of her debutante ball reappeared. She could feel what felt like a heartbeat down there, beneath the layers of skirts and pantalettes, loud and commanding. It shook her entire body, sending quivers through her.

And she wondered if Leander could feel it too.

"I do believe," Mary breathed, and before she could finish, Leander's eyes moved up from her hand and met hers. As he stared at her, the circling of his thumb picked up speed, as though it were moving with incredible urgency.

"What is it, that you believe, Miss Taylor?" he whispered.

"That I might actually be more comfortable with my gloves off." She could not believe the words as they left her mouth.

Were they even her words?

"Allow me to help you with that." Leander's eyes bore into hers.

Mary could no longer speak, but she gave a small nod to encourage him.

And with that confirmation, Leander Doucet began to remove Mary Taylor's glove.

He worked slowly, his thumb halting its assault on her senses momentarily as he ran his hand down the length of hers until he got to her fingers.

"You have beautiful hands, Miss Taylor," he breathed. "A lady's pair of hands," he confirmed, bringing her hand to his mouth and kissing the top of it softly.

He stared at her over the top of her hand, poised at his mouth.

The heartbeat in Mary's chest and in between her legs pounded in unison, as though they both desired the same thing.

Or rather, as though all *three* desired the same thing. For the manner in which Leander gazed at her could not be compared to anything Mary had ever experienced—even the attentions of Thomas Walker, trying his best to snare his piece of the Taylor fortune, paled in comparison to Leander. He looked at her with a boldness that was all at once commanding and vulnerable. He desired her attention—nay, he required her attention—for it gave him the ability to breathe.

And then Leander began slowly and meticulously removing her glove. He started with her smallest finger, softly tugging at the material to bring it away from her flesh before moving on to her ring finger, then her middle and index, finally working his way to her thumb. All the while he stared at her intensely, soaking her in an assault of undivided attention.

Once all the fingers were loose, Leander slid the glove from her hand easily, setting it on his knee.

"And how is that, Miss Taylor?"

"Much better," Mary heard herself say, though the words felt distant, as if spoken by someone far braver.

She wasn't sure what she wanted—not entirely—only that if his lips met hers, she wouldn't stop them.

Is this how Elizabeth had ended up in the barn with Charles's friend?

*Former friend*, Charles would undoubtedly desire clarified for the record.

"I am so grateful for your concern," Mary said, voice softer now.

"But of course," Leander murmured. "Any sister of Charles— "

Mary flinched.

"...Is a sister of yours?" She asked, the question catching in her throat as though it weren't hers to speak aloud. Her back straightened, but the rest of her body didn't follow.

"And... is this, how you would treat a sister?"

"I—," Leander paused, a bit startled, searching for words.

"Forgive me, Miss Taylor, I forget myself," he finally managed after a moment.

"It will not happen again."

At his words, Mary felt her ribcage contracting, threatening to crush her chest as the air disappeared from her lungs. The embarrassment welled in her eyes, tears threatening to stream down her face.

She looked down, as though her removed glove might offer some answers, but it lay limply on Leander's leg, a leg that sat far too near to her own.

"You... did forget," she murmured, unsure whether she meant it as an accusation or a question. "And perhaps you should decide... whether I'm just a sister, or..." She trailed off, not desiring to finish her declaration, for the words frightened her.

Somewhere in the depths of Mary's gut, she feared which option he would choose.

Before Leander could respond, Mary snatched her glove from his knee and put it on so quickly and aggressively she nearly tore the delicate lace. Then she rose to her feet.

"Elizabeth!" Mary called as she strode towards Charles's office door, declining to knock before pushing it open. "We need to be making our way back. We do not want to be late for supper, lest Auntie chastise us in a language we do not understand again!"

"What has come over you?" Elizabeth snapped as they stepped back out into the New Orleans street. The low sun cast a sleepy shadow over the town, the air chillier than when the ladies had first made their foray.

"Miss Taylor," Leander appeared at the door. Elizabeth turned but Mary did not, feigning that she did not hear him. Gathering her skirts, Mary looked both ways, before stepping out into the street, darting across so quickly it took Elizabeth and Leander by surprise.

"Mary!" Elizabeth called. "Did you not hear that Mr. Doucet was trying to speak with you?"

*He has already said what he needs to,* Mary thought, feeling the hot tears as they stung her eyelids. She blinked rapidly, trying to avoid the necessity of raising a hand to her eyes, for fear of giving away her shame and causing a scene.

For Southern society would hardly tolerate a young lady crying in public by herself. Any gentleman or lady of appropriate upbringing would be obligated to stop her and check to ensure she was okay, inquire if she required assistance, a glass of water, a chair to rest a moment, or any other nicety one could offer to a person in distress.

But Mary did not desire any of these gestures of goodwill. The last thing she wished was to become the girl from Virginia who had shed tears on her first day in town.

And besides, she did not even know what she would say!

*I am crying because a man made me feel desired, only to humiliate me by calling me his sister.*

How sad.

But there had been nothing brotherly in the way Leander had looked at her. Nothing fraternal in the way his thumb circled her palm, nor in the way he'd removed her glove with maddening, deliberate care.

Mary weaved through the crowd with as much propriety as she could muster while nearly blinded by tears. Was this the way back to Aunt Genevieve's?

She rounded a corner—and collided hard with something solid.

"Oy!" a surprised voice exclaimed.

Mary stumbled, the impact sending her to the ground.

"Oh, Miss, forgive me, I am so sorry," the voice continued, now closer, crouching beside her. "I was walking too quickly on my way to evening mass, and I am running late. I hope you are not hurt. Miss?"

The voice was familiar.

Mary blinked, her vision clearing.

"Mr. Rivera?"

"Why, Miss Mary Taylor," he said gently, smiling in recognition. He reached into his breast pocket and offered her a handkerchief. "Are you alright?"

"I..." Mary bit her lip, the tears returning with renewed force.

*Don't you dare cry, Mary Taylor.*

But the tears came anyway, slipping silently down her cheeks.

"There there, child," Mr. Rivera cooed sympathetically. There was something about the way he spoke, so paternally calm and unwavering, that always managed to disarm her. "Let us get you off the ground, my dear," he insisted, holding out his hands.

Mary accepted them, grateful it was Mr. Rivera and no one else.

Once on her feet, she dabbed at her face with the handkerchief, cheeks burning.

"I'm so sorry for making such a scene."

"Not at all, my dear. I am the one who knocked you to the ground," he reminded her. "Though I know those tears from my own daughters," he said with a sad smile. "You are too young and beautiful for tears, my dear," he insisted, patting her hand lightly. "May I escort you home, Miss Taylor? My son tells me that you are staying with the Defours, a distant relative of your mother's by marriage, if I am not mistaken?" he asked as though it were a question, though he already knew the answer.

"Oh, but Mr. Rivera, were you not on your way to church? I would not wish you to miss it on my account. And in any case, I have already made you so late."

"The Lord will forgive me," Mr. Rivera assured her, his black moustached face smiling good-humoredly. "I actually think he might condone it. No good Catholic man would leave a distressed lady on the ground in the street just because he is late to mass."

"Especially if he is the reason she is on the ground," Mary attempted humour.

"Well indeed, my dear. So you understand my desire to see you home is both selfless and selfish in equal measure. The Defour residence is in the French Quarter." He pointed with his cane across the street and to the left. "Shall we?" he asked, offering his arm to Mary and straightening his hat they made their way.

As they walked they talked, reminiscing about old times in that way that is so easy when the memories are happy and joyful. Mr. Rivera's cologne filled Mary's nose, that same citrus scent that she had remembered from childhood.

Mr. Rivera was nearly the same as in Mary's memory: a slight man of medium height and build, but of great dignity. He walked with a cane—he had for as long as Mary could remember—though he seemed to move like someone who did not especially need it. He was always dressed as though he was about to receive a guest, giving him an air of formality, but was known by the children in the town and on his plantation for carrying sweets in his pockets, which he was completely indiscriminate in distributing, making him a favorite of the children and a least-favorite of the mothers.

But his sweet good nature and old-world charm always meant no one could stay mad at him for too long. It was frankly impossible.

Mr. Rivera had, for as long as Mary could remember, always worn a suit of mourning and continued to wear his wedding band. Mary chanced a look at his left hand as they walked—it was covered in a glove, but even without seeing it she knew it was there; a pledge to his late wife of his continued love.

"I was so sorry to hear the news of your son-in-law," Mary offered quietly. "I hope Mrs. Sandoval is doing as well as she can in the circumstances."

"Thank you, my dear. She was as devoted to that man as I was to her mother. I suppose you could say that we Riveras, when we fall in love, we fall hard," Mr. Rivera explained with a heavy sigh. "It is a blessing and a curse, but I try to focus on the former, and try to convince my daughter to do the same."

"I think it's very admirable of both of you. I hope one day to find a love like that."

"I hope you do also, my dear," Mr. Rivera patted her forearm in fatherly affection. "It is the greatest gift in the world to love and be loved in return.

"Do you know she hated my pipe smoking?"

"Did she? How did you know?"

"Oh, because she missed no opportunity to tell me!" Mr. Rivera explained. "She'd hear me filling that pipe and was annoyed even before she smelled it. Insisted I would set the house on fire, which for the record, I have never done! She would say, 'Juan, I swear to Jesus Christ, if you light that pipe in this house, I will leave you!'" He mimicked, putting on a thick lady's Spanish accent.

Mary giggled, clasping a hand to her mouth. "And did she?"

"No, but she'd send me out to the porch. I'd sit on the stoop and the negros would laugh at me and say, 'Mister Rivera, have you been thrown out of your own home again?' And I'd say, 'It would appear I have.'"

Mary laughed, a large booming belly laugh that brought small tears to the corner of her eyes. She turned slightly and saw Mr. Rivera smiling at her fondly, small tears brimming his eyelids also.

"She still scolds me in my memory," Mr. Rivera admitted softly. "Even now, when I pack my pipe inside, I can feel myself waiting for it, but it never arrives," he continued after a moment, his voice lower, sadder. "I sometimes go and sit on the porch, just to feel like she's there. I still feel her presence in that house every day. Oh dear," Mr. Rivera gulped deeply. “I am sorry, my dear. Bless you for letting an old man run on the way I have.”

“Not at all,” Mary insisted, this time squeezing his arm comfortingly. “I am happy to listen. I love to hear about real love.”

“Well, it is not considered the most important thing for many families, and for some it is not a consideration at all. But in ours, it has always been a priority. That is why I will not push my Catalina to find another husband. She is still very young and very beautiful, but I will not pressure her into a life that she does not want.

“And yet…” he trailed off, gazing ahead. “I fear her grief will consume the rest of her life. And that would be its own tragedy…

“But I myself am no better,” Mr. Rivera reasoned, chuckling to himself. “I have been a widower many years now and have no intention of changing that.”

“If I may be so bold, I think it’s different,” Mary offered. “Your daughter had such a brief time with her husband, and her mourning is not only for him, but for a life they were promised and never got to share. You and Mrs. Rivera built a life together. You have children, and your children will likely have children. The evidence of your shared life lives on and is still a thing to be celebrated.”

Mr. Rivera looked at her meaningfully.

“That is very wise, Miss Taylor.” He nodded. “My Manuel is right to have taken such a keen admiration of you.”

Mary blushed furiously.

“Oh, do not tell me you did not know,” Mr. Rivera chuckled. “When I saw him earlier today, he told me he had invited you to church! I laughed and said, 'Hijo, have you ever heard of a Catholic Virginian?' His eagerness sometimes gets the better of him."

"I appreciated the gesture," Mary assured him. "Though before our journey my mother reminded me, quite firmly, that I am an English Protestant."

Mr. Rivera laughed. "Perhaps we should teach you some Latin, just to have a bit of fun."

"I fear losing my place in the will were I to come home reciting the Pater Noster."

"Ah, Mira eso," he chuckled. "One day in this city, and already you're starting to sound like us."

It was nearly dark by the time they arrived at the Defour house.

"I will leave you here, my dear, if it is all the same to you." Mr. Rivera stood at the bottom of the stairs, gesturing towards the door.

"Of course." Mary had all but forgotten that Mr. Rivera had offered to walk her home to a residence which he would refuse to enter.

Not that he would have been invited inside in any case.

But how could anyone have anything but good things to say about someone like Mr. Rivera?

"It was wonderful to see you again, Miss Taylor," Mr. Rivera removed his hat, and leaning forward, kissed both her cheeks lightly. "Though, I wish it had been under better circumstances. I promise in future to try not to knock you over."

"And I will try my best not to get in the way of you and your attendance at mass."

"Very good." Mr. Rivera smiled, eyes twinkling as he tipped his hat and began back down the street. "Oh, and Miss Taylor?" Mr. Rivera paused, turning on his heel. "I do hope my son was not the source of your distress earlier."

"Oh, not at all," her cheeks flushed.

"Good. I hope you would tell me if he were. He was not raised to leave a lady in tears."

"I assure you he did no such thing. Manuel is always the definition of a gentleman."

Mr. Rivera nodded, satisfied. "Good day to you, Miss Taylor."

"Good day, Mr. Rivera."

Mary did not even need to knock, for as she raised her hand to the door, it flung open dramatically, revealing the worried look of none other than—

Leander Doucet.

"What are you doing here?" Mary asked, forgetting her manners entirely.

"Miss Taylor, we have been worried sick," Leander insisted, reaching a hand around her back to lead her inside. "Are you alright?" His eyes swept over her, landing on the dust clinging to her coat. "Did something happen to you?"

"I tripped," Mary said flatly, brushing him off. She reached up and tugged the ribbon under her chin loose. Her bonnet came off in a huff of movement. Next came her gloves, stripped from her hands, and then she reached down and began unfastening her coat.

"Please, allow me—"

"That won't be necessary." She sidestepped his hands and tossed the coat over her arm, marching into the sitting room without looking back.

Leander followed.

"She's returned," he announced to the room.

"Oh, Mary!" Elizabeth leapt to her feet, sending her sewing tumbling to the floor. "Where have you been? We've been so worried! What is all this?" She gestured to the dust smudging Mary's skirts.

"She fell," Leander supplied.

Mary resisted the urge to throw him a look of disdain.

"Oh, you poor thing," Elizabeth cooed. "Are you alright? How did you get home?"

"I ran in to Mr. Rivera; he escorted me back."

Though which Mr. Rivera, Mary purposefully left ambiguous.

As though on cue, at the mention of the name, Amelié and Antoiné's spines stiffened.

"You should not be out with a gentleman without a chaperone," Amelié clucked. "The tongues in this town will be wagging about it tomorrow."

Yes, yours chief amongst them.

"While I, of course, tend to agree," Mary nodded, "for a young lady can easily find herself in a situation she did not mean—or worse, with a man who does not have her best interests at heart—I had little choice, considering I was lost."

"And injured," Elizabeth added, brushing a strand of hair behind Mary's ear. "How did you fall? Did you not hear us calling your name?"

"I did not. I apologize, Mr. Doucet, for not hearing you." Her words were cold as she finally deigned to glance his way. "Did you require something?"

"You had left your parasol." Leander gestured towards the wall where it had been propped. "I was also going to offer you both a ride home."

"Yes, Mary, why in the world did you run off?" Elizabeth asked. "We have been so worried! I would never forgive myself if something happened to you!"

*Because I am your sister, or because Father will never permit you to leave the house again if something happens to me?*

Perhaps she should just tell them all what occurred, Mary thought indignantly as she accepted her chastisements. Perhaps she should just tell them all about how Leander Doucet was no gentleman at all.

But even as she pondered the notion, dared to flirt with the unthinkable, she knew she would not. The consequences of a good upbringing meant that a young lady could often not say what she actually thought.

And in any case, what would she say?

That Leander Doucet winked at her, offered her a cup of tea, and then removed her glove in the most *intimate* of ways?

Hardly a scandal.

And yet...

The heat of embarrassment flared again.

"You are both very fortunate Mother was called away last minute to the children's hospital," Amelié sniffed. "She would have been furious."

"Well, then we will thank the Good Lord and Jesus Christ for our good fortune and all of us will agree not to say a word. Isn't that right?" Elizabeth demanded of the room, one hand propped on a cocked hip as she challenged anyone to disagree with her.

Antoiné nodded quickly while Amelié made a show of deliberation before agreeing with a sigh.

"Well, ladies, now that you are reunited, I will take my leave." Leander nodded to the room. "I am glad you are safe, Miss Taylor."

"Thank you for your concern, Mr. Doucet," Mary threw the comment over her shoulder, as though his concern was utterly inconsequential.

But her eyes—traitorous things—met his anyway.

And her heart began to pound.

Damnit.

"Good day, Miss Taylor." He nodded before turning on his heel and taking his leave.

He was a scoundrel.

Mary stared at the ceiling in the darkness, fury prickling under her skin.

Only a rogue would toy with a lady's heart that way. And worse—only a rogue would know how to make her feel like *that*.

He knew exactly what he was doing. She was sure of it.

Between her legs, the memory still burned—thirty seconds, maybe less, but enough to scramble her thoughts and upend her composure.

And it only takes that long to ruin yourself.

She glanced across the room. Elizabeth was already asleep, her breathing steady and soft, bordering on a snore. Mary considered waking her—surely Elizabeth would have insight. She *always* had insight.

*Men always desire what they cannot have.*

Hadn't Elizabeth said that once?

If Mary asked, Elizabeth would tell her to treat Leander like a brother. Be polite, maybe even lightly flirtatious. But then, parade a string of other men before him. Make him ache with jealousy.

The idea was wicked. And delightful.

Not ladylike, of course. But then again, Leander had hardly behaved like a gentleman.

Suppressing the more unsavory thoughts that came rushing back with the memory of his hands on hers, Mary turned her mind to Manuel Rivera.

He had been positively *delighted* to see her at her debut. And when they danced—had Elizabeth not dragged her away—she could have stayed in his arms all night.

The way he'd looked at her had made her feel like treasure. Not something to be toyed with.

But something to be cherished.

He was handsome. Polite. From a respectable family.

Yes, Catholic. But one must forgive some things in the search for love.

She remembered the way Mr. Rivera had laughed about Manuel inviting her to church. That had only been a few hours before he'd helped her up from the street.

Which meant Manuel must've told him she was in town almost immediately.

*He was not raised to leave a lady in tears.*

Those words stuck with her. She believed them. She believed *him*.

Manuel was no rogue. He wouldn't confuse, or tease, or tempt. He wouldn't make her feel foolish for believing his intentions might be genuine.

And that—*that*—was worth something.

Rogues had a way of slipping through a lady's defenses, charming their way into her thoughts, her heart, and then vanishing before she realized they had no intention of staying.

Mary had nearly let it happen again.

But no more.

Mary Taylor was too well-bred, too well-read, and far too intelligent to let a rogue turn her into the fool.

She may have been distracted—momentarily derailed—but she wasn't about to repeat her mistakes.

Yes. She would seek out Manuel Rivera.

And this time, she would not let herself be distracted.

And she would leave Leander Doucet exactly where he belonged—in the past.

# Chapter XI

"I cannot believe you've talked me into this," Elizabeth muttered as she and Mary briskly approached Santiago San Ignacio, their King James Bibles clutched like contraband.

Mary's had a second volume tucked beneath it—of course—because she couldn't leave the house without reading material. A lifelong habit that had earned her eye-rolls from young ladies and exaggerated sighs from Elizabeth. As though it were a crime to be well-read.

"I cannot believe I am the one trying to talk you into doing something, and you're the one protesting based on propriety!"

"It's not just propriety, Mary, it's the eternal salvation of our souls at stake!"

"You are aware that the God of Catholicism is the same God as ours?" Mary teased, trying to sound playful. The truth was, she was significantly downplaying how nervous the concept of entering a Catholic cathedral made her.

It really only came second to how furious her parents would be if they found out that they had attended Catholic mass on a Sunday.

Made even worse if they knew it was for the purposes of seeing a gentleman.

Could any man really be worth the risk of the Lord's wrath?

Mary certainly hoped so, though she was wiser than to say as much.

"I think we just have to somehow avoid communion," Mary rationalized aloud. "There are some... stark theological differences there."

"You mean cannibalism," Elizabeth offered, the distaste obvious in her voice.

"It is very odd, isn't it?" Mary asked. "I have wondered more than once if people actually, you know, really *believe* that it is truly changing into—"

"Do not say it!" Elizabeth pleaded, dramatically clasping her hands to her ears. "It is not so much that I ponder whether or not people believe it, but that if they do, they are still willing to eat the bread and drink the wine!

"What do we do if it is offered to us?"

"We politely decline."

"How do we do that without causing a scene?"

"I am certain it will not be *too* scandalous," Mary promised. "I mean, people who are not Catholics must visit Catholic churches too, right?

"For what purpose?" Elizabeth demanded.

"Perhaps, to see the architecture and admire the stained glass?" Mary suggested, knowing she did not sound overly convinced herself.

And if she couldn't manage to convince herself, the Lord knew she wasn't going to be able to convince Elizabeth.

"Do you really think people go to Catholic church just to see what it's like?" Elizabeth asked a bit hopefully.

"Oh, almost certainly!" Mary nodded vigorously.

Almost certainly not.

"Where did you get these, anyway?" Elizabeth asked, gesturing towards the chapel veils that both girls had draped over their arms.

"Gabrielle. I told her I wished to visit a few of the Catholic churches to admire the architecture, but wanted to ensure I was as respectful as possible, and she offered me these, along with, the strict instructions that we dress modestly." Mary's tone changed as she turned to look at Elizabeth. Despite her insistence of the need for humility of the flesh, Elizabeth had emerged from their bedroom in a short-sleeved and bright dress of golden yellow. The neck was cut so low, Mary had gasped.

*"That is precisely the reaction I am hoping for from the men," Elizabeth had giggled, twirling the parasol that was nestled over her shoulder prettily.*

*"Where did you get that?"*

*"I had it made," Elizabeth shrugged, peering down at her chest she cupped her breasts and yanked them towards the dress's neckline before releasing them again.*

*Mary stared at her sister's bosom, bouncing in pretty participation before casting a glance at her own situation. It was a relatively plain frock of deep navy—not quite black, but also not bright enough to draw undue attention to herself.*

*And it certainly had no prominent bosom to speak of.*

Now, next to Elizabeth, she felt even more like the drabby and unattractive little sister.

Which was a feeling that was far from foreign to her.

"Oh Mary, I love it," Elizabeth cackled, throwing her head back in delight. "Ever since your coming out, you have become so much more fun!"

"What do you mean?"

"The Mary I knew before would never have told a lie for the purpose of acquiring accessories." Elizabeth gestured again towards the veils. "All for the sake of "happening" upon a beau!"

"Well, it is not exactly a lie. I do wish to see the architecture."

"Oh, save your prissiness," Elizabeth dismissed her. "It is a little white lie and you know it, too, so don't try to make up some nonsense to convince yourself otherwise. And it's not going to hurt anyone, so don't you go and lose any sleep over it either!

"Though, in the spirit of confessing, as I'm certain that's something you do at Catholic mass, I am a little bit surprised you're pursuing Manuel Rivera this intently." Elizabeth threw a sideways glance at Mary.

"Why?" Mary returned her look. "Was not the entire purpose of coming to New Orleans to pursue Manuel Rivera?"

"I suppose in a sense." Elizabeth bobbed her head from side to side in consideration. "I mean, I was certainly not going to pass up the opportunity to visit New Orleans. You and I both know Mother and Father would never have let me come by myself."

"And here I have been laboring under the delusion that you came to help find me a husband." Mary did not even need to feign surprise, for it was, after all, very like Elizabeth to have some ulterior motives tucked away in her bosom.

In her ample bosom.

"Of course that is the reason I am here!" It was now Elizabeth's turn to feign mock offense, a hand flying to her breast dramatically. Mary raised an eyebrow and Elizabeth laughed. "And, it is a relief for me to not be immediately shipped back to North Carolina," Elizabeth finally admitted.

The Cathedral loomed in front of them, large and imposing, its bells echoing a deep hum which called its occupants to mass. All around the two ladies, hordes of men and women streamed up the stone steps and through the large wooden doors that stood flung open, somehow both inviting and menacing.

The flock of the Lord were a sea of muted colors—greys, dark blues, and blacks—their heads bowed in reverence. The women were dressed conservatively, sleeves down to their wrists and dresses to the ground, their heads covered in chapel veils of mostly black and white lace.

No one smiled, and an air of solemnity hung over the crowd as they entered the church, as though they all marched towards an expected reprimand.

Mary and Elizabeth quickly put on their chapel veils and followed suit.

Mary cringed as they entered the throng of people, for Elizabeth stood out like a bird on display in her dress of bright yellow, her bust unapologetically prominent.

"Do you understand now why I told you to dress modestly?" Mary hissed.

"Shhh," Elizabeth hissed back, tucking her Bible under her arm and placing her palms together she held them out in front of her in feigned sanctimony. "We are entering the house of the Lord."

"No one else is doing that," Mary insisted. "You are making a scene."

"SHHHHH!" Elizabeth hushed sternly.

As the girls travelled up the stone steps, Mary turned her face skywards towards the Cathedral. It was a grand structure, beautiful but imposing in nature. Aggressive, with large spires that plunged towards the sky, like a place that was purposefully built to intimidate and humble.

If that was the case then it has done its job, Mary gulped as they approached the large cathedral doors. In front of them, people paused, dipping their hands into a small bowl of water and kneeling they made the sign of the cross before processing in.

"Do we do that?" Elizabeth asked.

"I... I think we probably should?" Mary stared intently at the people in front of them, watching their movements as carefully as possible.

"Which way does it go?" Elizabeth asked desperately. "Is it down, up, left, right, or down, up, right left?"

"I always thought it was up first!"

"And then it is right, left or left, right?"

"I know not!" Mary admitted nervously, approaching the threshold.

Mary shook, dropping into a deep curtsy and making a quick sign of the cross—up, down, left, right.

In her haste, completely forgetting to use the bowl of water.

Elizabeth, on the other hand, plunged her entire hand into the bowl, soaking her glove in the process. Moving her hand so rapidly in the hope no one would be able to see and thus judge her movements, she inadvertently splashed water on the people behind her.

"Pardon me," she turned around, bowing her head in apology. "I just find myself so overexuberant when I visit the house of the Lord."

"Lord help us," Mary muttered to herself.

Inside Santiago San Ignacio the organ bellowed, a low dirge like sound that echoed off the high stone walls and ceiling. Large circular columns lined the aisles of the congregation, as wide as tree-trunks. Mary cast her gaze upwards again, staring at the domes created by the spires.

"Stop gawking," Elizabeth whispered, turning towards Mary. "You look like a tourist. Oh my gosh!" Elizabeth's eyes suddenly grew wide and Mary turned to her left to follow her sister's gaze.

"Oh goodness," Mary gasped, finding what had caught her sister's attention. Lined along the walls were stained glass windows filled in with deep and rich colors—they would have been beautiful had they not been heinously visceral and violent.

Mary ran her eyes along the left hand wall of the Cathedral—a man being stoned to death and beat with a club, another being eaten by a pack of animals, and another pierced with more arrows that Mary thought would have been technically necessary to kill a man.

What excess!

Mary cast her gaze around the rest of the cathedral, noting the bloody scenes everywhere she looked.

"This must be why Auntie is so fond of the notion of suffering," Elizabeth offered in bewilderment.

The Taylor sisters clutched their chapel veils under their chins tightly and scuttled into pews in the middle of the congregation.

"What are these?" Elizabeth asked, pointing at the small wooden boxes which lined the pews.

"I know not," Mary echoed for what she was certain would not be the last time, looking around to see if anyone was using theirs. "Is it a foot rest?"

The congregation turned as a man dressed in long white robes paraded down the aisle, swinging a lantern in front of him like a pendulum. Smoky incense filled the aisles as he processed, slowly and austerely, towards the front of the congregation. Once at the front of the church, he bowed his head in contemplative prayer.

"Do we wear these the entire time?" Elizabeth asked, gesturing towards the chapel veil as she competed with the bellowing of the organ as it reached its crescendo.

"What?" Mary leaned closer to her sister, cupping her ear towards her mouth.

"Do we wear these the entire time?" Elizabeth raised her voice as the entire church fell silent.

As if on cue, all heads turned to look at the Taylor sisters, Elizabeth, glowing like a canary on parade, and Mary beside her, coloring a tragic shade of scarlet. The room was utterly speechless as the congregation cast their reprehensible gaze at the two obvious intruders.

So much for remaining inconspicuous, Mary thought to herself, wishing the floor would open up and swallow them both whole.

Unable to take the awkward silence any longer, Elizabeth smiled at the people in front of them, who had turned to share in the crowd's silent judgment. "Good morning," she flashed her best smile. "How do you do?" She extended her glove soaked hand.

"Eh-hem!" The man clad in white at the front of the church cleared his throat, drawing the attention away from the Taylor sisters at long last.

"Well, you need not worry about finding Manual Rivera after the service now," Elizabeth whispered in consolation. "Because if he is here, he has most certainly seen us!"

"I believe your dress would have been enough on its own, even without the public humiliation."

"Shhhhh!" Both people either side of Mary and Elizabeth hushed them violently.

Mary folded her hands in her lap and stared at them intently, determined to spend the rest of the service as a quiet and respectful little church mouse.

After all, this was apparently the animal which most resembled her.

Up front, the service started, and the foreign words washed over her as her brain searched for sounds she might recognize from her Latin tutelage: Christus, Deus, Sanctus, Pastor. Mary silently cursed her lack of predisposition to learning foreign languages, catching the movement of the mass into Spanish, but failing to understand a word.

Next to her, Elizabeth stared blankly towards the front, a look of utter confusion plastered plainly on her face. She turned to Mary quizzically, but Mary shook her head in indication that she was similarly lost.

What an absolute disaster. Mary winced at the memory of their entrance. Aunt Genevieve was bound to hear about this, and then they would be—

*Thwack.*

Mary flinched, her hand flying to the back of her head. Had she just been... hit?

*Are they actually throwing things at us now?* She turned to look at the stained-glass depiction of the crowd hurtling stones at St. James.

*Have we created that much chaos?* She thought in desperation, averting her gaze back to the hands clasped in her lap, when a small slightly sparkling object caught her attention.

It was a gold button. A man's button.

Mary turned her head, looking around to see if someone was in obvious search of a missing accessory, but all the heads were bowed, eyes closed, deep in prayer.

"Eh-hem."

The sound came again, this time from above.

*Is God personally reprimanding me?* She thought in a panic, casting her eyes upwards.

High above the main doors, in a small balcony, sat the Rivera family.

And sitting in that balcony, as if he'd arranged the whole scene for his amusement, was none other than Manuel Rivera—smiling down at her with unabashed delight.

"Miss Taylor and Miss Taylor," Manuel swept the hat from his head and greeted the ladies with a bow as they surfaced from the dark cathedral into the bright sky of the early Sunday afternoon. "I must say, you both do know how to make an entrance."

"Why, thank you kindly, Mr. Rivera." Elizabeth curtsyed. "You Catholics do put on a very grand mass, though between you and me—" Elizabeth leaned forward as though confiding a secret, but as she bent down, nearly her entire bosom was on display. Despite the warmth of his complexion, Mary noted a subtle flush rising in Manuel's cheeks as he tried to return Elizabeth's beckoning without finding himself compromised by her choice of clothing.

Not a rogue then. She wondered if Leander Doucet would be able to operate with an equal level of self-control, especially when faced with such a challenging situation.

For Elizabeth did, undeniably, have a very nice bosom.

"I fear I cannot claim to have understood one word of it," Elizabeth confessed, to the surprise of no one. "But it was very ornate, and the cups and plates look very expensive!"

"I have heard that Protestant churches are less decorated," Manuel replied politely. "But I have never been myself, so cannot say I know for certain. Is mass in Virginia very different to here?"

"Oh yes, so very different. We do not have incense, and the service is all in English. What was the man in the white robes speaking Mr. Rivera? Was it Latin?"

"It was Latin and Spanish."

"And do you speak Latin and Spanish?" Elizabeth demanded.

"Well, we speak Spanish at home, but we were all taught how to read and write Latin, so as to allow us to understand mass." Manuel answered Elizabeth's interrogations patiently, his hat held politely in his hand as though he did not mind.

In fact, he gave the overall sense that there was nowhere else in the world he'd rather be.

"Do you now?" Elizabeth grinned. "My sister's very taken with languages!"

"Is she now?"

"Am I?" Mary asked incredulously.

"Do you not recall? You and Auntie were talking about you learning another language just the other day."

"I believe Aunt Genevieve berated our English ignorance for assuming everyone would learn our language, thus divorcing ourselves from the responsibility of learning another," Mary clarified.

Manuel threw back his head in laughter.

"I have heard your Aunt Genevieve is very spirited."

"And then when we discovered that a family friend spoke French, too, why, Mary here was so amazed she could not take her eyes off of him!"

"Is that so?" Manuel asked cautiously, eyeing Mary with a look that seemed to enjoy the idea of impressing her with his command of language.

"My sister often hears what she wishes and exaggerates the rest," Mary insisted. "She's famous for it. And if you can believe it, I told her to dress modestly—and *this* is what she chose."

"I think you both look lovely."

"Oh but Mr. Rivera, you must tell me." Elizabeth leant forward again. "Why are all the women dressed as though someone has died?"

"It is, as your sister says, for modesty," Manuel confirmed, a cheeky smile brimming at the edges of his mouth. "But it differs by culture. If you went to one of the French Catholic Churches, for example, the dress would be completely different. Less somber. I often feel the French see mass as an opportunity to showcase their latest imports from Paris. It is not dissimilar to a fashion show."

"French mass sounds so much more interesting."

Manuel once again laughed as Mary turned beetroot red.

"Elizabeth, really!"

"But do you not think it a bit odd that the people are meant to dress modestly, but then the church itself is so elaborate and ostentatious? I mean, even the man in the white robes was wearing a big golden cross—it was the largest piece of jewelry in the entire church!"

"That is a very interesting observation, Miss Taylor." Manuel pretended to ponder, "I had never thought about it quite in that manner."

"And these." Elizabeth pointed at the chapel veil still draped over her head, though doing little to lend a Virginius air. "When are we allowed to take them off?"

"If you can believe it, they are not actually required."

"Oh, well, we wish to be respectful." Elizabeth nodded insistently. "And when you do the sign of the cross, is it, down, up, left, right—"

"Manuel." A woman not even as tall as Mary and dressed in a long-sleeved dress of plain black velvet appeared next to him, touching him lightly on the shoulder. Mary could not make out her features, for her delicate black lace chapel veil hung over her entire head, covering both her hair and face and trailing down to her shoulders, almost like a veil at a wedding.

Catalina, Mary thought, as the woman said something in Spanish to Manuel, who responded.

"Catalina, these are the daughters of Mr. William Taylor. They are visiting from Virginia. Miss Taylor and Miss Taylor, this is my eldest sister, Catalina."

"How do you do?" Mary asked. "Please, call me Mary, and this is my sister, Elizabeth."

"Well, thank you," Catalina answered, politely but indifferently. "From Virginia, you say?" she asked, a small twinkle in her voice suggesting a smile was forming underneath the black veil. "This must be your first time attending Catholic mass?"

"Why yes, how did you know?" Elizabeth asked.

Catalina paused before answering, and Mary could almost envision her eyes travelling up and down the two obviously out of place ladies.

"Call it a woman's intuition," she offered with something between humor and condescension. "Manuel. ¿Dónde está..." Catalina turned back to her brother, speaking to him rapidly in Spanish. He responded with equal speed, and the Taylor sisters stood watching the exchange in silent awe.

"I wonder if they think in Spanish or English," Elizabeth pondered aloud.

"We are fluent in both, which means we think in both." Catalina turned, answering her in English. "And for the avoidance of doubt, even when we speak Spanish, we still understand English."

"Catalina, por favor!" Manuel tsked, clearly annoyed by his sister's rudeness.

"Qué? Honestamente, hermano..." They spoke animatedly for what was only a few seconds, but felt more like hours to the Taylor sisters as they loitered awkwardly.

"It was nice to meet you both." Catalina nodded mechanically. "Perhaps I will see you next Sunday."

Unlikely.

"You will have to forgive my sister," Manuel explained after she had slowly made her way down the stone steps to join a small group of people. "She is very traditional, and does not always see the humour in life the way she used to.

"But may I ask you both how you will be getting home, and whether I might have the honor of escorting you?" he asked, flashing a brilliant and genuine smile.

"Manuel Rivera, you sly dog." Elizabeth looped her arm around his left forearm as Mary took his right. "You just wish to parade us around town so that you can be the envy of all the men! And make all the women jealous in the process! Do not pretend as though you do not know of what I speak—and don't you go on trying to deny it either!" She wagged a finger at him playfully. "If you are going to escort us, I insist you at least be honest about your reasoning."

"Well Miss Taylor," Manuel blushed slightly. "I confess while that was not my conscious motive at first, I do have to admit that the idea has a certain appeal to it."

"And is there someone in particular you are looking to make jealous with our company?"

"Oh no, Miss Taylor," Manuel insisted. "My father would whip me with his cane if he ever thought I was deliberately running amuck with a lady's heart."

"You know, I always liked your father," Elizabeth clarified. "It is a shame more men were not raised like you."

"For my sisters' sake, I'm inclined to agree with you," Manuel nodded, "I just hope I can live up to the high expectation set for me.

"I hope that does not mean though, Miss Taylor, that either you or your sister have had any unfavorable experiences with New Orleans men? A man's status as a gentleman is not something that is taken lightly in this town, and if there were any men mistreating you, I would wager the good people of this town would desire to know about it."

"Oh, Mr. Rivera, you are so gallant, and we are so grateful to you. Especially because we are, as you well know, just simple country girls, and this is our first time in a big city..."

She was really laying it on thick, Mary thought, amazed that her sister possessed the stomach to air such helplessness.

"Oh, I believe that is my friend from school!" Elizabeth squealed pointing into the distance.

"Who?" Mary asked suspiciously.

"Why, my good friend Clarissa Thomas. I am certain that is her as sure as I am that God made the Earth! I must go say hello to her!

"I will just be up ahead, just there!" Elizabeth pointed straight ahead at nothing in particular. Before Mary could protest, Elizabeth had gathered has skirts and started, very unceremoniously, running towards this fictional friend, losing her chapel veil in the process.

"Your sister must have extraordinary eyesight." Manuel squinted, taking his now free hand and raising it to his eyes.

"Yes, indeed," Mary agreed, wondering if Manuel was oblivious to Elizabeth's ruse or just too polite to say anything.

Manuel paused to collect the chapel veil that had been forgotten and abandoned, and folding it carefully, tucked it into his coat pocket.

"Would you like me to hold yours also, Miss Taylor?" he asked, gesturing towards the veil that was clutched at her side.

"Oh, thank you, Mr. Rivera." Mary smiled, handing it over to him. "That is so kind of you."

"It is my pleasure. And please, allow me to carry your books also." He held his hand outstretched.

"Oh, Mr. Rivera, you needn't—" Mary's protests fell on deaf ears as Manuel's strong hand plucked the books from the crook of her elbow.

"I have never seen a King James Bible before." Manuel gently flipped it open and began to scan.

"You will read the Vulgate, I presume?"

Manual paused, looking up at Mary with a studied amusement.

"Miss Taylor, you are full of surprises. How have you found yourself to know that?"

"I read very often and widely." Mary sheepishly turned away, before returning to meet his stare.

"It would appear so." He gently closed the book, moving it to the bottom of the pile as he considered the second cover. "*The Rebels*," Manuel read aloud, raising his eyebrows. "Why, Miss Taylor, I had no idea!"

"It is not like that!" Mary insisted, her cheeks beginning to flush red as she clambered for the book back, but Manuel easily pulled it from her reach.

"Then pray, Miss Taylor, do tell me what it is *like*," he teased. "Is Miss Lydia Maria Child making a rebel of you?

"And is your father aware?"

"It is a novel, though her works include social commentary also—" Mary once again tried to wrangle the book from Manuel, who at her movement, held the book over his head. Instinctively, Mary reached for it, leaning herself forward and in the process brushing her chest against his.

Both their bodies went rigid, the entertained smile swept from Manuel's face as the gravity of the incident began to take form. Mary's heart pounded, the place where their bodies had met—most specifically, where her nipples had grazed him—sending a coursing warmness through her.

"Forgive me, Miss Taylor." Manuel lowered his arm, offering the book back to her in an act of repentance. "I believe I was momentarily taken back to our summers spent together as children.

"But you are no longer a child, nor am I." Manuel looked down at his shoes before chancing a look into her eyes. "You are a lady now, and ladies deserve to be treated with nothing but the utmost respect."

"There is nothing to forgive, Mr. Rivera." Mary placed her hands gently on the spine of the book and pushed it back towards Manuel, who tucked it underneath his arm before offering her his other.

Mary accepted, and they walked in quiet silence for a few moments more.

"Manuel."

"Pardon me?" Mary turned towards him.

"I would wish you to call me Manuel, if you desire to."

"Oh." Mary smiled, touched by the sentiment and what it meant. "Yes, of course, Manuel. And you might call me Mary.

"If you should wish to."

"Mary," he said, savouring the name on his lips like it was something extra sweet. "A queen's name."

"Who ended up beheaded," Mary said flatly, almost accusatory.

Manuel laughed.

"What is so funny?" Mary demanded. It had always bothered her that her parents had given her the name of a queen who was beheaded by her sister, Elizabeth.

If not foreshadowing, then she didn't know what was.

"I had not thought about *that* Mary," Manuel confessed. "Though I can understand why you might feel a certain way about that. I was actually referring to the Queen of Heaven."

"Oh, I see. I confess, Mr. Rivera, we don't have the same admiration for Mary, Mother of Jesus, that you do."

"I know, and I do not understand it," Manuel confessed in return. "Miss Taylor, I mean Mary." He smiled. "She is our most venerated saint. Honestly, it is amazing no one in my family is named Maria!"

Mary laughed.

"Some might say scandalous?"

"Some might!" Manuel agreed animatedly. "So tell me, Miss Mary, in all honesty, what did you think of mass today?"

"It was..." Mary chose her words with care. "Different."

"Please elaborate, Miss Taylor. I mean, Mary."

"Well, I will confess, it was perhaps a bit stressful because everything was so foreign from what we know. It would be easier to make a fair assessment had I known what we were supposed to do.

"But the cathedral is very... distinguished. Clearly well-constructed, and the artwork was very... colorful."

Manuel chuckled.

"It sounds to me, Miss Mary, that you did not enjoy it one bit."

Was mass actually meant to be enjoyed? Mary desired to ask, but thought better of it.

"Well, I do not know if I wish to say it *exactly* like that," Mary tried to be diplomatic.

"And while you enjoyed the colored glass, you could have done without all of the blood."

"Yes, and the violence and obvious suffering. Why, Manuel, is there so much suffering?"

"It is the Catholic way," Manuel nodded good-humoredly. "I believe my sister believes that it is a privilege to suffer."

"My Aunt Genevieve says something similar!"

"Ha, as is almost always the case, no one is as different as they believe themselves to be." Mary nodded her agreement, and the pair fell back into a shared silence.

"Miss Mary, will you permit me to ask you a question?" Manuel asked after a few moments.

"Of course."

"Would it be too presumptuous to flatter myself by believing that you attended mass today in the hopes of seeing me?"

Mary's heart pounded in her chest as her hands became clammy.

This was the most direct Manuel Rivera had ever been with her.

"I—." Mary paused midstride, slowly turning towards him. She tried to steady herself before chancing a look into Manuel's eyes, which she found expectantly waiting for her.

And when their eyes met, both inhaled sharply, as though in unison. There were his usual eyes, dark and kind, always filled with pleasure at seeing her, but today they also reflected back an anticipated, almost longing, excitement.

A magnetic tension that was so palatable, it made Mary's insides quiver.

"Go on, Miss Taylor," Manuel prompted, his voice low and husky.

"Mary." She corrected, her voice lowering to meet his as a whisper.

"Mary." He accepted her correction.

"I—I attended mass today to admire the architecture you had told me so much about."

"Ah, I see," Manuel played along. "That infamous New Orleans architecture. Quite worth dressing in disguise for, I hear.

"Though, If I do recall correctly, I had offered to provide you a tour of the architecture."

"You are correct, sir, that you did. Though, I found myself so eager to see it—"

"The architecture."

"Yes, the architecture, that I could not wait any longer."

"So you instead dressed in your most modest clothing, stole what I can only assume were your cousin's chapel veils, and made an unforgettable scene during mass, all because of...?"

"The architecture," Mary repeated. "I found myself with a deep desire to see the architecture."

"And you could not wait?" Manuel breathed.

"No," Mary cast her eyes down to where her hand was prettily tucked around his forearm before looking up to meet his gaze.

"I could not wait."

Manuel's eyes burst open a floodgate, that same look overtaking his face that Leander Doucet had given her, as though he wished to devour her.

That now becoming all too familiar sensation burned in her, sending an aching rippling through her body.

"Are you cold, Miss Taylor?" Manuel asked, concerned, mistaking the pulse of desire for something else.

"No, I am perfectly comfortable." Mary placed her other hand on his arm.

"If we were not in public..." Manuel ventured.

"Yes?" Mary heard herself say.

"Then I would so wish to, with your permission of course—"

"Miss Taylor."

The voice sliced through the moment like a blade.

Her chest went cold.

She turned—slowly—and there he was.

Leander Doucet approached, hat in hand.

"Good day, Miss Taylor." He bowed towards her. "It is a lovely Sunday, is it not?

"It is."

*What in the world is he doing here?*

Leander peered down at Mary with an expectant gaze, and was that a mocking smile on his lips?

Why yes, she believed it was.

What a rogue!

"Are you not going to introduce me to your companion?" Leander asked, his tone low and saccharine, dripping with insolence.

"Mr. Rivera, this is Mr. Doucet." Mary finally turned to Manuel, gesturing with her hand towards Leander, though she purposefully declined to introduce Leander to Manuel.

The height of rudeness, and she hoped he took notice.

"Ah, Mr. Rivera, I have met your father, but do not believe we have had the pleasure," Leander dismissed the snub, extending his hand with a smile. Manuel responded in kind, and as the hands clasped one another Mary could hear the slap of skin, as though they both had made an effort to shake as aggressively as possible.

In that most odd way that men did.

Especially when there was something to prove.

"The pleasure is mine, Mr. Doucet. I have of course heard of your business venture with Mr. Taylor."

"You are acquainted with my colleague Charles, are you?"

"Yes, my family are old friends of the Taylor family. Miss Mary and I used to play together as children."

At the mention of Mary's first name, Leander's eyebrows stretched towards his forehead.

"Is that so, Miss Taylor?" he asked pointedly, indicating to her that the informality had not been lost on him.

Good.

"It is indeed. Manuel is one of my oldest friends." Mary returned the familiarity, watching to see the expression on Leander's face.

He once again looked surprised.

Even better.

"Some of my earliest childhood memories are of playing tag in his father's study while Mr. Rivera tried and failed to work."

"I remember that." Manuel smiled at the memory. "And I can tell you nothing has changed—the plantation children still do the same."

"And does he somehow produce sugarcane from his coat pocket?"

"Yes, as if by magic!"

"And much to the fury of Millie?"

"Oh yes!"

"How nice that you can both be reacquainted after all of these years." Leander plastered a grin onto his face, the edges of his mouth quivering as he forced it to remain in place. "Though, Miss Taylor, as a friend of Charles's, I can't help but wonder if he would approve of you being out like this—unchaperoned, and in such... attentive company."

The words hung in the air, soft as silk but barbed like wire.

Mary felt Manuel stiffen beside her.

It was one thing for a man to call on a lady. Quite another to imply—publicly, no less—that he might be compromising her.

And coming from another man, unmarried and of no relation, it wasn't just rude.

It was insulting.

A direct challenge to his honor.

And coming from Leander Doucet, of all people?

The irony was almost laughable.

"Remind me, Mr. Doucet, where did you say you were from?" Manual finally managed with a feigned formality.

"Mobile."

"Ah, Alabama," Manuel nodded. "I cannot say I have ever had the pleasure, and as such I cannot comment on what social norms are considered acceptable in Alabama. Now, I fully understand that as a good friend and business partner of Mr. Charles Taylor, you will undoubtedly feel a familial, and perhaps brotherly duty to look out for his sisters, as though they are your own.

"And that, sir, is perfectly respectable, and would be the obligation of any gentleman.

"But, Mr. Doucet, I must caution you that the wrong person, perhaps one with a greater temper than mine, may interpret your sense of familial duty, especially when articulated in the lovely Miss Mary's presence, as a sign of disrespect.

"Which I am confident you did not mean," Manuel clarified before Leander could protest, his tone one of warning. "For I can only assume that any friend of Charles Taylor is as upstanding a gentleman as he is himself. Which is why I offer this caution freely and in good faith.

"Good day to you, sir."

Leander stood motionless, his mouth agape as Manuel and Mary continued their stroll towards town.

After a few moments, Mary chanced a glance back and saw that Leander stood in the same place they had left him.

Hat still in hand.

And for once, Leander Doucet had nothing clever to say.

# Chapter XII

The following evening, Mary, Elizabeth, and Amelié filed out of the house and into the carriage waiting to take them to the weekly sewing circle.

What had felt like a suggestion was made clear to them to be an absolute requirement by Aunt Genevieve, who considered service to others chief amongst their Christian duties.

"And is it in the cathedral?" Mary asked with a tentative caution, arranging her skirts as she sat down so that the other two women could fit in. The notion of trying to knit socks, a feat Mary would undoubtedly find difficult on the best of days, loomed even more largely with the thought of trying to work in a large cavernous stone church with the eyes of mutilated saints following her every dropped stitch.

"No, of course not," Amelié scoffed, as though it were the stupidest thing she had ever heard. "It is at Mrs. Lambert's house. She always hosts the sewing circles."

Oh, of course, how silly. Mary cast a sideways glance towards Elizabeth. Her sister was never one to appreciate a rebuke, particularly in the manner their cousin enjoyed deploying of withholding information and then presenting it as though it were obvious.

Though Elizabeth's extreme dislike for this trait was largely because she considered it her intellectual property.

Neither Elizabeth nor Mary were the most proficient sewists.

Well, to be technically correct, Mary was not the most proficient sewist, though she could be adequate if she concentrated very hard. Elizabeth, on the other hand, was naturally quite good, though she lacked the desire, discipline, or willingness to cultivate her skills into that of a great seamstress.

Much to her mother's dismay.

*"When the Lord has blessed you with a gift, the least you can do is make the most of it!" Anne Taylor had argued with her daughter.*

*"But Mother, if I become very good at sewing, then people will expect me to do it often!" Elizabeth had retorted. "And why would you wish that on me?"*

Mary hoped they didn't expect too industrious an evening. Between the tedium of knitting and the dread of gossip, she wasn't sure which she feared more.

Sewing circles were often a way for Southern women to come together and socialize, but in Mary's experience, it was largely a setting for the exchange of gossip under the guise of putting their needles to work.

Made all the more when one could claim it was all in the name of the Lord.

Neither gossip nor sewing appealed much to Mary.

In fact, she could not really decide which she dreaded more!

Perhaps a sewing circle in New Orleans will be different, Mary hoped.

Much to her dismay, it was not.

When the trio arrived, they were quickly ushered into the parlor of Mrs. Lambert's house, a large mansion on the other side of the French Quarter, no more than a ten-minute carriage ride from Aunt Genevieve's.

In the parlor, the ladies sat perched on chairs, stools, and sofas, their voluminous skirts gracefully spread out around them.

They looked like butterfly wings, Mary thought from her view at the doorway of the parlor, observing the multi-colored dresses of silk and chiffon.

On their entrance, all the women extended their introductions politely, bombarding the Taylor sisters with a slew of names, enhanced with details about their family relations as provided by Amelié, meaning that by the time they'd gotten around the circle, neither Elizabeth nor Mary could remember the name of even one of the other ladies.

Except, of course, for Mrs. Lambert, who appeared to be a kind and recently married woman, to a gentleman of prestige and fortune.

Mary noted as she scanned the room that while most of the women were in their late teenage years or early twenties, none of them wore wedding rings. It quickly became apparent to her that Mrs. Lambert, as clearly a good Catholic woman who had married a man of means, had been designated a de facto guide and guardian for the young ladies who also aspired to a marriage of equal esteem.

Being of good breeding themselves, the women in the room allowed Elizabeth and Mary to settle in to their seats and cast their yarn before the interrogation began.

"I have it on good authority that the Santiago San Ignacio had some unexpected visitors at yesterday's morning mass," one of the ladies, whose name Mary could not remember, offered to the group. Like a proliferated instigator, she leaned forward as she spoke, tossing the tidbit of information out into the center of the conversation, and then leaning back to watch the feeding frenzy ensue.

"Did you now?" Elizabeth's voice squeaked with feigned interest. "Pray do tell, what did you hear, Arabel?"

"It's Arabella," the woman corrected.

"Oh, A-brella, how charming." Elizabeth offered a smile far too sweet to be sincere.

"No, it's Ar-a-belle-a," the woman repeated, clearly annoyed.

But probably having gotten the message, Mary thought, looking back at her knitting.

"Oh, ahr-A-bella," Elizabeth intentionally butchered the pronunciation, but made it close enough that Arabella would likely let it pass.

It was a signal to the group that while she and her sister were new, they were not to be trifled with.

"You will have to forgive me. My sister and I are new to New Orleans, and we have never before in our lives encountered such exotic names!

"But I have interrupted you. Please do tell us, what is it that you heard about yesterday's morning mass at Santiago San Ignacio?"

"From what I hear, you would know better than us," another woman jumped in.

"Did you really go to the Spanish mass? How did you understand anything?"

"I will have you know, I understand Spanish just as well as I understand French," Elizabeth retorted, sitting up a bit straighter and raising her nose to the ceiling in an act of superiority.

Which was, not at all.

But the women, apart from Amelié, did not know that, and Amelié was smarter than to start a war with her cousin.

At least not in such a public setting.

"What was it like?" one of the girls asked, her voice laced with morbid fascination, as though she knew she was asking about something she shouldn't.

"It was smoky. And all the women must wear veils, otherwise they will not be allowed inside."

"Oh, how severe!"

Mary rolled her eyes at her sister's exaggerations.

Mary knew that Elizabeth knew very well that it was not a "requirement" to wear the chapel veils—in fact, Manuel Rivera had confirmed it. But if Mary knew Elizabeth like she did, she knew her sister would never turn down the opportunity to designate herself as expert in a group, especially on a topic considered both foreign and slightly taboo.

Even if she mostly spoke from a place of absolute ignorance.

Mary had decided long ago that her sister gained some sort of pleasure from feeding people nonsense, usually harmless, and watching them devour it.

"I heard that you made a scene," Arabella dared to foray back into the conversation.

Back for more, Mary sighed, studying her knitting. She had already dropped a stitch, despite being only a few rows in.

Where had it gone? She held the material up in search of it.

"Oh, yes, well, I had not quite understood the dress code," Elizabeth conceded. "I did not know that everyone was meant to be dressed in the manner of mourning, but apparently, that is part of Spanish Catholicism. You know, voluntary suffering for the Lord."

All the women nodded gravely.

"But me, I wore the prettiest yellow gown," Elizabeth chattered on. "It's new, with fabric imported from Paris, of course."

"It does not sound appropriate for any church," Arabella scoffed.

"Oh, well, Manuel Rivera seemed to think it looked mighty nice. And, you know, we Virginian girls don't like to toot our own horns too much, but after mass when we went strolling in town, a very fine man came and introduced himself to me. He said he saw me and just ran across the street to make my acquaintance, with no care at all for his safety," Elizabeth giggled. "He was a real gentleman. What was his name?" Elizabeth tapped her chin in thought.

"Dumas!" Elizabeth exclaimed, triumphantly stabbing the air with her needle. "A Mr. Francois Dumas."

The room immediately quieted to silence.

A stunned silence.

Mary paused, looking up to find that the faces of the women looked surprised.

Surprised, and perhaps the slightest bit amused.

"What is wrong?" Elizabeth asked innocently.

"Francois Dumas is my brother," Arabella finally responded, the words squeezing through her tightened lips.

"Oh, Abarella, I did not know!" Elizabeth clasped a hand to her mouth in mock horror.

But of course she did.

"And he is my fiancé," another woman answered with a voice as hard as stone.

That one might possibly be a surprise, Mary reasoned, as Elizabeth mumbled something along the lines of "Oh, good heavens".

"Well, rest assured, I only have the nicest things to say about the man."

In the delicate power struggle that emerged in every social setting where young unmarried ladies found themselves, Elizabeth had, without question, established herself as both the clear victor and the greatest threat.

"Oh, don't you mind it," the woman next to Francois Dumas's fiancée patted her hand comfortingly.

"Yes, don't you mind it one bit," Arabella agreed, casting daggers at Elizabeth. "My brother is a gentleman."

"And I can also attest to that," Elizabeth chimed in.

"Perhaps it would be helpful to educate the Miss Taylors on the current state of affairs in wider society," Mrs. Lambert suggested as cordially as possible.

Though the subtext was very clear, in Mary's mind.

"Of course." Arabella nodded her head vigorously, keen to re-establish herself as the leader of the group by taking on the role of keeper of the social norms.

"Perhaps it is not necessary," another woman offered. "If Manuel Rivera is your intended."

"Yes, he is a very eligible bachelor," another nodded.

"Perhaps a bit young for you, though," Arabella thought aloud, casting her eyes up and down Elizabeth.

"Bless you for your considerations of my interests," Elizabeth laughed good-naturedly. "But it is not me Manuel Rivera is interested in, but my sister, Mary."

At this declaration, Mary could feel all eyes in the room move from her sister to her.

How wonderful, the thought alone made her feel exhausted as she leant forward and stared at her knitting as though it were the most enthralling thing in the world.

It was no use. The stitch had completely disappeared, and she would have to unravel and start again.

"Well?" someone prompted.

"I beg your pardon?" Mary dared a glance up from her work, knowing it was expected of her.

"Is it true?"

"Is what true?"

"That Manuel Rivera has expressed interest in you?"

"Manuel and I have been friends since we were children," Mary began cautiously, eyeing the women in the room. Mary could not help but feel like a small animal, surrounded by hunters, for they all stared back at her with a keen undivided attention and eyes that looked, for lack of a better word—

Hungry.

It was not that she didn't trust them, but she was also not convinced that any of them had her best interests at heart.

Save Elizabeth, of course.

For a reason Mary could not very well explain, the face of Leander Doucet continued to appear in her mind. It had always been there really, lurking at the edge of her thoughts, no matter how tightly she tried to lock the door against him.

But now, as the ladies stared at her with giddy anticipation, waiting to hear more of her latest encounter with *Manuel*—a slip of informality on Mary's part that had certainly not gone unnoticed—all she could think of was the look on Leander's face at the bottom of the path as she and Manuel had walked away.

It was a face of mild surprise, perhaps for Manuel's boldness, but also included a hint of what Mary could only describe as suppressed forlornness in seeing her departure.

Or perhaps more specifically, her departure on the arm of another man.

"Well?" The annoyed insistence brought Mary back to the room.

"Well what?" she echoed politely.

"Is he your beau?" someone else demanded to know.

"The Riveras are a *very* good match," the woman next to Mary complimented, patting her arm in congratulations.

"And what do you think of that, Amelié?" Arabella asked, grinning wickedly.

"Oh, our family has a strict policy that we do not involve ourselves in the feuds of others," Elizabeth explained.

"Not even when it includes members of your family?" Arabella demanded, her mocked shock mixed with delight at what she clearly saw as a betrayal to a familial tie.

"It would not be seemly from a political standpoint for our family to become entangled in local feuds. Our father must remain as impartial as possible," Mary explained quietly. It was the way her father had always explained it to her, one of the reasons the Taylors were not known to have bad blood, unfinished business, or unsettled debts with anyone in the South.

Or the North, for that matter.

"Mr. Taylor serves in Congress," Mrs. Lambert explained to the puzzled stares of the ladies.

"Oh, but that does not mean anything!" One of them insisted. "My Uncle Richard served in Congress, and that did not stop him from taking sides in familial feuds. Why, I even think he stood in as second for a duel during his time serving in office!"

"Mr. Taylor is the Speaker of the House," Mrs. Lambert patiently elaborated. "And he executes the responsibilities that comes with that post with the utmost honor."

"Thank you, Mrs. Lambert, for those kind words about my father." Mary nodded towards her. "We are very proud of him."

"And we are proud to have that connection with the Taylor family," Amelié interjected. "Not to mention, our family's interest in the Taylor Mutual Fund."

"Oh, my family would never tie our money up in an institution like that," one of the ladies insisted. "Not that I mean any offense to your families, Amelié and Miss Taylor, and Miss Taylor," she insisted with what appeared to be a genuine smile. "But anyone who tries to convince me that a piece of paper representing our family's money is better management than a plantation full of slaves, livestock, sugarcane, and the land it stands on, is a charlatan if I ever did seen one."

"What you probably don't know is that most of these plantations all over the South have been used as collateral for debts, usually from private lenders. And when they find that those gentlemen's agreements they've made are useless and they're sitting on more debt than they feel comfortable with, why, they just go find an institution like Taylor Mutual Fund and try to sell that debt to them for pennies on the dollar," Amelié explained to the group. "Likely, if your daddy's ever taken a loan, it's been sold to a bank at some point."

Mary looked at Amelié with surprise and a new found respect.

She was right, of course. Even some of the largest and seemingly wealthiest plantations in the South were heavily in debt. Usually, so far as Mary could grasp, it came down to a lack of financial management.

Not to mention, that very human desire to always have the newest and most fashionable clothes, the fastest horses, and the most elaborate estate.

The Taylors, while very wealthy, had always lived more humbly than their means. It was most likely a function of their work ethic and tendency towards functionality over form, both inheritances of their English backgrounds and Protestant faith.

"I am sure, Miss Defour, that you are not insinuating that my family has such little business sense that they have spent themselves desolate," the woman who had pronounced her deep distrust of banks began heatedly. Her switch to Amelié's surname, indicating a return to formality, could only mean one thing—

That the night was about to become tragically soured.

"I am *absolutely* certain that I must be misunderstanding you."

"I doubt my cousin was intending to suggest that she was commenting on your family's personal situation or financial acumen," Mary interjected. "I believe she was simply speaking in a more general nature about the Southern states. Is that not right?" Mary asked, turning towards Amelié.

Amelié cast her gaze from her assailant back to Mary and finally to Mrs. Lambert, who watched the exchange with steely anticipation.

"Of course," Amelié finally nodded. "I apologize for the confusion. As Mary says, I was speaking in a more general capacity."

"I thank you, Amelié Defour, for clarifying," the woman responded, curtly but courteously.

Across the room, Mary saw Mrs. Lambert settle more comfortably back in her seat as the click of needles resumed—sharp, synchronized, and vaguely threatening.

The ladies whiled away the next few hours, making small talk, chief amongst the subjects was anticipation of the latest Parisian fashions and when, exactly, they would hit the streets.

Second, of course, only to the most enthralling of topics: the suspected courtships of the current season and whether or not they would result in wedding bells. Mary listened intently for any mention of Leander, who—while noted for his handsomeness and charm—seemed to be a mystery to all the ladies present.

As the evening wrapped up, Mrs. Lambert beckoned for Amelié to help her in clearing away the ladies' glasses. The two disappeared with their hands full of porcelain teacups, their heads pressed together in the manner of conspirators.

A moment later, Amelié popped her head back into the room. "Oh, Mary! Would you be a dear and help us with the last few cups?" Grateful for a reason to abandon her knitting, Mary rose and stepped carefully over skirts and sofas to gather the remaining tableware.

"Thank you so much, dear." Mrs. Lambert accepted the saucers.

"No, thank you for your hospitality, Mrs. Lambert. You have been ever so kind," Mary insisted. "It is so considerate of you to welcome us in to your home. My sister and I are new to town and haven't yet had the chance to make many acquaintances, so this has been lovely."

"You are very sweet to say so." Mrs. Lambert nodded. "Though, if I may, you do not seem the most eager knitter?"'

"Oh no, Mrs. Lambert, I fear it is a lack of ability as opposed to interest," Mary insisted in a manner she knew was not altogether convincing. "May I ask—what gave me away?"

"Let us just say that it developed over the course of the evening." Mrs. Lambert offered an all-knowing smile.

"Miss Defour and I belong to another circle," Mrs. Lambert explained. "And we thought it might be of interest to you."

Mary straightened, interested. "What sort of circle?"

"We meet on Wednesdays."

"I'll make sure she's there,"Amelié confirmed.

Mary hesitated. "And what sort of things do you discuss?"

"Ideas," Mrs. Lambert answered. "Some practical. Some quite dangerous."

Mary blinked.

Mrs. Lambert smiled kindly, with the faintest flicker of mischief. "Don't worry, my dear. I think you'll fit right in."

"She is a cat, but at least she is a smart cat," Elizabeth declared as she whirled around for Mary to unfasten her skirts and petticoats.

She was, of course, referring to their cousin, Amelié.

"Shhh!" Mary motioned. "She is only in the room next door."

"What? I called her smart!" Elizabeth insisted innocently.

"You also called her catty."

"I do not recall that," Elizabeth shrugged, motioning for Mary to spin around so that she could help her undress also.

Usually when Elizabeth undid the skirts , she tugged the strings with such zeal that they dropped to the floor before Mary could catch them.

But as Mary waited, she noticed her sister had paused, her hand on the small of Mary's back.

"What is wrong?"

"Shhh," Elizabeth sought to shush Mary this time. "Do you hear that?"

Mary stood still, even holding her breath, until she could hear it too.

Music.

Both the girls looked at one another, puzzled. Mary crept towards the door to the hall way, and opening it slightly, poked her head out—

The sound wasn't coming from there.

"I think it is outside," Elizabeth noted, walking towards the double doors that led out onto the second-floor veranda.

"You cannot go out there!" Mary insisted, yanking at her sister's arm.

"And why ever not?"

"Well for one thing, because you are in your undergarments!"

"Oh, it is dark anyway," Elizabeth half-protested.

Though Mary knew deep down that even this would have been a step too far in Elizabeth's constant battle with propriety.

Candle in hand, Mary opened the door to the veranda, and when she did, the sound of the music flooded into their room. Mary stepped out, carefully placing the candle on the banister.

Between her candle and the last flickers of the streetlights, Mary could just make out Manuel Rivera, strumming a guitar melodically outside of the Defour residence.

She gasped, a delighted fist pressed to her mouth.

This could not possibly be for her.

Emboldened, Manuel took a step forward and began to play, a melancholy melody rising through the warm New Orleans air.

And then—he began to sing.

The fact that it was in Spanish made it, Mary was certain, all the more beautiful. Even if she could not understand all of the words, the sound of the tune sent a crystal-clear message.

How could she be deserving of all of this? Mary gazed down at the handsome young man, his dark eyes full of depth and passion as her serenaded her.

"You honor me by listening so attentively," he declared on finishing, bowing deeply.

"Manuel, I am lost for words," Mary could barely choke out.

"Well, I regret, Miss Mary, that I told you so definitively that I could not call on your place of residence in New Orleans. But you flattered me deeply by coming to mass at my church, and I felt that such an act of intention deserved one in return," he explained, his voice sure, but something like a tremor underlying his words.

Could it actually be that Manuel Rivera was nervous?

Did she actually make this handsome and eligible man nervous?

"Your intentions have been received with gladness," Mary confirmed, leaning over the banister. "Though, to be clear, I did attend mass—"

"For the architecture." Manuel grinned back at her. "Yes, I am aware."

If he were there standing next to her, she did not think she could help but kiss him.

And she would not even care who saw!

Manuel's eyes darted towards the window next to Mary's, and when she turned, she noticed that the once-dark rooms had begun to illuminate around her.

"It appears you have woken the entire house," Mary giggled.

"I will happily accept whatever repercussions befall me, if only to see you smile like that."

She felt her heart trip over itself.

"I only worry you'll get into trouble."

"While I appreciate your concern, I must admit that in this moment, I do not care in the slightest whatever consequences might befall me.

"But, out of respect for your feelings, Miss Mary, I'll take my leave before I'm found out."

"Before you go—" Mary reached into her sleeve, and pulled out her monogrammed handkerchief. "I have nothing that can even come close to matching this. But I hope you will accept this as a token of my affection."

"It would be my honor, Miss Mary." Manuel smiled, reaching up to catch the white handkerchief as it floated down towards his outstretched hand. Once holding it, Manuel lowered it to his lips and kissed it before tucking it into his breast pocket.

They shared one last, lingering look.

And then Manuel swept into a low bow, which Mary returned with a curtsy.

And just like that, he vanished into the night.

"Good heavens!" Elizabeth snatched at Mary's arm from where she stood behind the curtain.

"You were watching?!" Mary demanded, annoyed at the lack of privacy.

"Of course I was!" Elizabeth dismissed. "And I can guarantee the rest of the house was as well!"

"Do not be dramatic," Mary insisted, a lump of concern catching in her throat. "Surely Aunt Genevieve would never tolerate a Rivera standing out in front of her house for long."

"Well, I am certain she is not *happy* about it," Elizabeth rolled her eyes, "but I doubt she is going to reprimand you over it."

"I think he left before anyone heard," Mary mumbled, obviously trying to convince herself as much as she was trying to convince Elizabeth.

Perhaps more so.

"Don't be a goose," Elizabeth laughed, throwing her head towards the ceiling in amusement.

Amusement at her expense.

Mary's heart began to sink.

"Oh, calm down." Elizabeth tugged at one of Mary's locks affectionately. "She knows Father wants nothing to do with the Defour-Rivera feud. She won't drag you into a proxy war."

That hadn't even occurred to Mary. Leave it to Elizabeth to be both maddening and insightful in equal measure.

"Tomorrow you will be the talk of the town," Elizabeth promised, and taking Mary's hand in hers, she spun her around, the way a gentleman might a lady during a waltz.

"Do not say that," Mary pleaded.

The thought of everyone knowing that Manuel Rivera had come to her window, the song he had played, and the words they had exchanged made Mary want to curl up in bed and hide until they found something else to talk about.

"Surely you are not embarrassed?" Elizabeth halted Mary mid-spin.

" It is not that I am embarrassed," Mary tried to articulate, a feat that always seemed harder under the interrogating stare of her sister.

"It is just that... it was our moment—mine and Manuel's. And I do not wish to have to share it with anyone else."

Elizabeth paused, considering this for a moment.

"How incredibly greedy of you!" she finally declared.

"H-How is that greedy?"

"Because," Elizabeth rolled her eyes, placing one hand on her hip in consternation. "One of the most devastatingly romantic things ever has just happened to you, and you wish to keep it to yourself. What do you think those books you so love to read are all about?" Elizabeth thrust her hand towards the pile atop Mary's bedside table.

"They're about women who not only marry gentleman, but find love too. Almost every young lady dreams of finding a handsome wealthy husband who adores her. They want to hear stories about these instances because it makes them feel like it can happen to them too!"

"These same ladies who would pine after my romantic serenade would also be the first to delight in any rumors of my downfall!"

"Well, that is true," Elizabeth conceded.

"Exactly. I do not wish my life to be the source of someone else's amusement."

"Then do not let it. Take control of it. It is yours, after all, and the only one you'll get."

"I am taking control," Mary crossed her arms in annoyance at sister's words. "Was it not my idea to attend Catholic mass?"

"Yes, but it was a safe risk, and you know it."

"In what manner is risking our internal salvation safe?"

"It was safe, dear sister, because you knew Manuel Rivera returned your affections. Which is fine, of course, if you desire to marry him or enjoy his affections for a time, then very well. But do not deceive yourself into believing you have any agency when you accept the pursuit of the first man who has ever paid you any genuine attention."

# Chapter XIII

*Elizabeth does not know of what she speaks,* Mary thought bitterly.

"What are you scowling about?" Amelié asked curiously.

*Or nosily, some might say.*

"I am not scowling," Mary insisted, plastering on her best fake smile and turning her head towards the carriage window.

Outside the streets of New Orleans passed by in a colorful blur.

At least they were able to leave Elizabeth at home. Mary sighed in relief, which was immediately followed by a pang of guilt.

*She should not feel good about leaving her sister out,* she chastised herself.

"I would expect you would be smiling after your late-night visitor." Amelié raised a suggestive eyebrow.

"Wh-who told you about that?" Mary quickly turned her head to stare down her cousin. "Was it Elizabeth?"

"I—No," Amelié stuttered, caught off-guard by Mary's unexpected hostility. "He was not exactly subtle. The entire house heard it."

"Oh." The hardness of Mary's face softened as she transitioned from annoyance to embarrassment.

"He was also singing in Spanish," Amelié explained tentatively, almost apologetically, as though she was sorry to be pointing out this very obvious fact.

"Of course." Mary nodded. "Forgive me, Amelié, I did not sleep well," Mary confessed, turning her head back towards the window. The bouncing of the carriage was starting to make her stomach churn.

Amelié nodded and silence fell between them.

"Do you think the entire town knows?" Mary asked after a moment, her eyes still staring out the window, focusing on nothing at all.

"I expect so." Her cousin tried to give a comforting smile. "But you needn't worry. Mother is of course not best pleased, nor would he be *my* choice, but he is hardly a beau to be embarrassed over."

Mary considered confessing to Amelié all of her confusions. How she had believed herself to fancy Manuel Rivera immeasurably until Elizabeth had cast aspersions over her feelings...

And how she had once believed she knew what she desired...

And now was only certain that she had no idea what she desired....

The words bubbled on Mary's tongue. It would feel so good, to finally get them off her chest. To speak them into existence.

But she did not dare.

"I just—I am a very private person. I do not wish everyone knowing every intimate detail of my life."

"Well, you came to the wrong town for that, dear cousin.

"But, if it is any consolation," her tone softened in response to Mary's expression of complete and utter despair. "I doubt anyone where we're going will have any interest in your late-night visitor."

"Oh?" Mary's face brightened.

If she could not escape it completely, she would happily settle for a temporary reprieve.

"Yes, they have better things to occupy their minds."

This somehow felt humorous to Mary, considering Amelié was one of the most prominent gossips she had ever met in her life.

"What?" Amelié asked, it being her turn to go on the defensive.

"It is just that I never considered you to be one who did not... appreciate knowledge of what was going on around town." Mary tried to choose her words with the utmost care.

"Oh, I do," Amelié assured her. "Life can be dull if one does not find ways to make it more entertaining. But that does not mean I don't also like to exercise my mind in other ways also."

Mary had never considered this.

"Where, exactly, are we going?" Mary inquired for the third time.

"Madame Lavigne's—and we have just arrived."

Mary squinted as they emerged from the carriage, shielding her eyes with her gloved hand from the bright early afternoon sun.

They were still in the French Quarter, Mary observed, staring up at Madame Lavigne's house. It was smaller than Aunt Genevieve's, though that was not exactly a surprise. The Defour household was, to Mary's more modest sentiments, beautiful but slightly obscene—it stretched nearly the length of a block on its own, not for any other reason than that it could.

Madame Lavigne's house was beautiful but more compact: a pink brick structure nestled at the corner of the road with a balcony up top adorned with an array of plants.

"And who exactly is Madame Lavigne?" Mary asked, opening up her parasol even for the short walk up to the door.

"Goodness, Mary." Amelié rolled her eyes. "She only hosts the most exclusive salon in New Orleans."

"Oh." Mary nodded, feeling incredibly stupid.

Mary had heard of salons before, for her brother Charles had frequented them often in his travels. From his letters, he had described them as a gathering place for intellectuals to meet and discuss literature, poetry, politics, and culture, a notion which had appealed to Mary greatly, for they sounded filled with like-minded individuals. In the romantic version of her life, Mary had imagined herself graciously answering invitations for her attendance at the most exclusive salons in Paris and Vienna, a place her mind might be as appreciated as her family name.

She had not ever actually expected to be attending one.

"Please do try your best not to embarrass me," Amelié clucked, gathering her skirts and marching up the steps to the house she knocked with the brass knocker.

The door swung open almost immediately, and there stood a tall negro man in a waist blue tailed waistcoat, white trousers, and a brown bowtie.

"Miss Defour," he said solemnly, stepping aside to allow the ladies inside.

"Hello, Matthew," Amelié nodded, picking up her skirts and stepping over the threshold into the house. "How are you?"

"Very well, Miss Defour. Thank you for asking," he responded cordially.

"And this must be your cousin." He bowed his head slightly. "Miss Mary Taylor."

It was a confirmation as opposed to a question.

"Yes, sir," Mary responded, dipping into a small curtsy. "How do you do?"

"Well, thank you, Miss. I trust our town is treating you well?"

"It is certainly an exciting change from Virginia."

"I can imagine." A smirk of amusement crossed over his face. "Though I have had occasion to visit Richmond and found it most pleasant. Not the hustling and bustling city we call home, but pleasant all the same."

"Oh, what took you to Richmond?" Mary asked with curiosity.

"Business," he responded curtly. "Now, please allow me to help you with your parasols and overcoats. The room is already filling up."

Surrendering their coats and umbrellas, the ladies followed Matthew through the house, the sound of music, talk, and laughter beckoning them nearer.

"Madame, Miss Defour and her cousin Miss Taylor have arrived," Matthew announced as the trio stepped inside a large parlor.

"Oh, delightful." A stout woman in an ornate armchair decorated with thread embroidered animals clapped. "Thank you, Matthew!"

"Would you like a drink?" Matthew asked the ladies.

"Some tea would be wonderful, thank you," Mary said.

"The usual please, Matthew," Amelié confirmed mid-stride, as she walked over to where the woman who had previously exclaimed at their arrival sat.

The woman who must be Madame Lavigne.

The room itself was large and bright. The walls were white on all three sides, apart from the one that faced the street, which was composed entirely of windows. The shutters had been opened, and the light from the spring afternoon streamed into the parlor. In one corner stood a beautiful grand piano, where two people, a man and a woman, sat. The woman touched the keys lightly, elegantly and nimbly, as the man listened, a glass of brandy clutched between his fingers.

Across from the door to the parlor stood a large marble fireplace, and a cluster of people stood perched, their drinks resting on the fireplace's mantle as they discussed something which appeared, to Mary anyway, to be keeping the party completely and utterly engaged.

The room was large enough to support two full-length couches; one stood against the wall of the windows, and the other in the middle of the room. The couches matched, both made of a green with gold flowers embroidered into the material. And littered around the couches were a slew of chairs: armchairs with large comfortable backs, dining chairs, benches, and stools.

And almost all of them were filled!

The room buzzed with the chatter of perhaps twenty people—some speaking English, others French and Spanish.

But perhaps the most magical feature were the shelves of books that lined the walls—

"Mary." Amelié beckoned from where she stood next to their host. Mary scurried over, mortified for her lack of etiquette.

One should, of course, always greet their host as a sign of respect.

"Madame Lavigne, this is my cousin, Mary Taylor."

"Madame Lavigne," Mary curtsyed low, her eyes on the ground to display her contrition. "Please forgive me for my rudeness. I am afraid I was struck by the scene and forgot my manners momentarily."

"Do not fret." Madame Lavigne waved a hand to dismiss any fears. "This is a place for people to both lose and find themselves.

"Mary Taylor, You are related to Charles Taylor?"

"I am." Mary rose, meeting her host's gaze with a smile. "He is my eldest brother."

Now seeing her up close, Mary noted Madame Lavigne was an older woman, perhaps twenty years older than her mother. She wore a dress of deep purple velvet, matched with a large pearl choker at her neck and complementary earrings. Her fingers, speckled with old age and rings of gold and gemstones, clutched the top of a brown cane.

Clearly a woman of status.

"Ah, but of course." Madame Lavigne nodded. "Charles is a wonderful man. Extremely bright and worldly, and very well brought up."

"Thank you, Madame." Mary bowed her head in appreciation. "My parents would be thrilled to hear you say so."

"Oh yes, I know your mother Anne." Madame Lavigne nodded, grinning at Mary's look of surprise. "She and her late sister used to come here with Amelié's mother.

"Though your father I have never met, but I have always heard nothing but good things about William Taylor."

"You are so kind to speak so highly of my family."

"I only say what I truly think," Madame Lavigne assured her.

"I also must thank you for inviting me to your splendid gathering."

"Please child, enough," Madame Lavigne insisted. "Sofia warned me you were smart but tripped over yourself to display the height of pleasantries."

"Oh, pardon me, Madame," Mary flustered. "I—in Virginia this is how we are raised to—"

"It is the same here, child," Madame Lavigne explained dismissively. "But the good Lord has only given us all a set amount of time on this earth, and I do not intend to while it away with needless pleasantries.

"Richard," Madame Lavigne turned to the man to her right, interrupting his conversation with the woman next to him. "Won't you be a dear and find somewhere else to sit so that I might speak with Miss Taylor here." She gestured with her cane.

"Of course, Ma." The man named Richard immediately rose and bowed to Mary before walking over to the other side of the young lady with whom he'd been having a conversation, perching himself on the arm of the couch.

"Here, dear," Madame Lavigne patted the now vacant seat next to her. "I want to hear all about Virginia and what is going on with those men in Congress."

Mary folded herself into the seat next to Madame Lavigne, arranging her skirts as non-intrusively as possible.

"Pardon me, Madame Lavigne, but I must go say hello to Madame Laveau." Amelié gestured towards a mulatto woman who stood in the circle near the fireplace. "I will leave you to interrogate my cousin. Though please do play nice with her, she has only just come out this season." Amelié gave a teasing smile.

"Yes, dear." Madame Lavigne dismissed with a wave of her hand. "Go get your tinctures and love spells."

Her tinctures and what?

"Pardon me, Madame Lavigne, but did you just tell my cousin to—"

"Oh yes," Madame Lavigne nodded, pointing with the bottom of her cane towards where Amelié now stood speaking with the woman. "That is Marie Laveau. She runs a salon in town, but she is also a very powerful conjure woman."

"A what?" She had heard of conjure, but it was never spoken of freely. It was, to her understanding, some type of magic, and it was especially popular amongst the slaves at their family plantation. Mary's mother and father, as traditional Protestants, both dismissed it as superstitious nonsense but also feared it with the kind of reverence reserved for things which one does not fully understand.

"A conjure woman," Madame Lavigne explained. "She is known all over Louisiana for her abilities."

"And what abilities are those?"

"To heal, to see the future, to bless and to curse," Madame Lavigne said matter-of-factly. "I was teasing your cousin earlier—the ladies in town go to her not only for the latest hair style fashion, but also for help with their beaux, wayward husbands, and unrequited love. She is a very smart, powerful woman. An entrepreneur if I ever met one."

"I see." Mary cast another quick look at Marie Laveau. She was of average height, slightly fuller in her build, with child-bearing confident hips and full breasts. She was dressed well, in an elegant black dress with an over jacket of ruffled orange chiffon, and her hair was piled on her head and wrapped in a yellow scarf. In her ears hung large golden earrings.

"And does it work?" Mary finally asked after a moment.

"Does what work, dear?"

"Her tinctures and her spells."

"They say they do. There have been many a young lady who has rumored to have gone to Marie Laveau for help with a beau and found herself married within the season. I myself cannot speak to the love magic, but she does provide me with tinctures for my aches and pains." Madame Lavigne absently reached for her knees and began to rub. "She is a godsend. I do not know how I would get on without her."

The time passed quickly as Mary and Madame Lavigne spoke about books, music, and politics. Other people, including Mrs. Lambert, popped in and out of their conversations, joining ad hoc and without invitation when they heard something that sounded interesting, controversial, or intriguing. It was all polite and non-confrontational, even when people respectfully disagreed, and Mary revelled in the free-flowing exchange of ideas. She found herself nodding thoughtfully, articulating herself passionately, and laughing continuously. It was, to her young seventeen years, the kind of environment she had always longed for.

Madame Lavigne had travelled wide and far in her youth, to France where her family was from, but also to England, Spain, Italy, and as far as India. She was the type of kindly older woman who had an equal interest in sharing her own stories and hearing those of others. She quizzed Mary on her time in boarding school, her views on the banks, foreign affairs, and slavery.

"I am of the personal opinion that it will be a matter of when, not if, slavery is abolished," Mary explained thoughtfully. "It is of course abolished in the North, its progress to the West has been stymied, and importation of slaves has been illegal here for decades. If these are not the signs of a nation looking to contain, with an eventual view to eradicate, this behavior, then I do not know what is."

"Interesting." Madame Lavigne nodded thoughtfully. "And how will you convince your Georgians, Alabamans, and Carolinans? Why, I am even certain Louisiana, more open-minded as we are in many parts, would push back strongly if these became more than theoretical discussions."

"Well, I would hope you could appeal to people on the grounds of morality."

"Ah, but my dear, it is not just a moral issue, it is also an economic and social one. How would these plantations operate without their slaves? What would become of the Southern economy if not built on the back of slaves? And even if, or when, as you would say," Madame Lavigne raised an eyebrow at Mary. "What would the nation do with all of these millions of people if plantations are no longer feeding and clothing them? Will they happily accept their new lot in life, or will they be resentful and take it out on their former masters?"

"I agree there are many questions which still require answers."

"For the record, I am not disagreeing with you." Madame Lavigne patted Mary's knee affectionately. "I am just asking the difficult things that need to be asked. I have found many young ladies of a similar upbringing to yours share your sentiments. And my question to them is always the same, which I shall put to you now: have you considered how your life will change when slavery is abolished? And would you be supportive of these changes? It is worth remembering that the mechanism that you declare a moral repugnance is that very thing that allows you to sit here today, wearing a dress made of Parisian silk, and contemplate and discuss these philosophical issues. Without it, you would likely find yourself sewing or knitting twelve hours a day or working a small farm with your siblings."

Mary opened her mouth to respond before pausing, mulling over Madame Lavigne's words.

"A very fair challenge," Mary finally conceded. It was not something she had ever thought about before. Her thoughts had always been focused on the issue at hand, as opposed to the aftermath of the outcome.

"In my experience, high morals are a wonderful thing. They speak to your good and Christian upbringing. But speaking of one's morals and living the reality of them are two different things entirely."

"I suppose, Madame, in line with my earlier insistence that this is a matter of when, and not if, I can keep you informed when I am faced with the consequences of my morals."

"You speak like the daughter of a Congressman," Madame Lavigne chuckled. "But a well-educated one at least. Now, please excuse me for a moment, dear." Putting the weight of herself onto the top of her cane, Madame Lavigne heaved herself to her feet. "I will be back in a few minutes."

"I might take the opportunity to explore your library," Mary confessed, casting her eyes towards the shelves of books.

If there was one thing she missed about Cana, it was their family library. Aunt Genevieve's was sizable, though nowhere near as large as theirs, and there was one slight but essential problem.

Nearly all the books were in French.

"Please do, dear," Madame Lavigne called, disappearing through the parlor door, the creak of her cane sounding on the wooden floor.

Mary carefully set her cup down on the small side table next to the couch and rose to her feet, smoothing the skirts of her dress before walking towards the bookcase nearest the piano.

"Would you like a turn?" The woman seated at the piano bench spoke with an accent foreign to Mary's ears.

"No, thank you. Though that is very kind. Honestly, you probably would not wish to hear me," she confessed with a smile.

This somehow felt like the kind of place where a lady needn't feel embarrassed to admit such a thing.

Mary looked at the books lining the shelves intently, running her fingers along the spines and allowing the leather to press against her skin.

This was probably just a very small portion of the household collection. Mary cast her eyes around the rest of the room. Four bookshelves in total, floor to ceiling, and fully lined with books and pamphlets.

Doubtless the library was even more grand.

That excited yet almost anxiety inducing sense flooded Mary as it always did when presented with numberless options of things to read.

She'd just have to dive in and pull the first book that met her eye-line out of the shelf.

It was a fairly new book, a heavy leather edition of poems by none other than Edger Allen Poe.

Mary smiled, amused that chance would have her pull Poe of anyone else on the shelf.

While from the North, he did currently reside in Virginia. And while she had not (and never would!) admitted it to a living soul, Mary had on more than one occasion fantasized about running in to him on the streets of Richmond.

It was silly, of course.

"I hear he is a drunk and a speculator," a familiar voice interrupted Mary's daydream.

She inhaled sharply, her hands immediately becoming clammy, and the book currently held open between her two palms all of a sudden felt like it was made of lead.

When had it become so heavy?

"I beg your pardon?" she asked, forcing herself to look up in only semi-feigned interest.

The way someone might if they have just been interrupted, and they desired their interrupter to know that they are not exactly pleased about it.

"Poe," Leander clarified, motioning towards the book in her hand. "Apparently he is a terrible gambler, essentially indigent, and finds solace for his bad luck at the bottom of a bottle."

"And are you, Mr. Doucet, the only sinless one amongst all of us?" she asked quietly, looking up to meet his gaze.

"I—"

"That you find it appropriate to pass judgment on the sins of others?"

"If I have offended you, Miss Taylor, I do apologize," Leander's cheeks began to redden. "I was simply trying to engage you in conversation."

"Well, I do not like that type of conversation," Mary explained, snapping the book closed and sliding it back on to the shelf. "I find gossip frivolous and cruel.

"Besides, from what I have heard, Mr. Poe has experienced a very challenging life from birth. I am not prepared to judge a man whose life I have not lived."

"You are quite right, Miss Taylor, and it is a testament to your upbringing that you have so vocally chastised my poor behavior, and not for the first time. It will not happen again."

Leander looked at Mary sincerely, clearly upset to have caused her distress and elicited such a harsh reaction.

"I am sorry, Mr. Doucet, I did not mean to be so severe in my reprimand."

"You need not apologize, Miss Taylor."

Silence fell between them.

But it was not a usual silence. It was not the normal kind that befalls strangers who are searching for an agreeable topic of conversation.

But rather the type that befalls a man and a woman when they know they have more to say to one another but do not know how.

Surely she had not made him nervous. Mary watched Leander as he shifted his weight, running a hand through his hair.

"And are you fond of him?" Mary finally asked, gesturing towards the book she had already reshelved.

"I am afraid not particularly, Miss Taylor," Leander responded quietly. Though his cheeks were still flushed, he met her eyes.

And when he did, Mary's heart pounded uproariously in her chest.

So loud she was certain the entire room could hear.

"May I ask why?"

"Well, I confess, Miss Taylor, it is a bit silly," Leander began tentatively. "But I do struggle to separate the man from his work."

"Ah, I see," Mary nodded. "You believe that art should not be judged by itself, separate to its creator, but as an extension of the artist, including their morals and values?"

"Ha, well, it is a good question." Leander nodded thoughtfully, raising a hand to rub his chin. "I suppose when it comes down to it, I do not wish to patronize a man I do not respect."

"I see. So you, Mr. Doucet, consider buying Mr. Poe's works a condoning of his lifestyle?"

"I feel as though I am on trial," Leander confessed with an uneasy chuckle. "If not condoning, Miss Taylor, it would be financing at the very least, and they do not feel worlds apart in my mind."

"I had never considered that. Is that why you frequent Madame Lavigne's salon? To allow you to read all of the books of the men who you do not consider gentlemen without having to buy their works yourselves?"

It was bold, and quite frankly outlandish, to accuse a gentleman of such miserly habits.

But Mary was feeling both, and besides, she had long ago decided that Leander Doucet was no gentleman.

"Miss Taylor, you see right through me." Leander clasped a hand to his chest. "Though I would beg you to please keep my secret between us."

"Certainly, Mr. Doucet. Though only for my brother's sake. His reputation by virtue of your joint partnership would be at risk if people learned of your frugality."

"I thank you kindly, Miss Taylor, no matter your reasonings."

They both smiled, chuckling lightly through closed lips.

"Who else on this bookshelf do you disapprove of so vehemently that you cannot bring yourself to purchase their works?"

"Let us see." Leander took a step towards the bookshelf, and in doing so, a side step towards Mary. Beginning at the top, he scanned the shelves methodically, his hands clasped behind his back.

"Well, beginning with the oldest," Leander pulled an enormous old leatherbound book from the top shelf and held it up for Mary to see.

"Surely you must be joking, Mr. Doucet... You do not approve of Homer?"

"I assure you I am not joking, Miss Taylor," Leander explained. "As an author, no, but to use as a large object with which one might prop open a door, I can see the merit in him."

"He is one of the oldest and most classic storytellers of all time!" Mary insisted.

"While I do not disagree with you, Miss Taylor, I am afraid I find him a terrible bore."

"How can you find him a bore? He writes of war, honor, and adventure!"

"Once again, I do not disagree with you, Miss Taylor."

"I had always assumed these were some of the favorite pastimes of men!"

At Mary's words, Leander laughed loudly, throwing his head back in amusement.

"Really, Miss Taylor, do you think these are the things that most matter to men? War, honor, and adventure?"

"Well, perhaps amongst a few others."

"Please do enlighten me, Miss Taylor." His eyes shone with amusement. "Horse-racing, shooting, and drinking?"

"Why yes, Mr. Doucet, I do believe that about sums it up," Mary feigned sincerity. "Are you saying there is more to a man's world than these things?"

"Well, any man's world, perhaps not," Leander conceded. "But a gentleman's world, certainly, Miss Taylor."

"Now it is your turn, Mr. Doucet. Please do enlighten me," Mary egged him on, placing a hand on her hip as Elizabeth might.

"Well, family, of course, should always be a gentleman's first priority."

"That is a good answer." Mary nodded. "And what else?"

"Well, of course the family you are born in to, but as most gentlemen would hope, the family you choose."

At these words, Leander looked at her intently, securing her gaze and holding it tight.

As though for dear life.

"And what else?" Mary asked in a quiet voice, barely more than a whisper.

"The family you create, if you are so blessed," Leander's voice was low.

"And what else?"

"And love," Leander admitted in a deep voice, as though a confession.

Mary's heart threatened self-destruction as they held one another's gaze.

"And you do not feel that Homer accurately represents all of these things?" Mary asked after a moment.

"I do not, Miss Taylor."

"But King Menelaus starts the Trojan war over the loss of Helen. Do you not believe this is because of his deep love for her?"

"I do not, Miss Taylor," Leander repeated. "I always interpreted King Meneluas's actions and motives as a man scorned, not one heartbroken."

"And Paris, is blinded by Helen's beauty," Mary offered.

"Agreed. It is lust and a sense of entitlement because Aphrodite has promised him the most beautiful woman in the world. Neither of those is love."

"And what about Odysseus, who returns to his wife after twenty years?"

"I suppose one could argue he is true to her in mind and soul," Leander conceded. "Though I am not particularly convinced. And in body, certainly not so.

"The only character for whom I have any respect is—"

"Penelope," both Leander and Mary said at the same time.

"She is the greatest victim of the entire affair. She waits faithfully for twenty years, despite multiple reports that her husband is dead and constant attempts by suitors to take his place."

"To be clear, Mr. Doucet, you dislike Homer because you find all of his characters morally repugnant?"

"That, and the fact that his stories are so long and repetitive. He uses the same words again, and again, and again."

"Well, I think there were smaller vocabularies then. I fear that is just a reality of the time, as opposed to a blame you can lay solely at the author's feet."

"But did he need *all* of this," Leander asked, slapping the cover of the book against the palm of his hand.

"I suppose he could have edited a bit more thoroughly."

"Perhaps he was being paid by the word?"

At his words, Mary laughed aloud, her lips stretching across her teeth in amusement she had completely forgotten to disguise.

"Forgive me, Miss Taylor. I have gone on and on about my views." Leander reached up his long arms and replaced the book where he had found it. "Who is your favorite author as of late?"

"I am not certain if I am brave enough to say after you assaulted the reputation of Mr. Poe and Homer so vehemently!"

"Please, Miss Taylor, do not force me to relive my ill manners," Leander pleaded. "I promise to behave this time, whoever your choice may be."

"Not at all. I do actually desire your honest opinion."

"Then you shall have it," Leander promised, gesturing towards the bookshelf.

Mary turned towards the shelves, tilting her head slightly to better read the spines.

"I fear you may roll your eyes," Mary prefaced, placing her fingers at the top of a book and tugging lightly. "But I have found myself enchanted by the work of—"

"Miss Austen," both she and Leander said together, and then laughed.

"How did you know?" Mary asked.

"A lucky guess," Leander shrugged, accepting the book from her outstretched hand and inspecting it. "She is very popular right now, especially amongst young ladies who enjoy reading."

And did he know this because he spoke to so many of them?

"Have you read her?" Mary inquired, trying to ignore the pang of disappointment which accompanied his declaration.

"I have not. Do you recommend her?"

"Oh yes. If you are interested in love, true love, and the societal and familial expectations that can sometimes come between that." Leander tore his gaze from the book in his hands to meet Mary's eyes.

Mary paused, almost frightened by the way his eyes burned into hers.

"Th-then you will find company in her novels." She finally finished quietly.

Leander looked at her a moment longer. It appeared to Mary that he was almost studying her, as though he were searching for an answer in her face.

Though to what, Mary did not know.

"Thank you for the recommendation, Miss Taylor." Leander placed the book back on the shelf. "I will be sure to look out for her works."

"And do you, Mr. Doucet, have a favorite author?" Mary asked.

"I—"

"Mary, there you are. Mr. Doucet." Amelié nodded congenially. "You will have to forgive me, but I have lost track of time, and if we do not leave now, we will be late for supper."

"Of course, Miss Defour."

"I have been boring Mr. Doucet with talk of literature, so I am sure he is in your debt for rescuing him."

"Not at all, Miss Taylor," Leander replied sincerely. "I just know how Mrs. Defour values punctuality. As any good Frenchwoman would. My mother is the same."

# Chapter XIV

"There is nothing more pleasurable for a man than to return from the country and find his parlor filled with fair young ladies."

"Mon fils!" Aunt Genevieve rose to her feet with an alacrity Mary had never witnessed from her measured and careful aunt. At her approach, Michel removed his hat, bending forward to allow his mother, nearly eighteen inches shorter, to place her hands either side of his cheeks and kiss his forehead with a solemn display of affection. With eyes squeezed shut she murmured a prayer in French, their foreheads pressed close together.

Suppressing the laugh that danced dangerously close to the surface, Mary threw a warning eye towards her sister, who sitting next to her had just made the most audible swallowing noise.

And it had not gone unnoticed, for Michel cast a glance towards the Taylor sisters where they sat on the parlor settee, a good-humored twinkle in his eye as he winked, before solemnly closing his eyes and receiving his blessing with silent attention.

And perhaps the tiniest bit of sarcasm.

At his gesture Gabrielle and Amelié rolled their eyes, so perfectly synchronized that it could only be borne of years of practice.

"Merci, Maman." Michel kissed his mother's cheek. "It is by God's grace and your prayers that we remain in health and wealth."

"Don't be so obtuse," Aunt Genevieve warned, giving his cheek a light slap of affection. "Where is Mr. Defour?"

"He has retired to his study. He requires some urgent messages to be sent before the sun sets."

"Very well, let us not bother him for now. Girls, come greet your brother and cousin," Aunt Genevieve called over her shoulder. "And I will go check on the status of dinner. Welcome home, Michel. Take off your coat, it is covered in dust from your journey."

"Of course, Maman." Michel made a nod of contrition, that did, in Mary's opinion, drip with jest.

As though there was a humor in everything, if one desired to see it.

"Well, the favorite child has returned," Amelié announced from her chair near the fireplace once their mother had disappeared down the corridor.

There was a frigidness to her voice Mary knew she would never have used in front of their mother.

"One would be wise, ma chère sœur, to not be so disparaging of the hands that put food on your table and clothes on your back." Michel slipped the coat from his shoulders in one effortless motion and with a flick of his wrist tossed it over his sister's knees. "Take care of this for me, s'il vous plait."

At the impudent gesture, Amelié turned the color of the sun, and shoving the coat off her legs with more force than was entirely necessary, she began a tirade in French.

Mary sat still, shell-shocked, for she had not expected this.

And nor had Elizabeth, for she now sat up a bit straighter, her eyes darting back and forth between their cousins in what could only be described as a twisted and bewildered entertainment.

"Paix," Gabrielle finally cut in, rising from where she had sat half-reclined in a chair near the window, watching the exchange with only partial interest.

Clearly, it was not an unusual occurrence.

"You give our Virginian cousins too much gossip to take home."

"Gabrielle, our stunning cousins would never be so indiscreet," Michel drawled, finally turning to the Taylor sisters with the full force of his devastating charm. Mary knew the delight her sister found in finally being under her cousin's arresting gaze, though Elizabeth would never be obvious enough to show it. Leaning back in her seat, she shrugged, turning her attention to a piece of hair that had fallen over her shoulder.

"Well I suppose, Mr. Defour, that does depend on the situation," Elizabeth acknowledged with a haughty disinterest.

"Oh?" Michel cocked his head to one side, and leaving his sisters, he perched on the arm of the settee next to Elizabeth, meeting her gaze. "In what situation would you sell your family for a moment of attention?" The words oozed from his lips, thick as sugar syrup as his blonde hair fell ever so slightly over his forehead.

Gabrielle crossed her arms, her eyes travelling to the ceiling in exasperation for her brother's overt flirtation.

"For I know, Elizabeth, that you do not require any help obtaining something as fleeting as a man's attention."

"Well, perhaps yesterday I would have agreed with you, but considering you have been here nearly twenty minutes and have not even bothered to greet your cousins..."

"Twenty minutes you say?" A skeptical—nay, mischievous—eyebrow reached towards Michel's forehead.

"Yes, at least." Elizabeth stared up at him from under her eyelashes. "And considering we have come so far to see you..."

"I believe I did declare you all very fair on my entrance."

"Get in line, Mr. Defour, for you are the fourth man today to make such a declaration.

"Perhaps the fifth. I have lost count."

"Well, I did not appreciate that there was so much competition."

"Either you overestimate your importance or underestimate the admiration of our qualities."

"I assure you it cannot be the latter, for you, my dear cousin, are the fairest lady in all of New Orleans."

At his words, Elizabeth squinted.

"In all of Louisiana."

Elizabeth's head cocked to one side.

"South of the Mason-Dixon."

"And what of my sister?"

"As I hear it, Miss Mary's charms are known far and wide, for news of her courtship by a certain name that shall not be spoken in this household, has reached even so far as Chêne Blanc." Michel extended an arm over the top of the settee, leaning over Elizabeth to tease his younger cousin with that merciless charm that came with such ease to him. "Maman is most displeased, as is Père, though he is too stalwart to acknowledge it. Were you not informed, Miss Mary, that part of your invitation to stay was on the understanding that you would be swept off your feet by one of our family and find yourself unable to leave Louisiana?"

"Well, Michel, how might my sister be swept off her feet if the only eligible male in the family is miles away, playing in the corn fields?"

"We grow sugarcane, Miss Elizabeth, as I know you know," Michel turned his attention back towards her, his words a playful reprimand. "As for myself, well, I have found that a lady's heart tends to beat most purely for a gentleman when he is not at all times available.

"After all, absence does make the heart grow fonder," he murmured, reaching for her hand and kissing it with an intensity that felt altogether far too intimate.

At the gesture Mary looked away, her eyes meeting Gabrielle's who had migrated back to her seat and held the most unimpressed look.

"Go to the servants' corridors if you wish to do that," Amelié grimaced, leaving the group with a look of utter disdain as she retreated from the room.

"You would not find it so distasteful if a gentleman had ever paid you such attention," Michel called back, still cradling Elizabeth's hand in his.

"Enough, Michel," Gabrielle snapped. "She's been worked up enough without your instigating."

"It is hard to help it when she makes it so easy," Michel returned Elizabeth's hand, and rising from his perch he settled into the chair Amelié had abandoned, lazing backwards in a manner he would never use in the presence of his parents.

"How fared the preparations, cousin?" Mary jumped in before Gabrielle could respond, desperate to steer the conversation towards something—anything—other than this.

"Perfectly smoothly, thank you for asking." Michel nodded towards Mary.

"Oh, were you not impacted by the heavy rains from last month? It is hard to believe, for it has been rather dry here, but I had heard that further north the rain was flooding the fields. I do hope it did not completely overwhelm the drainage system and spoil the crops?" At her questioning, Michel looked bemused, unearthing his pipe from his pocket and knocking it on the side table next to him.

"Do not flatter yourself into reading into her inquiry, Michel, for she truly inquires because she is curious," Elizabeth said, tone laced with the kind of bemusement usually reserved for children and fools.

"A woman of curiosity," Michel declared to no one in particular, digging through his trouser pockets for his tobacco. "What a curious concept.

"In truth, it is hard to say, sweet Mary, for sugarcane is a plant which requires patience. It has a lead time of—"

"Twelve to eighteen months," they spoke in tandem.

"You will make an excellent plantation wife for that Mr. Rivera of yours," Michel gave a half-amused chuckle as he packed his pipe.

At his declaration Mary's face flushed. Was it really that obvious?

And did everyone know?

Absolutely everyone?

"Oh, do not encourage her." Gabrielle dismissed the thought with a wave of her pretty slight hand. "It is bad enough he has come to our home to serenade her."

"Ha, yes, I heard about that. You must really have him hooked. The poor man probably never expected it from such a sweet little thing like you. Perhaps you can teach my sisters and yours a thing or two."

"You are insufferable."

"I will have you know, Mr. Defour, that everything Mary has learned has been at the hands of my wise counsel."

"Oh heavens, I do hope that is not true," Michel leaned forward in his chair, his elbows resting on his knees as he spoke in mock sincerity. "Little cousin, I implore you, if you ever do wish to marry, then do yourself a favor and do the opposite of what these two tell you." Michel gestured with the stem of his pipe to Elizabeth and Gabrielle. "For they are hardly role models. Spinsters, the lot of them."

"You're the devil himself—dressed in a once-fine, now travel-worn suit—" Elizabeth paused, the rest of the insult lost on her lips as all four sets of eyes travelled towards the ceiling, listening intently to the sound that seeped through below.

A woman's voice, raised, speaking quickly and rather furiously in what sounded like French.

"She lacks tact," Michel shook his head, placing the stem of the pipe in his mouth and lighting it he puffed on the end.

The smell of tobacco filled the room, reminding Mary of Cana.

"What does she desire now?"

"A new dress for the charity ball."

"Well, she won't have it," Michel rolled his eyes. "Father is on edge after the slow start to the year, and the autumn's harvest was hardly a symbol of the Lord's pleasure."

"Maman has suggested a pilgrimage if this one is not better." At Gabrielle's warning, Michel sighed, rubbing his forehead in dread at the notion.

At the sound of a raised male's voice, the room once again fell silent, eyes travelling once more to the floor above.

It was positively excruciating.

And it was about to get so much worse.

For when Amelié's volume met that of her father's, a door slammed from down the corridor, and as quickly as an apparition, Aunt Genevieve was scaling the stairs. She moved with such alacrity her footsteps were silent, her ascent presumably unexpected by the quarrelling parties until it entered the conversation.

And despite being such a slight woman, Aunt Genevieve had, when she desired, a voice that would rival the Lord's on the day of creation. Her words were commanding, crisp, and curt.

Ruthless.

Despite not understanding the words being spoken, Mary was confident that was the only appropriate adjective.

All eyes returned to the room, an awkward silence descending over the foursome.

"Was it really so urgent that she had to ask the evening he returned?"

"Yes, if she desired to put in a rush order with the seamstress."

"You ladies, with your heads full of fabrics, colors, and accessories."

"Pray, do not put me in the same category, for it was not I who demanded a new dress."

And upturned the household in the process.

"Why does she require anything new? I recall the bill for new trunks recently."

"It was the beginning of last season. She is worried, for everyone has already seen her dresses."

"Well, Lord have Mercy!" Michel shook his head in derision. "A lady, I'm sure, could never fathom leaving the house in an outfit a gentleman has already seen. Whatever would he think?"

"Mockery is a cheap form of humor," Gabrielle critiqued. "And you may laugh, but she has convinced herself that she has not received a proposal because none of her clothes become her."

"That is the silliest thing I have ever heard." Michel's words were detached, dismissive in their judgment of the absurdity of the notion. "Men do not care for such things nearly as much as ladies think. The notion that we might even recall what a lady wore a few months gone is absurd."

"You needn't lecture me, Michel, for I know this. But it is easier for her to believe her four seasons without a proposal is due to something as trivial as her dress trunk."

Kinder, perhaps too. Mary looked down at her hands, wrung tightly together as she considered her cousin in a manner she had not previously.

As the confrontation continued Michel and Gabrielle extended their spines, allowing their eyes to travel to the ceiling once more as they listened.

"Gabrielle, what are they saying?" Elizabeth whispered, much to Mary's horror.

"She is saying that the Lemieux ladies receive a new trunk once a year."

"Ha, an unwise example, for they are in debt up to their ears," Michel remarked with a shake of his head.

"No, but Hélène Lemieux is always dressed in the finest clothes!" Elizabeth insisted, a hand going to her mouth as she tried to hide her glee at the information.

"That does not mean her family possess the funds to pay for it. Look at you, dear cousin, delighting so in the misfortunes of others!" Michel chuckled, shaking his head with something between weariness and amusement. "Heaven help the man who finds himself on the receiving end of your affections—he will need both coin and constitution in excess."

"I simply do not believe people should be admired for living above their means," Elizabeth declared with a sanctimonious self-righteousness.

One might say, not the most challenging declaration for a Taylor daughter to make.

"Perhaps not, but a reverse of fortune can come quickly. It need only take a few bad harvests coupled with rising prices, and all of a sudden, one is borrowing to make ends meet. And it can be challenging for a family to change their lifestyle, especially when there are expectations of a certain manner of living."

Both internal and external.

"Pride is hardly an excuse," Elizabeth dismissed with a wave of her hand.

The irony of which was not lost on Mary, nor it appeared, her cousins.

"But what of charity, Miss Elizabeth? And forgiveness? Did you learn nothing in Sunday school as a child?"

"One always feels entitled to such gifts after one has been greedy and frivolous."

"Look how pious you've become, living under Maman's roof."

As if having spoken her name was a summon, the unmistakable rustle of a petticoat on the stairs once again plunged the group into silence.

Only this time, Michel straightened himself in his chair, Gabrielle reached for her sewing that had been discarded long ago, and both the Taylor sisters clambered after the book on the side table next to Mary. Aunt Genevieve paused, glancing into the parlor from the doorway at the suspiciously quiet inhabitants.

Mary studied the page in front of her, though she could not manage to make sense of the sentences. Stealing a glance at Elizabeth, her sister stared at the words with an intensity Mary had never before witnessed.

Especially between Elizabeth and a book.

"Michel." The name crisp and cool—a command.

"Yes, Maman?"

"Pick your coat up off the floor. You were not raised in a barn."

It was a somewhat long and arduous task for a household, specifically one made up of mostly women, to ready themselves for an outing such as the first ball of the season.

It was an even more arduous task to attempt to fit four ladies in full skirts into one carriage.

And that was even before anyone had accounted for Henri and Michel.

Antoiné, the youngest, having not yet been introduced to society as an eligible young lady, would stay home under the watchful care and attention of the house servant and Amelié, who had, following the events of earlier that week, refused to attend.

It was actually suspected that her mother had revoked the privilege of attendance due to her poor behavior, though no one was brave enough to pursue evidence of such a claim, and so it remained, much like most of the hushed whispers exchanged on Southern streets, a rumor at worst, and gossip at best.

In the end it was agreed that Michel would accompany Elizabeth and Mary first, and the carriage would be sent back for Genevieve, Henri, and Gabrielle.

The event was being held at the old opera house, a grand and ornate white building. Mary stared up at the structure as it came into view—the pillars reminded her of the ancient Greek temples she had read about in school.

Michel led the ladies up the steps, one Taylor sister on each of his arms.

"Michel Defour, you will be the envy of the ball," Elizabeth giggled, playfully slapping Michel's chest.

"Don't I know it, Miss Taylor." Michel's grin curved slow and sly, a perfect Cheshire smile."You know, I have had many of my friends approach me," he continued, a glisten in his eyes. "Asking after the status of the beautiful cousins of mine who all of a sudden appeared on the New Orleans social scene."

"Oh? And did you not think to mention it to us?"

"Forgive me, Miss Taylor, but it takes a very high caliber of gentleman to be good enough for my dear cousins," Michel gallantly insisted, smiling down at Elizabeth with a knowing look.

"Michel Defour, you absolute devil! You did not tell them because you desired to keep us for yourself!"

"Ha," Michel laughed, throwing his head back in amusement. "And if I did, Miss Taylor, can you blame me?" His eyes twinkled with the promise of danger.

"Oh no, not one bit. Though, it might be nice if you did give the other boys a chance."

"Ah, but Miss Taylor, I am certain you, of all people, must know that all is fair in love and war?"

"Well, that is very true."

They continued to flirt, Michel lavishing Elizabeth with overtures of their grace, beauty, and wit, and Elizabeth accusing Michel of being any combination of a rogue, devil, or rake.

Inside the opera house, a deep lush red carpet led guests into the main hallway, lit by delicately hung chandeliers, which sparkled, bathing the guests in a soft glow.

Mary cast her eyes around the entrance, looking to see if there were any familiar faces.

One chief amongst them.

"Miss Taylor, such a pleasant surprise." A tall figure appeared to her right.

Not the one she had been hoping for.

"Mr. Walker," Mary nodded courteously, hoping against hope that her face did not betray her distaste at seeing him once again.

At her acknowledgement, he bowed low, his body nearly creating a right angle. Mary fought the urge to roll her eyes at the display which she once took as affection and now knew to be pandering.

Mary Taylor was not someone who generally thought ill of people, but Thomas Walker, after the way he had pursued her and then spoken about her, was the absolute last person she desired to see.

Besides, what in the world were the Walkers doing in New Orleans?

"If you do not mind me saying so." Thomas reached for her hand, ignoring her slight resistance. "You look absolutely beautiful this evening."

Even though she knew he did not mean it, Mary did for once actually believe she looked beautiful. She had chosen a powdered blue dress of silk—the skirt cascaded in tiered ruffles in a way that filled out her figure more than most. At the top, the bodice was cut low, and white tulle sleeves looped across her shoulders, giving her top some broadness. And finally, a white silk sash was tied around her waist, accentuating its smallness and finishing prettily in a bow.

"Thank you, Mr. Walker. That is very kind." Mary dipped into the shallowest of curtsies.

Her upbringing meant that she could not entirely snub Southern etiquette in the way her sister was unafraid to, but she could make known her disinterest and even displeasure with subtle social cues that while small, spoke volumes.

And she hoped they did.

"I was hoping, Miss Taylor, that you might still, against all odds, have some space on your dance card for this evening." Thomas applied his best penetrating gaze.

The same one Mary had seen before.

Though this time, it lacked the original effect.

"I am afraid, Mr. Walker, that I will have to check."

Her tone was blunt, showing no sign of regret.

"Please do." Thomas nodded, seemingly sincerely, though Mary knew better. "I was so disappointed we were not able to dance at your debutante ball as originally planned. I confess, it is the type of disappointment that stays with a man," he bemoaned, with the type of extravagance that might once have made Mary's knees quiver.

But no longer.

"Well, I confess that I was not expecting to see you here."

A cool reply.

"Ah yes, with the spring races upon us, it's only natural we'd return. As I'm sure you know, Miss Taylor, our family is quite heavily involved in horse breeding and racing."

"Are you now? I fear this is the first time I've heard such a thing—"

"Miss Taylor." Manuel Rivera appeared on her other side. Removing his hat, he bowed low.

"Mr. Rivera." Mary allowed herself a large luminous smile before dropping into a low curtsy. While not the man she had originally hoped to see, he was the perfect candidate to extract her from the conversational agony imposed by Thomas Walker.

"You look radiant tonight." Manuel took her gloved hand, brushing his lips across her knuckles with a murmured, "Miss Mary."

"Thank you, Manuel. You look dashing yourself," she confessed, taking in his black-tailed velvet suit jacket, starkly contrasted by white trousers and a powder blue bowtie.

He was, undoubtedly, extremely handsome.

"Oh, it appears we have matched." Mary gestured towards his tie.

"It appears we have!" Manuel laughed heartily. "As you are the most elegantly dressed woman in the room, I am delighted by our fateful synchronisation."

"You are, as always, too flattering."

Manuel Rivera did have the most distinct way of making Mary feel like not only the most beautiful woman he had ever seen, but also like the only woman in the room.

"Mr. Walker." Manuel turned, extending his hand to Thomas. "It is good to see you again. I presume you are here for the upcoming races?"

"Yes, that's right, Mr. Rivera." Thomas clasped the outstretched hand vigorously—more vigorously than was entirely necessary. "Will you be in attendance?"

"Oh yes, I plan to be," Manuel assured him. "Any tips you can provide will, of course, be greeted with pleasure and treated with the utmost discretion."

"Mr. Rivera." Thomas shook his head in mock disapproval. "I know you, as a man of integrity, would never wish for information that might give you an unfair advantage."

"And I would not trust any secret he claimed to confide to you in any case," Mary muttered under her breath.

"What was that, Miss Taylor?"

"Pardon me, Miss Mary, but I missed that?"

Both the men had turned back towards Mary, competing to give her their full and undivided attention.

Did she really just say that aloud? She searched the faces of both men for any indication that they had heard, but they both stared at her, expectantly and mercilessly blankly.

"Nothing. I was just thinking to myself that I am ever so parched, and that I might go find the refreshments."

"Allow me to escort you, Miss Mary," Manuel jumped in before Thomas could. "Thomas, would you mind if we continued this conversation later? I do certainly hope that being the sole exporters of the Rivera plantation production will come with some advantages," Manuel made his desires known while holding his arm out to Mary.

"Of course, Manuel." Thomas nodded. "Miss Taylor," he turned his attention towards Mary. "I will await your confirmation on that dance." Thomas bowed once more.

"Good evening, Mr. Walker," Mary nodded curtly, taking Manuel's extended arm and allowing herself to be led away.

"What a treat it is," Manuel mused to no one in particular, a smile nestled between his lips in the most contented manner as he placed his hand atop Mary's where it lay delicately on his arm.

"Pray, do tell."

"To have won the attention of the most beautiful woman in the room," Manuel declared with a gallant flourish, reaching for his pocket watch that sat nestled in his vest. "And all within a matter of minutes of my arrival."

"Well, I confess, Manuel, I was surprised to see you in attendance. Had I known, perhaps you would not even have required to take that long."

"And pray, Miss Mary, why were you surprised at my attendance?"

"Only because I do not recall seeing an announcement in *The Verity* relating to its sponsorship." At her words, Manuel stiffened, his air immediately turning rigid.

"Yes, well, unlike certain other institutions in this town, we do not feel the need to self-congratulate our own charitable work. Though, for the avoidance of doubt, Santiago San Ignacio is a proud sponsor of this event, as is *The Verity*. We ran many advertisements—gratis, of course. We just do not believe in buying our way to heaven, contrary to the opinion of others."

"I—I sense I have offended you, Mr. Rivera, and for that I do apologize." She stared at his hand atop hers, the press of his palm all of a sudden felt like a weight.

A very heavy weight, in fact.

"Manuel," he corrected, and bringing her hand to his lips, he kissed it softly. "And please, Miss Mary, never apologize to me. Forgive me—my Spanish Catholic upbringing tends to make me a bit..."

Intense?

Perhaps the tiniest bit harsh?

If not condescending?

"Passionate.

"And in any case, I should not expect a lady to be aware of such matters as sponsorships and financing, and the wider nuances of when one might wish to remain silent in such endeavors."

Mary could feel the desire to disagree crawling up her throat, to point out that she had been listening to her father speak about federal and party financing for years.

And by party, she did mean the Democratic party, mind you, not a garden party.

Mary could imagine the words coming out of her sister's mouth, for Elizabeth was never one to back down from a battle.

Indeed, she often sought them.

Charles would point out that there is no need to antagonize a situation further and risk ruining what promised to be a perfectly pleasant evening.

As for Edward...well, Edward would have never made the observation in the first place. He did not care for reading and often declared that anything worth learning could not be done behind the feather of a quill and a bottle of ink.

And Mary?

What did Mary choose?

"And how is it that you know the Walkers?" Mary pivoted the conversation in a manner she was certain Father, Mother, and Charles would have approved of immensely.

She had chosen to lead with her head, as any well-raised young Southern lady should, but even this knowledge did not explain why she felt so hollow in doing what she knew was correct.

What was expected of her.

Not just by parents or the bounds of Southern propriety.

But by Manuel Rivera also.

"The Walkers and Riveras are long-time allies, Miss Mary," Manuel explained. "We send all of our production to the ports in Charleston for export."

"To Charleston?" Mary asked in surprise. "But Manuel, that is so far!"

"That it is."

"But there is a port in New Orleans," Mary ventured, before realizing her blunder.

There was indeed a port in New Orleans—it was controlled by the Defour family.

"Yes, you are correct, of course, Miss Mary," Manuel agreed awkwardly. "But, we prefer to send our production to Charleston."

"But, Manuel, it is so far," Mary reiterated in disbelief.

"That it is," Manuel repeated again, his voice becoming ever so slightly tense. "But it is what it is."

"To be clear, after you harvest, you incur further cost to ship your production to Charleston, I presume by rail, to avoid having to export via the New Orleans port?" Even saying it aloud felt like insanity.

Her father had always said it—family feuds were bad for business. "You are correct," Manuel nodded through tight lips. "It is all very long and complicated, Miss Mary, and unfortunately not very pleasant. Please, let us discuss something else."

"Of course," Mary agreed amicably as they arrived at a table of refreshments. An awkward silence settled between the pair of them as Manuel reached for a cup and poured some punch for Mary before doing the same for himself.

The seconds felt like minutes, cruelly elongating themselves as the pair stared awkwardly at one another over their cups.

"But Manuel," Mary finally could take it no longer. "Why Charleston? Even Savannah is closer, and is a key port city—"

"Miss Mary, please, I must insist we speak about something else," Manuel repeated, his tone terse and strained.

"Of course," Mary's eyes dropped to peer into her punch. "Pardon me, Mr. Rivera."

Was it that he did not wish to involve her in the family feud, knowing the Taylors' stance on such matters?

Or was it that he did not like being challenged on the sense of a decision that clearly cut the margins of his family business by significant proportions?

Whatever the reason, Mary did not like his tone—it carried a quiet finality, almost pleading, and it made her feel small.

"Miss Taylor, please call me Manuel, as you did before," he implored her, his voice low. "If you call me Mr. Rivera, then I will have to call you Miss Taylor instead of Miss Mary, and that will break my heart."

"Of course, Manuel." Mary looked up at him, pressing a smile out between her lips.

She hoped that it was convincing.

And it did seem to do the trick, for Manuel's shoulders relaxed again, a look of relief washing over his face at her reassurance.

But something about his name on her tongue did not feel the same as it had before.

In spite of this, Mary spent most of the night dancing with Manuel Rivera—he was an excellent dancer, and had they not had their earlier incident, Mary might have happily spent the night whirling around in his arms.

But try as she might to put it out of her mind, the incident continued to plague her. It followed her around the dance floor—the way Manuel looked at her, like the greatest prize he had ever won, felt somehow less appealing.

Not because anything about the way he was treating her had changed.

But because Mary's view of the way Manuel viewed her had changed.

Mary's dancing shoes echoed on the floor of the stage. She had never been to the opera, but she had always reveled in the idea of it. Not to be on stage, of course—that was only possible because the old smaller auditorium was completely abandoned and now used for storage—but to attend the opera on the arm of her husband. They could sit in one of those boxes. Mary cast her eyes to the balconies, trying to imagine herself seated there next to someone.

But who?

She closed her eyes, squinting them shut and trying to imagine a face, but it remained obscured, somehow grey and undistinguished.

"And what performance will you be gracing us with this evening, Miss Taylor?" A voice broke Mary from her contemplation.

She jumped, her eyes flying open in surprise, for she had not heard any foot treads.

There, in the main aisle of the auditorium looking up at her, stood Leander Doucet.

"Are you alright, Miss Taylor?"

"Yes. It is just that, you frightened me, Mr. Doucet. I did not hear you coming," Mary admitted.

"I do apologize, Miss Taylor." He bowed. "Never does a gentleman wish to hear that he has frightened a lady."

"It is alright, of course. I fear the problem actually lies with me, for I was in my own little world."

"I respectfully disagree, Miss Taylor, for I am certain you could never be "the problem"," he offered sincerely, studying Mary under a penetrating gaze that sent her heart pounding.

"You look like a natural on that stage," he said playfully. With a gallant swish, he folded himself into the nearest auditorium seat and made a show of settling in, placing the foot of his left leg on top of the knee of his right, the male version of crossing one's legs. Placing his hat in the seat next to him, he then turned his attention fully back to Mary and gestured with his hands for her to continue.

"You are very humorous, Mr. Doucet, but I am afraid I will have to disappoint you, for I have no such talents."

"Ah, I am sure you are being too humble," Leander insisted. "Your brother has spoken many times of your talents. He says you are very accomplished with a piano," he said and gestured with his head towards the piano which stood at the opposite end of the stage from Mary.

"And was this my brother Edward or my brother Charles, who is spreading such tall tales?"

"It is the eldest Mr. Taylor. Though I am sure he would not love to know that his sister is calling him a man of tall tales."

"No, of course not. My eldest brother is an honest man if there ever were one. That being said, when it comes to matters of subjectivity, he will always look to shelter one's feelings than provide a... shall we say critical assessment."

"Ha, very well put, Miss Taylor. It is clear you are a politician's daughter." Mr. Doucet nodded approvingly. Mary provided a mocking curtsy to his compliment.

"Perhaps if there were a showcase of literature or politics, I would find myself better able to impress you with my talents. But unfortunately, these do not tend to be the celebrated pastimes of most young ladies."

"Oh, I am not sure if I would say that," Leander disagreed politely, rising to his feet and plucking his hat from the chair. "You have attended Madame Lavigne's salon, and you will have noted that some of the most prominent members are ladies. Why, salons are often run by women. It is the same in France also."

"Have you been to France, Mr. Doucet?"

"I have, Miss Taylor," he nodded, slowly making his way towards the little steps which led to the stage.

"And is that where you became an expert on the concept of the salon?"

"Well, I do not believe I ever claimed to be an expert," Leander finished climbing the stairs, making his way towards Mary. "But I seek one out in any city I find myself spending considerable time in."

"I see. You must enjoy them thoroughly, in that case." Mary peered up at Leander as he approached her, less than a foot of room now separating them.

"I do," Leander agreed.

"And what is it that you enjoy so thoroughly about them?"

"Oh, the free exchange of ideas, the celebration of art, literature, and culture, and the general nature of being with like-minded people.

"And you, Miss Taylor? What draws you to Madame Lavigne's parlor?"

"I would say more or less the same reasons you articulated. Especially the last one."

"Mmm, yes. I believe that the soul finds solace in being around people who find the same joy and interest in the things that you do. It is part of human nature, I believe, to desire companionship that has depth to its connections."

"Yes, I agree." Mary looked up at Leander.

Was the distance between them shrinking?

Mary was sure it must be.

"And I think it is a human desire to be seen. It makes one feel less alone in the world."

"Indeed, Miss Taylor. It is a human desire to want the things that we hold dear in life to be the things others, our chosen companions, also hold dear."

"Yes," Mary breathed, her heart beginning to beat against her chest.

Silence fell between them as both Mary and Leander studied one another.

He was not looking at her in the way he would a sister—No, that same hunger had returned, looming heavy in his eyes, gnawing at the insides and making her feel hot and flushed.

But there was something else in his eyes too, a tenderness that she could not exactly place.

"Well, it would appear we are in agreement, Miss Taylor." Leander finally broke the silence, keeping his eyes fixated on hers.

"Yes, I believe we are," Mary whispered in response.

The moment held between them, suspending time and awareness completely.

If Mary had been aware, she would have reminded herself that it was considered completely inappropriate to be alone with a man who was not her father, brother, or other married relative.

Even further than inappropriate, it would have been scandalous. Finding unmarried young ladies alone with unmarried gentlemen was enough for a family to demand they became married.

And swiftly.

Or risk bringing ill-repute on both the young lady, and her family's reputation.

As Mary well knew.

But now, in this moment, these were not the thoughts occupying her mind.

Instead, she thought about the space between them, separating them, keeping them apart. It was not much. What Mary had first judged as a foot could now not be more than eight inches, ten at most.

But more than anything, she wished for a way to close that gap further, to bring their bodies even closer to one another.

Perhaps to allow them to touch.

Even if just for a moment.

What would she do, if he took a step closer?

Would she step back to discourage him?

Which would, of course, be the appropriate response.

Or would she stay still and hopefully in doing so encourage him to come even closer?

Or, would she step towards him also, closing the distance between them so that their bodies would be touching.

A statement, not a question.

And the thought of it made Mary's head spin. The clear message it would send—one of intent and decisiveness—made her body burn.

Mary looked into Leander's eyes with longing, willing him to take the initiative and move just a tiny bit to reassure her that the entire situation was not one of her own creation, existing only in her head.

But he remained still, his feet planted firmly on the stage, as though he were stuck in place.

But his eyes told a different story.

In his eyes, Mary could see that there was no space separating them.

No, in the eyes of Leander Doucet, Mary saw his arms wrapped around her, holding her tight.

Their bodies pressed into one another, their perfume and cologne mingling.

Mary could see herself running her hands up and down his arms and across his broad shoulders before finding his neck. He would respond to her touch in kind, pulling her by the waist even closer against his torso.

And even though she could not explain how, she knew she would be able to feel that he desired her, and that she desired him.

And when the moment was right, she would lean her head upwards, and his mouth would find hers, soft and tender at first, then the fire burning in both of them would transform their embrace into one of passion and impatience.

Mary finally broke the silence with two small words.

"Mr. Doucet," Mary whispered.

"Yes, Miss Taylor."

"Would you like to dance?"

"Why yes, Miss Taylor, nothing would give me more pleasure," Leander responded, extending his hand to Mary.

When Mary looked down, she could see that it trembled.

But it was not fear.

No, Mary knew it was desire.

For it was the same feeling she felt.

She reached out, placing her small hand in his. The sensation of his skin on hers sent an electrifying pulse through her body.

And when he finally stepped forward, placing his other hand on her waist, her entire body quivered at his touch.

They began to dance a slow waltz, led by the sound of the music drifting through from the ballroom to the auditorium.

In a normal waltz, the only contact that was technically necessary was for the dance partners to have their hands clasped, with the gentleman's other hand on the lady's waist, and her hand on his shoulder.

But somehow, and Mary could not explain how, the space that usually lingered between a dance partner had closed. Now as they moved, the bust of Mary's dress skimmed Leander's chest, and the rubbing caused a friction, a sensation Mary had never felt before. Her nipples felt hard and sore, and more than anything she wished Leander's hand would start a slow and steady ascent up from where it clasped her torso tightly towards her chest and cup her breasts firmly.

The thought made Mary blush, her breath disappearing from her lungs.

She tightened the hold of his shoulder, lightly digging her nails through his overcoat and shirt and into his flesh.

Leander responded, spreading his fingers wide across the small of Mary's back and pulling her closer.

So that their torsos were pressed into one another.

The heat from Leander's body sent Mary's heart beating with violent rhythm.

She was afraid and excited all at once. And she knew—if she tilted her chin up, just a little—their lips would meet.

Slowly and purposefully, she moved her gloved hand across his shoulder. When her hand found his neck, she wrapped her fingers around the base.

Leander inhaled sharply, responding to Mary's touch by pressing his body into hers, and with the hand wrapped around her waist, pushing hers into his.

Though he needn't have done it for her, for if he had not, Mary would have done it herself.

The sensation of something warm and hard pressed into the place between Mary's legs, and now it was her turn, her loss of breath so quick she did not have time to catch it.

Mary could not explain what it was, but she knew she desired more, knew that it made that cloying hunger burn so hot, she would do just about anything to satiate it. It was the same feeling she had felt the first time she had met Leander Doucet, only this time, she was certain he felt the same way about her.

The electricity between them heightened and they both lost track of the sound of the distant band, their dancing devolving into a slow swaying. The movement of Leander against her rubbed that place underneath her skirts in a way that was all at once both so satisfying and yet maddening. It teased—mercilessly, and she could feel her body responding, a soreness consuming her.

And Mary had a sneaking suspicion that Leander felt the same, for the more they moved, the harder and larger he seemed to become.

Finally, Mary raised her eyes to meet Leander's, tilting her chin up in that way Elizabeth had once told her would let a man know that a lady desired to be kissed.

And when she looked into Leander's eyes, Mary saw they were burning, like a man on the brink of...Mary was not sure exactly what, but she was sure she understood, for she felt the exact same way.

She was certain, that in that moment, she would do anything to chase that feeling that was just beginning to come alive.

"Mary," he breathed, squeezing her waist tightly.

"Yes, Mr. Doucet," she replied softly, willing his lips to meet hers.

"Please, won't you call me by my name?" he almost pleaded.

Smiling, she allowed the words to form on her lips, feeling them fully before speaking them into existence, quietly but clearly.

Assertively, as though he were hers.

"Leander." Mary exhaled slowly and deliberately.

Leander shuddered, clutching her to him and closing his eyes.

As though he were feeling both immense pleasure and immense pain.

"Mary, we..." He finally opened his eyes. "We should be getting back," he said softly, regretfully, as though the thought made him aggrieved.

Mary was certain she had not heard him properly.

"I said, we should be getting back," Leander repeated, this time with more insistence.

Mary's heart halted, and a sensation of someone kicking her in the chest pressed against her.

"I—" She began to splutter, confused and hurt.

"If someone finds us, it would ruin us both," he explained quietly, bringing their swaying to a halt.

"I see." Anger and embarrassment flashed across Mary's face.

And Father would force him to marry her, and he does not wish for that.

Tears began to well in her eyes and she dropped her arms, letting them go slack next to her body.

"Mary, please, do not be upset," Leander pleaded. "I am not saying this because it is what I desire."

"Is it not?" Mary stared at her shoes.

"No, of course not," Leander said softly, gently taking her chin and raising her face to meet his eyeline. "I would just never wish to put you in a situation where you are compromised and forced to do something you do not wish to do."

"But what if I did wish to do it?"

What exactly, Mary was not sure, but it seemed an unnecessary detail.

"Mary, I respect you too much to put you in that situation."

"But Leander, I want to," Mary insisted. "And I can tell... I am almost certain you do too."

Leander closed his eyes, inhaling deeply.

"Mary, I..." he faltered, his voice fraying. "I cannot."

And then his hand started to move, slowly and methodically it made its way up Mary's back, finally stopping at the nape of her neck. He cradled her, wrapping his fingers around the base of her neck while his thumb caressed her cheek, right below her ear.

Mary closed her eyes, breathing deeply.

This was the moment she had waited for, dreamed about but never allowed herself to believe would actually come true.

And then Leander Doucet placed a kiss, gently and purposefully, on her forehead.

Mary squeezed her eyes tightly, but the tears came anyway, falling down her cheeks in quick streaks.

Leander placed his chin atop her head and wrapped his arms around Mary, holding her as the tears fell. She rested her head on his chest, breathing in his deep musky scent and willing the moment to last forever.

"Mary, we need to get back," he said, louder this time, as though purposefully trying to break the spell that had been cast. "Your sister and cousins will be wondering where you are."

His voice was serious and concerned, and with perhaps the tiniest hint of pleading.

But it was not authoritative.

It was not a command.

"I know." Mary inhaled the scent of him once more before unearthing herself from his chest. "You are right, of course."

He was trying to be responsible.

But would it have been the most dishonorable thing in the world for him to have kissed her?

Yes, she reasoned. It would be.

If he had no intention of marrying her.

"I think it would be best if you made your way back first. And I will follow in a few minutes."

"Very well," Mary nodded, releasing herself from his grasp and taking a step backwards. "How do I look?" she asked, pulling off one of her long white gloves and running a finger under each eyelid to dismiss any remaining tears.

"Beautiful," he sighed, smiling sadly. Almost as though the thought was enough to bring him to pain.

"But not beautiful enough," the words escaped Mary's mouth before she could catch them.

"I sincerely hope you do not truly think that," Leander's response was stern, clearly hurt by her words.

"It is the only explanation that makes sense to me." She was trying to be flippant, trying to hurt him as he had hurt her.

Nay, mortified her.

"Mary, please. This is hard enough, please do not make it worse by saying such unspeakable things."

"But why is it so hard?" Mary asked, her voice rising as all the emotions came rushing out of her at once: frustration, anger, and confusion, all battling for prominence and being beaten by embarrassment. "Is it so hard to go to my father, or even my brother, and state your intentions and ask for their blessing?

"You know they would gladly welcome you into our family. And if those were your intentions, then a kiss would not matter in the slightest! It would make no difference—it would just be the first of many."

"A kiss, Mary, can lead to other things—"

"Don't," Mary interrupted, raising a hand to silence him. "It is only hard because you desire to kiss me, and perhaps more, but you do not desire to marry me. And you know that you cannot compromise the sister of your business partner, let alone the daughter of William Taylor!" She was now nearly shouting, her face red with fury.

"Mary, please," Leander quickly strode towards her, begging her to lower her voice. "Someone might hear."

"Answer me, Mr. Doucet," Mary's voice shook, quivering as she held back further tears.

"Mary, it is not that simple."

"Then help me to understand. Am I so young and foolish that I do not understand the difference between lust and love?"

"No," Leander responded firmly. "You are not."

"Then why, Leander? What makes it so hard?"

"Mary, I," he tried to speak but no words came out.

"I am sorry," he finally managed, staring at his feet. "But I cannot."

"Very well," Mary nodded curtly. "Good day to you, Mr. Doucet."

And with that she turned and walked out of the auditorium.

And though she wished to, with every fiber of her being, she refused to allow herself to look back.

# Chapter XV

Over the following week, Mary tried her best to keep herself busy. She steered clear of Madame Lavigne's salon, fearing she might encounter Leander, but instead threw herself into the latest charity project Amelié and Mrs. Lambert had concocted, which was, very creatively, knitting scarves for the less fortunate.

Mary's questioning as to whether the less fortunate required scarves at the brink of summer fell on deaf ears. So she sat with the other ladies and knitted, or at least tried to, which did apparently count for something from the perspective of gaining the respect of the ladies. Mary's scarves began neatly enough but quickly devolved into holey messes, growing in width as her distracted mind loosened the stitches. Still, she clacked her needles like her life depended on it.

And in a sense, it felt as though it did.

The constant motion kept her hands busy, even as her mind raced.

What in the world did Leander Doucet mean when he said:

*I cannot.*

The question gnawed at her, burrowing a hole deep in her chest that left her feeling hollow.

She had heard from her brother Charles that Manuel Rivera had called at the bank, asking after her.

"He is a very eligible gentleman from a good family." Charles eyed his sister over tea in the Defour parlor. "And he seems very taken with you. It would be a great match, Mary."

"Thank you for your insights, brother." Mary tried to seem warm, feigning a soft smile over her own cup. "I will keep it in mind."

"Do, and of course, there is no need to rush into things," Charles said a bit awkwardly. Mary could tell that he found his role as the de facto head of the family while their parents were so far away uncomfortable.

At least, when it came to feminine matters and those of the heart.

"But then again, you do not want to keep him waiting too long, lest your indecisiveness is taken for disinterest," he advised.

Elizabeth rolled her eyes in exasperation.

"Was there something amusing in my words?" Charles asked cooly.

"In a sense," Elizabeth chirped. "You place so much pressure on her, Charles. She has not even received a proposal yet!"

"Yes, but when she does, I think it best that she has considered these things beforehand. It is how responsible adults plan their lives, Elizabeth," he declared with a curt tone. "They have a plan—they do not just make it up as they go along."

"It does not feel as though we are speaking about our little sister anymore," Elizabeth said.

"We were—until just now. But you have a gift for turning things back to yourself."

"I beg your—"

"Thank you both for your suggestions and inputs," Mary spoke above them both, placing her teacup down with a purposeful clatter. "I appreciate the insights from all of my siblings. Now, if you will permit me, I believe I need to lie down for a bit," Mary excused herself, retiring to the shared bedroom.

When Mary awoke a few hours later, an invitation and a small package awaited her, left on her night stand.

The invitation was addressed to her and Elizabeth from Mr. Rivera, who was holding his annual garden party at the family plantation to mark the beginning of summer.

Turning to the package, Mary carefully pulled the brown string, unfolding the object from its paper.

Inside was a book of works by an author Mary had never heard of before—a man by the name of Alexander Pope.

Inside the carriage the Taylor brood made the quarter of a day's journey from New Orleans to the Rivera Plantation.

"Rice fields are often flooded," Charles offered to no one in particular as he peered out the window of the carriage, taking note of the deep wells of water. "This is done because rice paddies can still grow in water, and it means weeds are less likely to grow."

Mary nodded in agreement. The entire process of planting, cultivating, and harvesting rice had always been of interest to her.

"How laborious," Elizabeth thought aloud, "to flood an area and later have to drain it, just to flood it again."

"Someone has to do it. Rice is an enormous export, especially to the North."

"It is always very amusing to me how the North looks down on us Southerners and assumes were all uneducated and lawless, but they're not too good to buy our production."

"Well, they lack the climate to grow most of what we do," Mary offered, inspecting the large puddles. "Especially for rice. It needs to be kept fairly warm, including at night."

When the carriage finally pulled up to the Rivera household, the trio climbed out of the carriage as gracefully as they could manage, stretching limbs and rubbing backs as discreetly as possible.

"Mr. Taylor," Mr. Rivera welcomed them from where he stood out front to await his guests, clasping Charles's hand warmly. "It is a pleasure to see you again. We are so honored you made what I know is a long and arduous journey."

"Please, Mr. Rivera, Mr. Taylor is my father," Charles deferred to Mr. Rivera's seniority. "And it was our pleasure, we were honored to have received your invitation."

"Of course, Charles, we hold your family in the highest esteem, as I hope you know."

"We do, sir, and feel the same. And you may remember my sisters." Charles motioned towards the girls.

"Of course, Miss Elizabeth and Miss Mary." Mr. Rivera kissed both their hands. "A pleasure."

"Thank you so much for your kind invitation." Mary smiled at Mr. Rivera, peering up at him from under her parasol. "We are so looking forward to the day."

"As are we. And look how pretty you both look. I must remind you that this is meant to be a fun occasion, and I do sincerely hope you will try your best not to break the hearts of every man inside."

"Well, we can certainly try our best, Mr. Rivera, but unfortunately we cannot make any promises." Elizabeth winked, twirling her parasol that rested on her shoulder in playful flirtation.

"Ah, well, the only thing anyone can ask you to do in life is try," Mr. Rivera resigned with a sigh, his eyes sparkling with the mischief of coy words.

"I would love, Mr. Rivera, to see your orchards. I have such wonderful memories of them as a girl."

"Of course, Miss Mary, we will make sure it is arranged."

The festivities had been set up around the back of the house, where the family garden was kept and frequented. When the Taylors arrived, a large crowd had already gathered, men dressed in their Sunday best, colorful ties of lilac, yellow, and lighter shades of blue and green, signalling their desire for the warmer months. Similarly, the ladies wore dresses of bright floral colors, some embroidered with flowers and other delicate designs that beckoned summer. Those who were incredibly prepared held parasols which matched their dresses, tucked on their shoulders and held in place with small lace gloved hands.

Mary herself wore a dress of light seafoam green, stitched with pretty white flowers freckled on the skirt and a white sash that cinched her waist. Regrettably, her parasol was only white, so lacked the coordination of some of the other ladies in attendance.

But thankfully these trivial details rarely flustered Mary, for she did not think that the color of a parasol would make the difference between her finding herself a happily wedded woman or a spinster.

No, instead she scanned the crowd, looking for Manuel Rivera.

She had not seen him since the charity ball, when she had disappeared for an extensive amount of time only to resurface with that greatest of excuses that no gentleman could argue with, even those with the most quizzical of gazes.

*I fear I am not feeling very well.*

It was adequately ambiguous such that it could relate to anything, and most gentleman, for fear of embarrassing a lady by accidentally asking after something which might be linked to a certain—ahem—womanly process, let this vagueness go.

A lady's declaration of ill-health also immediately raised concern in a gentleman, and in doing so usually transitioned him into the role of caretaker.

Or protector, if you will.

All men desired to feel like a hero, and one of the simplest ways of doing so was to find a lady in distress and assist her.

And while Mary felt relief as Manuel Rivera fawned over her instead of undertaking his own version of the Spanish Inquisition, asking if he should perhaps find her cousins or take her home in his family's carriage, she also felt incredible guilt.

She had excused herself and found Michel, who had the driver escort her home.

Mary had wrestled with the events of that evening many times over, but even more confusing than her exchange with both Manuel and Leander were the feelings the exchanges left her to untangle.

It was clear to Mary that Manuel Rivera, with the right encouragement, would likely propose to her.

What was less clear was whether it would be a marriage of equals.

She thought back to their conversations and exchanges, always pleasant and polite, and most of all flattering.

But was that enough to last a lifetime?

Perhaps it would have to be.

For Leander, on the other hand, had—

No, she halted her thoughts before they could start down that road again.

It was clear Leander Doucet, for whatever his feelings may be, had no intention of marrying her.

And besides, she thought to herself, looking down at the small volume clutched in her gloved hands, Manuel had sent this with her invitation.

Mary did not exactly know why, she had even stayed up the entire night after receiving it, reading by candlelight into the small hours of the morning in search of the reason, maybe a hidden parable or truth buried in the text.

But she could not find it.

She had decided that it probably represented both a token and an apology. A gift, for Manuel knew well of her love of reading, and an indication that he did care about her opinions, and was even seeking them.

She must find Manuel and thank him. And find out what, exactly, it was about Alexander Pope that made him send this to her as a gift.

For despite her feelings at the charity ball, a lady should not overlook a gift from a gentleman suitor, especially one of such a thoughtful nature.

The party was abuzz with familiar faces—Alexander and Archibald Sinclair were in attendance. She did wonder what their connection with the Riveras was as she exchanged pleasantries with both of them warmly.

Similarly, Thomas and John Walker were also both there. John had, unsurprisingly, attached himself to the side of Elizabeth and did not give any indication of planning to let go. He tended to her like a puppy, asking if she required anything: a drink, some food, a fan.

"If you must stand here, you can hold this." Elizabeth thrust her parasol towards him. While fearless when it came to the sun, even Elizabeth was not foolish enough to flirt with the climate of a state she did not know, especially now that the sun was out for many hours of the day.

Elizabeth was, of course, hoping it would be a degrading enough proposition that he would refuse, but on the contrary, John Walker's face lit up and he clutched the parasol proudly, holding it aloft with an excited reverence.

"It is fascinating to me how that man does not mind being treated like a servant," Charles sighed, watching the scene from where he and Mary stood.

"I suppose love can make even the most levelheaded men into fools. And I am not certain whether the Walkers are level-headed in the first place."

A sideways smile peaked out of Charles's mouth.

"They are a very respectable family, but they do have some...regrettable tendencies," he finished vaguely.

"Yes, that is a good way of putting it."

They stood for another moment longer, taking in the colorful scene before them.

"I do know, you know," Charles finally said softly. "And I hope you know I do not approve."

Mary's breath caught in her throat, the hand holding her parasol tightening.

"Know about what, dear brother?" she asked, trying to keep her voice steady.

Did he know about her and Leander? Was this the reason Leander had insisted over and over again with those two maddening words:

*I cannot.*

"About Mr. Walker, and the manner in which he spoke of you."

Oh.

"Why did you not tell me?"

"Because it was embarrassing," Mary admitted softly. "And it would not have changed anything. The words were already said, even if they were never meant for my consumption."

"You handle yourself very well around them," Charles nodded approvingly. "Like a lady."

"Thank you, brother."

"I'm just sorry you had to experience that on your big day, and had to learn so quickly that sometimes people are bound to actions based on their circumstances."

"I understand," Mary managed through squeezed lips.

Of course, she understood. A family with no money but a good name and four children of marriageable age would find themselves tactically making the most of what they had to work with.

It was survival. It was not nice, but it was part of the game of life.

"Though that does not mean he had to say what he said about me. A gentleman should be judged by how he handles himself in a situation wrought with pressure."

"I agree, on both accounts."

"Brother, Manuel Rivera told me the most interesting thing the other day. He told me their family ships their rice to Charleston for export."

"Ha, yes, they do," Charles could not help but roll his eyes. "It feels very ludicrous from where we are standing, I know. But, this is why the Taylors keep themselves out of feuds—not only does hate rot the heart, but it is bad for business."

"Indeed," Mary concurred, relieved that Charles found the absurdity in it as well. "I mean, Savannah is much closer, why do they not ship from there if they cannot bear to send from New Orleans?"

"Dear sister, I know." Charles raised a hand to his head and rubbed it wearily. "I think we cannot try to make sense of it because it is an action born of emotion, not rationality."

"You are right, of course." Mary looked up at her brother. She had missed these conversations with him. They were similar to the ones she would have with her father.

And another man who shall remain nameless.

"I was also not aware that our hosts and the Walkers were such good friends," Mary offered, hoping Charles would bite.

"Well, yes, they became natural allies overtime when the plantation elite families fractured. The Riveras sent their goods through the Walkers' ports, and in return the Riveras helped the Walkers secure export to Spanish controlled regions of the colonies and even Europe.

"Now however, with indigo prices plummeting, the relationship is straining, at least a little, because the prices the Riveras' contacts were willing to pay before have moved as the value of the crop has declined."

Mary nodded her understanding.

"And despite that the Walkers and Sinclairs are known as having a healthy rivalry between themselves," Mary ventured. "And yet they are both here."

"Yes, well, after our bank financed the Sinclairs' movement into cotton, they are spending more time in New Orleans. They are a prominent family, and the Riveras are smarter than to snub them outright. Plus, they feel the pressure of their straining ally-ship with the Walkers, and need to be prepared with options, in case the need arises to change ports of export."

"To Savannah," Mary understood.

"Yes. Mary," Charles turned towards his sister seriously. "It is important to stay informed, but remain uninvolved in these affairs, for they are—"

"Bad for business, I know, brother. Then again, if I were Edward," Mary threw Charles a playful side-eye smile, "I would say that these are the types of matters a gentleman should be weighing in on, for they have to do with honor."

"And thank goodness you are not Edward." Charles shook his head. "He sees an opportunity to display his honor in almost every situation, and that will be his downfall. He is too emotional and not discerning enough."

Mary considered this, chewing it over in her mind. She had always viewed Edward as something of a romantic—a hot-head at times, no doubt, but also someone who went to bed every night satisfied, knowing he had lived and breathed his moral code.

Her thoughts of Edward instilling in her a momentary bravery, Mary mused on a question that she had dared not ask until this moment: what would Charles have thought if he had seen her and Leander at the charity ball? She could imagine the shock on her brother's face if he had walked in to find his youngest sister and business partner pressed into one another and staring into each other's eyes.

Leander was right; it would have been scandalous. Shame at the very thought of the idea washed over her. And perhaps out of respect for Charles, he did not wish to risk venturing down a path that would undoubtedly generate scandal.

But he could have gone to Charles. Or to her father, or even to Henri Defour as her guardian in New Orleans. It was not uncommon for a gentleman to find himself smitten with the sister of a friend. In fact, it was most common, and made practical sense, as the gentleman might have spent more time around the family than he might otherwise.

No, there was no rational reason for Leander Doucet to insist so vehemently *I cannot* unless he did not wish to marry her.

*Enough*, Mary thought harshly, pushing back down the tears that began to bubble underneath her eyelids. If she cried in front of Charles, she would have an awful lot of explaining to do.

As the afternoon petered on, Mary found herself making her way through the garden and towards the orchards. She had managed to dodge Thomas Walker, who was still chasing a wealthy mouse to marry. Thankfully, Charles swooped in with a conversation about horses before it dragged on.

She had not however been able to find Manuel Rivera. She had even asked Mr. Rivera, who had confirmed his son was expected soon.

So Mary took off towards the orchards, hoping by the time she came back, Manuel would have appeared.

The orchards were not far from the house, and wandering through them, Mary could remember playing hide and seek with the Riveras when they were all children. They would eat oranges and suck on lemons until their tummies hurt, returning back to the main house at dusk with sticky fingers and having utterly ruined their appetites.

Mary peered up at the trees, admiring the bright bursts of orange against the green bushy leaves. Perhaps it was the nostalgia of that sweet citrus smell that filled the orchard, but Mary found herself desiring one of those oranges. Locating the lowest branch she could, she extended her arm, but she could not reach. Pressing her toes into the earth, she tried to stand on her tiptoes but was much too short to even begin to reach one.

Perhaps if she jumped, she thought, staring up at the piece of fruit. But even with a running start, Mary was not convinced she stood a chance of reaching it.

"Allow me."

Startled, Mary jumped backwards, crashing into the body that had crept up behind her.

"Pardon me, Miss Taylor," Leander caught her with his chest, grabbing her arms to steady her. "I do have a terrible habit of startling you, though I promise it is not my intent."

"Mr. Doucet," Mary responded over her shoulder, declining to give him her full attention by turning around. "You possess the tread of a cat."

"Ha, thank you, Miss Taylor," he grinned, extending his arm up and easily plucking the fruit which had caused Mary so much trouble. "My mother ensured I knew how to dance from a young age, which I believe contributed to my light step."

His arm wrapped around her body as he presented her with the orange, held between his thumb and forefinger.

Mary had intended for her next words to come out harshly. She had told herself that when next face to face with Leander Doucet, she would be polite, but frigid. She would certainly not allow herself to be sucked into his seductive spell, especially considering she knew that there was no future with him.

But at his voice, his smile, his smell, and the feel of her back against his chest, the coldness dissipated.

"Yes, Mr. Doucet, I am aware of your proficiency on the dance floor," Mary said, carefully taking the orange and turning around to face him. "Thank you."

"My pleasure," Leander responded with a slight bow of his head.

"Have you just arrived?"

"Oh, no, I was inside playing cards with some of the other gentlemen. But I regret to say that once your sister found us, she cleaned me out—I left utterly disgraced and completely ruined!"

"That sounds like Elizabeth." For despite the coaching of her mother, Elizabeth resolutely refused to purposefully lose at anything.

Especially to a man.

And especially when money was at stake.

She was, to put it politely, a bit of a hustler, for who could resist when she threw on her ditzy charm, flapping her eyelashes furiously and asking the boys if they would let her play too. They always obliged, only to find their pockets empty by the end of the evening.

It was maddening to lose a game of cards on any day of the week, but it was unforgivably embarrassing to lose to a lady, especially a lady of such beauty.

But somehow Mary was sure that Leander did not mind in the slightest that he had lost the contents of his wallet to Elizabeth Taylor.

In fact, he seemed utterly amused by the entire affair.

"Ah, I see you received my gift." He gestured towards the book in her hand. "And what did you make of Mr. Pope?"

"I—your gift?"

"Yes, unless someone else has also gifted you a copy of my favorite author's collections. Or perhaps has taken credit for it?" His smile was playful, wily even.

"It arrived with another piece of mail, so I was not certain," Mary tried to explain. "Alexander Pope is your favorite author?"

"Yes, at Madame Lavigne's you had asked after my favorite author, but we had not had time to finish the conversation."

"Of all the great French thinkers, your favorite author is—"

"An Englishman, I know." Leander shook his head in mock horror. "I assure you, Miss Taylor, that the irony is not lost on me either."

Mary smiled at his humor.

"Well, I personally approve immensely of your favorite author being an Englishman."

"As I knew you would. I had hoped it would please you. I am glad it has."

Their eyes met, and the feelings from the charity ball came rushing back, filling the space between them.

"Thank you, Mr. Doucet, for the gift. It is very kind," Mary broke his gaze and looked back down at the contents of her hands. "And for the orange. I have found myself incredibly indebted to you, and I am afraid I am going to have to impose on your generosity at least once more, in the hope you can help me with something."

"Of course, Miss Mary," Leander breathed.

"Anything.

"I would do anything for you."

"Well then sir, I would be much obliged if you would be so kind as to help me with the meaning of this." She held the book up in her hand. "Because, in most circumstances, a lady would interpret such a gift as a token of affection."

"Your interpretation is correct, Miss Mary."

At his words, Mary looked up at him, meeting his gaze with eyes ablaze.

"But tokens of affection, sir, are usually delivered with intention. Is this gift one of intention?"

"Miss Mary, it is not that simple. I have matters I must attend to before I could be in a position to make formal declarations of my intentions."

"Please Leander, just explain to me what is going on." Mary closed her eyes wearily, his words running through her mind.

Before he could be in a position—

"Do you speak in hypotheticals purposefully?"

"Yes and no," he confessed. "Miss Mary, as I said, there are family matters I must attend to before I could be in a position to make formal declarations of my intentions."

"I see." Mary squinted her eyes together in concentration. "And once these matters are attended to, will you be making your intentions known?"

"It is not that simple."

"Well sir, I am certain if you explain it, I will be able to grasp the concept."

"I cannot, Miss Mary, for—"

"Miss Mary!" a voice called. Peeking over Leander's shoulder, Mary saw Manuel Rivera charging towards the pair of them.

"Manuel," Mary greeted him as energetically as she could manage.

It seemed altogether both the best and worst time for his interruption.

"You look absolutely stunning today," Manuel gushed, dipping into a low bow and kissing her hand.

"Thank you, Manuel. You look positively debonair yourself," Mary responded in kind, keeping her eyes firmly fixed on him.

If Leander was going to be maddeningly elusive, she would happily show him that she was not a lady devoid of options.

She *could* find herself a husband this season if she so desired.

"I confess, Manuel, you have caught me red-handed." She held up the orange.

"Ah, fruit theft," he nodded in mock sincerity. "A very serious crime. Punishable by obligatory accompaniment on a stroll through the rest of the orchard," Manuel explained with a playful gravity.

"Oh my," Mary brought a hand to her chest. "A heavy sentence, but I suppose not unfair."

"Shall we?" Manuel asked, offering her his arm.

"Thank you." Mary accepted it, prettily weaving her gloved arm through his and placing her hand atop his forearm.

"Oh, and Mr. Doucet, the men have decided to have a target match after lunch. Do come join if you wish," Manual smiled over his shoulder as he and Mary made their way deeper into the orchard. "That is, if you are feeling brave."

A target match was a favorite pastime of any country outing, equally enjoyed by both the gentleman and the ladies, for the former obtained an opportunity to showcase their marksmanship and masculine prowess, and the ladies delighted in watching the men compete with one another. If amongst the most upstanding of gentlemen, the competitors would remain cordial, and any man unhappy with his outcome had the good nature to bury his pride, conscious to not let his ill luck ruin the day for everyone else. But if the gentlemen in question did not possess such level-headed coolness, a target match could quickly devolve into heated words which could quickly escalate to a quarrel, which carried the potentiality of an all-out brawl, with those most important of Southern virtues at stake: pride and honor.

And while no one would say it, as the onlookers sipped their lemonade or afternoon tea, they all hoped, deep down, for the latter outcome. For who in their right mind would not wish to see a group of young Southern gentlemen argue over their assumed honor?

As the targets were set out—bales of hay with red circles painted on them—the participants lined up and the ladies crowded around. There were a number of men Mary knew participating: Manuel Rivera, of course, and his younger brother Miguel, both the Sinclair brothers in attendance, Alexander and Archibald, Thomas and John Walker, Leander Doucet, and Charles Taylor.

Mary gave her brother a sad smile, knowing this was the bottom on a long list of things Charles preferred to spend his time doing. It was the type of occasion where Mary knew he wished for the presence of their brother Edward, who would happily represent the Taylor family.

And would undoubtedly do a better job than Charles was going to.

He was an adequate shot, Mary reminded herself, but looking at the lineup of other men it was clear that adequate was not going to be enough.

It was common for Southern men to tend towards one of two categories: that of scholar or horseman. There was, of course, overlap, and many Southern men were both educated and proficient in such traditional manly pursuits as horses and guns. But Charles Taylor was a scholar and a businessman who had muddled through shooting lessons as a child because he knew it was necessary for a Southern gentleman to know how to shoot.

Much in the same way that Mary knitted scarves for the less fortunate because it was something she knew she ought to do.

"I wish Edward were here." Elizabeth appeared at Mary's side. "Charles is going to be the first one out."

"Do not be so pessimistic," Mary rebuffed her sister, though not entirely convinced herself. "I am sure he will stand up fine."

"Look at that lineup. Most of those men are country boys if God ever made one."

"Shush," Mary dismissed, though she knew Elizabeth was likely right. Thankfully, it did not matter one bit to Mary whether her brother went out first or second to last (for she knew he would not win, so did not even entertain this as an option). But clearly to Elizabeth, the Taylors not being knocked out in the first round was a point of honor.

"Though I don't know about his business partner," Elizabeth wondered aloud. "Do you think Mr. Doucet knows how to handle a gun?"

"How would I know?" Mary asked, more defensively than was entirely necessary.

"I was simply asking." Elizabeth gave her sister a suspicious look before turning her attention back to the event.

The rules were simple—all men took a turn shooting at the target, the goal of which was to hit the small circle in the center. The participant whose shot was furthest away after everyone had gone did not advance to the next round. The cycle would continue until a winner was found.

Manuel Rivera, as the eldest Rivera participating and the son of the host, went first. He calmly shrugged out of his brown overcoat, and handing it to a nearby servant he picked up the rifle, hoisting it to his shoulder in one quick movement. The crowd fell silent as he aimed and pulled the trigger. A clean shot, not more than a few inches from the bullseye.

The crowd clapped in impressed respect.

Next went the younger Rivera, who, while not quite as competent as his older brother, was more than adequate.

Archibald Sinclair made a show of not only removing his overcoat, but rolling up the sleeves of his cream cotton shirt to his elbows. His strong forearms flexed as he raised the rifle and swiftly fired with the confidence of a man who knew his mark.

All the while, a pipe stuck from the corner of his mouth. Lowering the weapon, he took a puff and then turned, flashing a grin before handing the rifle to his brother.

Alexander's shot was nearly on par with Manuel Rivera's, and the crowd roared, for who did not desire a close competition?

And, of course, the added thrill of a potential spectacle.

Both Thomas and John Walker were impressive shots. John did not even remove his overcoat, so sure was he in his abilities, even when his movement was impaired.

And he was right to be confident, for his shot beat Manuel Rivera's, much to the delight of the crowd, who clapped heartily.

On seeing John's shot had beat his own, Manuel tried to hide his grimace by taking a long sip of his whisky, kissing his teeth with his tongue in irritation.

When it was Charles's turn, he stepped forward stoically, an obvious dread in his movements as he slipped out of his coat and pushed the sweat from his brow up and into his hair. He squinted at the targets, and raising the rifle to his shoulder, he squeezed the trigger, his body flinching slightly at the rifle's blowback.

It was not a horrible shot, Mary reasoned, ignoring the comments Elizabeth muttered under her breath. He had made it onto the board and into the first ring, so there was nothing to be too heinously embarrassed over.

Last was Leander, who stepped up with a carelessness that he wanted on display—as though he wished for the crowd, and his hosts, to know that this event was of no consequence to him. Taking off his jacket, Leander took one more sip of his drink before accepting the rifle. He shot quickly, handing the rifle back to the servant without even taking a moment to judge the accuracy of his shot.

It was only marginally better than Charles's, Mary noted. This meant that Charles would not be progressing past the first round (which she was certain was a blessing for her poor brother), but also that he had not been the obvious loser, for the shots were so close, Mr. Rivera had had to call someone else over to help judge which gentleman had gotten off the better shot.

"Oh, Mr. Doucet, you are clearly going to be heavy competition," Manuel goaded over the rim of his glass.

Leander levied a menacing stare at his host's son that he held for just a moment too long.

Despite his unimpressive start, once Charles had been removed from the competition, Leander Doucet returned for the following rounds with a vengeance. The crowd gasped when his second shot was so close to John Walker's, a second and third judge were forced to come inspect who was closer to the center.

Slowly, the other gentlemen began falling out of the competition—Archibald Sinclair was the next to follow after Charles, then Miguel Rivera and Thomas Walker.

In a heated round, Alexander Sinclair was booted by Manuel Rivera by nothing more than a hair of difference, so slight that Mr. Rivera had called Alexander's brother Archibald to weigh in on the validity of his judgment, to ensure that no ill will or accusations of foul play would ensue.

This left Manuel Rivera, Leander Doucet, and John Walker as the final contestants.

By this point in the day, the afternoon sun was beating down on all the guests. The women stood sheltered under their parasols, but the men, especially the three contestants, stood baking underneath the bright sun. All three men had lost their jackets by this point, and their sleeves had been rolled up to their biceps.

Manuel Rivera stepped up, squinting he raised the rifle to his shoulder and got off a brilliant shot a mere inch from the centre bull's eyes.

John Walker accepted the rifle from him, patting him on the back with the confidence of a man who knows he has the upper hand. Beads of sweat dripped off John's face, but when he raised the rifle and pulled the trigger the bullet pierced the bullseye dead in the center.

The crowd exploded in cheers, delighted by the first bullseye of the afternoon.

As Leander approached the designated shooting line Mary tried not to stare at him—the veins protruding from his forearms in the heat or the bulge of his bicep as he took hold of the rifle, the sweat glistening off his skin.

When Leander pulled the trigger, the crowd leaned forward in anticipation. The shot was close, very close, to Manuel Rivera's.

Mr. Rivera walked over to the target, leaning close to inspect the bullet hole. When he looked back up, his face appeared puzzled and perhaps slightly amused as he announced that Leander's shot had hit the exact same point as Manuel's.

The crowd laughed, delighted with this unexpected outcome.

"In that case, let us go again," Manuel declared, taking the rifle from Leander.

But when both men had gone again, the same thing appeared to have happened—Leander's shot hit exactly in the same place as Manuel's.

"Ha, what are the chances?" Leander smirked, handing the rifle back to Manuel.

"Indeed, very fine shooting, Mr. Doucet," Manuel said, forcing a smile that didn't quite reach his eyes.

And when it happened a third time, the crowd began to buzz with the implications—it was becoming clear that this was no accident. Leander Doucet was purposefully hitting Manuel Rivera's marks, though why he would antagonize his host in such a way, the crowd could only theorize.

It was the kind of drama Southern guests could only hope for.

"What in the world is he doing?" Charles asked under his breath, watching the scene with wide eyes. It was, of course, completely ungentlemanly for Leander to be so provocative.

A lump formed in Mary's throat as she watched the two men line up again.

And again.

This wasn't about a bullseye anymore. This was about proving something. And the target wasn't the hay—it was one another.

What started as excited entertainment in the crowd quickly morphed into a tense feeling of unease as the tempers of both men began to rise. Manuel began insisting Leander go first, with Leander feigning offense at the suggestion that he would break with social decorum in allowing anyone other than the representative of his host to go first.

"Please sir, I am certain you do not mean to offend my good upbringing with such a suggestion," Leander quaffed, reaching for his glass of whisky and bringing the cold cup to his lips.

"I do not," Manuel answered stiffly. "But I do mean to put an end to this nonsense."

"Excuse me, sir?" Leander lowered his glass. "I am sure I do not know what you mean."

"Oh, I am sure you do," Manuel responded, one of his hands clenching into a fist at his side. "You would be much more a gentleman to win gracefully."

"Sir, I fear we have been standing in the sun too long." Leander took a sip of his glass before slamming it down on the small table the servants had brought out for their drinks. "For I am almost certain I just heard you accuse me of not being a gentleman."

"You are right, sir, in that you have been out in the sun too long, for I did not accuse you of not being a gentleman, I accused you of acting in an ungentlemanly way."

"Is that so?" Leander asked through clenched teeth. "It is much easier to say such things when one is holding a weapon." Leander gestured towards the rifle at Manuel's side. "But pray sir, put it down, or get me one of my own so we are evenly matched, and we can settle this—"

Before Leander could finish, John Walker stepped between the two men, and in one swift motion, yanked the rifle from Manuel Rivera's hand. Raising it to his shoulder, he released the contents of the barrel into the target, hitting a bullseye every time.

"There, it is finished." Mr. Rivera stepped forward, accepting the rifle from John. "John Walker is the clear victor of the day."

"Thank you, Mr. Rivera. You are such a generous host," John bowed to him gallantly. "And if I may, sir, I would like to dedicate this victory to the most beautiful lady here.

"Miss Taylor," John announced, gesturing with his hand.

"What?!" Both Manuel and Leander gawked, turning their heads in unison.

"As in, the elder Miss Taylor," John clarified.

The crowd clapped, relieved for the event to have come to a peaceful end.

Elizabeth rolled her eyes in annoyance.

"Thank you, gentleman. You are both very worthy opponents," John confirmed, holding a hand out to Manuel and then Leander, who both shook it, all the while staring daggers at one another.

"Now you two," Mr. Rivera said gruffly. "Shake hands." Both men eyed one another wearily, neither wanting to be the first to extend an offering of peace.

"For goodness' sake," Charles huffed before striding towards the men. He grabbed Leander by the arm, and while Mary could not hear what he was saying, she could see he was angry, fuming even, speaking furiously and sternly. The hardness in Leander's eyes slowly softened and was replaced by the shame of his behavior, as articulated by his business partner.

Finally, Leander held up a hand, gesturing for Charles that he could cease, and turned back to Manuel with his hand outstretched.

"I humbly ask you to forgive my poor behavior, Mr. Rivera," Leander said stoically. "I confess that competition gets the better of me—one of my many shortcomings."

"There is nothing to forgive, Mr. Doucet." Manuel met his hand and clasped it. "We are cut from the same cloth, for I too lose myself in the heat of a competitive moment."

Mr. Rivera looked relieved, beckoning Manuel inside to clean himself up. As though on cue, the conversation of the audience exploded as the participants dispersed.

"That was a close one," Mary heard someone comment, though she was not sure if they said it with relief or disappointment.

"Anyone who lets Southern men compete with firearms, in the heat, after whiskey—," one guest shook their head. "It's all fun and games until someone pulls a pistol."

Or worse, makes a scene.

# Chapter XVI

For nearly two weeks afterwards, New Orleans was abuzz with talk of the scene at the Riveras' garden party. Those who were not there asked everyone they knew to recount any series of events they had heard from actual eye witnesses, and those who were there elaborated their tales—innocently, at first, but soon outrageously, as was often the case when one found themselves in a position of such gossip-inducing authority as to be the owner of a firsthand account.

In Mary's opinion, perhaps the gentleman most flustered by the entire event was her brother Charles, who it appeared could not make sense of his partner's poor behavior. He was clearly embarrassed Leander had stooped to such a level of pageantry designed to emphasize his masculine prowess. And if this was not bad enough, the victim of his displays was their host's son!

What Mary did not know was that Taylor Mutual Fund was in the process of courting Mr. Rivera as a client. He had, on more than one occasion, expressed an interest in expanding his plantation. Charles had planted the seed of re-mortgaging the Rivera plantation or borrowing the money from their bank and using their plantation as collateral for the funds.

There were two primary obstacles, so far as Charles could see. Number one, it was no secret that Henri Defour was an investor in the Taylor Mutual Fund, and while Mr. Rivera was too well bred to speak publicly about the family's feud, he would balk at even the indication that he was lining Henri Defour's pockets; and number two, he had a general distrust of anything that he could not see with his eyes and touch with his fingers, unless of course, it had to do with the Lord. And unfortunately for Charles Taylor, Juan Rivera was certain that banks, with their numerous financial instruments, had nothing to do with the good Lord.

But neither of these obstacles had seemed insurmountable, at least, not to Charles. Charles knew the Rivera family and respected them deeply. They were not only educated, but possessed good sense (when not blinded by slights of the past, that is), and he was certain he had begun winning Mr. Rivera round to the concept, even if it did mean trusting his assets to a Virginian of English heritage and a French Alabamian.

That was, of course, until said French Alabamian had humiliated his son in their own home.

Honestly, the shame by association brought color to Charles's cheeks every time he thought of it.

Leander, for his part, was fortunate that the Riveras were the type of people who usually allowed cooler heads to prevail.

He was equally fortunate that John Walker had been wise and gracious enough to shut down the situation before it escalated further.

No, Mary could have guessed at Charles's feelings of disgrace, but she was not aware of the courting of Mr. Rivera for his business.

Which was why she was surprised as she stood silently in the doorway of the bank, hearing from Charles's office as he berated Leander for his foolishness and short-sightedness. Leander took the verbal beating as well as one could. He did not once bring up the fact that Manuel had been the original provoker, or that he had performed so poorly on the first round to spare Charles the embarrassment of being the worst in the group by a long shot.

No, instead he acknowledged Charles's words, apologized profusely, and promised that he would make things right between themselves and the Riveras at the upcoming races.

"I will purposefully lose respectable amounts of money to them," Leander promised.

"Do," Charles responded firmly. "But in a discreet way, so that they do not catch on and take even further offense."

"Hello, Taylor Mutual Fund, I am looking for Charles Taylor," Mary announced loudly, opening the already shut door a small crack so that she could dramatically close it again.

"Mary." Charles burst from his office in a flurry. "We were not expecting you! Are you in town by yourself?"

"No, Elizabeth is next door at the seamstress, but I thought I would pop in and say hello."

"At the seamstress?" Charles asked, clearly exasperated by the news. "Again?!" Elizabeth Taylor had the most maddening ability to spend through her allowance at an alarming rate and then have the audacity to come demand more.

When this well had dried, she had begun requesting the bills be sent to Charles directly.

Charles shook his head, reaching for his hat off the hook near the door. "I will be back in a moment, Mary. Leander is just in there." He gestured towards his office. "I will not be a moment," he promised again, disappearing through the door, and due to his annoyance with his other sister, slamming it harder than was technically necessary.

Mary grinned, the notion that Charles was going to require only a moment to shut down one of Elizabeth's unnecessary shopping sprees proving quite amusing.

Inside Charles's office, Mary heard Leander stirring, and she quickly looked down and ran a smoothing hand over her dress. The weather had warmed to such the extent that an overcoat would be far too hot, especially under the New Orleans sun.

"Miss Taylor." Leander appeared at the doorway, smiling warmly. "I trust you heard all of that exchange?"

"More than I would have admitted had I not been asked directly," Mary confessed. "If you had been a character in one of the classics you so like to criticize, you would have found your behavior most disappointing." Leander chuckled, amused by her answer.

"Leander, what were you thinking?"

"Yes. It was...regretful behavior," Leander admitted. "I blame the drink, the sun, and the way men become when they are competing with one another, especially if that competition involves horses or guns."

Mary stared at him, eyes narrowed, attempting to interrogate with her view.

"Is that all?" she asked quietly, looking down at her hands.

"What do you mean?"

"I mean, did you and Manuel Rivera end up in such a situation because of the heat, the sun, and the competitive nature of men, especially where guns are involved, or was there something else that made you embarrass your host's son in front of a crowd made up of some of the most prominent names in the South?"

"Mary, what do you want me to say?" Leander asked, his footsteps sounding on the stone floor, indicating he was coming closer.

"The truth," Mary insisted, taking a step back and putting a hand out to halt his progression.

He paused mid-stride.

"Leander, I am so very confused," Mary whispered. "I have replayed the events again and again, and what conclusion could a lady reach but this: that you are a rogue who would have his way with me if he could, but will not—for fear of losing your business partner."

"Mary, do not say that," Leander pleaded. "You know that is not true."

"And why should I know that?"

It was the most maddening thing. Mary finally knew what she wanted—and now—

"I fear, Mr. Doucet, that you do not know what you want."

"It is not that," Leander cast his gaze to the floor. "I know what I want—Mary," he said her name loudly, as though an announcement. "But it is not that simple."

"Why? What can be so complicated that it would stand between us?"

"It is a very complicated family affair. I have not told a soul, not even your brother."

"And will you tell me?" She ventured a step nearer him.

"I, I would if I did not think it would mean you would think less of me."

"You men." Mary shook her head. "You are always speaking of honor and pride as though they are these guiding forces, and yet you let them run your life, hiding behind them as excuses for your poor behavior. You would rather cling to some obscure and intangible concept than go out and live your own life and take what you want from it."

As the words left Mary Taylor's mouth, their irony was not lost on her. They were not dissimilar to something Elizabeth had once said to her.

And Edward.

And her father.

Mary sighed as the realization dawned on her—in life, knowing what you want was no guarantee you would get it.

It might just slip through her fingers, the way sand did on the beach.

But that did not mean that she could not try.

She would never forgive herself if she did not try.

"Leander." She stepped towards him, closing the space between them. "I do not know the nature of this complicated family matter, and I suppose, deep down, it does not matter. For the question remains the same either way: do you intend to speak to my father?

"Because if you do, then I will be the happiest woman in the world," she confessed, reaching for his hand and placing hers atop his. "But if you do not, then I require you to tell me now. I require you to stop sending me tokens of your affection and seeking to embarrass my other beaux because you are envious of the attention they give me, for it is not fair. If you do not wish me for yourself, then you must set me free. A lady's heart is not a plaything made for your own amusement."

"No, of course not, and that was never my intent," Leander assured her, placing his other hand on top of hers. "I must speak with my family before I can speak to yours. But I promise I will."

"When?"

"After the races. My father is sending some of the new breed to compete this year, and I am required to be here to represent the Doucet entries.

"But I promise, I will be on the first train that leaves the following Monday morning."

Over the following days, Mary found herself in a daze of excited sedation. Every time she thought about the eventuality of becoming Mrs. Doucet, a giddiness overtook her, spreading through her body like an electrical current and forcing her lips into a permanent smile which, try as she may, could not be concealed. It all felt like a dream—she felt light, as though she was walking on air, and she never wished to be placed back on the ground.

Not to mention, that feeling seemed to grow more and more urgent as the days ticked by. Even inside the bank, when Leander had promised to go to his family, Mary had tilted her head towards his, closing her eyes, hoping that this would finally be the moment she had waited for.

But instead, he had placed a kiss on her forehead, a chaste and familial gesture reserved usually for fathers and brothers.

"I would rather wait to kiss you when I can claim you as completely mine."

While Mary had been touched by the gesture, it did only intensify the frustration that had begun to build.

It cloyed—an unbearable, unladylike word for a feeling that wouldn't leave her.

She supposed it would be like this until they were married, the thought more than a little bit insufferable.

Perhaps she should ask Elizabeth. Mary eyed her sister who sat across from her in the carriage as they bumped along towards Mrs. Lambert's.

Surely men do not expect their wives to know what to do on their wedding night (in fact, if a lady did know, this might be a cause of some concern), but surely she would receive some level of preparation? From either Mother or perhaps Aunt Genevieve or Elizabeth, if she had been married first.

"What is it, dear sister?" Elizabeth demanded, clearly a little bit annoyed.

"What do you mean?"

"You have looked at me at least four times in the last few minutes. Do you require something?"

"No, I apologize. It is just that you look so pretty this evening," Mary tried to deflect.

"Thank you." Elizabeth rolled her eyes. "But you do insult my intelligence. You know I am certain that you learned the art of deflection by way of offering a compliment from me!"

"It is nothing," Mary's cheeks grew red at the idea of bringing the topic up to her sister. Even if she tried to be innocuous, she was certain that Elizabeth would find her way to the root of the question, and quite quickly as well.

"I will ask you later," Mary said definitively, casting a discreet side-glance over towards Amelié. There was little point trying to divert Elizabeth's attention now that her interest was piqued, but the least Mary could do was delay the conversation until they had more privacy.

Due to the official start of the social season, the sewing circle had more attendees than ever before. And being some of the last to arrive, Amelié, Elizabeth, and Mary found the room cramped full of young ladies, all chattering excitedly as they wove and poked their needles through their various projects.

The return of the sun, and with it the longer days coupled with the anticipated social season, always livened up gatherings, leaving the young ladies in high spirits. All three of the late arrivals wedged themselves in, scattered amongst the group of many old faces and a few new as gossip flew around, bouncing off the walls from one end of the room to the other.

Mary and Elizabeth, by virtue of having been at a recent large social event which was not only deemed exclusive but had produced stories good enough to retell, quickly became the centre of the conversation.

"Miss Taylor, I hear that Mr. Walker dedicated his victory in the target shooting at the Riveras' garden party to you," one woman offered.

"And where did you hear a thing like that?" Elizabeth asked, looking up from her sewing with scrutiny.

"Why, from Miss Marianne Fleming, who was there herself!"

"Well, if you have heard it from Miss Marianne, why do you need to hear it again from me?"

"I just thought it was romantic. Most women would be delighted to be the honoree of such a victory."

"I am afraid I do not much care for Mr. Walker," Elizabeth informed the group. On this declaration, she was immediately bombarded with instigations and prying questions. "And that is all I would wish to say on that matter," Elizabeth announced, much to everyone's dismay.

"How about you, Miss Taylor?" the same woman, clearly only momentarily flustered by Elizabeth's harsh response, moved on to Mary. "I hear Manuel Rivera is quite smitten with you."

"As I think I have told this group before, Mr. Rivera and I are longtime friends from childhood."

"Well, I have it on good authority that you were seen walking through the orchards of the Rivera plantation on his arm," another woman reported.

"I also hear he came to your window one night and serenaded you when you first arrived in New Orleans," another squealed.

The group devolved into telling and swapping different accounts of Manuel Rivera's courting of Mary Taylor. Some were accurate, or fairly accurate, while others appeared to be shameless exaggerations and in other instances, outright falsehoods. It was surreal, to sit and listen to others recount stories from one's own life, but Mary sat quietly, concentrating on her stitching and letting the stories wash over her. Her fingers shook with excitement for the secret she kept inside, and more than once, she nearly poked herself with the needle.

"Was not your intended at the Riveras' garden party also, Noémie?" A woman asked, turning towards a young lady who Mary thought to be new to the group, for she had not recognized her.

"Yes, that's right," the woman named Noémie answered. She was pretty, with shoulder-length blonde hair and large blue eyes.

"Oh, who is your intended?" Elizabeth asked, interested in gossip that did not revolve around John Walker and herself. "Perhaps we know him."

Elizabeth had no problem being the centre of gossip, but if she was going to be, she wished it to be with someone she considered worthy!

"I believe you do, Miss Taylor, for he is your brother's business partner—

"Leander Doucet."

Mary's needle stilled midair. The thread pulled taut. Her mouth opened, but no words came. Her vision fuzzed at the edges, a low buzz rising in her ears as though the whole room had been dropped underwater. Noémie's words repeated in her head, but they sounded as though someone else had said them, in another lifetime.

Leander Doucet has an intended.

The words didn't make sense. They didn't fit. Like a puzzle piece being jammed into a place it didn't belong. She looked down at the thread in her lap—tangled, useless. Just like her thoughts.

Somewhere, distantly, she heard Elizabeth's voice.

"How interesting," Elizabeth declared, looking Noémie up and down in what was a display of skepticism. "We see Mr. Doucet often, by virtue of calling on the bank to visit with our brother Charles, and he has not once mentioned you."

Mary looked over at her sister in gratitude, clinging to her voice like it was the edge of a dock and she was being swept out to sea, relieved that Elizabeth's natural nosiness meant she would ask the questions Mary could not.

She silently vowed to never speak an ill word or think an ill thought of Elizabeth's nosiness again.

"Yes, well, perhaps you are not as close as you think. It is not a secret—everyone in Alabama knows." Elizabeth eyed Noémie critically. She hated not being in the know when it came to a piece of gossip.

Mary's heart pounded, trying to catch up with the flood of memories—his hand at her waist in the orchard, his voice thick with promise, the book he'd sent her. The dance. The closeness. The way she had looked into his eyes and seen—no, *felt*—something real.

She squeezed her eyes shut, but the tears still pressed forward. Her chest burned. Her cheeks flamed.

Had she imagined it all?

Had he used her?

*Was it a game?*

Next to Mary the wheels of Elizabeth's brain were turning, piecing together the oddities— the fact that Leander appeared to never call on young ladies, and none had reported him as being their beau. At events he was always respectful but distant, often in attendance, but rarely requesting a dance of any ladies, apart from those older married women, who delighted at the chance to dance with a handsome young man while their husbands were off at the bar or playing cards.

"And what brings you to New Orleans?" Elizabeth asked cautiously, still clearly unconvinced.

"The races," Noémie responded. "The Doucets have a few horses entering this year. I came over with the horses as a surprise to Leander."

Mary couldn't breathe. Her skin was hot and prickled with a sweat that had nothing to do with the Louisiana heat as the room began to spin.

How could this be?

How could he do this?

A voice in her mind, low and cruel, whispered the answer.

*Because you are not the woman he chose.*

She sat perfectly still, needle frozen, thread tangled in her lap, her face blank and composed—because if she moved, even an inch, the illusion would shatter. The room would blur. The tears would come. And everyone would see—

Mary Taylor had been a fool.

And the worst part?

She had let herself become one.

“Do you not find it odd that Leander Doucet never once mentioned his intended?” Elizabeth asked Mary as they helped one another get ready for bed.

“Perhaps some people are very private,” Mary offered in a half-hearted attempt to engage.

“Hmm, perhaps,” Elizabeth considered, tapping her chin with her finger in thought. “But it is still *odd* to live in New Orleans for so long and never mention it to anybody! Not even once!”

“Perhaps he did mention it to Charles.” Mary yanked her nightgown over her head with an aggressive pull, biting her lip in an attempt to hold back the tears which seemed inevitable.

“No, he did not, because I specifically asked Charles if Leander had an intended.” Elizabeth explained over her shoulder from where she sat at their vanity, brushing her hair. “Oh, Mary, what was it you wanted to ask me?”

It was an innocent question, completely devoid of ulterior motive, but it folded Mary all the same, reducing her to sobs as the tears came quickly. In a moment Elizabeth was by her side, cradling her head into her bosom and patting her hair.

"Mary..." Elizabeth urged gently, brushing the hair from her sister's tear-streaked cheek. "Tell me. Please."

And so she did, and the truth, as it so often does when it has built up for so long, came pouring out. Elizabeth and Mary sat where Mary had crumpled on the floor as she recounted the scene in the bank when they had first arrived at New Orleans, her and Manuel's encounter with Leander after their disastrous trip to Santiago San Ignacio, their discussions at the salon, their dancing at the charity ball, the gift she had received from him, the scene in the orchard at the Riveras', and finally, her latest visit to the bank.

When he had made his intentions known that he wished to marry her.

# Chapter XVII

It was an unforgivably warm day for May, and particularly warm for a day spent outside at the races. Races were specifically scheduled for spring and fall to avoid the debilitating heat of summer. But this year, the weather had clearly been too eager, and by late morning, the temperatures were already above what one would find comfortable, especially if one intended to spend the entire day outside.

Mary had made up her mind that she did not wish to attend, that the thought of facing Leander and his intended was too much to bear, but Elizabeth had insisted.

"First of all, Mary, you have done nothing wrong," Elizabeth had declared more than once, and had even made Mary repeat it. "But men should be held accountable for their bad behavior. If you decline to attend, then Leander Doucet gets to spend the day at ease in the knowledge that he will not have to face you. But you will not give him that satisfaction—you will attend, looking fabulous, and remind him why he wished to marry you, and that you *know* he is no gentleman. No Mary, you do not have to hide because of his disgraceful behavior—he should be the one ashamed, and he can only feel the full extent of that shame if you attend."

As always, Elizabeth did have plenty of reason in her logic.

But just because Mary should not be the one embarrassed or who felt ashamed does not mean she did not.

Now, in the carriage on the way to the race tracks, Elizabeth reached for Mary's hand, which sat clenched and sweaty in her lap and squeezed it tightly, offering her a reassuring smile.

"You look beautiful."

Mary looked down, having forgotten what color dress she was wearing.

Lilac. The same color as her debutante dress.

The ladies unfolded out of the carriage, stepping out sideways so as not to bend their straw hats, and immediately unfolded their parasols.

In this type of heat, it was best to be especially cautious.

Mary could feel herself holding her breath as they entered through the bottom of the race stands and made their way up the stairs to where attendees could observe the races, move around freely, and obtain refreshments.

"Mary." A hand lightly touched her arm. At the contact, Mary jumped, nearly tumbling backwards and treading on someone's foot in the process.

"It is me." Charles caught her from behind and placed her back on both feet.

"Oh Charles, pardon me. You startled me."

"Are you alright, Mary? You look a bit flushed."

"Yes, I am just a bit warm."

"Perhaps we should find you some water. Leander has just gone for some refreshments. I will try to catch him before he gets to the front of the line."

"No!" Mary blurted, extending a white gloved hand towards Charles. "I am fine, thank you." Charles's eyes narrowed, clearly assessing Mary's actions as, well, bizarre.

"I just—I would rather wait for my escort. I do not wish to be rude."

"Oh, very well," Charles nodded in understanding. "I expect he will be here soon. Ah, Leander, we were just speaking about you." Leander and Noémie emerged through the door to the refreshments bar.

"Miss Taylor and Miss Taylor." Leander nodded, handing a drink to Charles. "I apologize, I did not know you had arrived. Please, allow me to get you something to—"

"No thank you, Mr, Doucet, we are perfectly hydrated," Elizabeth said in the stoniest of fashions, so clipped and curt it could only be interpreted as unforgivably rude. Charles turned towards Elizabeth with a puzzled look and a face that begged the question:

Why were both of his sisters acting so oddly?

If you only knew, Charles.

"As you wish," Leander nodded, and silence descended amongst the group.

Noémie feigned a cough, looking at her intended with expectant eyes, but Leander did not notice. Mary could feel his stare, imploring her to meet his gaze, but she had turned her undivided attention to her shoes, studying them with such an intensity one might believe her life just about depended on it.

And indeed, it did.

"Leander," Charles finally broke the awkward silence, offering a small chuckle. "Were you not going to introduce my sisters to Miss Mercier?"

"Pardon me, I have forgotten myself. This is Miss Noémie Mercier—"

"Yes, we have met," Elizabeth cut him off with a snarl, like a rabid dog protecting its meal.

Charles threw her another look.

"Nice to see you both again," Noémie nodded.

"Oh, it is *our* pleasure," Elizabeth insisted. "Truly, our deepest pleasure. For we have spent such considerable time with Mr. Doucet, and would you believe, he did not mention you—not even once! Why, we were totally unaware of your existence until...what day this week did we finally have the pleasure of your acquaintance?" Elizabeth asked, her voice laced in sarcasm.

Mary stood silently, her hands clammy underneath her gloves as she continued to stare at the ground. She could feel the palatable tension from Leander's stare, imploring her to look at him, but she dared not.

For she was not sure what would happen if she did chance a look at him.

Would she burst into tears?

Scream at the top of her lungs?

Tell his intended of the things he has said to her?

The promises he has made to her.

Or the way he had held her close?

"Mr. Doucet and Miss Mercier, congratulations on your intended marriage," Mary finally managed, her voice almost steady.

Almost.

A single tremor crept in at the last word, and she cleared her throat delicately, as if the heat had caught her, not heartbreak. "I sincerely hope that you are both very happy together." She chanced a look up and immediately met Leander's eyes.

"Thank you, Miss Taylor," Noémie nodded and offered a kind smile, perhaps relieved to finally receive a normal reaction to news someone is to be married.

Leander looked pained but when he opened his mouth, no words came out.

"Now if you will excuse me, I believe I see that my escort is arriving," Mary motioned to where Manuel Rivera and his party were coming up the stairs.

"Miss Mary," Manuel exclaimed, beaming at her presence as he rushed over to join the group. "You look absolutely stunning." He smiled, taking her sweat-soaked hand and kissing it warmly.

Mary plastered on her best smile, fighting the sinking sensation that threatened to drag her to the floor as she tried to meet Manuel's enthusiasm.

When the invitation had arrived from Manuel, she had snatched at it without a moment's thought, clutching it to her chest with a crazed zealotry that she knew was, shall we say, uncharacteristic.

And certainly not normal.

Or ladylike, for it lacked any shred of dignity.

But at this particular moment, that was the least of Mary's concerns.

For the thought of attending the races at all had plagued her greatly, but the thought of attending them alone after everything that had passed, well, that was absolutely untenable.

But she reasoned she could do much worse than to be escorted by Manuel.

And besides, Manuel Rivera was a gentleman, for he had enough good breeding not to notice how horribly wet her hand had become.

Or if he did notice, he declined to mention it or react.

Manuel exchanged polite greetings with the rest of the group before turning his attention back to Mary. "Miss Mary, can I interest you in a refreshment?"

"That would be lovely, Manuel," Mary accepted his outstretched arm.

"And Miss Taylor, may I get you something as well?"

"Yes please, Mr. Rivera, if it is not too much trouble, I would appreciate it immensely, for I am terribly parched." She turned a set of dagger eyes towards Leander.

"Then I will do my best to be as quick as possible!" Manuel declared, leading Mary into the room with the refreshments stand.

"Are you looking forward to the day, Miss Mary?" Manuel asked politely, placing his hand over hers and squeezing it. "For I am. I am so happy to see you again."

"And I you," Mary forced a smile.

"Manuel, there you are," Miguel Rivera called, running up to where Manuel and Mary stood in line. "Miss Taylor." He bowed. "I do apologize, but I will require my brother momentarily. There appears to be a small incident which requires your attention."

"Is it the horses?" Manuel's brow narrowed with concern.

"I am not sure if it is appropriate to say in front of Miss Taylor," Miguel admitted sheepishly.

"Oh, please do not trouble yourself on my account."

"Well, it is not the horses, but the jockey—"

"Let us finish this conversation in private," Manuel cut in. "You are quite right that Miss Mary does not need to hear of such things.

"Miss Mary, I apologize. Please will you permit me a moment?"

"Of course, Manuel. Take your time." Manuel gave an apologetic bow and dashed off with his brother towards the jockey lounge.

"I thought you had promised me that you were going to keep him out of the bars!" Mary could hear Manuel castigate his brother furiously.

"It is not the drink this time. It's the laudanum!"

In more normal circumstances, the exchange would have left Mary extremely irritable—as though as a lady she might be scandalized by mentions of overindulgence and laudanum!

But it did not matter—as it turns out, very little matters.

Including promises of intention.

Such promises are meaningless unless they come with tangible assurances.

Mary did not remember waiting in the line or ordering the drinks, but when they were placed in front of her, a hand appeared, paying the cashier before she could.

Mary was afraid to turn.

And she need not, for she knew whose hand it was already.

"Thank you, Mr. Doucet. That is very kind," she answered tersely, continuing to stare at the barman.

"Allow me to help you," Leander said quietly, picking up the two additional drinks while she took her own. "And please permit me to speak with you a moment," Leander begged once they had stepped away from the bar.

"I am afraid I do not wish to speak with you, Mr. Doucet," Mary snapped, finally meeting his eyes.

Leander's brow was scrunched, as though he were holding a permanent grimace, his eyes filled with a perpetual misery.

Mary did not care.

"Mary, please. I do just wish to explain—"

"I should hope so, for you do have an immense amount of explaining to do, but as I have already stated, I do not wish to hear it."

It wasn't entirely true—there was a part of Mary, a very large part of her in fact, that did want to understand how, and why, Leander could have kept this from her.

Whether the words he had said were true or fabrications which only felt like truth in the heat of a moment.

But she was also afraid of hearing it, for the truth can be one of the most terrifying things in this world, especially when it is about one's self.

Leander began to speak in hushed quiet whispers, leaning close as he spoke, but the words did not register in Mary's brain. The stifling heat of the day had begun to take its toll, and she looked down at her dress and its many layers, considering what she might be able to remove.

Perhaps I could remove the hat, she thought to herself. And the gloves.

But scenes from that first day in the bank flashed back to her mind, and she resisted the temptation. She would not allow the words and actions of this man to lead to her removal of clothing.

Not again!

"Mary?" Leander asked, looking at her with concern. "Are you alright?"

"I would prefer if you would call me Miss Taylor," Mary responded sharply, the edge faltering as she swayed, her knees briefly betraying her. Leander tried to reach out to steady her, but Mary dodged his attempt at help, and in doing so threw herself off balance even further.

"Oh, Miss, be careful!" The barman ran from behind the bar and steadied Mary, walking her over to a nearby chair and helping her to sit down. "Miss, this heat is unforgivable today. Please promise me you'll be careful in it."

"Yes, thank you. I do apologize."

"No need to." The barman smiled warmly. "Is this gentleman your escort, or your husband or brother perhaps?" he asked, pointing to where Leander now hovered helplessly, his hands still full of drinks.

"He is not. I am afraid I do not know this man very well," Mary glared at Leander, allowing the declaration to wound the way she had intended. "My escort is Manuel Rivera, and he has just—"

"Miss Mary!" Manuel called in distress, reappearing in the door and registering the scene before him. "Miss Mary, are you alright?" he asked, kneeling down to be level with her face.

"She's just a bit overheated, sir, but I'll caution you to make sure she has plenty of water and stays out of the sun."

"Yes, of course. Thank you for your assistance, sir." Manuel shook the barman's hand. "I can take it from here.

"Oh, Mr. Doucet, thank you," Manuel looked up, noticing Leander for the first time. He took his drink without it being offered. Reaching his hand into his inner breast pocket, he brought out a wad of bills, and peeling one of the top, tucked it into Leander's coat pocket.

But Manuel Rivera was not finished mortifying his foe. Perhaps the events of the garden party still lingered in his mind, or perhaps he was simply just a bit petty by nature, for having placed the bill in Leander's breast pocket, he proceeded to pat his chest, in a manner that could only be described as condescending.

Some might even say savage.

Leander gaped at Manuel, caught between incredulity and fury at the indication that he was waiting around to be paid for the drinks.

"That other one is for Miss Taylor, if you do not mind delivering it to her?" Manuel threw the comment over his shoulder, returning his attention to Mary. But Leander remained where he stood, expressionless, watching Manuel fawn over Mary.

"Mr. Doucet, is there something you require?" Manuel looked up at him irritably, his eyes flickering in frustration. Leander met his stare for a moment longer before finally conceding.

"No, pardon me," Leander somehow managed to unearth his manners. "Miss Taylor, I hope you feel better soon."

After a few minutes of sitting in the shade of the bar, Mary was insistent she was recovered enough to make her way back into the stands.

"I do not wish you to miss any of the races."

"I would not care if I did," Manuel promised, easing Mary slowly to her feet.

Mary and Manuel settled into shaded seats with a view of the track. They made polite conversation with passersby—the Sinclairs, Brynes, the rest of the Riveras, even the Walkers—each exchange blurring together, her focus drifting with every glance toward Leander's looming figure.

When the Defours wandered by, they did not stop to extend extensive greetings, but they nodded cordially to Mary.

Thus displaying the height of civility in the presence of a Rivera.

As the races drew nearer, Charles and Elizabeth joined Mary and Manuel in the stands, accompanied by the Sinclairs.

And with them, much to Mary's dismay, also came Miss Mercier and Leander.

Correction, Mr. Doucet.

"You folks feeling blessed this fine morning?" A man walked by, lists of the order of races and participants rolled up in his fists. "How about you, sirs?" He stopped in front of their party, leaning forward in a conspiratorial fashion. "Have you placed your bets for the day?"

"We are feeling immensely blessed, but have no interest in—"

"Oh yes we do!" Elizabeth cut Charles off. "I have it on good authority that Rooster is going to win the second and fifth races."

"And where have you heard that?"

John Walker.

"Does it matter?" Elizabeth motioned for the bookmaker to hand her one of the sheets.

"Elizabeth, really!" Charles looked around in disbelief before snatching the paper out of her hands and offering it back to the bookie.

"Charles, don't be such a bore!" Archibald Sinclair bemoaned with a raucous twinkle in his eyes, gesturing for some leaflets which he distributed to the party. "Let the ladies have some fun!"

"My brother, Mr. Sinclair, believes having fun a failing, especially if it's the kind ladies might enjoy. Why, I'm certain he despises it altogether!"

Mary tuned out the bickering which ensued and glanced down at the paper in her hand as Manuel Rivera looked over her shoulder.

"You will not misunderstand my interest, Miss Mary—," he spoke into her ear, gently repositioning a piece of her hair. At his touch, Mary's body went rigid, clutching the paper in her hand as she stared at the entries with her undivided attention.

It was, quite possibly, one of the most horrible feelings she had ever experienced.

Though, shockingly, not the worst of the day.

"For I confess I am not a betting man and do not intend to begin now, especially in your presence. But I cannot help my desire to see the odds on my family's entry."

"I understand, a curiosity, and nothing more."

"Yes, though my late mother would have argued such a curiosity a weakness of the mind." He extended an arm around her torso, allowing his sleeve to graze her as he scanned the list with his finger until he landed on the Rivera family entry—Azul.

Mary could feel his breath against her neck, hot and sticky in the heat, leaving dews of sweat plastered to her skin.

She steadily raised her eyes from the paper and was immediately met with a pair of murderous eyes, staring at her—or rather, her escort, the paper in between his fingers clenched so tightly it crumpled at the sides. Mary was certain she could see his heart pounding through his linen shirt and day coat, the hair around his temples wet and pressed against his forehead due to the heat of the day.

Or perhaps, due to the heat of the moment.

Mary lowered her gaze, the self-loathing momentarily giving way to anger as she feigned listening to Manuel's explanations of how bets were placed (not that she had asked, nor did she require to be told).

What right had Leander Doucet to look at her in such a manner? She seethed, her heart picking up pace as the outrage of the entire situation bubbled to the surface.

When he sat not two yards away with the arm of his intended tucked into his.

"I'll place twenty dollars on Rooster for races two and five." Elizabeth finally declared.

"Twenty dollars?!" Charles failed to hide his horror, both at the notion of his sister betting in public and at the sum in question.

"Oh, don't be such a spoilsport, Charles," Archibald Sinclair insisted. "Now, I'm going to back you, Miss Taylor, but if this information of yours proves itself to be a falsehood, you will be in my debt," he warned with an impish grin, as though the idea of having Miss Elizabeth Taylor in his debt delighted him immensely, before declaring, "Fifty dollars on Rooster for races two and five."

"I think, Mr. Sinclair, you will find that when you go home a wealthier man than when you arrived, it will be you who are in my debt," Elizabeth tossed over her shoulder with a mischievous smile.

Archibald Sinclair nearly fell off his chair.

"Leander, tell me, are these horses of yours any good?" Alexander presented a request as a demand. "And please, sir, keep in mind that it is considered extremely bad manners to hustle your own clients."

At the question, Mary quickly scanned the page until the name came into focus: Doucet. They had three entries: Duke, Sugarfoot, and Romeo.

How appropriate.

"There are no better horses in the south than the Alabamians," Noémie declared. "Isn't that right?" She turned towards Leander, squeezing his arm in hopes of being praised for her wifely loyalty.

For wives were best performing if they took every opportunity offered to flatter their husbands.

In fact, it wasn't just considered good manners, it was entirely expected.

"Quite right." He gave her a stiff nod.

"I do not believe I have ever once heard of a great horse from Alabama. From Charleston, yes, of course. But Alabama?" Mary glanced up to the group with narrowed stony eyes. "It feels as though you might be telling us tales, Mr. Doucet."

Leander stiffened, his hand twitching at his side, suppressing the urge to reach for her. His gaze pierced, a mix of fury and helplessness. He opened his mouth to respond, but mercifully, Charles jumped in.

"Mary, just because you have never heard of the prowess of Alabamian horses does not mean they have none," Charles offered with caution, eyeing the exchange with weariness.

"I suppose there is some reason in that," Mary nodded in consideration. "But the absence of evidence is hardly evidence in and of itself. If I were to declare to you, Charles, that rice grown in Boston is some of the best rice you have ever tasted, would you simply assume that just because you have never heard of Bostonian rice, that does not mean it is not the fluffiest and most delicious rice your lips have ever tasted?

"No, you would perhaps consider the facts: that Boston is far too cold in the winter for a reasonable rice yield, that the city has no space to support such a claim as being the secret cultivator of the best rice in the world."

"Where are you going with this, Mary?"

"I simply mean that just because someone says something is true, that does not make it so."

"A skeptic!" Archibald Sinclair slapped his knee heartily. "How delightful. You rarely meet a lady these days who looks at things so critically. What a head you have on your shoulders, Miss Taylor," Archibald complimented, very obviously amused. "It would appear, Mr. Doucet, that Miss Taylor here has called your bluff."

"It would appear so," Leander responded with a quiet resignation.

"Oh, don't be sour about it," Archibald chided as his large hand slapped the back of Leander with a great clatter, causing Noémie to jump. "It's no fun if you become sour."

"I would like to place five dollars against Romeo for races seven and twelve," Mary declared, reaching for the small reticule tucked into the folds of her skirts.

"Miss Mary," Manuel laughed, catching her hand and not allowing her to remove the bills as he tried to dismiss the notion. "You have dealt your blow. You needn't participate in such unseemly activities as this—"

"Oh, but I think I do, Mr. Rivera. In fact, I find that I must." Mary yanked her hands from his and forfeited the bills over to the bookie, who quickly scribbled her a receipt as the entire group sat in awkward silence.

Even Elizabeth seemed shocked by Mary's obvious antagonism, and it was only Archibald Sinclair who found the entire situation the height of entertainment.

"If I make such an utterly audacious declaration, surely it is only appropriate that I prove my sincerity by putting my money where my mouth is," she explained, accepting the receipt from the bookmaker. "I am nothing, if not a woman of my word."

The day passed by akin to a dream, or perhaps more appropriately, a nightmare—one that moved slowly, like wading through molasses in the summer, but one from which Mary knew she would not wake up.

She watched the races, detached, barely able to react when Elizabeth's inside information returned her a hefty profit, and Archibald Sinclair an even larger one. Mary did not even find it amusing when Elizabeth talked Archibald out of a portion of his own winnings, for he would have won nothing had it not been for her sage advice. Nor did she have the strength to shake her head when John Walker repeatedly asked Elizabeth if he could take her for a walk, and finally convinced her that it was the least she owed him following her victories which were, thanks to his insights.

"You really do know how to hog-tie a lady," Elizabeth grumbled, stepping down from the stands and opening her parasol. "One lap, Mr. Walker." She wagged a finger at him.

"Miss Mary, if you are feeling up to it, may I interest you in a walk also?" Mary nodded, heaving herself to her feet and taking Manuel's extended hand as he helped her down from the bleachers.

"What a pleasant day," Manuel mused as they strolled arm in arm through the promenade, nodding and waving to friends and acquaintances seated in the stands above.

"Yes," Mary heard herself say, though she was not sure where the words were coming from. "And a good day for your family's horse."

"My father is a romantic, as I am sure you know," Manuel confessed. "And he has always wanted to make his way into horse-breeding. Why, he is actually considering expanding the plantation for this very reason."

"How interesting," Mary nodded, declining to mention that she was aware of Mr. Rivera's considerations.

She somehow suspected that Manuel would not be thrilled to know she was aware of his family's affairs. He was the type of gentleman who wished a lady to know exactly as much as he cared to share.

But at this point, it mattered not. She had stooped so deeply into despair and self-loathing that the attention of any gentleman, especially one who was, objectively speaking, handsome, kind, and wealthy, was not something she was going to throw away.

On the contrary, she was going to cling to it for dear life.

For at least Manuel Rivera did like her. He found her interesting and beautiful, and perhaps most importantly, he was not, so far as Mary was aware, anyone's intended.

Which in normal circumstances would have felt like the absolute bare minimum requirement, but after the events of the last few weeks, Mary was happy with any gentleman who she was certain would not break her heart.

And whilst she was not certain that Manuel Rivera saw her in the way she had always hoped a gentleman would, she was certain he was no rogue.

Which was more than she could say for some other gentlemen.

"Miss Mary, are you alright?"

"Yes."

Why was everyone constantly burdening her with that question?

"Shall we get you out of this heat?" Manuel suggested, leading her down the stairs from the promenade and underneath the stands where the air was cooler and they were adequately shielded from the sun.

The area was deserted, apart from a few benches and some debris from discarded snacks and the contents of used tobacco.

"The jockeys sometimes sit here to escape the heat," Manuel explained, slipping out of his overcoat and putting it on the bench, gesturing for Mary to sit.

"Oh Manuel, but your coat will become filthy."

"I would rather that than the same for your dress." Manuel gallantly placed a hand on her back and guided her to the seat. At his touch, Mary could feel the sweat which laced her back pressing into her skin. She perched on his coat and Manuel took a seat next to her, their legs touching.

"Miss Mary, may I confess something to you?" Manuel asked, holding out his hand in request for her own.

Mary looked at him stupidly. If she had been in her right mind she would have seen where the conversation was going the moment their thighs had touched. But her current state of confused and sedated detachment gave her the appearance of an innocent who knew nothing of the desires for which Manuel was about to speak.

"Please do," Mary prompted him, placing her hand in his.

"I hope you will forgive my forwardness, but ever since your debutante ball, I have not been able to stop thinking of you."

"Is that truly so?" Mary asked quietly, staring into Manuel's eyes. There she saw hunger, adoration, perhaps the tiniest hint of anticipated fear, and an overwhelming desire to protect.

All the things that any sensible woman would desire.

"It is, Miss Mary," Manuel confirmed, bringing her hand to his lips and kissing it. "You fill my thoughts wholly and completely," he confessed, lacing his fingers into hers and resting her hand on his cheek tenderly.

"I do believe I have fallen in love with you."

"Have you?" Nothing more than a whisper.

"Yes, and I have found myself wanting—no, needing to know, Miss Mary, if you feel the same way."

The sadness and despair that had built up in Mary's heart began to dissipate, making room for something else that she recognized—hope.

Someone did want her. And not just anyone, but a gentleman of good name and good breeding.

Who gave a damn if it wasn't Leander Doucet.

For she was a Taylor and a Taylor would marry a gentleman.

And Leander Doucet was no gentleman.

"Manuel, before I confess to you the contents of my heart, I must ask you something."

"Of course," Manuel nodded. "The contents of a lady's heart are not something to be taken lightly. Ask whatever you feel you need, Miss Mary."

"In making these declarations to me, what are your intentions?"

"Oh, Miss Mary, I would have thought that would be obvious." Manuel looked taken aback. "I regret to say that I find myself almost offended that you would feel the need to ask such a thing.

"Is that your opinion of me, Miss Taylor?" he asked with a quiet sadness, returning her hand to her lap.

"No, Manuel, of course not." Mary nearly leapt from her seat in panic. A very curious sensation overtook Mary as she grabbed for Manuel's hand, squeezing it in attempted reassurance.

For someone she was sure she did not want with all her heart, the thought of losing him was now unbearable.

"Please forgive me," Mary insisted, leaning towards Manuel and placing her hand on his cheek affectionately. "I just...I could not bear to misunderstand your intentions."

Not again.

"I am certain it would break my heart past repair."

"Oh, Mary," Manuel breathed. Meeting her gaze, he took both his hands, cradling her face. Slowly and yearningly, he traced his thumbs along her cheek bones, across her ears.

And then, over her lips—first once, then twice, and on the third time lingering, brushing them slowly and seductively.

Mary gasped, inhaling sharply at the moment as that space in between her legs began to burn.

"Do you want me to stop?" Manuel asked softly.

If she was to get over Leander Doucet, this must be as good a start as any.

Mary shook her head.

Manuel's eyes roared with anticipation, running his fingers along her lips once more.

And then, as his thumb made its way back to the center of Mary's mouth, she opened it, slipping her tongue over his thumb in a motion she could not explain.

For it had come from a part of her she had only begun to understand.

At the touch of her tongue, Manuel halted, his eyes now ablaze.

And leaning forward, he brought his head to meet hers. Mary closed her eyes, inhaling deeply as their lips touched.

It was chaste and gentle at first.

But Mary felt nothing.

Pressing her eyes closed tighter, she pressed her lips against his harder, waiting for that burst of clarity or explosion of her heart that she was sure was meant to accompany a lady's first kiss.

But it did not come. Her head remained foggy, unable to comprehend what was happening. Confusingly, that space between her legs continued to burn the more Manuel Rivera pressed his lips to hers.

And in that moment it became clear to Mary that her body was responding to Manuel's kiss, but her heart...

Well, her heart would not be swayed.

His tongue slipped into her mouth, and for a moment, she froze.

Then—mechanically—she moved with him. Mimicked the motions. Let herself be pulled along.

His hand ran up her arm, fingers curling just under the edge of her bodice. Her skin prickled at his touch.

It was thrilling.

Exciting, even.

But it was wrong.

All wrong.

For it was not what she desired.

All of a sudden, Manuel fell backwards, pushed from the bench with such a force that Mary yelped with a start.

In one swift motion, he was picked up from the ground and hurled against one of the wooden supports of the stands, his body knocking against it with a large thud. Mary blinked rapidly as the scene unfolding began to take shape—Leander advanced on Manuel, fist cocked, but as he raised it Manuel ducked at the last moment, causing Leander to make contact with the wooden beam.

Seizing his moment, Manuel charged at his assailant's torso, tackling him to the ground.

"Stop!" Mary shouted as the men continued to fight, throwing fists and dodging with duck and rolls.

The sound of a gunshot startled everyone, causing them to freeze as they looked around for the source. Was it from the track? Or was it from—

"You devil!" A voice roared, charging into the scene and grabbing Leander by the shirt he dragged him to his feet, only to throw him against the wall of the stands.

"Edward?" Mary screamed, registering the third man as her brother. "What are you doing here? Stop!"

"Edward, it's him you want!" Leander insisted, pointing accusingly towards Manuel. "When I found them, he was violating your sister!"

"How dare you?" Manuel raged, flying towards Leander in a fury. "I was violating no one, and Miss Mary will confirm that—"

"Hold your tongue!" Edward growled at Manuel. "If you were kissing her, Mr. Rivera, then I can only assume your intentions and will hold you to them.

"But you," he turned his attention back towards Leander. "You are no gentleman. You have embarrassed my family past forgiveness!"

"Edward, please," Mary insisted, grabbing at her corset, which all of a sudden was feeling far too tight.

"What are you talking about?" Leander demanded, bewilderment and fear mixed into his face as he feigned ignorance and perhaps expected the worst.

"Don't you dare play the fool with me. You are a devil, but you are no fool. Or perhaps you are, if you really believed your actions would bear no consequences."

"Edward, please don't!" Mary begged, gasping for air.

"Edward, let us speak with Charles. I am sure this is just a misunderstanding—"

"A misunderstanding? You mean, the manner in which you courted my sister and made promises of intentions to her, when all the while you were intended to another!"

"What?" Manuel exclaimed.

"Edward, no, I—"

"And for that, Leander Doucet, I will kill you."

And then everything went black.

# Chapter XVIII

Mary awoke in her bed in the room she shared with Elizabeth at Aunt Genevieve's house. She was unaware of how she had gotten there, or how long she had been unconscious, or if the events at the horse races had even occurred.

Surely not.

It was all just a dream.

A horrible, terrible dream.

But once she had thought of it, the scene came rushing back to her like a tidal wave—kissing Manuel, the fight, and then—Edward's vow:

I will kill you.

Mary sat up quickly, yanking the covers off and swinging her legs out of bed.

Did Edward kill him? Mary thought in a panic, planting her feet on the ground. But when she tried to apply the weight of her body, the room began to spin again and she fell back onto the bed.

"You are finally up," Aunt Genevieve declared from the doorway, a cup of tea in her hand. "I was coming to sit with you."

"Auntie, what—"

"Lay yourself back down this instance, Miss Taylor," Aunt Genevieve snapped. Mary obediently slid back into bed, allowing her aunt to fold the blankets back over her body.

"You are dehydrated, and the last thing we need is another fainting spell," she said, making sure Mary understood the drama she'd caused.

"I am sorry, Auntie," Mary mumbled, accepting the glass of water from the nightstand.

"All of it, and then we will get you another," Genevieve instructed, watching carefully as Mary drained the glass.

"You, my dear, have caused an immense amount of trouble," Genevieve sighed, combing Mary's hair with her fingers tenderly. "I hope you know how mortified I was to write to your mother and father. It was not what I expected from you. From your sister, well, that would have been another story. But Elizabeth would have known how to control the situation."

Mary nodded, tears welling in her eyes. Aunt Genevieve was right, of course—she had played with fire, believing she could chase what she wanted like a man might, and this was her punishment.

A mess.

This big terrible mess.

Perhaps even a scandal.

"Auntie, please," Elizabeth appeared in the doorway. "Can we wait to berate her until she is at least back on her feet?"

Aunt Genevieve threw Elizabeth a look before rising to her feet carefully and walking out of the room.

"Oh Mary, she is right, you know," Elizabeth whispered, taking Aunt Genevieve's place on the edge of the bed and petting Mary's hair. "It is all such a mess. I have been avoiding Charles like the plague. Have I not told you before that it's fine to kiss a beau, but you must do it in secret!"

"Elizabeth, Edward said he was going to kill Leander. What passed?"

"Calm, dear sister. Leander continues to breathe...for now. From what Edward has said, the moment you fainted, the men momentarily forgot their vendettas."

"And does everyone know?"

"No, not as far as I am aware," Elizabeth assured her. "They all have far too good of upbringings to publicize the incident, which is very fortunate."

"Elizabeth, do you mean to tell me you are in support of the suppression of gossip?" Mary attempted a jest, though it felt like the least natural thing in the world in these circumstances.

"Yes, when it involves my little sister," she answered back with a snark.

"Honestly Mary, no one looks particularly good coming out of this. Manuel Rivera was kissing you, despite not having spoken to our father; Leander Doucet punched him without provocation; and Edward made known his desire to kill Leander due to the way he treated you. None of these men are going to be eager for retellings of their behavior to make the rounds."

"Well, Edward out of all of them acted the most honorably."

"Yes, but he would have to explain *why* he wishes death on his brother's business partner, and that will drag you into the spotlight as well, which, as your brother, he does not wish upon you."

"Do you actually believe he intends to do it?"

"Do what?"

"Kill Leander."

"Possibly," Elizabeth shrugged, as though it were a matter terribly inconsequential to her. "Our brother takes affronts to our family very seriously."

Mary nodded gravely.

"But, look on the bright side—you have three men fighting over you!"

"Yes, but why, is the question."

"What do you mean?"

"I mean, I understand why Edward would be upset," Mary paused, looking at her sister through narrowed eyes.

She had not yet asked *how* Edward knew.

"Elizabeth, did you write our brother?"

Elizabeth met Mary's gaze with her own.

"It is possible it came up in our correspondence."

"Do not take me for a fool—you are a horrible correspondent! I wrote you ten letters for each one I received in return when you were at school."

"And I treasured each one," Elizabeth said breezily.

"But why would you do such a thing?"

"Because it was a wretched thing for Leander Doucet to do," Elizabeth answered, her cheeks flushed with passion as she spoke. "And I knew that Charles would have done nothing. But Mary, it is a terrible wrong you have suffered. For a Taylor to be treated with such insolence, well, it simply cannot stand.

"But I did not know he would be showing up to the races. I wrote to him asking for advice, and whether we should involve father."

"And he showed up and punched Leander instead."

"And probably would have killed him had you not fainted."

Mary closed her eyes and shook her head.

"Alright," she continued wearily. "That is one mystery solved."

"Wonderful. How many remain?"

"One."

"Which is?"

"Why would Leander behave in such a manner?"

"Oh Mary, you goose." Elizabeth rolled her eyes in that condescending way that was her own. "It is because he harbors feelings towards you. Romantic feelings."

"He has an intended, sitting upstairs, not a few feet away no less, and yet he still—"

"Because he is positively stark raving mad," Elizabeth cut in. "All men are."

"That they are," Mary agreed, her eyes closing in exhaustion.

Mary spent the next few days in bed, waking every so often to drink or nibble a few small bites of food—though her appetite remained non-existent. Aunt Genevieve, upon noticing the food trays returning to the kitchen untouched, imposed a rule: the plates must be cleaned before they were allowed back. This forced Mary and Elizabeth into elaborate schemes to dispose of the food—feeding bits to the Defour dogs, tossing scraps out the window, or hiding them in the veranda's potted plants.

Sometimes Mary awoke to find fresh flowers on her bedside table, though she did not ask who they were from.

She did not wish to know.

After nearly a week confined to her room, she finally felt well enough to venture into town. But the moment she stepped into the streets, she sensed it—that unmistakable prickle of being watched. Wherever she turned, people seemed to glance too quickly, then just as quickly look away, suddenly fascinated by signs, windows, lampposts, anything but her.

Were they whispering about her?

Surely not. Neither Manuel, Leander, nor Edward would have publicized what happened. They wouldn't dare implicate themselves.

But if they were not speaking about her, what was it that they were whispering about?

Mary turned towards Elizabeth with the intention of asking her the same question, but Elizabeth was wide-eyed, scanning the streets ahead of them with a fear borne of recognition.

"Mary, they know," she breathed.

"But how?" Mary asked, her voice barely audible over the thudding of her heart.

"I know not. Come, let us call on our dear brother Charles and see if we cannot collect ourselves," she said through gritted teeth, pushing Mary towards the bank.

Mary allowed Elizabeth to drag her across the street. The thought of facing Charles made Mary wish the world would open and swallow her whole. It would be almost as terrible as facing her father, for she knew neither men would be able to conceive of such behavior.

And the thought of seeing Leander was...

Everything.

And at the same time nothing.

"Good day, Mr. Treewell," Elizabeth and Mary greeted him as they stepped inside.

"Good day, Misses Taylor. I'm afraid your brother is not here, he—"

"Miss Taylor and Miss Taylor," Leander emerged swiftly from his office, bowing to them both. Mary stiffened at his appearance, noting when he rose that his face bore the yellowing remnants of a bruise and a thin, healing scar above his eye.

Clearly Edward had done a number on him, Mary thought with more satisfaction than she knew was technically ladylike.

"Mr. Doucet," Elizabeth replied icily. "How is your fiancée?"

"She is my intended, not my fiancée," Leander corrected quietly but firmly.

"Well, one tends to lead naturally on from the other, does it not?"

Leander opened his mouth, but no answer came.

"What do you think, Mr. Treewell?"

"Yes, Miss Taylor, I would say that's usually the way it goes," Harrison confirmed, eyeing the exchange with a weary trepidation.

"Mary, I think you need to stay here." Elizabeth turned to her sister. "And I will go see if I cannot get to the bottom of what is going on out there."

"Elizabeth, please don't." The thought of being alone with Leander Doucet made Mary want to scream and cry all at once.

"Mr. Treewell, would you be so kind as to watch over my sister for a moment or two?" Elizabeth asked, turning towards him with her best smile. "It's just that our dear Mary hasn't been very well as of late, and I do not wish to overexert her by dragging her from shop to shop. Surely you understand, Mr. Treewell?"

"Yes, of course, Miss Taylor," Harrison smiled, the way men smiled anytime they were graced with the gift of doing a favor for Miss Elizabeth Taylor. "Your sister is welcome here as long as she likes—it is her name on the door, after all!"

"Oh, you are so right," Elizabeth laughed. "But Mr. Treewell, do you promise to look after her? It is just that there are so many men in this town, men who give the air of being a gentleman, but are actually the devil is disguise. Do you know the kind of which I speak, Mr. Treewell?"

Mary chanced a look at Leander, who observed the exchange with a practiced blankness.

"Yes, Miss Taylor, I reckon I do. But I also reckon that our Miss Taylor here has a good head on her shoulders, and I'm sure she would be able to tell a scoundrel when she saw one."

"Yes, well, you just never know. Thank you ever so much, Mr. Treewell. I won't be more than a few minutes, I promise."

Harrison very graciously set Mary up in Charles's office, fetching her a cup of tea and insisting she call for him should she need anything at all.

Mary sat in one of the chairs opposite the desk, for it felt a bit too presumptuous to sit in her brother's chair. She could feel the tenseness of her body, rigid as though it were about to be under attack as she tried to sip her tea quietly.

The soft knock on the doorframe startled her when it came, though she had been expecting it.

And though she had been expecting it, she still had no idea what she was going to say.

"Miss Taylor," Leander called quietly. "Can I get you anything?"

"No, thank you, sir. I have everything I need," she declared, declining to turn around to make eye contact with him.

The sound of footsteps tapped the floor gently as Leander walked over to the desk and took the seat next to her. Mary could feel his eyes on her, the smell of his cologne filling her nostrils—familiar, infuriating.

But as before, she once again declined to acknowledge his presence. Continuing to stare at the wall straight in front of her, she raised her teacup to her lips and took a silent sip.

"Mary, please, will you look at me," Leander pleaded.

Lowering the cup, Mary carefully nestled it back into the saucer before slowly turning to meet his gaze.

"I am sorry." Everything about him—his tone, his voice, even his eyes—was melancholy. "I never meant to hurt you."

"I am not sure how you could have expected a different outcome considering your circumstances. You have made a fool of all of us—yourself, me, and your fiancée."

"She is not my fiancée," Leander corrected again. "But my intended."

"Mr. Doucet, do you really think me so foolish that such a distinction would mean anything at all to me?" Mary demanded, offended that he would believe such a technicality should make any difference.

"Mary, we have been intended since we were children," Leander exhaled as the words came out with a quiet resignation. Not in anger, but in surrender—like something that had clung to the inside of his chest for years, and only now clawed its way free. "It is an old family tradition to maintain the bloodline and ensure the family wealth is all kept in one place. On my eighteenth birthday, I was told my second cousin, who was nine at the time," he raised an eyebrow for emphasis, "would be my future wife. And then you are sent off to make your fortune and return to marry your intended once she is of age and continue on the family lineage."

"I see."

"Perhaps unsurprisingly, I had no interest in marrying my child cousin. And I still do not. I regret that I have been a terrible coward. I have purposefully spent long and extensive spells away from home in the hope she would demand another match.

"But it did not happen. I suppose her entire life has been spent waiting—first to reach a certain age, and then for me to return."

“But she is a grown woman now. She must have at least eighteen years. Surely you cannot look on her as a child anymore.”

“She has nineteen years, but I still cannot help but view her as a child.”

“She has more years than I do—surely you do not see me that way.”

“No, of course not. But the difference is that I did not know you as a child. I did not care for you and watch you when your parents went away. I feel a more paternal instinct towards her,” Leander explained. “And cannot imagine being her husband.

“I am afraid we are not kindred spirits, she and I. We share a family name—but little else. A lifetime together would be congenial, tepid at best... but it would not be shared. We would coexist—bound by proximity, not intimacy—never truly knowing one another.

“I—I desire more from marriage than that.

“I desire a partner who sees me—and perhaps, chooses me anyway. Who loves me, despite what they see.”

Mary nodded slowly to show her understanding. She could feel her body releasing, the hardness melting as the full picture came into view.

For she felt the same.

“And none of this excuses my behavior. I had every intention, after our last conversation, of going to my father and telling him I would not marry Noémie. But her arrival took me by surprise, and everything escalated from there.” Leander put his head into his hands and rubbed his temples with a weary resignation of how terrible the situation had become. “And now I do not know what to do. Your brother has challenged me to a duel, and I fear...," he swallowed.

"I fear I've lost the woman I love."

"You—you love—"

"Mary!" Elizabeth burst in. "It was Thomas Walker," she announced furiously. "He saw the whole thing at the races and told *everyone*. That snake!

"The Riveras are livid to have been treated this way by their business partner," Elizabeth paused, considering the weight of her next declaration. "And Mary—I have it one good authority that Manuel intends to propose."

Mary's stomach dropped.

"What?" Mary asked, her heart in her throat.

"What?" Leander echoed Mary's words.

"Well, he is acting as a gentleman in his position must," Elizabeth reasoned, placing a gloved hand on Mary's shoulder. "Sister, it is not a bad match—you both could have ended up in a far more unfortunate situation.

"But this is exactly why I told you to do your kissing in secret!"

"Leander Doucet!" A voice roared from the front of the bank, drowning out the attempted pacifications of Mr. Treewell. Loud footsteps pounded the floor, and in a moment, Edward Taylor stood in the doorway behind Elizabeth.

"Leander Doucet. Tomorrow, at daybreak! At the hill behind the old factory a mile south of town. Name your second." He turned towards his sister. "Elizabeth, arrange for a doctor."

"Edward, I have no desire to duel you."

"Well, sir," Edward reared towards Leander with menace. While both large and imposing men, Edward was a true-blue country boy and was formidable even when assessed against the most impressive of opponents. "You might have thought of that before you embarrassed my sister beyond repair!

"And if I were your fiancée's brother, I would be on the first train from Alabama to tear you limb from limb!"

"That is enough!" A deep, commanding voice cut in. Everyone in the room turned to see—

William Taylor.

Stood in the doorway, cane in hand, the weight of his authority draped over him like a cloak. Charles stood silently behind him.

"There will be no duel," Mr. Taylor announced.

"But Father, he—" Edward began to protest.

"Edward, you are always so bloodthirsty," William sighed, stepping into the room and approaching his son. "I will not permit you to start a war for the sake of it. There are no victors when families kill families.

"Plus, son, they are Alabamians," Father whispered. "Have you ever heard of anyone feuding with Alabamians?"

"No, sir."

"Exactly, because no one is foolish enough to do such a thing. You fight one of them, you fight all of them. I fought aside Alabamians in the War of 1812. I assure you, it is best to have them on your side."

"Yes, sir," Edward nodded, biting his lip to hold in his anger.

"Though that is not to say that a demand of a duel is an inappropriate response to your behavior, Mr. Doucet," Mr. Taylor turned his attentions towards Leander, eyeing him with a stern look, in itself a reprimand.

"Yes, sir, my father would say the same," Leander agreed, staring respectfully at the ground.

With the confidence of a man who controlled any room he entered, Mr. Taylor invited himself to the seat behind Charles's desk. Removing his hat, he tossed it aside and slipped out of his overcoat, hanging it over the back of the chair before settling into it. Finally, he unbuttoned the sleeves of his cream shirt, rolling them to his elbows.

As though some strenuous work lay ahead.

"Now," he finally began, turning his attention back to the room. "Where shall we start? How about with you?" He pointed at Leander as the rest of the party silently obeyed and filed out of the room.

Mary waited outside with the others, wringing her hands in anticipation.

She watched as Leander emerged, head low as though like a dog who had just received a beating. Without needing any provocation, Edward dutifully rose and entered the office next, closing the door behind him. Leander had stopped at the doorway of the office to speak to Charles, who had stood, arms crossed as though he were guarding the door.

"He's obviously eavesdropping," Elizabeth had insisted, and Mary smiled for the first time in a long while.

It was such an Elizabeth thing to say.

And she was almost certainly right.

Mary watched their conversation, wondering with a burning but terrified curiosity about what was being said. After a few minutes, they shook hands, and Leander dipped into his office to retrieve his hat before heading towards the door. He stopped in front of Mary and Elizabeth. Turning first towards her sister, Leander bowed, but Elizabeth did not respond, staring him down with a stony impudence. Leander seemed unfazed and turning to Mary, his hat in hand, he held out his free hand. Mary considered it, remembering the moments when those fingers had wrapped around her neck, had tangled into her hair, and had held her against him. She stole a glance upwards, meeting his eyeline, and noted, for the first time, that his hand shook.

This time, due to fear.

Finally, she placed her small hand in his outstretched palm. Leander repeated the action, bowing low and once eye-level with Mary, brought her hand to his lips and kissed it softly. They held one another's gaze for a moment, and then another.

And then, too soon, Leander was returning to his standing position. He gently placed Mary's hand back into her lap, donned his cap, and disappeared through the door.

By the time Mary's turn arrived, she was exhausted with anticipation.

"Mary," Mr. Taylor sighed, leaning back in Charles's chair and rubbing his eyes wearily. "I never did expect this from you. From—"

"Elizabeth, yes, but she would have been able to control the situation better," Mary finished the sentence for him. "Aunt Genevieve has already informed me of all of this."

Mr. Taylor stared at her, stunned, unsure if he should laugh with amusement or be perturbed at her impudence.

After a moment, Mr. Taylor removed his glasses, tossing them on the table next to his hat, and chuckled.

"Yes, that does sound like your aunt," he concurred. "She is furious, as I am sure you can imagine."

"Yes, she informed me, the moment I gained consciousness."

Mr. Taylor allowed the tiniest grin to form at the sides of his mouth, shaking his head and once again rubbing his eyes.

"That woman," he mused momentarily, before turning his attention back to Mary. "Daughter, this is a very serious situation."

"I know, Father."

"And if you were your sister, I'd sit here and deliver a full lecture—on your conduct, your reputation, the impact to our family's name. But I know you. And I can tell you already know it all. You've punished yourself far more thoroughly than I ever could. So, in light of this, we will be expediting to solutions."

"Thank you, sir."

"You are fortunate," he continued, folding his hands together on the desk, "that you display good judgment in the gentlemen you associate with. Despite his ungentlemanly behavior in engaging in acts that are, let us say, traditionally reserved for matrimony—Manuel Rivera has done the right thing. He came to me this morning and asked for your hand."

"My hand." A statement, a question, borne of denial.

"In marriage."

Mary reached for a breath, but her lungs came up empty.

"And you will of course, be accepting it."

"But, Father, I—"

"And that," he interrupted, voice like steel, "is the end of it."

# Act III

*A Resolution, of Sorts*

# The Verity (excerpt)

*In which the engagements of the season—both social and otherwise—are proclaimed*

**An excerpt from *The Verity***

## Social musings (societal update)

Juan Rivera of Hacienda Ofrenda is delighted to announce the engagement of his son Manuel Rivera to Miss Mary Taylor of Cana, Richmond, Virginia.

The union will join two longtime allies of great prestige into one.

A private celebration of this joyous engagement will be held at the New Orleans residence of the Rivera family on the evening of the 3rd of August, with the Taylors travelling in from Virginia and staying with their relatives to be.

# La Libération (excerpt)

*A collection of congratulatory notices and editorial observations, delicately worded—with the strictest attempts at civility*

## An excerpt from *La Libération*

### Crème de la crème (societal update)

The Defours wish to extend their congratulations to Miss Mary Taylor on her intended engagement. Publishing such announcements so early in the process clearly speaks to a lasting love—and admirable confidence in the outcome.

# Chapter XIX

A sense of impending doom overcame Mary Taylor as she sat at the dressing table, staring at the reflection it produced. She carefully inspected the figure's hair, the tight curls that had been primly pinned either side of her head, gathered with a light white silk ribbon tied into bows. Her eyes travelled down as she considered her skin—a wet film of sweat lightly covered her chest. She tried to breathe deeply, but her breath could not find its way past her throat. Closing her eyes and bringing a hand to her torso, she inhaled as insistently as she could, but the breath stubbornly remained at the surface, refusing to give her any reprieve.

She reached for a small table mirror, but her hands shook too violently to steady it—the image inside jumped like a skittish fowl.

She just needed something to keep her mind occupied. Mary looked desperately about the room. There was still nearly an hour before guests arrived, and if she did not find something to do, she was certain she would go mad.

Mary's scan proved fruitless, which while frustrating, was unsurprising, considering this was not her Aunt

Genevieve's house. It was a slightly unorthodox situation, for an engagement party to be hosted by someone other than the bride-to-be's family.

But then again, the nuances of the situation as a whole could hardly be described as usual. For it was not common for a lady to be marrying into a family with whom her extended family had an ongoing feud, and it was certainly not common for a lady's engagement to be preceded by a brawl of three young gentlemen.

*"You will be setting the new trend, dear sister,"* Elizabeth had tried to convince her when Mary had emerged from her talk with her father, his verdict fresh on her lips. *"No young lady will feel a gentleman truly desires their hand in marriage unless he is willing to knock another man to the ground over her."*

While it was frowned upon that the entire town knew that Manuel Rivera and Mary Taylor had been found engaging in premarital relations of kissing, it was not as uncommon as the old guard of proprietary Southerners would lead the younger generations to believe.

And besides, as Mr. Taylor had said himself, the fact that Manuel Rivera had come to him on his own accord and asked for Mary's hand spoke to his good breeding and honor. There was no requirement for the Taylor men to hunt him down, and he did not act as one being led to the gallows.

On the contrary, Manuel Rivera appeared incredibly pleased with the outcome. According to Elizabeth, the word around town was that he had sent for an enormous diamond ring from Spain and would be presenting it to her this very evening at their engagement party.

Mary looked down at her gloved hands, imagining her ring finger weighed down, dragging towards the floor, under the weight of a large rock.

A promise of a life to come and to be shared.

Then why did it feel like a tether?

Mary had not seen or spoken to Leander since that day at the bank. He had disappeared through the door of Taylor Mutual Fund that afternoon, and even Charles claimed he did not know of his whereabouts. But when her brother spoke of his friend, a pained expression crossed his face, his brow wrinkling into a state of distress. After a little while, Mary had ceased to ask, aware of the displeasure it clearly brought him.

Not to mention, the further strain such inquiries placed on their own relationship, which had not even begun to recover from the scandal caused. Mary had always perceived the worst part of a scandal must be the social ostracization, the knowledge that tongues wag excitedly when they pass you in the street, but now she knew better. It was the impact the scandal bore on your relations with those you cared most for that dealt the heaviest blow.

At one time his favorite sibling, Charles now barely looked at Mary—he stopped calling at the Defour residence to visit, citing the additional workload with Leander's absence as the cause, and when Mary tried to call at the bank she was nearly always informed by Mr. Treewell that Charles was with an important client and had asked not to be disturbed.

Once having confided in her sister her fears that Charles had been avoiding her, Elizabeth had strong-armed their way into Charles's office. Mary had gasped at the man who looked up from the barricade of papers, his hair unwashed, his shirt requiring an iron, and his eyes sunk deep into his face, a slightly crazed look that seemed to ask "what, in God's name, could it possibly be now?!" plastered across his face—an expression that felt both accusatory and condemning at the same time.

She had brought on him this stress, her actions had caused the depart of his business partner, and now she could not even give him a moment of peace.

"*It is not your fault, Mary,*" Elizabeth had insisted time and again. *"It is only scoundrels who lack the bravery required to speak the truth."*

And yet, despite the rift that scoundrel had caused, Mary could not bring herself to stop thinking about him. Even when she tried her best to suppress thoughts of him, burying memories of the moments they shared the instant they began to emerge, they still always managed to wiggle their way through.

Which was why, now, on the eve of her engagement party, when Manuel Rivera and Mary Taylor would formally announce their engagement to wed, Mary felt hollow.

For she liked Manuel Rivera, respected him, and appreciated the way he made her feel.

Or rather, the way in which he believed he made her feel.

The way he believed all young ladies wished to feel.

"But I do not love him," Mary admitted aloud to herself in the mirror in nothing more than a whisper.

Even as she spoke the words into existence her heart pounded, for the consequence of the evening was not lost on her. She stood at the precipice, staring down the barrel of the rest of her life, all the while knowing that it would be spent with a man whom she did not love.

*"You will learn to love him,"* her mother, having arrived from Virginia the day before, had promised. *"Love sometimes takes time."*

*And what if I love another?*

It was not only that she felt numb for herself, but for Manuel Rivera she felt... sorry. Sorry that he was marrying a woman who, deep down, did not wish to be his wife. The Rivera family had such a rich history of true love stories, ones which Mary drank up gluttonously, that left her feeling full and hopeful. But now, when it was her turn to join this rich tapestry, she felt like a fraud.

Manuel had not once asked why Leander Doucet had attacked him. When pressed by others, he explained that he had regrettably found himself carried away with the charms of Miss Taylor, and Mr. Doucet, as a close friend of the Taylor family, had reacted impulsively, out of a brotherly instinct to protect.

Which while misplaced, was honorable.

Mary had wondered more than once whether her father and Charles had spun that tale for the Riveras themselves, and how much convincing had been required before they had agreed to accept it. As for Edward, his frequenting of bars and houses of ill repute had easily cast doubt over his claims, and while New Orleanians accepted this explanation at face value, secretly they continued to ponder what had actually happened the day of the races.

Mary stood up from the vanity, smoothing the front of her pink dress with her gloved hands.

*But did it not bother him?* The question gnawed at Mary's insides.

Did it not bother Manuel to lack the truth, to so readily accept a story that lacked satisfaction and closure? Would it not pick at the edges of his brain, perhaps subconsciously at first, before burrowing into his consciousness and demanding an answer?

Could a man really be satisfied living that way until the end of his days?

Or a woman, for that matter.

Elizabeth opened the door without pronouncement or without permission.

As was her way.

"Look at you," Elizabeth went to her side, and the sisters stood facing the mirror, gazing into their joint reflection. "You look beautiful." Her smile lacked conviction as she gently busied herself with fixing a lock of Mary's hair with her fingers.

One that did not, by Mary's estimation, require any fixing.

"What is it?" Mary tried to meet her sister's eyes in the mirror, but Elizabeth's attention could not be caught, particularly when she did not wish it to be.

"You do look absolutely beautiful," she repeated, finally meeting her sister's gaze—though the uncertainty in her voice had nothing to do with Mary's choice of dress.

"Elizabeth, what is it?" Mary caught her sister's hands, forcing them to hold still.

"I am just so happy for you," Elizabeth tried to insist, though her eyes told a different story.

"Then why do you appear so distressed?" Mary followed her sister's attention to the floor.

It was so unlike Elizabeth to fear speaking her mind.

"There is something I fear I must tell you," Elizabeth finally admitted, looking up to meet Mary's eyes. "For I feel you should know, though I know it will bring you difficulty, and I should not wish that on you.

"Especially today, of all days."

At her words, Mary swallowed, and holding her breath she motioned, for Elizabeth to continue.

"I saw him." The words fell from her mouth like a confession, a pained expression crossing her face.

Mary did not need to ask who.

Nor did she dare.

It was all at once, the only and last name she wished to hear—especially on today, of all days.

"You are certain?" Mary breathed, her heart pounding.

"Yes, for I spoke with him."

"You spoke with him?"

"He was exiting the bank. Mary, he—he asked after you."

"What did you say?"

"I told him of this evening," Elizabeth admitted, brushing a piece of nothing off Mary's dress.

"He asked if you are happy." At her words Mary inhaled, holding her breath as she waited for Elizabeth to continue, though she did not.

"And? How did you respond?" She finally found the words.

"I asked him what lady would be anything other than happy on the night of her engagement party."

It was a fair question—an excellent question in fact, and one to which Mary had no answer.

"Come in," Manuel called, startled to see Mary's face peek through the door. "Mary!" He quickly stood from his desk, abandoning the pen and paper in front of him and meeting her at the door. "I was not expecting you. Is everything alright?" he asked, looking at her swollen eyes. "Dearest, what's the matter?" he insisted, leading her over to a couch and sitting her down, taking the seat next to her.

"Manuel, I—" Large tears dripped into Mary's lap. Manuel reached into his pocket, producing a handkerchief.

Her handkerchief, in fact.

The one she had gifted him as a token of her affection.

He carried it on his person always, in his breast pocket.

"*So that is it close to my heart,*" he had explained on more than one occasion, without provocation.

It was clearly to Manuel Rivera a great treasure—a living, breathing symbol of their shared love story.

And to Mary a constant reminder of the consequences of one's actions.

"Is the thought of marrying me so disagreeable to you?" he asked, attempting to mask his disappointment behind a sad smile.

"No, it is not that. I just fear that if I tell you the truth, it will hurt you."

Placing a hand atop Mary's, Manuel inhaled, turning his attention straight ahead of him for a moment as silence settled between them. Finally, when he spoke, he continued to stare at his desk, his voice far away, almost dreamlike as he made his own confessions.

"My sister Catalina married a nameless soldado, a soldier in the Spanish army. He called one day to speak with my father and found himself unexpectedly and undeniably smitten with his daughter.

"'She was the most standoffish and severe woman I had ever met'," Manuel echoed his late brother-in-law's words, chuckling at the adjectives used to describe his sister, "'and I knew from the moment I saw her that something larger than us had crossed our paths. Something larger than us had given me, a man so undeserving of this woman, a chance to be chosen by her.

"'And if I could manage to win her heart once, just once, then I would do anything to be chosen by her every day.'"

"That is the kind of marriage my family knows, Mary." Manuel finally turned towards her, squeezing her hand. "The kind that chooses one another every day.

"I would not wish you to marry me out of requirement," Manuel spoke with a soft gentle tone. "I would wish you to marry me because you chose me.

"Would you, Mary, have chosen me?

"Do you?" He finally breathed.

Mary studied her lap, the weight of Manuel's large hands engulfing hers felt heavy, like a burden, an untold secret, an unconfessed sin. Finally, inhaling deeply, she turned to meet Manuel's gaze.

"No," she declared, a single final tear escaping her eyelid as she finally divulged the contents of her heart. "I am afraid I love another."

With a heavy effort, Manuel nodded, turning his gaze from hers and towards the window where he allowed his stare to linger. Finally, he eased himself to his feet, and clasping his hands behind his back, he walked towards it. He stood against the early evening light, the shadow of the sun elongating his slender frame as he inhaled deeply.

"Then you should go to him."

In the uproar and confusion of Manuel Rivera calling off their engagement, Mary slipped out of the Rivera townhouse. She had not had time to grab her overcoat or hat—or at least, had not risked the moment it would take.

For Father would be furious, his direct order discarded.

Mother would be left utterly speechless.

And Charles would sit in stunned disbelief for his youngest sister's waywardness.

Yes, there would be music to face tomorrow, Mary acknowledged, pausing for only a moment to inhale the evening air, revelling in the feeling as her lungs filled and expanded.

But tonight, she would dance while she was still able. Gathering her skirts in her fists, Mary bolted down the steps, taking off down the street as though for dear life.

And indeed, if you had asked her, and if you asked her still to this day, she would say that was exactly what she was running for.

Away from the life chosen for her.

And towards the one she would choose for herself.

"Mary!" A voice called from behind her, but Mary did not stop, nor did she look back. She pushed herself onwards, her legs moving at a desperate speed, her hair falling free from its delicate ties.

Up ahead, people on the street paused to stare at the richly dressed young lady hurtling down the Spanish district, her hair flapping behind her and her little silk slippers ruined from the cobblestones.

But Mary did not care.

The calling of her name continued, the voice insistent, pleading even. It was closer than before, and Mary willed herself to go faster as her heart pounded against her ribcage.

She did not think about what would happen if the voice caught up with her, for it was not a possibility she was willing to entertain. Good luck to the man who tried to reason with her.

And God help the man who tried to drag her back to her own engagement party.

Without knowing how or why, Mary found herself falling backwards, her arm being pulled from her socket as she stumbled, her back falling into the torso of her pursuer.

"Mary, it is me," the voice pleaded.

The plea a promise.

Mary's heart stopped, and she whirled around, only to find herself face to face with...

Leander Doucet.

"Leander, I...what are you doing here?" she managed at long last.

A stupid question, really.

But at this point, Mary Talyor was certain she had learned her lesson when it came to making assumptions based on behavior.

"I happened upon your sister in town today and she told me that you were to be engaged after this evening."

"And what was your intention, to ruin my engagement party?" Mary demanded, unsure if she intended to be jovial or accusatory.

Perhaps a bit of both.

At her words, Leander reddened, well aware that it was a dastardly thing for a gentleman to ruin a lady's engagement party.

"In truth, the thought had crossed my mind," he finally confessed after a moment. "Though, it would appear to me, Miss Taylor, that you are doing an awfully good job of that on your own.

"Where are you fleeing to, on this, what is supposed to be one of the happiest evenings in a lady's lifetime?"

"I will answer you if you answer me this, Mr. Doucet," Mary returned his cheek. "What are you doing gawking outside a lady's engagement party—

"Particularly when you have explicitly not been invited—

"And especially when you are intended to another?"

"I have no intended. Which is what I came to tell you," Leander confessed, shame filling his eyes, an acknowledgement of the extent of his selfishness.

"And yet you did not make your presence known."

"I was still deciding if it was appropriate," Leander confessed, casting his eyes to the ground.

"Are there any circumstances in which ruining a lady's engagement party is appropriate?"

"Well, perhaps yes."

"Please, do enlighten me then."

"If the lady in question is marrying a rogue, for example."

"Of which Manuel Rivera is not one."

"Indeed."

"When else?"

"If the lady in question is marrying another, but you have found yourself tragically in love with her."

Mary's questioning froze and Leander raised his eyes from the ground to meet hers as he continued.

"But you have been a terrible coward, and you do not know if she will wish to see you. For she would have every reason to not... And the last thing you wish to do is ruin this moment for her, but you also know that you will never forgive yourself if you do not try to tell her how sorry you are," Leander breathed. "And how much you love her."

Mary stood frozen, allowing his words to wash over her, bathing her in disbelief as she willed it all to be real.

Finally, after a moment, Leander asked,

"Does that answer your question, Miss Taylor?"

Mary nodded, slowly, almost stupidly as she processed his words.

"Your turn."

"Pardon me?"

"It is your turn now. I have answered your inquiry as to when it is appropriate to ruin a lady's engagement party. It is now your turn to tell me to where you were fleeing."

"I left to find you." The words tumbled from her mouth, shameless and raw, but the embarrassment at her lack of tact had left her. Taking a step towards him, Mary placed her hands on his chest. He was firm and warm, and underneath her palms, Mary could feel his heart pounding.

"Did you?" His voice was no more than a whisper, an exhale, as though he could not believe it to be true.

But it was. Her words confirmed it.

"Oh Mary, I was certain I had lost you."

"I couldn't bear it," She admitted.

"Mary," Leander murmured, wrapping his arms around her waist and pulling her close.

And this time, when Mary leaned her chin upwards, Leander bent down to meet her. They pressed their lips together, gently at first, and the smell of Leander filled Mary's nostrils, sending flutters through her chest and down to the tips of her toes. After a moment their bodies moved closer, their lips pressing into one another with a bit more force as their mouths opened in unison. Mary's hands travelled up his torso and wrapped around his neck, clinging to him so tightly she hoped she would never have to let go. At her instigation, Leander pulled her into him until they were one body, pounding in unison for one another.

It was the moment she had been waiting for, for in that moment Mary felt not only desired—

But seen.

"There is one thing we need to make clear, Miss Taylor," Leander pulled himself away from her lips and murmured into her ear.

"Oh? And what is that?"

"I told you I was certain I had lost you once, and I will not ever risk that again.

"I need to ruin you," he declared, nibbling the bottom of her earlobe. "Completely and utterly ruin you," he teased, absorbing her gasp with his own mouth. "So that no man can take you from me."

Mary paused, pulling her mouth from his and studying Leander for a moment, as though considering his words.

One could argue that Leander Doucet had already done a fairly robust job of ruining Miss Mary Taylor—being in public and unaccompanied, standing at a proximity that should be reserved only for the privacy of one's home, and not to mention, kissing most intimately underneath a streetlamp which only illuminated their ill behavior.

Especially on the night of the lady in question's engagement announcement to another, which had been published in the papers not twelve hours earlier that very morning!

Yes, one could argue that Leander Doucet had already torn her reputation to tatters.

But then again, Mary was not one to argue.

At least, not in this moment.

"Do your worst, Mr. Doucet," she finally declared, finding his lips once again.

# Chapter XX

The large oak door of the bank closed with a heavy thud, the click of the lock crisp.

A sign that they were alone, truly alone, at long last.

Even cast in darkness and from where she stood leaning against the edge of Mr. Treewell's desk, Mary could see the way Leander's eyes swept over her as he turned around. She knew her appearance could only be described as dishevelled, her hair completely free-flowing, and a light film of anticipation coating her white chest, which gleamed pearlescent in the unlit foyer of the bank.

And she also knew that he did not care in the least.

In fact, she was almost certain he thoroughly enjoyed the look of her.

With purposeful steps, Leander closed the space between them. He moved slowly, and Mary savored the sound of his footsteps on the stone floor as he approached, moving with an expectant revel, borne of a knowledge of what was to come, and a lack of necessity to rush it.

Towering over her, Leander stared down at Mary, soaking her in as he gently raised a hand either side of her shoulders and ran them down the length of her arms. Mary inhaled, closing her eyes and allowing herself to become lost in his touch. A thumb pressed against her chin, beckoning it upwards, and when she tilted her head, she was met with his lips.

They were soft but passionate kisses, the kind that sought to relish a moment, especially a moment one had waited for so patiently.

Mary felt her arms reach for Leander's torso, gently tugging him closer, and at her insistence, he immediately responded, closing the gap between them as their bodies pressed together. The feel of his body against hers awoke in Mary that urgency that Leander Doucet had stirred in her so long ago, and reaching for his neck, she pulled him somehow closer to her still, her kisses hungrier as something within her pressed her on.

Leander responded by pulling her closer still, and when he did, his manhood pressed into her, firm and pounding with an insistence of its own. He trailed his mouth down to her neck, his body responding to the soft moans that escaped Mary's mouth as he pushed into her, causing them both to rise and fall in tandem.

The feeling was like nothing Mary had ever experienced, and she knew she desired it again.

And whatever else came with it.

Instigating this time—for if the last few months had taught her anything, it was the necessity of pursuit of one's desires—Mary pressed into him while moving her hips from side to side. At the sway of her body, Leander inhaled sharply, his manhood growing larger and harder. Without hesitation he reached for her breasts, cupping them gently. At the squeeze of his hands, Mary's entire body rose and fell, melting into his touch. Dipping his finger into the top of her dress, he flicked her nipples lightly and pressed her into him as she moaned in pleasure.

"If you like what I can do with my fingers, Miss Taylor," he whispered, his tongue laced with what could only be described as wickedness.

Delicious, indulgent wickedness.

"Imagine what I can do with my tongue."

At his words, Mary gasped, urgently pushing herself into him as the space between her legs throbbed with desire.

Leander took this as an invitation, and trailing his fingers lightly along the tops of her breasts once more, he teased her before placing a hand either side of Mary's dress and tugging the material further down her torso. As the top of her bustier emerged he slipped his hands inside, caressing her nipples in slow, sensuous circles.

Mary moaned, her head falling backwards as though her neck had snapped. She was certain she could not feel more delight in her life until Leander's mouth continued its assault downwards, nibbling at her collarbone before pausing at the top of her chest. Mary's eyes flew open, meeting Leander's mischievous gaze. He held it for a moment, meeting her anticipated stare with one of his own. Finally, he slowly lowered his head, and pulling her even nearer by the waist, he traced her right nipple with his tongue. At the action, Mary quivered in his arms, her body losing its ability to support itself, but this only seemed to delight Leander, who glancing up at Mary once more, took her entire nipple in his mouth and began to suck. He sucked and teased, whirling his tongue around her nipple and gently tugging it with his teeth as she cried out in breathy desire.

"Mary," he said as he moved to the other nipple, pressing his body into her with his own urgency this time as he steered them away from the door and walked them backwards.

They were still standing in the doorway for heaven's sake!

Once inside his office, Leander lit a lamp, placing it carefully on the rung on the wall. In the dim light that the fire cast, Mary took him in. His hair was ruffled, a product of her own roving hands, his cheeks flushed with desire.

And that place between his legs was enlarged, pushing against the material of his trousers with such force, Mary could not believe they still held together.

Leander followed her gaze, and broke into what could only be described as a devilish grin when he realized what had captured her attention.

"That," he said in a low growl, closing the distance between them, "we will get to in due time. But for the moment, I believe we need to do something about this dress." He placed a hand either side of Mary's shoulders and found her lips once more.

"Really, Mr. Doucet, do you think the dress is the most pressing matter?" Mary asked coyly, looking up at him. Leander paused, returning her look.

"I am still wearing my gloves," she declared, presenting them to him.

"That you are, Miss Taylor." He took her outstretched hands, and lightly tugging them, walked her further into the office. "Let us see if we cannot do something about those also."

Picking her up with ease, he placed her on the edge of his desk in one swift motion. Then he turned his attention to her gloves. Starting with Mary's right, he slowly peeled the gloves from her hands, finger by finger. As he did, he pressed his body into her legs, and without being told, Mary moved them apart, allowing him to nestle in between. As he did, she could feel his manhood, hard and stiff, pushing into her, lightly at first, barely a graze, but then with more force, and finally with a necessity that she was sure would consume him.

For she felt it too.

He moved to her left hand, gently tugging at each finger until both the gloves were off, discarded over Leander's shoulder in a dramatic show of desire.

"Now, about this dress..."

"Tear it," Mary heard someone say.

And she did not think it a bad idea.

On the contrary, it sounded like a rather sensible idea.

Perhaps the most sensible thing she had ever heard in her life.

"Pardon me?" Leander's eyes burned at her words, desirous to hear them again.

"Tear it," Mary pleaded.

"But, Mary, how will you—"

"I do not care," she insisted, reaching for his torso and pulling him into her with more urgency than she had ever felt before in her life. "Tear it."

Something altogether animalistic came over Leander. Not needing to be told a fourth time, he took hold of the material in between her breasts and pulled. The soft wisp of the tearing sound filled the room, and when Leander had finished Mary sat in her pantalettes and bustier, her skin glistening from the light of the lantern. She had expected to feel exposed, but on the contrary, she felt magnetized, drawn for dear life towards the man in front of her. She was nervous, of course, for what was to come, but assured by a comfort in knowing that Leander would take care of her.

And that he did.

Leander paused, soaking her in under the soft glow of the firelight. His skin was flushed with the excitement of anticipated passion, but the way he looked at her with those wide eyes, urgent yet somehow also deep and tender, made Mary feel like the only woman in the world.

"Mary." Leander placed a hand either side of her thigh, squeezing them lightly. "Would you like to stop?"

"Why?" The question caught her by surprise—it felt a quite absurd thing to ask after he had just torn her gown past repair.

"I just do not wish you to feel pressured or uncomfortable," he explained carefully, a sincerity in his voice though it also trembled.

Mary could tell that these were the words of a man competing with his own body.

And perhaps, because of his love for her, his mind was winning.

"Am I suitably ruined?" Mary asked, cocking her head to one side. A smile slithered across Leander's face and he chuckled. Taking a step back, he tapped his chin, feigning consideration.

"Because I am not sure I am," Mary heard someone say.

At her words, Leander's eyes grew large and he stepped towards her, closing the space between them once more.

"Is that so?" Leander purred the question into her ear as his hands started at her knees and began to travel up her thighs. They moved slowly upwards, but also inwards, until his fingers were tracing the insides of her legs. At his touch, Mary inhaled sharply, her heart pounding only second to her womanhood as he inched closer and closer to it. He teased her, caressing the outsides of the area in the most maddening way before finally touching her gently.

Mary moaned, melting into his fingers as he massaged and tantalized. The fire that had built in between Mary's legs escalated at his touch—she wanted more, his fingers but also something... more. He responded to her sounds, making his way to her crest and swirling the area with the tips of his fingers. Mary gasped, and natural instinct took over as she tried to close her legs, but Leander wedged them back open with his torso. Placing a hand around her waist, he gently began to lower her back onto the desk, pressing her down and in the same motion moving her further onto the desk, until nearly her entire body lay flat against it.

In a quick motion, Leander was atop her, his legs straddling her body as he continued to rub her womanhood. Mary stared at him, eyes wide in excited bewilderment. She had already decided to surrender completely and wholly to whatever it was he had in store for her.

Still caressing her with one hand, he reached for the strings of her corset and began to tug, all the while, keeping his eyes locked with hers. He did it slowly at first, as though waiting for her to protest, but when she did not, he pulled with more force, allowing the string to pull through completely. Holding it between his thumb and his forefinger, he dropped it to the floor, and Mary watched as it tumbled out of view.

Along with her innocence.

Now that her torso was completely bare, Leander paused his assault on her womanhood and gently pulled the corset out from under her before placing her back on the desk.

"Oh Mary," Leander breathed, leaning forward so their faces were only inches apart. "You are absolutely beautiful."

It was both a declaration and a promise.

Mary reached up, cupped his head with her hands, she pulled his face towards hers, kissing him with a hunger she had never known. He pressed his body into hers, and she could feel his manhood beating against her. And when she wrapped her legs around Leander's torso, pressing herself into him harder, a quiver shot through his body as he paused suddenly.

"Miss Taylor," he warned playfully, shaking his head. "You will pay for that."

Another promise.

Mary's eyes bulged as Leander returned to a straddling position. Unlooping himself from his suspenders, he reached into the top of his trousers, pulling his shirt up over his shoulders. Mary gaped at his bare skin, the broadness of his chest and the ripples of the muscles in his arms, glistening with a soft film of exertion.

But Leander wasn't through shedding clothing. Reaching down, he fingered the band of Mary's pantalettes, and with a maddening slowness, began to tug them down until her womanhood was exposed.

"This, Miss Taylor, is when I ruin you," he growled, reaching his finger down to that place between her legs. Mary could feel herself wet and ready for him, but nothing could have prepared her for the sensation of his bare fingers against her lips. He trailed a single finger through her, revelling in her wetness before finding his way back to the top of her, to that small ball of passion. At his touch, she opened up like a flower, closing her eyes as he caressed her. Her back arched towards the ceiling, pushing her chest upwards and towards Leander, as though an offering.

An invitation.

And he did not need any further encouragement.

His teeth found her right nipple, tugging lightly and sending electric shocks through Mary's body while a hand cupped her other breast. Leander massaged, cupped, and sucked her all at the same time.

The sensation was overwhelming, all-consuming, and Mary bit her lip as the pleasure built and built, pushing her towards the edge of something—what exactly, she did not know, but she was certain she was about to find out.

Until finally it erupted, sending her body reverberating as she gasped, reaching out for Leander for dear life.

But he was there, and as she clung to him, her body rigid, he held her tightly, kissing her cheek and neck with a soft tenderness.

"La petite mort," Leander said to no one in particular.

"Pardon?"

"It means 'the little death'."

"La petite mort," Mary repeated after a few moments.

"Very good. It is of course best to start practicing now, considering you will need to learn French."

"Will I?" Mary demanded playfully.

"Oh yes," Leander murmured, kissing her neck. "Our children must grow up speaking their native language."

"I think you'll find, Mr. Doucet, that we are speaking my native language right now."

"Ha, indeed. But I'm afraid it is a prerequisite to becoming Mrs. Doucet. I trust that will not be a deal breaker?"

"I wish I had known of this requirement before I went and ruined myself."

"Oh," Leaned tilted his head, the light from the lantern illuminating a puckish grin. "And would that have altered your feelings on the prospect of becoming Mrs. Doucet?"

"Well, it does seem like an awful lot of work." Mary met his mischievous expression with one of her own.

"I promise that it will be worth it," Leander whispered into her hair as he began kissing her neck. At his movements, Mary's body burned, pressing into his torso with a yearning that caused Leander to pause.

"I promise you, Mary, that you are suitably ruined," he insisted with caution. "We do not need to—"

"But what if I wanted to?" Mary asked, her eyes bearing into Leander's.

"This could wait until our wedding night," Leander replied softly.

But his body trembled.

"Can you wait that long?" she dared to ask, completely unaware of the power of her words and the effect they had until she saw Leander quiver with desire.

"It would have to be a quick wedding," Leander leaned down, biting at her neck. "For who knows the consequences of our laying together."

"That will be slightly scandalous," Mary admitted in a whisper, pressing herself into him and wrapping her legs around his torso once more. Only this time when she did, she thrust herself against him, and Leander gasped.

"Do you know, Miss Mary Taylor, what you do to me?" he demanded.

"I am not sure I know in words," Mary admitted slowly.

"But you can feel it." Leander finished, his voice low and husky.

"Yes," Mary whispered.

"And do you wish to know more?"

"Yes.

"I wish to know more."

"Very well," Leander responded, slipping a finger between them and reaching for the hair of her womanhood. "I do find myself helplessly bound to fulfill your desires," he spoke into her neck, wetting his finger in her before pausing suddenly. "Mary," he asked, his tone serious. "Do you know what transpires between a man and a woman?

"Or rather, a husband and a wife?"

Mary bit her lip, shaking her head slowly as she looked to the side.

"Do not worry," Leander touched her hair with his other hand. "I will take care of you. But please, you must tell me if it hurts. Or if you wish me to stop." Mary nodded.

And with that confirmation, Leander slipped two fingers inside her. Mary gasped at his entrance, her body stiffening at first at the foreignness of it. But Leander coaxed her open, entering again and again with a lightly applied force, each time pressing deeper and deeper into her.

Mary's mouth opened in surprise—it felt good.

No, it felt great.

But she was certain there was more to it.

"Leander," she breathed his name. He paused, staring at her as though she held his life in her next words.

"I want you."

A declaration.

"I am yours."

A promise.

Leander climbed off of Mary, and once standing, unbuttoned his trousers and pulled them from his toro. At the sight of his cock, Mary's eyes grew wide, a hand immediately coming to her mouth.

It was so large. She stared at the erect member. How was it ever going to—

"It will fit," Leander assured her, as though reading her mind. "But you must tell me if it hurts," he insisted again, climbing back on top of her and lowering himself towards her. At their proximity Mary's womanhood throbbed, desperate for him.

He began by touching her with his tip, rubbing against her wetness and pressing into her. When Mary opened for him, he slowly and, as gently as possible, pushed into her, meeting the expected resistance with a patient tempo of back and forth.

Mary wrapped her arms around Leander's neck, holding on to him tightly as he progressed into her further, going deeper and deeper until finally he was fully inside of her. He began to move back and forth, slowly at first, pressing her against him and using his mouth to bite her neck, to tease her nipple, and to kiss her lips.

"Mary," he murmured. "Does it hurt?"

"No," she breathed, revelling in the feeling of him inside of her and the notion of their bodies being one.

"Would you like me to go deeper?" he asked, his voice low. At the strain in his voice Mary paused, noting the almost pained expression on his face, the way his eyebrows scrunched towards his nose.

"Are you alright?" Worry shadowed her brow, momentarily disregarding his question and placing a hand on his face.

"Yes," he breathed, but his voice was hoarse, as though he were in a terrible amount of discomfort.

"But you look to be in pain—"

At her words Leander gave a mournful laugh, shaking his head.

"My dear Mary, if only you knew when you do to me," he sighed.

"What does that mean?" she demanded.

It was never nice to be laughed at by a gentleman, but in this particular circumstance, Mary found it utterly unbearable.

"Pardon me, I did not mean to laugh," Leander insisted, kissing her softly. "It's just that I desire you very deeply, Miss Taylor... with all of my mind, body, and heart. And it is taking every ounce of self-control I have to not simply take you.

"My head knows that this is your first time, and it can be uncomfortable for a lady, especially on her first time. And my heart wants to make love to you, but my body...

"My body wishes to ravish you."

"Yes," Mary whispered in his ear.

"Yes?"

"Yes, I want you to go deeper," she insisted, wrapping her legs around his torso. Leander plunged into her, and Mary gasped, clutching his shoulder. He paused, looking at her for direction.

But she wanted more.

"Again," she told his ear, and he obeyed, thrusting harder and deeper.

"Again," she commanded.

"Again."

"Again," until he needed no further direction. He plunged into her with deep passionate strokes whilst caressing her crest. The sensation of both was more than Mary could handle, and when she died again, she let out a scream. Leander thrust once more and then gasped, his body going limp on top of hers.

"I never knew that death could be so pleasurable," Mary confessed from under Leander. Propping himself up to meet her face, he smiled.

"Oh yes," he grinned wickedly, leaning forward and kissing her. "And there will be plenty more where that came from, Miss Mary."

"Please, call me Mrs. Doucet."

# Epilogue

*Featuring a final excerpt from La Libération—interrupted, of course.*

## An excerpt from La Libération

## Crème de la crème (social update)

The Defours proudly extend their congratulations to their niece and cousin, Mrs. Mary Doucet (formerly Taylor) and Leander Doucet on the birth of their son. The child is to be christened this coming Sunday, at—

"Do you think he will be most upset?" Mary asked, looking down at the small bundle in her arms and bouncing him lightly in her lap.

"I think he will be surprised," Leander poked his head around from the newspaper he held sprawled open to offer his wife a reassuring smile. "But Charles is too much of a gentleman to say so."

"Yes, but that almost makes it worse. At least if it were Elizabeth we had hurt, she would tell us—"

"Very directly," Leander added.

"Indeed," Mary smiled at his added detail. "But I fear Charles will feel disappointed and never speak of it."

"Men and women are different, Mary," Leander folded the paper in half, and discarding it on a side table, he rose from his seat and joined his wife on the couch.

Even before Mary had become pregnant, this had been their ritual—they would take turns reading to one another. Whether it was the papers, a novel, or a volume of history mattered not, for the simple act of indulging in one of life's greatest pleasures along with the love of one's life felt so—

Right.

"A gentleman should bear his pains wordlessly, for they are his and his alone." Leander gazed down at the small sleeping boy in Mary's arms and rubbed his cheek affectionately.

"That is your Catholic suffering speaking."

"Yes, well, even if it is. It is most traditional for a child to have godparents, not one, singular. Your sister Elizabeth is married, your brother Charles is not. It need not be more complicated than that."

"I suppose you are right. I just cannot bear the thought of hurting my brother."

Not again, she wanted to say, but refrained. Mary had never spoken to Charles about her marriage to his friend and business partner, nor had they even discussed the scandal that predated their engagement. He had seemed his familiar polite and congenial self, celebrating their wedding with his usual reserved happiness, but Mary could not help but fear there were things left unsaid.

"Charles is not and will not be hurt," Leander promised her, reaching a hand up to pet her hair. "And you should give your brother more credit. If he truly has something to say, he will say it."

"How do you know?"

"Experience," Leander answered simply, holding out his arms and motioning for Mary to pass him their son. As she did, Mary thought back to that scene in the bank the day William Taylor had arrived in New Orleans to adjudicate on their behavior, untangle their messes, and dish out punishments. Mary had often wondered what had been said between Leander and Charles after Leander had received his reprimand but had never dared to ask.

But if the last year had taught her anything, it was that you do not receive in life what you do not seek.

"Leander." At his name, he looked up from gazing at their son and met his wife's eyes. "That day in the bank, when my father arrived—do you recall it?"

"Of course."

"I have often wondered," Mary looked down at the skirt of her dress. "What you and Charles discussed."

"Mary, must you bring up such unpleasant memories on the day of our son's baptism?" he bemoaned lightly, but his tone was not harsh or reproachful.

"I just wish to know, because I have never been able to shake the idea that I have disappointed him terribly."

"Oh Mary, Charles would be heartbroken if he knew you felt that way," Leander assured her, leaning forward and meeting her lips gently. "Let us see." Leander closed his eyes, hankering back to that moment now a year gone. "We discussed the future of our joint business venture and agreed our partnership could continue. He rebuffed my behavior, obviously," Leander opened his eyes and threw Mary a sideways smile. "And laid the blame for everything at my feet, which was fair."

*"Leander, you are unequivocally the instigator and perpetrator of this entire situation." Charles shook his head with a resigned sadness.*

*Worse, with disappointment.*

*Despite being slightly shorter than and less built than his business partner, Charles commanded an authority when he spoke which left no confusion about who was calling the shots. He was, through and through, his father's son.*

*"You are not wrong," Leander responded. "I never meant for any of this, Charles. I came to New Orleans hoping that Miss Mercier would grow tired of waiting for me and demand another match. It is why I never mentioned it to you, though also why I never courted any other ladies. I resented my family obligations—"*

*"And respected them all the same. I understand the challenges that familial obligations can create," he admitted. "Though I am lucky enough not to find myself in a situation such as yours.*

*"But you did act out of cowardice and implicated my sister in the process."*

*"You are, once again, not wrong," Leander rubbed his neck, casting a glance toward where Mary and Elizabeth sat, their heads pushed together in hushed whispers. "It was never my intention, Charles, to develop non-familial feelings for your sister. I had only started coming to terms with the idea that I was going to have to marry Miss Mercier when Miss Taylor appeared like something out of a dream," Leander explained quietly. "It was like seeing what my life could be, if I were not bound, tethered by these obligations. Charles, they weighed so heavy," he confessed, turning his eyes back to his friend. "Like chains."*

*"Many gentlemen must endure such obligations and do so without causing unforgivable scenes or blotting the reputation of young ladies who are not and can never be theirs," Charles responded, sternly but not unkindly.*

*"You are, as always, not wrong," Leander repeated, casting his eyes to the floor. "I meant what I had promised to Mary—after the races, I was to go to Alabama and speak with my father, I had even purchased the ticket." Leander reached inside the breast pocket of his jacket and produced a piece of paper, which he surrendered to Charles.*

*"I recall you told me a family affair had arisen which required your attention." Charles declined the offered evidence.*

*"Honestly, Leander, I find it all a shame. A damn shame." Charles shook his head, casting a glance over towards Mary. "My sister is special."*

*"That she is."*

*"And she does not always see it, and even when she does, she does not believe it. Not fully." Charles sighed, returning his gaze to Leander's. "I do not begrudge you your feelings,*

*for I understand both the tether of familial obligation and circumstances which dictate whether or not a man can follow his heart.*

*"But Leander, know this: she is to marry Manuel Rivera. My father has decreed it, and I would ask that if you actually love her, you let her go."*

*Leander opened his mouth, but found no words.*

*"She deserves to find happiness."*

*"Of course, that is all I would wish for her. But will she find it with him?" Leander dared to ask.*

*"I know not," Charles acknowledged, his chest rising and falling with a heavy sigh. "But I do know she will have no chance of it if you are around her constantly, reminding her of a life she wants but cannot have. It is not fair, Leander, to hold her heart captive when you cannot give her yours."*

*"Oh Charles," Leander shook his head, "she has my heart. She has for the longest time now."*

*"Very well, then your person," Charles clarified. "If you cannot give yourself to her completely, then you must let her go."*

*Leander nodded his understanding. "What would you have me do?"*

*"I would ask you to leave, only for some time. Return to Alabama and make peace with your family. This will be handled swiftly." Charles gestured towards Mary. "Father will make certain of it. Harrison and I can handle things here while you are away, and once things cool down you can return and take up your place again."*

*"I am not certain I have anything to say to my family," Leander admitted in a low mumble.*

*"Well, be that as it may I am certain they have plenty to say to you." Charles raised an eyebrow, attempting to sound jovial. "And in any case, you have the ticket already."*

*"Very well," Leander agreed, extending his hand which Charles took, grasping it tightly.*

*"And Leander." Charles grabbed his arm. "Were circumstances different, I would have welcomed you as a brother-in-law."*

A tear rolled down Mary's cheek as that shadow that had hung over her slowly began to dissipate.

"And what did he say when you told him we were to be engaged?"

"He was glad," Leander reassured her, placing a hand on her knee and squeezing it lightly. "Well," he paused, considering. "He was glad in a sense. He was also furious because perhaps unexpectedly, we did lose the Rivera account."

"Ah," Mary nodded. She had not seen Manuel since their called-off engagement; he had temporarily left New Orleans, as she had heard, under the guise of escaping the heat of summer, but had failed to return with the cooler months. She often wondered how he fared—and hoped he bore her no ill will. The thought of such a nice gentleman resenting her was saddening in a way she could not describe.

But Mary knew, in her heart of hearts, that it would have been far more cruel to marry a man she did not love.

Especially if that man loved her and was devoted to her—

Mind, body, and soul.

No, that type of love required reciprocation—even more, it demanded it. And Mary knew that Manuel Rivera would find it.

She had once thought love was something bestowed upon a lady, a fate handed down from family or fortune.

But no—love was a choice.

For those bold enough to choose it.

# A Most Grateful Pause

A lady always knows when to express her gratitude, though I must confess, the exact nature of my thanks in this instance is a matter of some delicacy. In this case, I must offer my deepest appreciation to a distinguished gentleman who, with the frame of a bear and the patience of a saint, has been my most steadfast companion on this journey.

Though he may not yet know the role he plays in my own story, I owe him thanks for his steady hand in both editing and support, always offering guidance and assistance without once asking for anything in return. He is, after all, an excellent listener—and an even better critic.

And while he may blush, frown, or shake his head in disapproval over some of the more—let us say—spirited actions of the ladies within these pages, his support has always remained unwavering. I dare say, the poor man might now be wondering if there's anything he can do to keep me from writing such scandalous ladies into my stories!

Though, as a gentleman of the written and lived world, he knows better than to try and change a lady's mind, especially once it has been made up.

# About the Authoress

Lucine Elizabeth Watson, named for her mother, aunt, and grandmother, is a lady of regal name, undistinguished lineage, and modest means. She passes her days keeping the books of her brother's business—an occupation both practical and, some say, unseemly for a lady—and her evenings writing love stories, quietly hoping that life might pen one for her in return.

Her work has been described as "far too detailed to be entirely fictional," but Miss Watson wishes to assure readers that any resemblance to living persons—especially those with connections to the region's more decorated families—is purely coincidental... even if there are, admittedly, some unfortunate resemblances.

Still, as Mr. Wilde once remarked, "Imitation is the sincerest form of flattery."

And really, who is she to argue with a man of such wit?

# A Most Courteous Final Note

*From Lucine Elizabeth Watson*

Ah, but of course, the story cannot end with Miss Mary Taylor alone, can it? For the observant among you will have noted that while one tale comes to a close, another is just beginning—*how terribly convenient!*

Elizabeth Taylor has always said that marriage is but a *formality*. But what happens when a lady like her finds herself bound by duty, and a future that's *far from* her choosing?

What man, I ask you, can truly be worthy of Elizabeth Taylor? And when the world insists she must marry, how will she reconcile the path ahead with the pride that has always defined her?

Now, I'd be loathe to give too much away—*where would the fun be in that?*—but suffice to say, in *An Unlikely Union*, Elizabeth's world is about to change, in ways she may not be ready for.

Will she embrace the future laid out before her, or will she fight against the world's design?

But, as with all things, time will tell. Do stay tuned—*this* adventure is far from over.

Yours in anticipation,

Lucine Elizabeth Watson
*A lady of ink and intrigue*

P.S.—Should you find yourself still troubled by questions, or inclined toward commentary (delicate or otherwise), Miss L. E. Watson may be reached—one might call on her at her brother's general store, where she is known to assist with the accounts and only occasionally rearranges the ledgers to suit her narrative needs.

For those with a taste for ongoing scandal, whispered dispatches from society's fringes, and a desire to know precisely what the next chapter of *An Unlikely Union* holds, one may subscribe to her newsletter—and explore further mischief—at **www.MissLEWatson.com**

She awaits your correspondence with a quill in hand and an appetite for intrigue.

Printed in Dunstable, United Kingdom

68868542R00229